734-580-
2181

D 15
chaotic
Hair

Bria-
3.30

GOLIATH

GOLIATH

SUSAN WOODRING

ST. MARTIN'S PRESS

NEW YORK

GOLIATH. Copyright © 2012 by Susan Woodring. All rights reserved. Printed in
the United States of America. For information, address St. Martin's Press, 175 Fifth
Avenue, New York, N.Y. 10010.

www.stmartins.com

ISBN 978-0-312-67501-1 (hardcover)
ISBN 978-1-4299-4153-2 (e-book)

First Edition: April 2012

10 9 8 7 6 5 4 3 2 1

For my children

Acknowledgments

Many thanks to my agent, Peter Steinberg, who plucked this book from the slush pile and tirelessly advocated for it and for me. Also, I am forever grateful to Elizabeth Beier, my brilliant editor, whose heart and wisdom and enthusiasm guided this novel to the place it needed to be. Thank you to Michelle Richter and others at St. Martin's Press who have invested their time and talent in this book.

I am indebted to a number of fellow writers for their encouragement and support. Many thanks to Mary Akers, whose Zoetrope office is such a treasure to me, and to the members of Terri Brown-Davidson's Zoetrope office. My friends from the Queens University MFA program continue to bolster me—thank you, all of you, so much.

I am a member of the world's most wonderful writers' group. Priscilla Cutler, Rosemary Jones, Gwynyth Mislin, Sheryl Monks, and Karen McBryde: I don't know what I would do without you. I am so grateful for your friendship and your encouragement, for all these years of workshopping and retreating and AWPing and talking about our lives and our lives' work.

I want to add an additional word of thanks to Sheryl Monks and Karen McBryde, who were this book's first and most enthusiastic readers. Their feedback has been immeasurably valuable to me, and their friendship is one of my life's greatest blessings.

Thank you, Caldwell and Burke Counties, for welcoming me into your communities and for sharing with me your factory stories, hopes, and heartaches. Thank you, Martha and Danny Foster, for letting me borrow the history of your hometown, *Brookford Memories*. Many thanks also to Winona Childres, a native of my community and a church nursery volunteer who recounted so many of her Drexel memories to me when my son was a baby. Winona also lent me her copy of a written history of our town, which has been so helpful in the creation of my fictitious Goliath.

Many, many thanks to my family. Thank you to my parents, Bruce and Arlene Yergler, who believed in me from the first and have given me everything I needed and so much more. Also, thank you to my in-laws Rita and Jerry Sutherland, who love me as their own and who have unfailing faith in my talent as a writer. Rita and Jerry also support me in a very real, practical way: they babysit . . . constantly! It is no exaggeration to say that I could not write if it weren't for their help.

Which brings me to my everyday family, the people who live with me and put up with me and so generously make room for my work. Thank you, Abby and Aiden, my sweethearts, and my husband Danny, the biggest sweetheart of them all.

ONE

A teenage boy coming in from a morning of lighting fires along far-flung creeks was the one to find the body. He stopped shock-still, uncertain of what he saw splayed out there on the mud. But the clean white sunlight shone down on it same as it did on the bent weeds and the grass-and rock-stubble field leading up a hill, across a gravel path littered with junk parts and gutted automobiles set on cinder blocks, a white box of a house beyond. What he saw was true. A handful of black-birds flung themselves up at the sky, crossed over in a shifting amoeba, and lit on a telephone wire, strung over the highway beyond the house. The boy stood looking down the set of silver railroad tracks glaringly bright in the sunshine. The sky above him was made of color so thick, it seemed he could plunge his open hand into its blueness.

He came back to himself and turned, hurrying across the field. The boy, Vincent Bailey, did not feel his feet move over the uneven earth and the bulging roots of old trees. All he could pay mind to was his heart thudding hard against his rib cage and the rush of air coming in and out through his lungs. He reached the house and stepped inside, the screen door clattering shut behind him. His father was in the living room, watching television with a plate of scrambled eggs balanced on his lap.

Vincent told him what he had found. "It's Percy Harding," he said.

His father set his plate aside, slow to believe. "Are you sure?"

Vincent was certain, and his father moved to the kitchen telephone to summon the police. They went out front to wait. His father did not speak, though he watched the boy in silhouette, then turned his eyes to the bend of road where the squad car would arrive. Vincent stared into the sun until it smeared purple when he blinked.

Some moments later, a patrol car and an ambulance sloped down the long gravel drive to where Vincent and his father stood. Neither vehicle had its siren turned on, and, to Vincent, it seemed the world had been sucked clean of true sound. Even when his father spoke to him, he just saw the movement of his father's lips beneath his eyes squinting in the sun. The three men—Vincent's father, the police chief of Goliath, and the coroner—nodded at one another and then turned to Vincent, who led them out to the field.

He worried the body would be gone, mysteriously up and left, but they came to it directly, and it was worse now, even more still, as if it were possible for a person to grow more dead in a half hour's time. Though it was the beginning of October, the air felt as mild and new as on a spring day.

The boy stood back with his father, who folded his arms across his chest and leaned over to spit into the mud. The police chief, a patient, solid, grim-faced man who was slow in his movements, and the coroner, a pudgy fellow with a wide forehead that beaded with sweat despite the cool breeze riding across the trees, spoke quietly over the body. It was quickly determined that the deceased,

struck by the train, was Percy Harding, just as Vincent had reported. His father stepped forward to hazard a closer look but
kept his expression hard. Vincent, wanting the relief he had expected to feel when the situation was safely in the hands of the
police, kept his eyes turned away from his father's. He searched
the sky for more blackbirds.

Later, after the body was taken away and the men had left,
Vincent sat at the kitchen table with a supper of cornbread and
beans, ladled off the stove by his mother. She and Vincent's sisters had just returned from morning church services, and she was
still dressed in pressed pink linen, a summer dress. She set the plate
down and lingered a moment, her hand on his shoulder. The girls,
all older than Vincent, fluttered about the kitchen, hoping to catch
the details of what Vincent had found. Finally their mother shooed
them away, and Vincent was left alone with his father, who sat
across from him and looked from his own plate to his son to the
window.

"It's going to be a hard thing to forget," he said. "What we saw
today."

Vincent didn't answer. Outside, the clouds swept across the sky
in quick-time, blossoming orange, then pink, then blue gray.

The Baileys lived in a ripple of wooded hills threaded with county
roads a few miles west of the town of Goliath, where Percy Harding had lived and presided over Harding Furniture Company
and where Vincent Bailey, riding the county school bus, had just
begun attending high school. There in town it had been a blessedly ordinary summer of modest white nuptials and giant insects
and bloated afternoons spent in kiddie pools and backyards, the
neighborhoods of Goliath filling with the greasy smells of charred
meat and bug repellent. During these months, the heat saturated
Goliath and the people sat behind electric fans set on front porches,
the ladies' hair tied back in bandannas. They passed around garden

tomatoes, which grew heavy and red on their vines all the way through the end of September.

They weren't prepared for the sad news when Vincent Bailey found it on the first Sunday of October, the weather just beginning to cool. The sorrow of it went out in glittering gusts like the old-fashioned purple and pink insecticide clouds sprayed through the streets in years past. There was a sheen to a tragedy this grave, this mysterious. It began with Clyde Winston, the soon-to-retire police chief, going out to inform the widow.

Clyde left the Baileys' house after the body was removed and drove into Goliath, passing the two-pump gas station, the huge gray rectangle of the Harding Furniture Factory, the railroad tracks, the downtown shops, the post office, and the great white Baptist church. Beyond the church, the roads split into narrow neighborhood streets with cracked sidewalks and gray and blue houses hunched over splintered front porches.

The Harding house was a monstrous brick structure sitting atop a hill looking over the residential end of Main Street. The gentle slopes of the Goliath Cemetery—just a few graves shy of full capacity—lay across the street. The house was reached by a private graveled avenue labeled Redemption Lane. A long driveway led up the sparsely treed hill and came to a semicircle a few steps from the heavy wood door, flanked on both sides by intricate stained glass, vine- and leaf-patterned. Years ago, factory workers, called there by Martha Harding, the namer of the private lane and the factory president's wife during the post–World War II years, had stood waiting in that same spot. They had been called there for a prayer meeting, which Martha herself administered from her leather chesterfield inside.

Lela Harding, Percy's wife, opened the door clutching a glass of amber-colored liquid, slender ice cubes floating on top. She was a petite woman with glossy black hair and a powdery-white complexion. Clyde Winston pronounced the news, disclosing as

few details as possible. "No," she said, shaking her head. "*No.*"
She stood motionless for a moment, then turned and stepped into
the house, and Clyde, after a moment's hesitation, followed her.

"I was just about to take the car out," she said.

Clyde was unsure of what to do or say to console her. They
sat without speaking a space apart on a thickly upholstered sofa
in a room made of shining brass and gleaming old furniture. She
drank and touched her face with her fingertips. Her husband had
been the most powerful and the most beloved man in town, but
Lela had mostly kept to herself. Few knew her well. The music,
a far-off radio, changed from song to song, back to the announcer,
back to song. When her glass was empty, Lela held it up to Clyde
to refill, gesturing to an unlocked cabinet where he found the
bourbon. Returning her refreshed glass, he sat next to her on
the couch and she bent a tiny bit closer to him. He thought of
Martha Harding, whom he had seen only at her viewing—she was
hollow-looking, carefully embalmed. It was the first dead person
young Clyde, then fifteen years old, had ever seen.

"It's too big. It's like driving a bus."

"Ma'am?"

She looked at him. "He must have left early," she said. "I was
still asleep."

The elevator music continued, interrupted again by the announcer's lilting voice. Clyde did not argue with Lela, but instead let her sit there and come to understanding. She closed her
eyes, and he began to move his hand up and down her back. At
another time the gesture might have seemed too familiar. Now,
though, in the moment of her stark grief, her drinking, the awful,
shapeless music, this seemed the only thing for Clyde to do. He
was a widower, ten years on his own now, and was unpracticed in
the art of offering sympathy. His palm moved slowly against the
small knots of vertebrae and Lela Harding seemed more fragile
with each passing.

She touched her temples. "I wish we'd get some rain."

Clyde left after dark, the radio still playing, and unwilling to return home, looped the streets of town and the outlying county roads until dawn. He drove past his son's trailer, in the woods behind the school, past his neighbors' houses, past the factory. The downtown shops were silent and dark except for the soft buzzing of the streetlights and the perennial blue glow of the Pepsi fountain inside the Tuesday Diner.

The body was brought to Thompson's Funeral Home, and in the morning, Holland Thompson, the undertaker, set about preparing it for internment. Holland was a slow, methodical man who would have been a surgeon except he preferred a cleaner, more exact succession of tasks. He worked alone in a room furnished with only the table and his instruments, the cabinet, the industrial sink, and a portable radio tuned to a station that played covers of old pop songs. His married, childless daughter Celeste came, knocked shortly on the door, and then opened it without invitation. Her father, irritated at the interruption, turned sharply to her, and though Percy Harding was barely recognizable in his mangled state, she knew at once who it was laid out there on the cold steel table.

She gasped. Though the daughter of a mortician, she had never seen such a corpse. The body was so completely dead—simply *emptied* of life—and yet so untouched. His skin had not yet turned waxy and unreal, and he wasn't terribly bloody. Instead, the body was rumpled, a misshapen scattering of broken bones sealed over by skin and a blue jogging suit.

"It was a train," Holland said unnecessarily—Celeste had already heard what had happened, indeed had been the one to answer the phone. She had known Percy Harding, now dead, was coming to them. Her father shook his head over the particular violence of the tragedy, the degree of technical skill his job now required of him. He turned to his cabinet to select a thin, sharp needle and a spool of wire. He gestured to his daughter with a pair of surgical scissors.

"You keep this to yourself," he said.

"All right," she said, and hurried out.

She was still clutching her car keys when she whispered her discovery to the checkout girl at Lucky Grocery. "One hundred percent *crushed*," Celeste told her.

The checkout girl, a can of green beans in her hand, stopped, looking up at Celeste. The buyer of the green beans, a woman with two small children at her knees, asked, "What did you say?" though she'd heard Celeste well enough. She picked up the littler of her two boys and listened: Celeste, in a whisper, described what she had seen.

The news began swirling out, Celeste and the checkout girl and then the mother of the little boys and the bag boy all speaking of it there at the front of the store. Of course many had already heard that Percy Harding had died—it was in the local papers—but few had spoken to someone who had actually seen the body. Celeste repeated again and again, "One hundred percent *crushed*," and nodded at the blank faces, their brows wrinkled, their mouths half forming questions as the image settled in. Those coming in and those leaving heard and lingered; with time, a murmuring knot collected there. There were shoppers who had come off third shift a few hours earlier: the women still had their hair tied back. The men had their work boots on. Some were off work this morning, come in blue jeans and sweatshirts to pick up groceries for tonight's supper, and a few were in dressy slacks and sweater vests, late for their office jobs, dropping by to pick up coffee and pastries for their coworkers. They listened to Celeste describe what she had seen, and they began to understand: Percy Harding had been struck—*destroyed*—by a train.

The shock and sorrow of it clung to them as they stood by the automatic sliding glass doors, too numb to move. After a time, though, they remembered themselves and started to leave, some with thoughts of going to retrieve their children early from school, some to wait for the day-shift workers to come down the hill from the factory at four, and some to go home and sort it out, this horrible thing that had happened here, in their own small realm of church, friends, and work. Each recollected an actual encounter with the man, or at the very least, a sighting, and those remembered moments were absorbingly macabre now. The people recalled what they could of Percy Harding and looked, through time passed, for some foretelling, some hint, of the present disaster.

"He was a rock," one worker told another, and they both nodded. It was true—Percy Harding had been the town's single greatest support—but this was also the beginning of the kinds of legends people create after a passing.

"Harding will never be the same. *We* will never be the same," another said.

"It's true, it's true," came a response.

They referred to the incident as an accident, though many went home to confront their loved ones with the chilling uncertainty as to how a man might be struck by a train without either lying down for it or else standing resolutely on the tracks. People speculated. One man recalled a scene in a movie where a woman's shoe got wedged between the ground and the rail and the woman had struggled to free herself in time.

Clyde Winston stopped by the post office on his way home from the station late that afternoon. Hearing one of his neighbors speak of Percy's death, relaying a description, largely distorted, of the condition he was found in, he remembered the granite look of Lela Harding's eyes, how fragile the bones in her back had felt under his hand. From the post office, he went to his son's mobile home behind the junior high school rather than return to his own dark cave of a house. He leaned against the kitchen sink with a tepid glass of water and said, "It just don't make sense." He took a drink, shook his head, and said again, "It just don't."

"You're right there," his son agreed. "A man does not stand in the way of a train unless he means to get hit." He was still a moment, thinking, watching his father. "Or unless he's crazy," he added. He stood gripping the back of a kitchen chair, opening and closing his fingers to ease the tension in his knuckles. Ray Winston was a large man, his sturdy limbs and broad chest in proportion to his more than six feet of height. He wore his curly brown hair longish, just over the collar of his county-issued work shirt. In a softer tone, he continued, "And no one even guessing at it, not even knowing he was capable of it."

The two were quiet for a moment, considering the dead man's intentions. A chill breeze seeped through the slipshod hinges of the aluminum trailer even as sunshine beat through the uncurtained windows, lighting up dirt smudges here and there across the pane. Ray Winston was the groundskeeper for the county, mostly keeping up the yard of the junior high and high school, built on neighboring lots, and the grade schools across the way. He was also a part-time preacher, ordained by the power of the Spirit and none other, bringing the good news to the poor, the downtrodden. He kept his own worldly load light. He belonged to no church and did not do his preaching while lounging on a leather chesterfield in a great house on a hill, but instead stood on the doorsteps of Goliath, visiting the physically ill and the spiritually unwell. Now, also unlike Martha Harding, he kept his silence, waiting to see what else Clyde needed to say. He had learned that much—the ministry of listening—from his father.

Clyde had served the town of Goliath for decades. He had dealt with any number of domestic squabbles, drunken insanities, and break-ins. There had also been acts of vandalism, fits of meanness, and episodes of blatant stupidity. He had seen other suicides. But there was something different in this one. It was as if every person in town had put their own bodies in way of the train and were all broken now, spiritless.

After a moment, Clyde set his glass down and spoke.

"A person goes that far," he said, "he takes the rest of us partway with him." He stared squarely into his son's eyes. "You can't unsee a thing like that, you can't unlive it."

The Harding family assembled itself in Goliath a day and a half after the Bailey boy's discovery. Percy's oldest brother, Anthony, made the unnecessary announcement about Percy's passing in the factory's lunchroom at noon; by then, everyone knew. Anthony Harding was a commanding figure, as tall as Percy, yet with a more deeply lined face, his eyes watery behind gold-rimmed spectacles. He stood in front of the employees in a dark blue suit, clearing his throat between utterances of grief and regret. The workers, in flannel and worn denim, stirred. There was sawdust on the shoulders of those who worked in the rough room, and the back of every finisher ached.

"Let us," he said, "come together during this time of loss."

The employees were let off early to prepare to attend the viewing, and they moved out in small knots into the breezy fall day. Rosamond Rogers, Percy Harding's secretary, remained at her desk, her fingers resting on the smooth green keys of her electric typewriter. She had already attended to the tasks the family had asked of her and had supplied a list of phone numbers they could call—business associates and friends, acquaintances Percy's family might not think to include. She had made a number of the calls herself earlier this morning, and had already given over the list, all the rest. She had thought they might need something more from her, and she had offered to do more: type up the program for the funeral, begin cleaning out his desk—though she wasn't at all sure she could do that, handle Percy's things—but nothing more had been required.

Now suddenly Rosamond was experiencing a momentary loss of memory. It was too much, Percy dying; she dreaded the viewing. Dreaded standing in the long, long line with all the others—the ones who felt as though they had known Percy Harding only because they had lived here in Goliath, or even just near Goliath, in the same county—and shaking the widow's hand, the son's hand. Offer her condolences, receive the condolences of others.

She had her daughter, just returned to Goliath after a failed college career, and that was all. Her husband, a salesman, had left years ago. Certain material entities were blotted out now in her mind. She knew the thing before her was called a typewriter, but she was unsure about what it was doing there, or what it was used for. She blinked, fearful, then closed her eyes tight, seeking to regain herself, and opened them to find small familiars, the flower-patterned coffee cup, her papers, the manila file folders. Restored, she rose to check on things.

The offices were still, and in the factory beyond sun motes floated over stopped machines. The halls made tiny pings of silence. She returned to her desk and took her coat, a single-breasted orange felt cutaway, and set out, the sidewalks spotty with sunbeams and bits of shadow. There was a bit of time, a few hours, for her to rest up before walking down to the viewing at the funeral home.

Rosamond began down the sidewalk, past the downtown businesses. There was the bank, the diner, the pizza place, the drugstore. One street up from the drugstore was a junk shop that a generation ago had been a department store. Above that, there was a truncated street with a shut-down bowling alley and a dingy bar masquerading as a hole-in-the-wall restaurant— Rosamond had not been inside it in ages. Coming up on the

large white Baptist church just this side of downtown, she paused
to adjust the collar of her coat. It was barely cool enough for the
coat, but she kept it on. Her feet, pretty in their vintage red
pumps—circa 1954—were not properly outfitted for so much
walking.

Across from the church was the grade school with its great
oak looming tall, the branches stretched out across the scratchy
lawn as if to protect the children who sat there in groups on
warmer days, eating their lunches or awaiting their parents. Rosamond, years ago, used to stroll by on her lunch break to watch
her daughter Agnes pick apart her bologna sandwich. The other
first-grade girls arranged themselves in a complicated-looking
game that involved running and screeching away from some boy
who looked both perplexed and ashamed, more than a little annoyed to find himself the unwitting villain. It had always pained
Rosamond to watch Agnes playing with the other children, even
when they appeared to like her. She was a pretty girl, but disheveled, everything askew, and entirely too serious. Rosamond
had never been able to fix Agnes's hair up right or get her to keep
her shirttail tucked in. Throughout her childhood years, and even
now, Agnes seemed half complete, a person who couldn't tie her
shoes without getting distracted by her own thoughts.

Rosamond walked down the hill past a string of ordinary
houses, all with brick faces and painted cement porches. Below
the high school, in a patch of woods, was the site of the house,
now gone, where a movie star had lived. Dorothy Blair had
grown up here, in these streets, and had run away to Hollywood
as a teenager. Rosamond often thought of her, imagined what it
was like to be famous and, at the same time, to remember a childhood in Goliath.

Agnes had recently surprised everyone—including her
mother—by dropping out of college and returning home. She
had taken a job at Lucky Grocery, at the checkout. Rosamond

didn't understand why. There were better jobs to be had, even in Goliath. Agnes had come to live not with Rosamond, but with Rosamond's aunt, Mia Robins, who had throughout the years taken in a number of wayward relatives.

A few more houses, and she came to her own. A 1957 blue Cadillac sat in the driveway. The car was nearly three decades old and still in pristine condition. She had not driven that car nor any other in more than a decade. She stood at her front door and felt for her house keys inside her coat pocket. She had believed her own daughter might go out and do something spectacular in the world. Rosamond touched the doorknob, and the instant she made contact with the house, empty inside, she discovered she could not enter. She looked toward the house next door, where her best friend had lived before she died several years ago. Her friend's husband, the police chief, lived there alone now. Clyde Winston, a solitary man. The day was hushed save the thrusts of new autumn wind shaking the boughs of trees, still mostly green, changed at the top as if they had been uprooted, dipped partially in red or yellow paint, and set back in the earth again.

Returning to the sidewalk, Rosamond headed east, in the same direction she'd just come from. The shadows from the houses and the telephone poles were stretched long across the street. The day would soon begin to lose its light.

She arrived moments later at the drugstore, prompting the tinkling of a little bell as she stepped inside. The store smelled of plastic packaging and cleaning liquids. There were no other shoppers inside and the proprietor, Charlotte Branch, was perched on a stool behind the cash register, thumbing through a movie magazine. Charlotte wore her gray hair in short, tight curls; Rosamond pictured Charlotte sitting at her kitchen table in the morning, her hair wrapped in an assortment of plastic rollers, her eyes narrowing to focus on her newspaper as she leaned over to read. She raised her eyebrows now at Rosamond, nodded shortly, and returned to her reading. Rosamond knew, though, that Charlotte kept her eyes on her even as she appeared to study the celebrity pages, their evening gowns and divorces.

Rosamond examined the cellophane-wrapped squares of chocolates and mints, and, on a shelf devoted to Christmas pretties, a variety of plastic snow globes depicting the nativity. October had just begun and Rosamond had not yet begun to think about Christmas. Picking up one of the globes, she flipped it, then righted it, and saw that the baby Jesus had come dislodged and was floating and swirling about in the fake snow, finally coming to rest, upside down, beside the virgin Mary. There were painted wood tree ornaments and, the next aisle over, teddy bear figurines, pocket flashlights, and lingerie drawer sachets. Rosamond picked through the gadgets and flummeries. More snow globes, seashell jewelry boxes, miniature sewing kits. The store was unusually quiet and still for this time of day.

She finally made her selection—a letter opener, its wooden handle carved and painted to look like a red cardinal. Percy, she remembered, had been an admirer of birds. *They're never still,* he had once noted, turning from the window in his office. *Even at rest,* he had said, *they jerk their heads around, looking. They lift off the branch in an instant. Gone!* She moved to the counter, taking out her wallet to pay.

Charlotte laid her magazine down on the counter to ring her up. She studied Rosamond for a second, remarked, "Awful, what happened." Rosamond agreed yes, a terrible tragedy. "Pretty," Charlotte said, picking up the letter opener to examine it, glancing up again at Rosamond and giving her a second to respond. But Rosamond only shrugged. Charlotte punched the numbers into the register, announced the total, and then wrapped it in tissue paper, turning it over and over again. The small, happy energy of the task, the purchase, the idea of bringing a gift warmed

Rosamond, and she ignored Charlotte's questioning look. She picked through her change purse, taking out five dollars and thirty-three cents, exact change, and, accepting the bag, turned to leave. She had never before done this sort of grieving, never sought to comfort a widow who wasn't so very old—Lela Harding couldn't be much older than Rosamond.

"The whole thing makes you wonder," Charlotte continued in a measured tone, "about people. Impossible to tell what they're really thinking." She paused. "I'm real sorry, Rosamond. I know this is a great loss to *you*."

Rosamond thanked her and hurried away. She found comfort in the spunky click-click of her heels on the sidewalk. This, she decided, touching the sharp point of the letter opener, wrapped in tissue paper and settled into her coat pocket, was the least she could do.

Main Street was a long stretch of storefronts, houses, and schools. Finally she came to the cemetery and Redemption Lane, but when Rosamond drew close to the start of the long road, it seemed to have come too soon. She hesitated, then set forward again.

As she began the climb, cursing her beloved shoes with every pinching step, she thought of the letter opener, of the tiny bird, that brightly colored ornament, of how it would find its place inside the fancy house up on the hill. She wondered how Lela Harding would receive it, maybe holding it long, for its heft, its solidness, looking closely to admire it, maybe slipping it into her own pocket or leaving it on an end table in the living room. Rosamond had been to the house maybe half a dozen times in her thirty some odd years of working for Percy Harding and could picture the brass and deep wood expanse of the room, could see the letter opener casually left on one of those shining pieces of furniture. The letter opener was pretty and red, a specific item she had chosen and touched and carried. It would live among the Hardings,

Rosamond's own scrambled message to the people inside—the children, the grandchildren, the rest. Rosamond was sure no one knew Percy Harding—in certain ways—as well as she did. God help her for even thinking it, but it was true.

When she was a girl, Harding Furniture had been world-famous. In those days, Goliath was the site of the manufacture of fine handcrafted furniture, a town of skilled artisans. The railroad tracks tied working towns to big cities across the country, and trains carried the furniture away. Goliath had Easter parades, those years. Dorothy Blair, the movie star, was making her way on the big screen at the furniture company's height of glory, first playing, fittingly, a teenage girl from a small town who finds herself, wide-eyed, on the streets of New York City. After that, she had starred in a string of pictures, portraying everything from a stripper to a nun, and had played opposite all the famous leading men. This was thirty years ago. Dorothy Blair had since turned obscure. Rosamond, who loved her still, once read an interview where the actress spoke of her hometown. *A little place called Goliath,* she had said.

Rosamond came to the steep driveway and started up, leaning forward a bit for balance. The house above her was going dark in the small light of late afternoon, its windows glinting gold with the sun's setting across the street.

She reached the heavy wooden door, narrow panes of stained glass on either side. The house was a mammoth stone and brick structure, impregnable. In Rosamond's mind, it was overdone, unfit for human habitation. She thought of church, of museums she would likely never visit, of the jaunty, earnest look of Percy Harding at his start. She smoothed the front of her coat, pressed her lips together, checked her pretty shoes. Stepping forward, she pressed the bell.

After barely a moment, the door opened and a tall, thin boy with an untroubled, childish face stood before her. His hair was so pale it nearly matched his skin, and the only distinction of color was his silent blue eyes, so purely blue they seemed unnatural, like colored glass. It's the family, Rosamond realized. She had, in her fervor over purchasing a gift, forgotten about them, that they even existed out there away from Goliath, that now they had returned, come together from their scattered places across the country, ascending now in a thick plume of opulence, dense in the house before her.

The boy said nothing, simply raising his eyebrows in an unspoken question. *Yes?*

"It's Rosamond Rogers," she said quickly. "I . . . worked with Mr. Harding." She stopped. "Oh, it's you." She stared. This was no boy, but a man of nearly thirty, some years older than her Agnes. Mr. Harding's son—his *son,* that gorgeous boy. Rosamond gaped for a moment, then, embarrassed, collected herself. "Ryan." He smiled, but there was still the question on his face. And also here *he* was. The sweet pale swag of hair falling down over his eyes, that beautiful man, young now, stepped out of his coffin and across time, come back to her. Ryan was dressed in a navy suit, ready for the viewing. Flushing, Rosamond tried again. "It's me, Ryan. Rosamond Rogers." The polite, uncertain look remained, and Rosamond winced at its blankness. "The secretary," she prompted, her voice coming out shrill and unpleasant.

At this, Ryan nodded. "Of course." He grinned—his father's grin—then stepped back, inviting her to enter. "Come in."

He held out his hand, here's the way, but Rosamond remained where she was. There was the viewing. The family would be going, of course, and she was holding him back. He needed to finish dressing. Behind Ryan, the house was warm and complete, soft light shining outward, a thin stretch of private grief hanging about his shoulders, and Rosamond crept back inside herself, shrinking away. She shook her head, and Ryan's face slipped over to confusion, then mild annoyance. Rosamond spoke, apologizing.

"I shouldn't have come," she said, stepping back. Her shoe scraped down the first step, and she stumbled, grabbing hold of the wrought iron handrail to catch herself. Ryan stepped forward to help, but she smoothed her coat, said, "I'm all right. So sorry, so . . ." Smiling, she leaned forward to squeeze Ryan's thin, warm hand; then, letting go, she turned to leave.

Percy's boy, standing at the top step, called out to her. "Mrs. Rogers?"

She hurried away. The afternoon was beginning its lapse into darkness as she staggered down the driveway onto Redemption Lane. Down she clattered. The front door finally blinked shut as Rosamond stopped at the bottom of the hill, looking back.

She took her shoes off to walk home, taking the long, zigzag way through the neighborhoods. She would not be attending the viewing, she decided. She *couldn't*. When she finally arrived back on Main Street, her pantyhose were torn through, and the town was absent, gone to the viewing. There was only Clyde Winston there, sitting on his top porch step next door, his neck bent back as if to soak up the last of the day's light. She had known Clyde for years. Carrying her shoes in one hand, the letter opener a snug weight in her pocket, Rosamond nodded hello as she went up her front steps. Clyde nodded back and didn't seem to notice she'd been crying, or was too polite to show it, or that her feet were bare, or that she, like Clyde himself, was not in the place she was supposed to be.

TWO

Some years ago, a man in a black jumpsuit came to town in a single-engine airplane. It was a high-winged, compact, glorious contraption with a broad red stripe and the number 46 painted on its side. The pilot, called Ringer, set himself up for business on the high school football field on a Saturday morning, offering three-dollar rides above Goliath in his amazing flying machine.

At first only the children wanted to go. Ringer had an assistant, a sleek-haired woman in a matching jumpsuit with smoker's gravel in her throat. She remained on the ground and took the money, organizing riding parties of four.

"Ever been above the clouds?" the woman asked the waiting children, flattening the dollar bills across her palm. "Ever touched the sky?"

Lines formed in the football field, little ones who were too excited to stand still and their fretful mothers, yanking their children into place and squinting hard at the tiny airplane lifting up almost tentatively, rising before the bleachers and hovering over the trees. On the sidelines, teenagers flung their arms into the air, waving them like castaways. The old men from the diner, freshly barbered, stood back and shook their heads at the flying dune buggy, as they termed it. They judged the safety of the apparatus. "No bigger than a gnat," one said. "We'll see if it doesn't crash," another added, laughing.

Other spectators worried. They'd ridden in airplanes before, some of them, but nothing like this: it was hard to believe in something so small, so noisy, so unbecomingly *mechanical*. The stands filled with old people and young couples with babies. They held their breath, waiting to see if the airplane would drop onto the rooftops or lose its place when it circled back, shifting sideways in the sky.

Rosamond Rogers watched the children being hoisted into the plane through its square door, more than two feet off the grass, and saw there would be little hope of her mounting the thing gracefully should she choose to do so. Pastor Grady, who had just turned old at sixty-five, shuffled past her, shaking his head and muttering to himself. "Fools," she heard him say.

Her little girl Agnes was angling for a spot in line, but Rosamond was unsure. There was the grumble of the engine and the whirl of the propellers, the commotion of the waiting children, jumping and pointing. Agnes hazarded a step away from her, toward the others.

After the first few trips, the groups of children and their mothers were returned unharmed, though dazed—motion-sick in a couple of cases—and the desire to go up in the wobbly cloud-buster spread through the crowd. The shipwrecked teenagers went up, and then the young couples, leaving their babies with the grandmothers, who turned the babies' faces toward the sky and pointed out the sputtering *tut-tut-tut* progression of the plane arching above. Finally the old men from the diner left the bleachers and decided, with mocking courage, to have a go at it themselves. It was a fresh yellow-green day in the spring.

The people in the airplane saw the tops of the trees in the woods beyond the factory. They flew over the factory itself, looking down at its long, flat roof, the circle of the dust collector tower, the loading dock, the parking lot, the water tower. They looked down upon the gray ribbon of asphalt through downtown and into the neighborhoods, the highway, the rooftops of the houses, nearly identical, the boxy green yards, the school, the cemetery. The fliers witnessed the river and the railroad tracks, running parallel on either side of town, trailing off to other towns, growing smaller.

From above, they viewed the town they knew so well they could walk its streets blindfolded. Seeing everything as small and tidy as a line of colored boxes on a board game was both marvelous and unsettling.

Mia Robins remarked, "Why, I could just reach down there and change everything around!" For years she remembered the sight, and she could always recall exactly what it was she had said. "Change *everything*!" she exclaimed, clasping her hands together. Much later, she was still telling her niece Rosamond and her great-niece Agnes, "You have no idea how *small* everything really is."

That day Goliath became a trinket in the minds of its people. It was awe-inspiring and terrifying to see everything from above, and it gave them pause to reconsider their devotion to what, in miniature, they saw below them.

Rosamond, entreated by her daughter, finally hazarded to hitch her skirt up and let that slick pilot help her onto the plane. Once settled in her seat, then jarringly launched, she looked out the dirty window and knew she would never leave those minute, winding streets, the square clapboard houses, the nickel-and-dime grocery store. It didn't occur to her that Agnes, seated beside her, was thinking anything but the same. Agnes, however, only seven years old, looked beyond instead of down, peering as far into the distance—gray highway, green mountains—as possible. It was her first inkling that she would someday *have* to leave.

Clyde Winston, the police officer, was slightly nauseated by the sensation of his body rising up from the ground, and he felt something of what Rosamond felt, that his spot on this earth was Goliath and Goliath alone. His son Ray, just a little boy, would not look away from the window, his fingers smudging the Plexiglas, already grubby from the fingers of other little boys who had ridden the airplane across the skies of other small towns across America. As he gazed outward, he wished his mother had been there with him. Penny Winston was still living then, but she did not want to go up in the itty-bitty airplane and had resisted her son's pleading.

"Oh, no," she said when Ray tried to pull her to the line, "these feet are best kept to the sweet green earth." She stomped her shoe onto the football field, in a small, dancing sort of way, smiling at him. The spark of cancer had just lit inside her chest, but it would be years before the tiny mass would cause her a moment's trouble. Today she was feeling fine, like the others. "No, thank you, little man," she said.

But even Penny ultimately chose to go, young Ray taking her up for his second trip, them waving down at Clyde for as long as they could see him on the ground below. The passion for flight became irresistible and communicable. The more people went up, the more wanted to go up. In the end, there were only two people of any notice who did not go up in Ringer's airplane that day.

One of them was Pastor Eugene Grady from the Baptist church. The next afternoon, after the plane had left and the previous day's adventures was all anyone could talk about, the ladies

who met up at the drugstore discussed the pastor's unwilling-
ness. They pointed out to one another that it would not have been
dignified for a man of God to strap himself inside that tiny
plane. There might have been something sinful about it, or perhaps his doctor—Eugene was taking various medications for his
weak heart—had forbidden such excitement. Or maybe he had
simply stepped aside so as to free up a space for a youngster's
third or fourth trip up. Pastor Grady was a quiet, dull man, ago-
nizingly slow but kind, bent toward indulging young children
and white-haired ladies.

"I'm *glad*, really," one of the ladies, the mother of teenagers,
declared. "It seems the good pastor has more pressing matters on
his mind."

"Of course he does," another agreed.

Rosamond did not particularly care what kept the old man
down. She assumed it was simple fear. She saw him in the stands,
head bent, eyes closed, hands gripping the concrete step he was
sitting on as if to keep his body from inexplicably shooting up
into the blue. The truth was, plane day or not, Eugene Grady
always looked half terrified. The few times Rosamond had bothered with church—one or two Easter services, a smattering of
funerals over the years—Pastor Grady had delivered his sermons
with trembling in his voice. His eyes darted fitfully over the faces
of the congregants.

But it was fine for the mild-mannered pastor to be afraid.
What stopped Rosamond, who was still a little unsteady from
her own turn in the sky, was the sight of the only other person
in a similar state of panic. Standing apart from the others with
the heft and chill of a stone statue was Percy Harding. Beneath the
blue-bright sky filled with high white clouds, Percy, tall and thin
and presidential-looking, radiated panic. The cords of his neck
stood rigid and his eyes were wild with searching fear. Rosamond
could taste the grit of clenched teeth in her own mouth.

It had to be more than a fear of flying. She tried to catch his eye, but he wouldn't turn her way, and she felt uncertain about approaching him. She didn't know what she could be seeing, Percy so afraid it seemed beyond the scope of any present danger; there was a greater power of soul-wrenching doubt, or rather belief—any horrible thing could happen. What she glimpsed of Percy there on the high school football field that morning—the toy airplane rising, turning in the sky above them before it came back, landing in a fog of noise and exhaust—spooked her very bones.

Dusk came, Ringer and his woman packed up to leave, and the people of Goliath left the football field feeling peaceful and accomplished and exhilarated, all of the anxiety from earlier in the day forgotten. Rosamond, however, felt uneasy as she and Agnes walked home together. Her husband Hatley was away on a sales trip, and she rose from bed late that night, unable to sleep. She scrubbed at the shelves in her Frigidaire, half hoping to wake her daughter so she could have a little company. But then the night passed and she went to work the next morning, typed letters and filed the purchase orders, answered the phone, saw to Agnes's homework, and years went by. In time, the particular worry of that day faded. Percy had always had his dark moods, and she did her best to buoy him. She was his secretary, and that meant that she spent more time with him than anyone.

She didn't give the incident much thought for years. Yet she woke early the second morning after Percy's death—the morning of the funeral—with a sudden and clear memory of the long-ago day. Speaking aloud to break the maddening quiet of her empty house, the sky still gray beyond her bedroom window, she recalled his frozen panic standing there amid all the freehearted adventurers. "He was terrified," she told her empty house. In picturing the day, conjuring up the green buzz of the fresh, sun-blazed grass, the gauzy blue of the sky, the pale anxieties of the old men, the very real terror of first, the pastor, and second, her own Percy, she caught a clearer sense of what had truly frightened him that day. It was, she realized, the same fear that caused him to fall into his silences, his guarded stiff moments: Percy had been afraid of *himself*.

Percy Harding, a man whose presence was still so familiar to her: even now she couldn't believe he wasn't already at the office, flipping on the coffeemaker. Rosamond had always filled it for him before leaving at the end of each day so he could make do—or at least make coffee—until she arrived at nine. Even at this distance, only half believing he was truly dead, she took comfort in the solidness of him, how sure he was, how tall. In the alcohol-woodsy scent of his aftershave, the crispness of his white shirt, somber tie, the crackle of his neatly trimmed hair, the hairline at his neck so sharp she could swear his barber used a ruler to cut it. He'd had a weight about him that kept her own thoughts in place.

But here she stopped, getting up from bed and going down to start her breakfast. She concerned herself with heating the pan for eggs, with stepping out to fetch the paper. She was unwilling to travel the thread of what had caused Percy's death, to unravel it completely. She snatched up the paper, pulled the rubber band off it, and began reading it right there in the driveway to keep herself from thinking it through. She didn't want to know that Percy had feared his own impulse to jump. She didn't want to see it all too clearly. Yet she knew it. Already, all those years ago, his course was set.

The funeral was likely to be as well attended as the viewing had been—people had lined up out the church, around the corner, all the way to the post office—and Ralphie Thompson, brother to mortician Holland, was secretly thrilled. He was seeing to the memorial service of the greatest man in present-day Goliath, maybe even the greatest man in the town's long history. He was awake and at the church before Rosamond, who was taking her time with her eggs and coffee, had even finished reading the paper. It was a historic day.

Eugene Grady, the pastor, arrived early from the parsonage and took a seat at the front pew, fingering a bundle of index cards tucked into his breast pocket. A bit later, the organist, Johnsie Smith, who was deaf in her right ear and as a result always played the treble too loudly, waddled down the center aisle and settled herself at the organ bench. She folded her hands and waited.

Celeste Bradshaw came nearly half an hour early, alone since her father, the mortician, almost always kept to home, and her husband Ronald was superstitious about churches. The furniture executives began arriving in their dark suits, tidily dressed wives on their arms. Members of the Harding clan, their faces calm and deliberately unknowing, began filtering in. Many of them had not been in Goliath in years, and they felt they were stepping across an era, entering the church.

Ralphie Thompson shook their hands and led them to their seats, offering again and again his deepest sympathy. As he greeted guests and directed Johnsie to begin playing, first by nodding and then by touching her back, by whispering to her, and finally by placing her hands on the keys and pointing to the music in the stand, he watched the double doors at the base of the church with growing anxiety. The widow and her son had not yet arrived.

Others came. Here was Clyde Winston, the chief of police, who took a place in the back. His son Ray, the sidewalk evangelist, arrived in army pants and a clean white shirt, nodded first to his father, then to Eugene Grady, and chose an empty spot about halfway up, awkwardly folding his long limbs into the pew.

A moment later, the great doors opened once again and two figures entered, but neither was the widow. Rosamond had eaten her breakfast slowly and dressed with care and now she and her daughter had arrived. She wore a pale blue dress that fit her well and white gloves. Agnes looked the opposite in a black knit dress and matching boots, her hair a long tangle down her back. They took a pew across the aisle from Ray Winston, who looked up, nodded at Agnes, then bowed his head in prayer again.

The entire place smelled of dry heat from the antiquated heating system and mint, the individually wrapped green candies found in crumples of tissue in old ladies' pocketbooks.

It seemed Johnsie Smith would keep playing the same hymn forever, and that the aged pastor, Eugene Grady, who sat crumpled up in a gray suit in the front pew, would nod off in sleep, and the people in the pews would be stuck there, in polite suspension, for hours. But the heavy door opened at last, and everyone turned to look: Lela Harding was led down the center aisle by her son Ryan, and his plump, pretty wife, who gripped a little boy and a little girl by the hand on either side, followed. As Lela passed, the people in the pews leaned forward a bit, staring. Celeste Bradshaw whispered to the woman next to her, "It can't be."

But it was. Though Lela Harding kept her coat on and though she carried herself with her back straight, head held high, several inches of a blue flowered nightgown were visible below the hem of her coat, and a lace edge emerged from her sleeve. Her eyes were bare and small and threaded with red veins, blinking behind her sparse lashes. Her dark hair was uncombed, standing up a little in back. She had hastily tucked the loose strands around her face behind her ears. Rosamond touched Agnes's arm but said nothing. Everyone in the church was silent, watching.

Ryan Harding's neck burned pink as he showed his mother to her pew, but he seemed to puff up a little in determined dignity as he took his place beside her. His wife, perfectly coiffed and dressed in a simple navy dress embellished with a strand of pearls, slid in next to them, the children neatly tucked beside her. The two little ones looked about them, and though even they, at their young ages, understood there was something the matter with their grandmother's wearing her nightgown to church, they were unaccustomed to having so many eyes on them, and they stared back at the gapers until one by one, gazes were averted to the dense crimson carpet, the crisp white programs, the ancient Eugene Grady who was rising now, preparing to lead the assemblage in a hymn.

He trembled before them, his hands clasped to the podium, calling out the hymn number. Johnsie Smith played out the opening notes, and he sang it by heart. Pastor Grady saw that Lela Harding was a mess and that the entire room was pressing in on itself, watching, but he understood these things to be little more than tiny figurines, far off, as if he were observing everything through the wrong end of a telescope. They finished the first verse and Johnsie prepared to dive into the second, but Eugene turned to her, shaking his head, and addressed the congregation.

"We are gathered here," Pastor Grady began, then corrected himself. "We are here in the Lord's house this morning to celebrate the homecoming of our dearly departed, our friend and valued community leader." He paused here, peering out at the people crowded into the pews. He clutched the sides of the pulpit. "And also to mourn his passing." His hands shook as he drew his index cards from his breast pocket.

He began his sermon. "Lazarus was dead four days when the Lord went to him and expressed first his utter humanity—he wept. Yes, dear brothers and sisters in Christ," Pastor Grady continued, saying words that he did not so much issue as recite. The words were familiar to most of the people assembled there. This was his standard funeral sermon, and even Rosamond recognized it. His voice shook a bit now, though, and it registered as a whine at the close of each sentence. "Our Lord and Savior understood the grief we all share when one of us departs this life . . ."

He drew a breath, about to go into the bit about Christ showing his divinity in raising Lazarus from the dead, but Lela Harding suddenly rose from her pew and began to cry into the sleeves of her coat.

Ryan stood and awkwardly touched his mother's back. He whispered something to her and she paused, sniffing, steadying herself, then looked about the room, opening her mouth as if to say something but then stopping. She closed her eyes. Sunlight streamed into the sanctuary through the stained glass, and no one could speak or move.

Lela crumpled a bit further, whispering—the church was quiet enough for those several pews away to hear—"I can't," and turned to the side aisle. She shuffled past her son and daughter-in-law, past the children. Every eye was on her as, nightgown fluttering below her coat, she escaped to the aisle and moved swiftly past the pews of mourners to the back of the church. She opened the door, dazzling the congregation with a flash of sunlight, and left.

Ryan stood a moment later, following after her, though his wife remained seated, a hand on each child. Clyde Winston rose to his feet and left, too, and everyone else, the entire assemblage, dissolved into shock. People unfroze and turned in their pews, buzzing.

"Percy Harding," Pastor Grady said, finally recalling, "was a great man." But no one was listening. They looked about, wondering if they should leave or stay, if instructions would be forthcoming. Ray turned toward Agnes across the aisle, and, in answer to her questioning look, gave a meager *who knows?* smile. Rosamond pressed a tissue against her closed eyelids. After a moment, Ralphie Thompson thundered down the center aisle, sweating out what might be done to save the funeral.

The answer to that question, of course, was nothing. Pastor Grady stood blinking out at the congregation, and people began gathering their coats and drifting through the aisles, spilling out onto the church steps and into the parking lot.

Ray and Agnes walked on either side of Rosamond, who would accept no comfort, and gave each other little knowing looks, a sort of telepathy they had worked out long ago. The two had been friends since they were babies.

Around them, the sun was bright but not especially warm, turning the sidewalk bright white except for where their shadows fell. A few cars floated by. Rosamond paused to touch a tissue to her damp nose. She was still unnerved by the vividness of the memory she'd woken with and was trying now to focus on how unseemly Lela's behavior had been.

"She made such a mockery of everything," Rosamond said. Her face was blotchy and tear-streaked, smudged with dissolved makeup, her eyes gummy and red. She had come to regard Ray as a piece of scenery, a sort of walking tree, and she addressed all of her comments to her daughter. "Terrible behavior."

"Or grief," Agnes told her. "It could be she's horribly sad, unable to function."

"One functions," Rosamond insisted. "It's just what one *does*." They walked a few moments in silence, passing the neighbors' houses, lawns gone brown and tired by the long months of summer. Now dry fall breezes scuttled through the trees. "I wish I had been there," Rosamond said suddenly. "I would have stopped him."

Here Ray, who since the sidewalk was too narrow for all three had been walking a half step down in the gutter beside them, spoke up. "You couldn't have. No one could have."

"The widow," Agnes began.

"She didn't even love him," Rosamond said. "*That's* the worst part about this. She didn't even love him, and look how she carries on."

"We're not to judge," Ray said, "but to love. Can you love this woman?"

Rosamond snorted. She coughed shortly into her fist. To Agnes, she said, "Did you see how she carried on?"

"Then," Ray continued, walking in his subdued-giant way, his shoulders slouched as if to make himself appear smaller, his loping arms loose at his sides, "you will be judged. Those who don't love, who *won't* love, will be judged by their own measure. What fault you find in others will also be found in you.

"Tell me, Rosamond"—he paused for a car passing too close; even Rosamond, though pretending not to see, started—"what makes a person good? How do *you* count goodness?"

She turned to him in fresh anger, her eyes snapping. "I count it grief. You should miss the ones you love when they are gone. You should miss them. *And* keep your dignity." She shook her head, as if to dismiss Ray, all his "goodness and love" talk. Around them, in the yards they walked past, the trees were going bright with gold and deep purple. The few cars on the road, drove by at Ray's elbow. To Agnes, she said, "That woman doesn't love him. She never did."

Once home, Ray stood about, quieted, while Agnes helped her mother get the tea things ready. They used an old tea set with an ancient bone china teapot. There were stains around the spout and the flowers on the handle had faded from frequent use. Rosamond always took tea upon returning home from an outing; Agnes imagined she had picked up the habit from some old movie.

They drank their tea sitting on Rosamond's mustard-colored furniture, the late afternoon sunlight flooding through the windows, filling up all the gold-colored spaces, the velvet throw pillows, the dull beige carpet, the pinkish-taupe fleur-de-lis-patterned wallpaper. It was, in Agnes's view, a spectacularly gaudy room. The rest of the house was still gold-touched—gold-tone fixtures in the bathroom, a chest of drawers with brass handles in the bedroom—but not nearly as light-concentrated, as *heavy* as this one. Agnes would have preferred they sit in the clean-white, green-curtained kitchen, but she knew her mother wanted them to sit here, in all this comfort. Inside the beautifully papered walls.

Rosamond said little more about Percy, even less to Ray, though she set out the tin of shortbread cookies on the spot of coffee table closest to him. She prattled on about the odd bits of information she picked up on morning news shows. First, there were a hundred and one ways to cook an egg—"I've *never* poached," Rosamond said, and from there, she drifted to the strange things people ate in other countries. Liver pudding in England. Headcheese in Sweden, she said, her cheeks sucked in as if she could taste these oddities, as if she were suffering, that very moment, from their gelatinous textures.

"One of my uncles eats chocolate-covered ants," Ray contributed. "Mail-ordered from Vietnam."

Rosamond winced. "Ants?"

She looked at her daughter, limp on the sofa beside Ray, their arms touching. Agnes pressed the back of her hand against Ray's arm, some private signal, and Rosamond looked away.

"He really was a wonderful man," she said.

After a time the light through the window began to fade, and finally Rosamond was tired enough to let Agnes go. "I'll be glad when this day is over," she said, rising.

At the door Agnes squeezed her mother's hand, leaned close, and said, "Try to get some rest, Mom." Rosamond checked her daughter's voice for any mocking note. She found none, and nodded, letting loose a long sigh. The air, thick with sunlight, was too much even for her. She was drowsy from breathing it all afternoon, from talking into it. She kissed her daughter, lightly touched Ray's shoulder, and closed the door behind them.

The pair stepped out into the early evening where the sun, which had been overheating Rosamond's living room for so many hours, had cooled, and now the light breeze of the afternoon had a chilly bite to it. Agnes huddled close to Ray, hooking her arm to his as they walked. They had been babies in the same playpen while their mothers, close friends, played cards and drank iced tea, laughing themselves weak. Agnes remembered Penny as a tiny woman with a sudden, ringing laugh. She and Ray grew up together, were fellow misfits in high school, and then drifted away from each other when Agnes went off to college. Now she was returned, and she was relieved, with all she'd encountered out there, away from Goliath, to find Ray exactly as he always had been: *here.*

"I cannot stand another moment of sadness," she confessed, pressing her face into his work jacket. It smelled of leaf-pile fires and damp earth. "Let's go find something happy and stupid to do."

After the children left, Rosamond changed into her nightgown and arranged herself on the chair by the window in the living room. The day's light dissolved away in under an hour, but once the sky was completely dark, the window let in a fair amount of glow from a nearby streetlight. It was enough for knitting, though barely. She worked, pulling the yarn this way and that around the needles. She knitted too tight, as she was prone to do when she was agitated. It seemed she would never finish this sweater for all the times she had stopped to unravel a mistake, or, judging the garment too small or too large, took the whole thing apart and started all over again. It was meant for Agnes, though she would probably change her mind and keep it to save herself the trouble of watching Agnes's face arrange itself in uneasy surprise when she gave it to her.

She sensed Agnes would not stay in Goliath long. While she

was up at that college, she had married a boy in a loose sort of way. From what Rosamond could gather, the two went and stood beneath a tree and promised to love each other for all time. Rosamond had not been invited to the ceremony, but Agnes had told her no one had been invited. It had been just the two of them and the tree. "How *nice*," Rosamond had said, and Agnes had only looked curiously back at her, willing herself, Rosamond could tell, to ignore the sarcasm. It *had* been nice, Agnes insisted. Even now, the marriage ended, she persisted: the wedding had been nice. Rosamond's own wedding had been in the courthouse with her cousin as a witness. Hatley was older than she, and he had seemed confident of himself and exceedingly certain of all his decisions. *Too* certain, Rosamond later decided.

Agnes had said even less about the end of the marriage, though Rosamond guessed Agnes had been the one to do the leaving. Since she was ten years old, Agnes had been fluent in the names of distant cities. She had wall maps of the world; a tourist's map of Boston; a map of the Eastern world, of Columbus's world, of the ancient world; one of Australia, turned upside down; one of Sicily from an Italian restaurant menu. They were taped to the walls of Agnes's basement apartment, kept on the refrigerator with magnets, scattered on the stack of soda crates she used for a coffee table.

No, Agnes would not stay. Rosamond knitted. She was glad of that. She wanted Agnes to go off, do things. But she wanted *home* to matter. She pictured Agnes invisibly tethered here, always returning. Outside, darkness settled, and the town was rubbed over with fog as the hours moved toward morning.

What Agnes hadn't told her mother was that she sensed, with a gut-level instinct, that there was something significant she needed to get from Goliath before leaving again. It was more than a resting place, as her mother guessed, or a last resort, as Ray might have predicted. Goliath was a spot on the earth just like any other, and it held every moment lived there, what survived and what died out, what was lost and what held on, its history just as long, just as significant as that of any other. The timing of her return now seemed prearranged. She had been there working her shift at Lucky Grocery when Celeste Bradshaw announced it: the most powerful man in Goliath had ended his own life. The planet shifted to accommodate a bit more sorrow let out into the world.

The happy and stupid thing she and Ray found to do was to play four rounds of hearts and then settle onto her couch, drinking instant hot chocolate from mismatched coffee mugs, similarly chipped, until she finally lay her head on the armrest and fell asleep. Ray watched her sleeping for a bit, then brought her a pillow and a blanket. Having settled her, he locked up and left. He walked across town to his trailer, cracking it open against a seal of cold when he turned the key and pushed in the door.

Clyde Winston, though not on duty, patrolled the town all night, mostly just parking down the hill from the Hardings' house and looking up at a lit square of window.

Late that night, down Main Street and beyond, the people of Goliath slept soundly inside their matchbox houses beneath a cold, deep moon shining clean on the rooftops. In every dark basement, a clunky old furnace rumbled on for the first time of the season, laboring against the chill in the air, which dropped even colder as the night wore on.

Rosamond finally fell asleep and at once began dreaming of flying day. She watched Pastor Grady—Percy was nowhere in sight—standing out on the field on the bright spring morning, waiting a few paces away from the crowd. His hands were in his pockets, and he was calm.

This time the pocket-size plane touched down on the football field, its engine idling tinny and canned through the heavy wraps of Rosamond's dream-conscious, and Eugene Grady held out his dollar for the woman in the black jumpsuit to take. He was the only passenger to board the plane, the others staying outside the window, waving and cheering and stamping their feet. They *loved* him.

The sun shone against blue sky as the plane gathered speed and lifted, the pilot nothing more than a dark shape in the cockpit, for there existed only what was outside the windows. Airborne, Eugene looked down at the streets, and Rosamond saw through his eyes the miniature cars like insects, the houses and trees looking so much simpler and neater for the distance. The plane went still farther, pressing against the bright seam of the sky, bearing hard through the clouds, coming out into night darkness. He unhooked his seat belt, crawled out of his seat. In the dream Rosamond was unsurprised, and she knew what was going to happen next. Strong-arming the swing lever at the door, he wrestled his way out. He drifted, weightless, and it took him hours to fall, Pastor Grady strolling along commonplace and miraculous on the star-glow layers of black and gold and the deepest blue.

THREE

Rosamond kept to herself those first days after Percy's funeral. She moved through the rooms of her house and listened to the nothing-noises, the nearly soundless creaks and sighs of its joints and walls settling into middle age. Most of the houses in Goliath had been built during the late forties and early fifties, when young families settled in and the downtown shops opened. Before that, the town consisted of the factory, the railroad, and a coarse motel where the factory workers, all male at that time, stayed. There were loggers in the woods. A hundred years before that, there was only the river, moving swift and strong, and the trees growing tall all around it.

Rosamond did not attend the second funeral, that of Eugene Grady, who had died in his sleep the night of Percy's funeral. She had no recollection of her flying-day dream but felt a wary sort of unsurprise at Pastor Grady's death. Well, she told herself, he *was* an old man. Besides, surprise seemed an unlikely response to any news at the moment. Shock—who could be shocked?

Mia called incessantly, though she did not come to visit; she was old and disliked leaving her house. She worried Rosamond would catch absentmindedness, a condition she believed to be borne of spending too many hours alone. She told Rosamond, "Sometimes, I don't know if a sound's in my head or happening for real. That's dangerous territory, I'll tell you—when you start to doubt your own senses."

Mia was Rosamond's mother's sister, and Rosamond sometimes felt a twinge of the impatience her mother used to feel for Mia when she called. Rosamond told her it was all right; she was going back to work next week. She couldn't stay home forever, even if she wanted to. Mia had four children, but only one lived close by. Her son Donald brought her science magazines she looked through in the afternoons, after the daytime game shows, before she stepped outside to tend to her jungly wild flower garden. Mia loved her telephone—her lifeline, she called it. She had a separate line installed downstairs when Agnes moved in and rang Agnes on it when she needed her rather than walking down the steps.

Often Rosamond let the phone ring and ring. She was waiting for something. She moved through the rooms in her nightgown, bending to pick up a piece of lint from the carpet, reaching to straighten a curtain. She peered inside drawers and cabinets, opened closet doors and stood there, looking. There was *something* for her, she was certain. She examined the cracks in the plaster ceiling in the living room; she touched the towels folded and stacked in the linen closet. Though she couldn't recall a time Percy had actually been inside her house, she believed he had managed to leave behind a message.

She entertained a fantasy, then half convinced herself it was real: Percy had entered her house the morning of his death. She pictured it from a vantage point outside her own body, saw her house in the gray predawn hours, watched the front door from inside. It opened, and there stood Percy wearing the kind of

business suit he typically wore to the office instead of the jogging suit he was found in. In her dream's eye, she saw him enter
the house and walk down the dim hallway, silent. She could
even see the dark form of herself, upstairs in her room sleeping.
Each time the waking dream revisited her, she peered closely,
concentrating, but she could never see just where he went inside
the house. Her focus returned to the front door, and she watched
it, motionless, while Percy moved about the house. She could
hear his footfalls and the small clicks and shuffles of him touching things, opening and closing closets, drawers, she didn't know
what all. Then the front door opened again, and she saw the
back of Percy in the dimness of early light, leaving.

It occurred to her that perhaps what she was seeing in her
imagination had actually happened *after* his death. Maybe it was
yet to come. Maybe he would yet appear in his navy suit, the
one he usually paired with the chevron-patterned maroon and
ivory tie. He would come in while she was sleeping. She knew
she was making herself crazy, thinking this way, but she couldn't
stop. Whenever she tried to be more realistic, another voice insisted: *but maybe.*

Finally it became too much for her, and on the third evening
of her seclusion, she felt compelled to do as her aunt Mia had
instructed: to seek out a flesh-and-blood person. She had no
girlfriends, and her parents were gone. Mia had her ways, and
Rosamond truly loved her. But she would look at her too carefully, too worriedly. The man she had loved even more than Percy
had left one morning fifteen years ago to sell outdoor lighting
fixtures to a recreation center in Georgia and had not yet returned. Agnes would come if she called, but she didn't want to
wade there, into her daughter's doubtful looks and quiet judg-
ments. She needed someone who would not ask a thing of her.
Who would just let her *exist.*

Rosamond dressed hastily and stepped outside. The sky had

deepened into purple, the first stars appearing, and she crossed the lawn to stand on her neighbor's doorstep. She wanted a drink—it had been ages since she had wanted a drink—but she planned to ask Clyde Winston only if she might borrow a tea bag. Goliath had a tiny scrap of a bar a street up from the post office; years ago, she used to go there often.

After the days she'd spent inside, it felt strange to be away from her house. She stood in the open, nothing but wind—*nothing*—between her body and the far-flung stars, the half-moon, waiting for Clyde to answer her knock. It was ridiculous for her to be here, and she hesitated, looking back toward her own house across the lawn.

She and Clyde had not known each other well when the two couples—Penny and Clyde, Rosamond and Hatley, the salesman—were together. The couples were linked by the women's friendship. The two men had little in common but talked sports and fishing and made a go at easeful silence, gazing out from their lawn chairs onto the smooth surface of the lake during the group's Sunday-afternoon outings at the state park. At that time, Rosamond hadn't liked Clyde. He was too serious and fretful, eyeing the teenagers who picnicked on the other side of the lake, the girls in bikini tops and cutoffs, the boys teasing them. Penny, who saw Rosamond's impatience with Clyde, caught her eye and drew on her cigarette. She shrugged, letting out a thin flat spiral of smoke. *He loves me,* she told Rosamond at other moments. *He's devoted.* She in turn did not care much for Hatley. He told tall tales about stupid, proud men and gruff, bovine women in the holler he'd grown up in. He was too slick, urban-like from his years on the road, imploring her to dance with him when a favorite song came on the radio. He winked at her. She pointed her cigarette at him. *You watch your manners, sir.* She laughed, a little viciously, and elbowed Clyde.

Secretly, though, Penny had told Rosamond: *You put our hus-*

bands together, you get the perfect man. The way Clyde loves, the way Hatley dances. Rosamond had betrayed the comment to Hatley, and he was pleased. *The devil and the saint,* he'd said and whistled. His speech was loose that way when he'd been drinking. He pulled her onto his lap. *You got yourself a devil,* he whispered into her ear.

Clyde, who was not religious and would have disputed that word *saint,* was soft-spoken and contemplative. He had a poet's soul, Penny said. But Rosamond had rarely seen such depth in Clyde. In those days he seemed at a loss as to what to say to Rosamond. He asked her how work was going, made weather predictions. Useless talk.

After Hatley left, and later, during Penny's sickness, he and Rosamond had come together over practical worries, their children. Clyde could hardly boil an egg on his own. Rosamond had trouble getting her lawn mower started. But he was resigned to his life and his grief in a way that made Rosamond edgy. He accepted his loneliness with long-suffering regret, while Rosamond made efforts to burst out of hers. After Hatley left, she simultaneously hated and adored every man who crossed her path.

The door opened at last, and Clyde appeared wearing slacks and a wrinkled button-down. He was in his stocking feet, which was of course completely natural—he *was* in his own home—but it struck Rosamond as being too casual somehow, even a little indecent.

"Come in," he said, stepping back for her to enter. He seemed unsurprised to see her, as he always was, regardless if it had been two days or two years since her last visit.

"I've come to beg a tea bag," she said.

Clyde frowned, then observed, "Awful chilly out there." He stepped back, inviting her into the house. "I don't know that I have any tea, Rosamond." She and Clyde rarely spoke except in passing and when she sought him out—he never came to her. It occurred to her now, following him into the house, that he had probably been expecting her this time. Since Percy's accident.

"Yes, it's bad out there," she said, dropping the pretense of the tea bag. She felt coarse and old standing there in his house. She found she could not shed her coat while he was watching her—his black socks, the silver-and-black stubble on his cheeks—so she kept it on, fiddling with the sleeves.

"Sad, too. It's terrible sad out there, it seems." He kept his hands in his pockets a moment, frowning at the carpet, then looked up. "Beer?"

She shrugged, yes, and Clyde disappeared into the kitchen.

With him gone, she shed her coat and dropped it onto the couch. She looked around. There were signs of bachelorhood everywhere. A pile of newspapers up to her knees was stacked beside the door leading out to the back porch, on which there was only a single rusty lawn chair. Years ago, she remembered, Penny had kept potted plants out there, even in the wintertime. Always something blooming. Inside, the carpet seemed clean enough, and the vacuum cleaner had been left out, as if to testify that it was used with some regularity, but there was a layer of dust on top of the television and on the end table. Beside the easy chair, on the carpet, there sat a half-full cup of coffee, its oily surface dull and black, gone cold hours or maybe even days before.

He returned and handed her a beer and a napkin. "Have a sit." He gestured toward the couch, seating himself in the easy chair.

She sat, then lifted her beer as if to toast. The can was so cold, she didn't hold it bare in her hands but wrapped the napkin around it. She took guarded little sips. "You must keep them in the freezer," she remarked. It tasted good, though, and she found herself starting to relax.

"Baseball," he began, "is a fine sport."

Clyde had always been a sports guy, watching the games on television, making predictions as to which players would save which teams. But now sports of any flavor was the last thing Rosamond wished to discuss. She took a drink of beer and listened impatiently.

"Rosamond," he said seriously, "can I share with you? I have a vision—"

She covered her nose with her fingers. "Tonight is the first night I like beer. Strange how that works, isn't it? Yesterday I hated it." She squinted at the can. "Tonight is a different story."

He shrugged. "I always thought you liked it."

Their visits usually went like this: She gave him recipes he never tried, and he told her useless facts he discovered in science documentaries and sports hero biographies. Later the bits of science anomalies and Hank Aaron stats would come back to her at odd moments; she'd be pulling wet towels from the washer and thinking of a bit he'd told her about sea spiders, a newly discovered species, he'd said. The difference between him and his son Ray, whose words about judgment and love from a few days earlier still nagged at her, was that Ray pretended to know something about the way the universe worked—all of it providence, everything foreknown—while Clyde remained appropriately baffled. *Sea spiders,* he'd said, amazed. When it first became apparent that Hatley had left for good, Clyde had said, "There's nothing right about his doing this. Nothing that makes sense."

After Penny died, they had made a halfhearted attempt at a love affair, which ended almost as soon as it began. For a time, though, they ate dinner together in the evenings, and he kissed her lightly when she said good night and left. But she found she couldn't stand the silences, Clyde's retreating, and she couldn't bear his hopeful looks, his philosophizing. He was always searching, trying to tunnel through the end of every dilemma.

Now she said, "Baseball," and snorted. "All-American. All that. Sure." She drank some of her beer, then heard herself voice one of the thoughts she'd been thinking by herself inside her empty house. "What I don't get is how can a body destroy it-self," she said. Clyde said nothing, and she continued. "I mean, I understand the desire, we all have our desperate moments, our sadnesses. Life *is* hard. Yes, it makes sense, just end it." She took another drink, unpeeling the napkin from the can and laying it, damp, across her lap. "But for the physical, the actual *body,* to do it? The mind, the heart, yes. But the body? The body wants to keep going. Everything about it says *keep going.*"

She didn't know what she was saying. She plucked the tab off her beer can and pressed the pad of her finger to the sharp opening in the can, a perfect, machine-cut oval.

"A body needs to run," Clyde said. "A *person* needs hope."

"Its job is to keep you alive. It's *biological.*" She put her hand to her chest.

He nodded, sighed, leaning back in his chair. "Rosamond, I don't know. I don't know what calls a man to such a place. I don't know what takes him there."

"I can't believe it's happened. I can't believe he's gone."

He nodded. "I went to tell Lela. I was the one to have to tell her."

They were quiet for a space then, the mention of Lela Harding stalling their talk. Rosamond still wished for Percy's ghost and began to worry absurdly that he was waiting for her across the lawn, in her gold-colored living room. He would find something to read, stand up and walk around—he had always hated to just sit and wait. He might nose around her kitchen, try to make a pot of coffee. She observed the workings of her own body, noting the tiny thumps of her pulse in her wrist.

"I've been thinking about a town game. The whole town. Everybody coming out to play." Clyde shrugged, as if to dismiss the idea and champion it with the same gesture. "A body needs to run," he said again.

Rosamond nodded. "Sure," she said, though she was still

thinking of Percy's ghost, and then, strangely, of soup. Before
Agnes had gone away to college, she had assembled some sort of
soup most evenings and left it simmering on the stove until they
were both home, mother and daughter eating together at the
kitchen table. In her old, old life, when Hatley was still there,
she had cooked a real supper every night: roast, potatoes, green
beans. Now that her house was empty, she subsisted on saltines
smeared with peanut butter. Tuna straight from the can. Rice
cakes. What tiny comfort her body could take from such skimpy
provisions. Clyde said, "Lela Harding is a good woman," and the
comment felt random, disconnected, but only because Rosamond had not been listening. Her nerves were loosened by the
beer but the relaxed feeling had left her, and now she felt unfas-
tened and dull.

"I've been up to see her since then," Clyde said. "Evenings.
Just to lend a little comfort. Just to be with her."

Their try at a love affair had begun for the same reason it had
ended: they were each searching for a bit of Penny in the other
person. To staunch the gaping, uncloseable loneliness. It brought
acid to back of her throat for Clyde to now speak of Lela Harding. She couldn't stay, not with him talking like that.

"Thanks for the drink," she said, rising.

Years ago, as a teenage girl, she had left the dinner table in
the same abrupt manner and her father, that dear, dear man, had
been confused, himself rising from the table. *Rosamond?* What
could be wrong? She would go home now, eat something, try to
get her mind together. *Sit down,* her mother had said. *Don't you
walk away from me, little miss.*

It couldn't be that easy, kill the body to extinguish the soul.
No, no—Percy was still out there. The soul, the heart was not so
easily shaken off.

Clyde stood. "It's sad for all of us. You're not the only one."
He was going bald, Rosamond saw suddenly, the tufts of dark

hair around his crown lit up by the lamp's yellow glow. He nodded to the door. "It's here now, in Goliath, a colossal sadness. I
don't know how we'll stand it."

"I'm just tired," she said, closing her eyes for a moment.
"Tired and hungry." She opened her eyes and blinked at Clyde,
surprised. "Why, I'm famished."

"Come on," he said, his voice going soft. "Stay. Finish your
beer. Cook something. Let's have a meat loaf."

She looked hard back at him, thinking on how she might really stay. He might never get rid of her, her staying and staying,
lounging about in an old nightgown, drinking his beer. If she
ever did stay, that was exactly how it would happen. She would
sink into his couch and never rise up from it.

"No," she said simply, "but, thank you. Thank you, Clyde."

She left her can there, sweating coaster-less on the coffee table,
and struggled back into her coat. Leaving, she paused, one hand on
the doorknob. "What's wrong," she said, "is no one cares about
it. Percy is gone and there's not a person in this town save me
who really cares. Everyone's shocked, that's all. He was a great
man. No one even seems to know it."

She stepped out into the thin black night, unable to string
one thought to the next. They went: soup, blood, chicken, death,
flowering cabbages. A body's irrational bent toward undoing itself. Every impulse was suspect. Crossing the lawn, Rosamond
again felt exposed to the reaches of the universe, and she hunched
down inside her coat.

The people of Goliath would not have been surprised to hear
that Rosamond Rogers was holed up in her house that weekend,
waiting for a ghost. She would take a man however she could get
him, they believed. They knew she had taken up with Clyde
Winston before his wife's body had even gone cold. There had
once been a doctor from nearby Winnie she'd trounced about

with. She and the doctor—a *doctor*—had carried on at Dalton's Bar, up behind the post office. Tucker, the doctor's name was. People suspected, too, that she had tried to start something up with Percy Harding. In public, the secretary and boss had had a familiar way about them. She picked the lint off the sleeve of his suit and the two often exchanged quick, knowing smiles.

Rosamond had always been an odd one, those vintage dresses, her solitary twice-daily journey along the sidewalk on Main Street, walking up in the morning, down at quitting time. Most could not remember how Rosamond, who had lived in Goliath all her life, had come to be regarded as an outsider, forgetting or never knowing that her parents had never been much for church potlucks or community picnics. Her father had worked at the factory, her mother had stayed home. At some point, there had been an older relative who lived out her final days in their house. Rosamond was younger than Clyde had been when she saw her first dead body; her aunt Belle had died when she was thirteen and had been laid out in the dining room all night. Rosamond was in her bed down the hall, both trying to sleep and trying not to.

Most forgot the family of Mia Robins, who had been popular as a young person, a respected schoolteacher as an adult, eccentric but truehearted and dear now, an old lady with tissues tucked into her sleeves. This Mia Robins had once been Mia Hampton, sister to Lila Hampton. Lila Hampton married a quiet man and had three sons who left as soon as they were old enough and one daughter, Rosamond, who stayed. Those who remembered Rosamond as a child remembered her quieter than she actually had been, and then, when she was a teenager, wilder. The women remembered that she had made out with their boyfriends in high school, though she hadn't—not all of them.

People remembered she had shacked up with a traveling salesman when she was young; she had just started working for Percy

Harding, who himself was new at the job. He plucked her up from a pool of girls in the mailroom. She had been living at home with her parents when the salesman came along.

He worked his way across town, pitching sewing wares and upright vacuum cleaners, and had made a pass at Rosamond Lewis in her parents' living room. Lonely girl, people said. It was said she fell for him right away, before he even did his dirt demonstration, though that part was pure rumor. The other part, about her and Hatley staying at the King's Motel, was sworn to by witnesses who saw them coming and going, she with her hair tied down in a new scarf every day. The salesman's gifts, the women said. He kept a close shave—his cheeks were as soft as a baby's—and his hair was oiled and combed straight. The King's Motel was down the highway, beyond Lucky Grocery. Today there was a waterbed and pool-table warehouse where the motel once stood.

Rosamond had never been one to attend church. It was unknown—even, in many ways, to Rosamond herself—just what she believed. Nearly everyone else in town was Baptist.

Most attended the First Baptist Church, an expansive brick and white-pillared building huddled just east of the downtown shops, across from the high school. Nearly all of the town's social activity was centered around the events of First Baptist, their potlucks and missionary yard sales. A few Holy Rollers went up to Sonrise Baptist, a tiny clapboard church just outside of town, perched in the wooded hills dotted with scrappy houses with skinny goats grazing on the slopes like something in a prophet's dream. It was where the mother and sisters of Vincent Bailey, the boy who had found Percy Harding's body, went to church, though Vincent, like his father, stayed home on Sundays mornings.

The preachers of Goliath held to a similar doctrine of good works, faith, and an unflinching allegiance to God Almighty.

They differed only in emphasis. Pastor Ray was all about repentance and acceptance of God's grace, the holiness church called for separate living, and the standard First Baptist preaching sought a balance of good works and mercy. What not a one of them could preach out of Goliath, though, was a hold to superstition and a general fear of bad luck. If God's ways were mysterious, then at least the sinister whims of luck had its warnings. Spilled salt, the appearance of a black crow at dawn, spying a quarter moon through cracked glass were all signs of misfortune coming soon. And death, as it did everywhere, came to Goliath in threes.

The wives who gathered in Charlotte Branch's drugstore in the late afternoon while their children were at basketball practice or at home watching television; the old ladies who met to can or bake in Opal Mercer's kitchen; the old men, whom the old ladies called the Morning Glories because they rose early as a habit born of their working years and were the first customers at the Tuesday Diner, drinking coffee and recapitulating the day's headlines—they all spoke of it. They counted and recounted to each other all the times in the town's known history that three mortalities had come in quick succession. The first two were often unrelated, happening in the natural progression of a life, but the last came from nowhere, descending upon the unlikeliest of victims, as if the first two had opened up a spot for the third. In some cases, a full year united the deaths, and in other instances, there were three funerals in one month. The Morning Glories retold the story of a week in 1919 when twin sisters were killed by the influenza outbreak, and, that same week, a perfectly healthy girl the same age died in her sleep from no discernible cause.

In the days following Percy Harding's suicide and Pastor Eugene Grady's heart attack, many were afraid to go to sleep for fear they'd dream of muddy water, a sure sign death was on its way. The burial of Percy Harding was seen to the day after the failed funeral, and this time Lela Harding appeared on time, appropriately dressed and outwardly grieving, as the ladies from Opal Mercer's kitchen agreed she should. Eugene Grady's funeral was held a few days later, with junior pastor Dale Myers delivering the sermon, a treatise on suffering and faithfulness from the book of Job. It was a solemn, respectful service and the viewing the night before was well attended, but it was a timely passing—Eugene Grady had been in his eighties—whereas Percy Harding's death remained unreal and haunting.

The weather grew unreasonably chilly as October progressed, and Ray Winston revved up his sidewalk ministry, arriving on doorsteps across town, presenting the Gospel, leading many in the decision to follow Christ and thus be assured of eternal paradise. Besides his words of hope, Ray's presence, gigantic and tender, had a calming effect on those he visited. Throughout town, people were consoled, though ever watchful, and they gathered in tight bunches to pass the comfort around and muster talk about ordinary things, high school football and the price of gasoline.

Still, there were those who would not be consoled. The Baptist ladies commenced lengthy prayer sessions, and Marty Pickard, who had hugged Ryan Harding's wife too hard at the visitation, sobbed the sermon away that Sunday at church. Celeste Bradshaw, the mortician's daughter, finally after two years of trying got a positive result on a pregnancy test, and she spread the happy news along with scraps of Marty Pickard's overblown depression. Janice, Marty's wife, snuck out nights to drink at one of the restaurants the next town over. Celeste mostly talked about her baby, the size of a grain of rice inside her. "Already this baby is changing me. I'm puking my heart out for her, and she's still so little, so *minute*." She told her friend the checkout girl, "Marty Pickard is overdoing it. He's sad. We *get it*."

People were worried about whether Harding Furniture could

go on without Percy. "Seems almost like blasphemy, to think of starting up again," a few of the workers remarked to one another. There had long been rumors of the company's going under, and Percy's death heated them back up again. They didn't want to think about stopping production. "Seems more like blasphemy *not* to start back up," the men gathered in the break room that first morning back agreed. "He'd be upset we'd waited this long," they told one another.

They were relieved to see Ryan Harding, young and squeaky blond, in a gray suit and *pink* tie, occupy his father's office that first day back at the factory. The pink tie was odd, but who were they to judge? It was a mercy, his being there. Though he was no Percy, he was at least a Harding. Long ago, being a craftsman in Goliath was a great honor. There had been Harding furniture in the nicest houses across America, in the best hotels. It had not been strictly factory work in those days; they were truly artisans. These past years, though, everyone could see there were fewer orders to fill, less furniture to go out, fewer workers hired. Ryan Harding was a godsend.

Rosamond, returning as secretary to the new president, was not convinced he would be the salvation of Harding Furniture. "What I'd like to know is what's in it for him?" she asked Agnes, calling her during her lunch hour. "What does *he* stand to gain?" she asked. Agnes sighed into her end of the phone. "Mother," she began—she'd started calling her that, *Mother,* since she'd returned home. Rosamond hated it. "Try not to get yourself too worked up over this, okay?" Agnes urged. Rosamond opined: "He's in it for the power. For some people, that's more important than money."

Those early days of the changeover, she took note of his work habits. Some time near nine o'clock, he strolled down the long corridor, dressed in a crisp suit and a tie—no longer pink after that first day. The tie would be loosened by ten o'clock, when he emerged for his second cup of coffee. He went to the same coffee island the secretaries used rather than ask Rosamond to fetch it for him, and he then returned to his office, where the door remained closed again until lunch. He came out for coffee once more at two, and left early, at just past four. Ryan rarely summoned Rosamond, but he took the calls she patched through and signed the papers she brought him. She nearly always found him on the phone with his feet propped up on the desk, his jacket off, bobbing a pen between his fingers. Each time he glanced up quickly, attended to whatever she brought for him, and dismissed her with a pert nod. She found it almost unbearable, after the intimacies she had grown accustomed to, and she found herself despising him for the way he cradled the receiver against his shoulder, the way he leaned back and clasped his hands behind his head, the way he laughed too loudly at whatever it was someone was saying on the other end of that telephone. His cool blue eyes were always blank at first seeing her, as if he'd forgotten, a number of times over the course of the day, just who she was.

"You'd think he'd been doing this all his life," she complained to one of the other secretaries, a young girl who always managed to look simultaneously surprised and completely bored. The girl adjusted the cuff of her sweater and shrugged. "You'd think he'd been here for decades, the way he owns the place," Rosamond said.

Percy had once been as maddeningly boyish as his son Ryan, but it was different in those days. Rosamond was young and pretty then. She wore blue dresses and silk stockings purchased with her modest wages. He had just taken over for his father then and he loved the business. He fairly *sprung* into the work each day. Rolling up his shirtsleeves, he sat on the edge of the desk and started to give dictation. In those days, there was only charting the profits and numbering new markets. Percy wangled a deal to get his furniture featured on a daytime game show where contestants put historical facts in sequence. Young models in gauzy pastel evening dresses displayed the prize Harding bedroom suites with vivid floral bedspreads, pillows stacked high, the living room sets complete with record players set in bookcases and gleaming brass lamps on end tables.

The problem was, she was not in love with Ryan Harding. His acts of arrogance could not be forgiven. A second problem was Rosamond knew better than most just how bleak things were for Harding Furniture. Once, the year before, Percy had failed to make payroll. After that, she'd patched through more and more phone calls from the board members, the family. Now they were calling Ryan. Those in accounting must have known it, maybe a few of the other secretaries. But nobody spoke of it, no one let on just how close real trouble was coming.

What was most bothersome was that she could not concentrate on the matter long enough to work up the necessary amount of misgiving. All her life, it was worry alone that had staved off the unthinkable. Now she sat at her desk and stared at the desk calendar, but instead of playing out the many ways the company might collapse, her thoughts kept going back to the same predictably morbid thoughts she'd been struggling through all day. Just exactly *what* kills a person when he is crushed to death, she wondered. One could live without air for a few moments. Brain activity might proceed—for a short time, perhaps—even after the heart has stopped beating. Residual thoughts, disconnected flashes. It was said he had died instantly, but just how quickly could it have happened? If there's time, one passes out when in such pain. Blessedly, the mind knows when to shut off consciousness.

These speculations brought on an instant, powerful headache that was still pulsing relentlessly when she finally left work that afternoon, just minutes after Ryan left for the day. The headache was so intense that her sight had gone shimmery in spots, smudging out the street, the trees, the houses, the cars parked in driveways and carports, those half hitched up on the sidewalk, her reaching out like a blind person as she navigated around them.

She took a right on August Street, toward Mia's house instead of going farther down on Main Street to her own house. The afternoon was bright and cold, the trees shaking their brittle leaves in the wind.

She found her aunt kneeling in the weeds near her mailbox, a netted bag of flower bulbs beside her. Aunt Mia, a self-taught horticulturist, tended her tiny yard, a mess of tough green vines, overgrown shrubbery, and heavy-headed stalks of wild flowers, black-eyed Susans, and tiger lilies. She ordered her seeds and bulbs from catalogues and was pleased with her successes: unwieldy rose-bushes, growing spiky and beautiful in their thorny disarray; a clump of English heather, dusty with purplish pollen; dahlias with blooms as large as a dinner plates.

Rosamond came up the driveway calling hello. Mia's station wagon was alone in the driveway; Agnes wasn't home. The old woman looked up from her work and wrinkled her nose in greeting.

"So you've come to wish me luck with the fall planting," she said.

Rosamond stood on the driveway, her hands in her coat pockets, stalling in the way she'd done as a child—she and her cousins had hated the dirty, itchy work of gardening—before she gave up and fished around in Aunt Mia's wheelbarrow for a second digging spade. She squatted next to Mia, her high-heeled pumps pushed into the dirt. Above them the clouds burned orange, but the sky was already going gray on the other side of the street. Mia clucked her tongue. "Mmm," she said, putting all of her ninety-odd pounds into pressing the point of the spade into the dirt. Mia always smelled of body talc and sweat.

After a time, the old woman rose creakingly to her feet and stretched magnificently. She dropped her digging spade in the dirt and sat on the nearest spot of empty driveway. Rosamond joined her. The cement was cold and rough through her stockings, and the dusk air had grown chilly. Together they watched the new circles of bald earth among all the reckless vegetation, the unseen bulbs below beginning—in their microscopic slowness—to soften into the earth. Rosamond's headache had gone away, but she was left with a sort of dark numbness. She willed herself not to think about Percy, and she didn't want to speak of the difficulties at the factory. Mia seemed to be waiting for Rosamond to say something, to explain why she had come or to relay the details of her grief. But Rosamond remained quiet, her gaze cast across the street at the dimming houses. Finally Mia broke the quiet.

"It will be a cold winter," she said, and she reached across Rosamond's lap to touch her hand. She held it. "Good for the daffodils."

Later, Agnes still gone, the sky turned gray, Rosamond slipped her hand out of her aunt's grasp and stood. She stretched and then helped Mia into the house. Mia turned on the porch light, a lamp inside, the television, and Rosamond nosed around in a drawer in the kitchen for a flashlight to carry on her way home.

FOUR

Halloween came, and the grade school children attended a costume ball at town hall during their lunch hour. The older students carried on with algebra and the Constitution until they were released at three. Then they dressed and prepared to meet up in one another's basements. This year bobbing for apples was making a comeback, and the teenagers planned to watch horror films from the 1950s on late-night cable. They talked about the old drive-in theater down the highway that had been torn down when they were kindergartners, aeons ago.

Rosamond handed out candy and waited for it to grow dark. The Snow Whites, the ghosts, the devils, the pirates, the cheerleaders, and a lone Mae West came and went, and close to eight, she turned off her porch light. She wandered about her house for a time, checking each of the rooms, still burdened with ghost visions and hopes of the unearthly, the *special*. She filled the tea-kettle and turned the stove on, then stood waiting for it to boil. Halloween was dying down outside, the sidewalks emptying.

She had learned how to forget time and make it go away from her mother, an unimaginative woman whose only success, counted daily, was a quiet, sleeping house. Rosamond and her teakettle, the water just starting up its boiling sounds like thunder in miniature, were the only warm things in the house tonight—no sleeping bodies. The house itself had become a distinct entity, a sort of blinking presence. Its quiet had grown as fragile as eggshells, and the glow from the light fixture reverberated dully off the pale countertop, the porcelain saltshakers, the face of the clock. It was as if something had quickened here since Percy's death. The house thumped soundlessly, a pulse beating in its walls.

She kept the letter opener she had meant to give Lela Harding in her robe pocket. Smoothing her fingers over the hard, dull blade kept her from feeling as though her front door would sweep open and she would be sucked out and away, into the sky. She had experienced more instances of forgetfulness the way she had the day of Percy's death when she'd sat at the typewriter and was unable to think *typewriter*. Now it was the refrigerator. She stared at it until it became a harmless blear of white.

The teakettle sang and she lifted it from the heat, switched off the burner. She dropped a tea bag into one of her coffee mugs— she used the teacups only when she was serving real loose tea, from the china teapot—and poured the water, watching the dark color seeping from the bag in swirls. She touched the countertop, the plastic blue tulip napkin holder, a jelly jar made of clouded glass. The sky through the window was black and there was a small wind tonight rustling the trees. She dunked the tea bag and the water darkened.

She had begun moving the small household things from their places. The windup alarm clock was in the refrigerator, beside the butter, and she'd put a pair of shoes in the linen closet in the hallway outside the bathroom. The sugar bowl was upstairs on her night table. She had no good reason for any of it, other than everything felt different, and she was trying out new combinations. On her way home from work today, she had stopped by the drugstore for a bottle of nail polish and had also purchased a straight razor, the kind her father had used, simply because she couldn't believe they were still selling them. Who used a straight razor these days?

She squeezed the tea bag out against a spoon and dropped it in the wastebasket. Mia had told her where the spot of railroad where Percy died was. A boy in a family named Bailey had found him, and there had been information exchanged in town and among the ladies in Mia's neighborhood, who could pinpoint the house exactly. There was a broken fence and a maple tree, squat and very thick, its branches spread over the lawn. The house behind it was simple: two-story, white, a painted metal glider-rocker on the porch. "A *child* found him," Mia said. "A boy, they say, fourteen years old."

Rosamond took a sip of plain tea with no milk or sugar. There were moments when the house seemed to nudge her to leave as much as in other moments it bid her to stay. She had lived alone in this house since Agnes went to college, and she had known a number of quiet, still nights here throughout her marriage, Hatley always on the road. He sold vacuum cleaners first, then lamps, and last she knew, life insurance policies. Now she drank her tea, and her house, as it had the night she had stepped across the lawn to visit Clyde, urged her to leave. Rosamond felt certain there was *something* for her to discover.

She had been thinking about the boy, Vincent. She had never seen him, didn't know his family, but she found herself searching for him every time she went out. For a description, Mia had said only, "Skinny, I hear. And brown-headed."

The house ticked once more, and she left her tea, half drunk, on the counter. She flipped off the kitchen light. In the closet, she found a pair of walking shoes and her coat. She slipped the letter opener inside a coat pocket and locked the door behind her.

The sky was crisp black. She remembered a past Halloween when Agnes was little and it had been unusually warm for late October. She had let Agnes go out in her princess costume, no jacket, and Agnes had skipped up the sidewalk, free as sunshine. She had had a cardboard magic wand with glued-on circles of glitter that dusted off as she sashayed up the walk. Rosamond had had to remind Agnes to make her trick-or-treating stops at the houses, she was so dreamy, so lost. Agnes turned back, startled, at her mother's call, and Rosamond could still remember the sight of her on the sidewalk, a pink-winged girl in the gathering darkness.

She started down Main Street, toward the factory. The trick-or-treaters were gone, tucked in their beds by now, and if there were older goblins lurking about, they had successfully hidden themselves. Down the road, two houses across the street from each other had toilet paper strewn over the branches of their trees. The thin white draping bouncing lightly in the breeze was strangely picturesque in the darkness, like streamers on a parade float.

The downtown shops were dark and empty. Even the Tuesday Diner was already swept and locked up. Rosamond stepped over the railroad tracks, listening for a train. It was cold out, but she was beginning to warm a little from the walking. She passed the factory, a square dark shadow against the sky, and picked her way through the weeds at the side of the road. A few cars passed by, the beams of their headlights flashing over her, bright and sudden enough to leave her blinking through the afterspots. Though she was likely to be recognized whether she hid or not, she turned her face away from the cars when they went by. There was no good reason for her to be out here, but she persisted onto the county road that sloped up away from town, then north, the road curving left as it climbed. Now she had fallen into real darkness, the streetlights behind her. There was only the moon, nearly full, and the lights from the houses, spaced farther and farther apart.

The princess costume had been Agnes's last, though she had been only eight years old then. The next year, at age nine, she begged Rosamond to take her off to a haunted house in someone's rickety old barn. The creaking structure was scarier to Rosamond for the mice and other vermin that most likely occupied the scattered pieces of wood and spent tractor pieces than for the supposed haunting noises. Agnes had gripped her hand tightly the whole way through. That night, though, and ever since, Agnes had feigned fearlessness. At eighteen, she drove herself to McGraw College, a folk school so unconventional no one else from Goliath would even consider attending. When she withdrew from her classes, her short-lived "marriage" behind her, she moved back to Goliath, but not back home. She had called Mia beforehand and set it all up before Rosamond even knew she was coming. "This way," she had told her mother, "we can each still have our space."

Space. Rosamond believed people allowed too *much* space between them. We move away from the people we love, she understood, not because of what they need, but rather because of what we lack. We feel incapable. We *are* incapable, we *do* lack. But to her, it seemed the greater failing, this moving away, this giving of space. All this room to breathe. To stretch our arms out into thin air, to touch nothing with the tips of our fingers. It was too little, Rosamond knew, to give a person—a child—an empty refrigerator in a basement apartment with a lock on the door.

Yet she hadn't argued. Instead, she had insisted on a small thing: she would make Agnes's bed. It was a full-size mattress and Rosamond had purchased and laundered the sheets herself.

The day Agnes moved into Mia's apartment, Rosamond was there in the tiny bedroom, which was hardly large enough for the bed. She stretched the fitted sheet across, tucked everything together. She laid a blanket she'd taken from her own linen closet across, smoothing it down with her palm.

And then she'd left Agnes on her own to unpack the rest.

Rosamond, unlike Agnes, readily admitted she was afraid of many things—spiders, darkness, strangers. Once when she was very young, she had reached into a wooden box in the garage and touched a thin green garter snake nesting there. But the real fears began when Agnes was born. It was the price she paid for becoming a mother, these new eyes she had for seeing every danger, the chance she'd taken from the beginning. Loss, in any form, was nothing more than the other side of love.

She continued walking. It was black farmland all around, the fields textured with cut cornstalks, the air smelling of damp earth. She found the long gravel drive. Beyond, she could see the fat maple, the small light from the moon striking one of its monstrous branches, tufted with dry leaves stirring in the wind. Probably its roots went all the way beneath the house on one side, out clear to the highway on the other. She knew Percy would have stopped here because of that tree. Stopped here just to look at it. It could be this was his normal jogging route. There was no telling when he had ventured out beyond the house and saw the tracks there. Maybe he had happened to hear the early train passing through months ago, beyond the house, and returned to it. Above her, black telephone poles stretched upward, their wires strung across.

She moved through the black quiet, drawing nearer the tree and the gray house behind it, slipping through one of the broken places in the fence. She looked up at the house, thinking of the boy, his mother. How was that boy faring in all of this? What had it cost him, discovering Percy like that? She imagined it was innocence he had lost and fear he had gained. But then maybe he was already hard; even young people sometimes were. Some had already gained the sort of knowledge that could hurt them just by possessing it.

After Hatley left, she was a single mother, an anomaly in a town like Goliath. Years later, a doctor named Tucker started coming around, and they had a good time together before his daughters married him off to a lady from their church. Rosamond still thought about Tucker, though. He had been a fierce, tiny man who once literally swept her up off her stool at the bar in town she used to sneak away to late at night during Agnes's adolescent years. It had been for a joke, her teasing him that he wouldn't dare, but he carried her away right through the door out to the open street.

It was her association with Percy Harding, though, and not the presence of a man that ultimately made living in Goliath bearable. She had been plucked up, made special. Percy himself had come down to the mailroom to drop a letter and stretch his legs. He did that often, especially in those days, when he had just taken over from his father. He walked the different offices, the factory rooms, the warehouse, the loading bay, observing. The other girls were nervous when he came; they quit their chattering and turned their eyes down to their work, but Rosamond hadn't been chattering in the first place. She just kept working. Percy strode around the room, nodding and making chitchat with the other girls. He made a joke about how incompetent he would be at their job—every letter would be returned to sender, at his error—and the girls laughed, but Rosamond didn't look up. He'd lose all the billing statements, he said. Rosamond kept sorting mail.

"I'd be utterly hopeless," he said, but this time the girls' laughs had quieted. Now Rosamond looked up; he was standing a few feet away, arms crossed, watching her. He was jacketless, and his tie was loosened, that shock of blond hair falling into his eyes. He grinned like a boy.

"Sir?" she said.

"Madam," he answered, bowing slightly. He was teasing her, and she smiled uneasily. The other girls looked at one another— what to think?—and waited. He took a step toward her, put his finger to his lip, considering.

"I'm wondering," he said at last, "can you spell *efficient*?" She could and did. "All right then, what about numbers? Two plus two and all that?" To this she only nodded. "You type?" Yes. "File?" Yes. "Have a friendly disposition?" Friendly enough, she supposed.

"Good, good," he said. He nodded to himself, deciding something. Later, she would learn the full story, how he had already determined to ease his present secretary—a chalky older woman who had worked for his father for decades—into retirement, how he had a mind to do his own hiring. In fact many of the higher-ups under his father's administration were phased out in that first year. He was twitchy, yet confident and daring. This was the modern age: *anything* was possible. He was already spinning out new ideas for the next decade's catalogues. He wanted swiveling juror's chairs and high-back bar stools and kitchen tables that were elegant for their simplicity. He could see all the way into the next century. Upholstered headboards. Dining room tables made of sleek lines, their surfaces so beautifully varnished, they'd gleam like water.

That day he looked up to nod good-bye to the other girls, then, leaning down over her station, he whispered, "Follow me."

She hadn't cared a thing about the president of the company until that moment. Before, all she'd wanted was a safe job like this one, away from the lines. But now he'd *chosen* her. He led her down the corridor and up the stairs to a whole different stratum. Above the ground, to a desk and a chair with rolling casters on its legs. Nothing would be the same for Rosamond after that. No matter what people said or thought of her, from then on it was understood: she had her place in this town. She settled right into it. She did good work for him, and Percy started telling people that Harding Furniture couldn't run without her. He was still saying that all the way up to the end.

Tonight Rosamond had thought to wear comfortable shoes, well-cushioned athletic types with a bit of sheen to their white nylon fabric. They showed bluish in the small light. Inside her coat pocket, she held tight to the blade of the letter opener, its hard edges digging into her palm. She picked her way across the grass around the monstrous tree, past the house. The windows were unlit, though she could sense the presence of sleeping bodies inside, and she kept her steps as quiet as possible.

She used to take Agnes for drives out here in the country when Hatley had first left them. Rosamond tucked her into the passenger's seat with a soda and a blanket, and the two of them drove out to the house where her parents lived when they were still alive, and out to the county line in one direction, then, turning, to the start of Highway 64 in the other. They stayed out long hours, sometimes using up half a tank of gas, sometimes getting lost upon coming home. In those times, Rosamond simply drove until she found a highway she knew; all these small towns were attached at one place or another to the same highways. She was reckless about it; somehow she felt they *couldn't* get all-the-way lost. Often they were out so late that Rosamond let Agnes sleep in the next day, making up excuses for the school office.

Several months of this, and Rosamond had worked it all out of her: her compulsion for driving blindly into tangled country roads, for getting lost. One morning she went out to take Agnes to school and to drive herself to work, and she found she could not make herself open the door of the Cadillac. It seemed vaguely hostile sitting there, all pale blue and lit up bright and huge in the morning sun. It was monstrous and unbearably public, that car. She told Agnes, "Let's walk." Agnes, twelve at the time, stared at her mother. She wouldn't go, and Rosamond had to lie to her, said she'd been out to start the car already and it wouldn't crank. "It's dead," Rosamond said, kicking at a tire in one of her delicate thrift-store shoes. She had just started with the vintage clothing. "It won't move unless we push it," she said. Agnes gave her a long look, but then trudged down the driveway. Rosamond understood that for Agnes, and perhaps for Rosamond too, the end of the country drives, the last night of the Cadillac, the final vanishing of her father—all of it was part and parcel to their final giant step away from the town. The Cadillac sitting cold in their driveway was a proclamation: we're different, we're alone, we're fine this way.

People thought they knew all about it, what happened between her and Hatley all those years ago, the King's Motel and all that. They didn't know a thing. In the beginning, she and Hatley only lay side by side in the dark, not touching. He drank rum mixed with water from the bathroom sink and they talked over the plots of the movies they'd seen. He told her war stories, though he'd never fought in any war; these were the stories he'd picked up along the way. Truck stops, he said. Diners. He was forty; she was twenty-three. Sometimes after a long time of talking, he would kiss her, and Rosamond could taste the alcohol on him.

Percy said, *It's the trouble with people.* What is? she'd asked. *Everything is. All the trouble happens because people don't know how to be. They don't know how to* persist. It was when Hatley had left, when his son Ryan had married and moved away to Baltimore. Years after the morning he, full of confidence and youth, rescued her from the mailroom. *We should have been the ones to leave* them. *You and me,* he said. *We should have been the leavers.*

That'll do, Ryan had said to her at the close of the workday. *Have a good one.*

And Clyde: *It's here now, in Goliath, a colossal sadness.*

What of colossal sadness to a boy stumbling upon a dead body in his own backyard? What of that boy, the one who had *seen*? It was ironic, of course. Rosamond saw that. That Percy Harding, the one who had stepped in front of that train, had spoken of persistence. Ultimately, though, what Percy had done was only to bow to another brand of persistence. An altogether different power of the inevitable.

She made her way around the house and the patch of junk parts behind it and was walking out across the rocky field of red clay, the moonlight spreading out across the clearing. The railroad tracks, she knew, were up a ways beyond. She felt she was reconciling a long-abandoned landscape, that there wasn't another soul for miles.

Yet she wasn't alone. Another person was looking on the same things. The boy Rosamond wondered over lay awake inside the house she had just passed. The field of junk parts was all that separated them.

Inside the house, the moonlight through the window turned a space of the boy's bedroom wall blue. The house smelled of the pork chops his mother had fried for dinner, and it contained an inaudible static, as if all the family's conversations and activities were stored up and muffled tightly inside.

He was the only one in the house who wasn't asleep; his mind kept turning back, experiencing anew what Rosamond could know only in her imagination. *That* day. Sunday-morning sunshine spilled all over everything. The cool wind crept down his collar. The railroad tracks laid out plain and straight into the trees. He saw the dead man's arm twitch. He knew he had seen this, and he also knew he hadn't. Dead is dead. Now the silence—the house's energy restoring itself—took on its own sound, like cotton expanding in his ears. He didn't know anyone was out there. His thoughts were much louder than anything he actually heard.

She crossed over the deeply rutted field, across the frosted dirt, slippery in places, and finally came to the railroad tracks. The moon lit them silver. She climbed up the bank, stepping across the gravel. The near-full moon hung above the fields. She stood, her eyes closed. The air around her was freezing cold and she felt she was standing in nothing. Dissolved away. There was only the pain in her hand.

Something like a soundless call—a stirring from outside the house—prompted Vincent, and he rose and crossed the carpet to look through the window. He saw nothing, though, only the depthless shadows of late night, the high round face of the moon. He could not see Rosamond for the darkness and the muddled outlines of the trees. Distant, he heard footfalls. The thumps were so soft, so removed, he couldn't tell for sure if they came from the outside or from within his head, brain-settle, nerve-settle.

The train would not come for hours. Rosamond took her hand, stiff from gripping the letter opener, from her pocket. She could not move for a long moment, standing there in the very center of darkness. She opened and closed her fingers to work out the cramp.

Above her, in the house, Vincent Bailey was experiencing a moment of hypersensitivity. He felt everything, even the prickle of his T-shirt tag against his neck. He felt more than the reality of present sensations, actually: he felt a chill that was not in the house at all. It was *there,* in the field. Rosamond was nearly numb, unaware of her very limbs.

There suddenly, distant in the trees, pieces of the darkness unhinged themselves, silvered, came together and rose up in the sky, sparked alive—bright—into a quivering, fleeting oval shape, like spilled mercury. Then, breaking again into shimmering pieces, it glittered away.

Vincent stood alert a while longer, but the sparkle-fire did not return. He didn't know what he had seen or if he should believe it. He felt the snug fit of the elastic cinching in the hem of his sweatpants, his bare feet on the carpet, the cool painted wood of the window ledge under his fingers, his eyelashes brushing together when he blinked.

Rosamond held fast, waiting for another streak of light. *This* was the other-earthly, the unreal she had suspected. She had known it was coming, and now, just as suddenly, it vanished. She did not think it was cosmic or explainable. She knew it was a *person*, someone seeking her.

But it was gone now, and at last she climbed off the tracks and trudged wearily back over the field, picking her way around the jumble of spare parts. She shivered, moving slowly, stopping from time to time to catch sight of the sky, the stars, checking to see that all was still in its place.

She was exhausted the next morning as she made her way down Main Street toward the factory. It was the busy hour in Goliath, full of departures by car and sidewalk and children congregating at street signs for bus stops. The sky was gray, but brightening quickly, the enormous sun just breaking through the spaces between the houses. The grass was frosted, the air chill and damp.

She was thinking over what she'd seen the night before. It was such work, the thinking, the walking. This morning, she hardly believed she'd actually walked all the way out there, inching through the darkness to the railroad tracks in the country. She recalled the sight of the thick-trunked tree, the pale house, the quick-dazzle of light rising from the far-off trees. It reminded her of an eye-trick, like closing your eyes against a bright light and seeing its burnt image, a skeleton of light, against your eyelids. Rosamond wished for a day of normal things; today was All Saints' Day. When she was a child, her teacher had instructed the class to draw a wreath of candles on the first of November. She taped the finished pictures to the wall, saying, *In remembrance of those who are gone.*

Rosamond lifted her hand to shade her eyes. She saw that a few houses down a road that crossed Main a group of people was collecting. She heard the buzz of their voices meshing together, a confused and excitable swarm. Rosamond stopped. It was Marty and Janice Pickard's house.

The fights, sometimes staged in the couple's front yard, sometimes at the Tuesday Diner, once at a PTA cakewalk, always went like this: Janice threatened to leave, Marty pleaded his voice away, begging her to stay; and Janice succumbed at last.

Rosamond, after a moment's hesitation—she really was so tired—crossed the street and began walking toward the house. She saw, drawing near, that the neighbors collecting out front were all watching the roof of the house. There, appearing almost fragile for his distance from the ground, stood Marty Pickard, one hand gripping the chimney, the other on his chest. He looked down into the crowd. The house was not large, only one story, a box made of brick with a simple gray-shingled roof. Janice stood in the driveway next to her white Datsun, packed to bulging, the trunk tied closed with twine. Rosamond noticed how prepared Janice was to actually leave this time—she couldn't remember Janice's having gone to such trouble before. Standing below, Janice appeared solid and unmovable. She stared hard up at her husband. The sun struck the rooftops and Marty, holding tight to the edge of the chimney, squinted.

People clumped together and murmured. Marty had never threatened suicide before. The closest was when he had stood in front of Janice's car as she tried to speed away, calling to her that she would have to run over him in order to leave. *You're going to have to kill me,* he'd said.

Rosamond looked about. Those closest to her were quiet, but

others, beyond, talked. Two police officers with staticky walkie-talkies and pistols in their belts had arrived, and they and a handful of other youngish men—younger than Marty—stood back with their arms crossed, comparing rescue plans. Clyde was there. He stood a few paces apart from them, staring Marty down and muttering to himself. He glanced at Rosamond, but she pretended not to see. Cars crept by, the drivers craning their necks to see what was happening. The old men from the diner stood a ways apart, noting the persistence of Janice's pansies, blooming through the frosted grass around the mailbox.

"Come on now, Marty." This came from Wally Thumb, who had left the diner untended to come see. He stood in his brown cardigan and green corduroy slacks, his head cocked back to call up to the roof. "Come on down," he said.

"Not until she promises to stay," Marty called back. He let go of the chimney. "Not until she swears she'll never leave again."

His eyes moved over the crowd. Janice kept her place next to her car and shook her head very slowly, *no*. Rosamond pulled her coat closed tighter around her, recinching the sash. She wanted to leave but couldn't. Partly this was because she was too tired: it was easier to stand here and wait than to wade through the crowd and move on to work. She blinked through the bright sun. Clyde was speaking with one of the officers, issuing commands. Rosamond remembered what he'd said about the colossal sadness, and she saw he was right—and how pathetic such a mighty sadness appeared on a cold day so bright with sunshine, in a town as tiny and old as Goliath, in a man as child-hearted as Marty Pickard. She could understand what Janice was doing, and she was alert to Janice's newfound resolve. Rosamond found herself hoping Janice would actually do it this time. Someone, she thought, needs to *do something*.

Agnes arrived in her black coat and blue jeans. Her hair was still damp from the shower, pieces of it freezing into slender cords around her face. "What's going on?" she asked, nodding at Marty on the roof as if Rosamond might not understand what she meant. A handful of children drawn to the scene on their way to school organized themselves into a game of tag in the neighbor's yard. They were sick and spazzy from all the candy the night before. One boy took something from his pocket, a wrapped toffee, and threw it up at Marty, missing him by several feet. The boy ran away, hollering. Teenagers lined the street, and one was dancing soft-shoe in his own sideshow. The Morning Glories scowled, tired of the pansies.

Rosamond touched her daughter's frost-hardened hair. "You'll catch pneumonia."

Agnes ignored this. "That man's going to jump."

His eyes were closed, and he was mumbling something no one else could hear. The sky was pale blue now, gauzy and cold.

"People die of pneumonia," Rosamond said. She was thinking of the evening before, her walking through town in the middle of the night. She wondered if she'd been seen; no one said anything to her now. She remembered the gathering of silver light in the trees and wanted to tell her daughter, but Agnes coughed into her fist and looked away.

Celeste Bradshaw, who was standing nearest the house, told the others he'd been up there since at least seven-thirty. "I was the first one," she said. She moved over to Janice, who was weeping softly into the sleeves of her sweater. When Celeste put her hand on Janice's back, Janice crumpled into her, sobbing. Everyone had turned quiet, the teenager no longer dancing. Only a cluster of middle school kids, oblivious to everything outside their circle, were still talking and laughing. Rosamond hadn't noticed Ray Winston's arriving, though she could tell from the way Agnes glanced back at him that she had seen him come. He knelt in the grass behind them and bowed until his forehead touched the ground, praying.

Rosamond realized they were missing something. Each one was acting out a half reality, and they didn't know there was a full meaning beneath it all. There was *real* sorrow, like another, denser earth beneath the asphalt, the dry grass. The trees in the lawns were in full autumn now, lush with color, a few already past their prime, their leaves spilled out on the ground below.

Down the street, the mail truck, having completed its delivery and taken on a new load of outgoing post, made its morning departure from the Goliath post office. At the grade school, the cafeteria ladies were dishing out scrambled eggs onto the plates of the free-breakfast students, who came early, and the janitors were unlocking the doors to the gym. The first-shift workers had been at the factory since six, and they were going about the business of sawing, sanding, piecing, gluing, and varnishing pieces of wood into furniture.

Vincent Bailey, hollow-eyed and heavy-footed, slouched off the steps of the school bus, squinting into the sun. The cool air ruffled his hair and he shook it out of his eyes, shuffling along, following the other students up the walkway toward the building, most of them talking. He was silent. His jaw was clenched against the chilly breeze and he pulled his hands into the sleeves of his jacket. Nearing the school, he suddenly turned hard to the right, taking a path out behind the school, into a patch of woods maybe half the size of the gym inside. Small but densely wooded, a shock of trees in the middle of town. The others filtered into the building, and no one seemed to notice his departure.

His thoughts were not altogether different from Rosamond's—he sensed the same town-wide ignorance, a stumbling over the significant, the true—but he didn't linger on these thoughts. Unlike Rosamond, he did not want to sort out what the light rising from the trees might have been or speculate what the source of the light had been. Whether or not it would flash across his window again on another night—maybe *this* night. Vincent, standing alone

GOLIATH   73

in the woods, was in free fall, frightened of what his brain might try to think, to picture next. In his jeans pocket he carried a few Winstons he had pinched from his old man's pack.

Among the trees, he selected a spot to sit and pulled the half-crushed cigarettes from his pocket. He lit up and exhaled upwards into the branches. On Chester Street, Rosamond looked into the sun, small and cold. Janice opened the car door, slipped inside. Celeste stepped back, unconsciously putting a hand to her middle, protecting a tiny yet unseen life, as the ancient Datsun protested once, then fired up. Marty inched closer to the edge, the chimney no longer in reach.

"He's going to do it," Agnes said.

Vincent took the cigarette from his mouth, judged the length from butt to tip, and took a long, slow drag. Janice's reverse lights came on and her car eased down the driveway, onlookers stumbling out of her way. Ray stopped praying, pulled himself to standing, and came to stand close to Agnes. Rosamond, on Agnes's other side, caught her breath. Vincent, tucked into the scrap of woods, braced himself, then folded the cigarette unto his tongue, extinguishing it, pushing it to the back of his throat, then down. The Datsun butted out into the street, changed direction, and pushed past the onlookers.

"He's really going to," Agnes said as Marty Pickard stepped off his roof.

FIVE

Weeks passed, Thanksgiving came and went, and the weather stayed cold and dry. The trees were bare, and the young people hoped for snow. Marty Pickard had broken his arm when he fell, but nothing more. To Rosamond, it seemed a great loss to go to such lengths and have nothing tragic happen. His wife Janice stayed gone.

In the schoolyard, the children made a choo-choo line, holding on to one another's shirttails as they hollered through, the caboose a listless slow boy who was always at the end of every line. Finally the teachers, made uncomfortable by the mocking reprise of a train, stopped the game, though the children still played, unaware, when no grown-up was watching. Celeste Bradshaw began wearing her husband's baggy button-downs around town, even though her pregnancy wasn't showing yet, and Mia Robins's mums finished blooming. At the factory, workers took their time coming in, lingering in the warmth of the locker room, slowly unwinding scarves from their necks. Though they, bit by bit, returned to the everyday rhythms of work and chitchat and late-afternoon weariness, nothing felt exactly right. The streets outside were blustery and bright, but inside, the coffee in the break room was weak, less like the substance it was supposed to be.

It had been weeks since Percy's death, but the shock of it still lingered. Some of the people of Goliath were struck with an odd impulse. In the gray chill of late November, amid the waxy, unreal light of life after tragedy, they began to seek out the company of one of the most unknowable people in town. They looked for Rosamond Rogers.

None of them could say outright why they were seeking her, what they hoped to gain by talking to her. Maybe it was that she still wore the luster of tragedy, of sadness. Her face was still pained; they saw their own heartaches hidden there, like to like. It could be people understood she would keep their secrets. Rosamond, unmarried, not directly connected to anyone except her daughter and her aging aunt Mia—who would she tell? More, it could have been that they recognized, knew instinctively, the mercy of unburdening yourself to a person as isolated as Rosamond Rogers. Rosamond of the antiquated fashions—white gloves! Rosamond, who never engaged completely in conversation, who looked confused and innocent and haughty all at once. Who had been secretary and all that that entailed—confidant, typist, provider of coffee—to Percy Harding, benevolent, unknowable man. Who seemed to *always* be on that sidewalk, walking. Telling her a secret was like speaking it into a mirror. It was like telling no one, and yet still having the relief of the confession.

They sought her, those weeks after Percy Harding's funeral, and they found her in the supermarket and at the factory, on the streets and in the post office. She was always alone, huddled into her orange cutaway coat. One by one, they took their secret thoughts to Rosamond. They simply gave them to her: their small pains, their nagging worries, and even their thimble-sized joys, their minuscule yet momentous triumphs. These they handed to her, hurriedly, but also with great care, with *focus*, each one like pressing a warm coin into her palm.

It started on a morning when the air outside was so sharp and cold, it hurt to breathe. One of the other secretaries, passing Rosamond's desk, stopped to tell her, "I heard the train whistle this morning, and I can't shake the headache it gave me. It's *killing* me." At the drugstore, Charlotte Branch leaned across the counter and confessed a suspicion she'd kept to herself for years: "Opal Mercer's husband steals candy." A Morning Glory bought Rosamond a cup of coffee and told her about the storm that had knocked over his grand oak a few summers earlier. "Came up roots and all," he said. He chuckled softly, but then confessed, "It was almost scary, I'll tell you. Big as that tree was. Took up half the lawn with it."

They said these things to Rosamond even though they'd never shared such thoughts with her before. It seemed the quiet she'd carried with her for so many years had become an invitation, drawing others in. A man in the lunchroom, one of the foremen, said, "It's Leeann's birthday." Leeann was his wife. "I bought her a necklace. I don't know. It seems there's something else I should be doing for her. You know?" The man shrugged. "There's something I'm missing," he said.

Rosamond said little in response and went home to drink hot tea in the chair by the window. She rubbed out a stiffness in her fingers, then picked up her cup, touched its rim to her lips, didn't drink. She had somehow caught the young secretary's headache and the old man's unease. How strange that Frank Mercer—old, prickly man—stole candy bars, and even stranger that Charlotte Branch felt the need to tell her. All of it left Rosamond feeling anxious and, oddly, more alone than ever. Twice she rose to slip across the lawn to Clyde's house, but she remembered his stocking feet, his forgotten coffee. What he'd said about baseball, about

Lela Harding. This house was old; frosty air seeped in through the spaces between the window frame and its glass. Soon it would be dark and she would be left to contemplate exactly what that silver light rising from the trees had been; she would search the black sky and wonder. She started back in working the cold out of her fingers. She checked her watch. In an hour she could call Agnes. Likely she would be home from work by then.

"You'd think we'd get some snow," Agnes complained to Ray later that night; she'd missed Rosamond's call. Rosamond had left a message with Mia, but Agnes had dialed Ray's number instead. It made her tired, literally drowsy, to talk to her mother. And she was tired enough, in a restless, impatient way. Tired *and* bored. She didn't want to sleep, but she didn't want to think either, or to be alone. Ray let her grumble. He let her sigh hugely and prattle on about the smallest things.

"The problem is," she said, "it's *too* cold. This kind of cold is beyond snow."

Ray was teasingly sympathetic. "Poor Agnes," he said.

The next afternoon he showed up at Mia's back door in his camouflage work jacket and a pair of flannel earmuffs. He was ready to take Agnes up to the mountains to search for snow.

But there was precious little even up there, just patches along the highway, clumps of dead leaves showing through. Still, they gathered what they could, scooping some up from the hoods of parked cars and fences and dropping handfuls into the bed of his truck. As they drove, tiny scraps of white escaped into the air. They stopped at a roadside stand to buy boiled peanuts and to pick through a lot of yard ornaments, angel statues and garden gnomes. There Agnes caught a glimpse of a man in a plaid sports jacket slouching back into his car, which was bright red among the gray mist, the mountain fog. She told Ray: "I know that man." He asked her who he was, but she turned elusive. "I know a dozen ways to make pecan pie," she said. She shrugged. "Occupational hazard. People at my checkout tell me recipes all day long."

She looked out the window as Ray's pickup wound its way down the mountain, and bits of snow kept floating away. The scraps looked like the smallest white feathers drifting past the window. "We can *pretend* it's snowing," she said. It would have to be the smallest bird, she thought, to shed such tiny feathers.

"All right," Ray said. "Let's pretend."

When she wasn't working or studying her maps or talking to Ray, Agnes walked the town: the sidewalks, the streets, the backyards, the parking lots. She didn't see the hurts same as Rosamond, but she felt something Rosamond didn't. There was a vacancy there beneath her, in the soles of her feet, in her very bones—so much of the town had fallen away. In years past, when her mother was a child, they had held grand parades in the springtime, complete with homecoming queens and American flags. She told Ray, "I can't stand to live here any longer." But she *would*. She was stuck in Goliath somehow, fastened down. Ray sat with her out in front of the grocery during her afternoon breaks. She watched his long thin fingers fold together, his leaning forward to prop his elbows on his knees while he looked out across the parking lot. It was drizzly out, and the sky was the color of smoke. Ray waited, but Agnes didn't mention the man at the roadside stand, and she spoke of her ex-husband only once, when Ray finally hazarded to ask.

"He was foolish," she said, then drained the last of her coffee. Ray carried that word with him; it seemed a peculiar, almost antiquated thing to say. *Foolish*. And yet it pleased him, this word she'd used. *Foolish,* he said to himself. Agnes's ex-quasi-husband, a very foolish man.

Since the townspeople had begun telling her things, Rosamond found herself hiding away more and more. It wasn't just because what they said often brought her discomfort, or that she found many of their ailments, their headaches and bouts of insomnia, contagious. It was rather that she always felt at a loss. What to say to the elementary school teacher who had unaccountably—and only momentarily, she assured Rosamond—forgotten her students' names? How to share in the small and ridiculous joy of Celeste Bradshaw's pregnancy-induced indigestion? "The baby doesn't like spaghetti," Celeste said, grinning hugely.

If she *had* followed her inclination to visit Clyde the other evening, Rosamond would have discovered he was still—exactly as she had feared—dreaming of baseball. It would have annoyed her, how obsessed he'd become. These days he was thinking about baseball and Lela Harding nearly all the time. Clyde was longing for a townwide game.

His final day as chief had been marked by a department gathering with sheet cake, and there had been a short farewell piece in the *Goliath Star*. The next day, after breakfast at the Tuesday Diner, he spent his time watching the news and choosing his dinner from the deli section at the Lucky Grocery. All around him, the town functioned. The old men sat for long hours at the diner counter, clearing out just before the younger lunch crowd set in. The Baptist ladies played bridge in the church basement. The mothers of school-age children gathered at the bus stops and kept on chatting there for some time after the children had been carted away. The teenagers were sequestered at the high school, on the sports fields, at their part-time jobs. Children played on the sidewalk and on the school's playground, spending time there during off-hours, in the late afternoon. Everywhere people moved through common spaces, keeping tight to their own circles. Seldom did those circles overlap.

"It could work," Clyde told Ray. "Baseball could be just the thing."

He began prospecting for a baseball diamond but found none.

At the high school, there was only a football field, and at the junior high, the only outdoor space was for soccer. No pitching mound, no chain-link fence, no home plate. The vacant lot where Clyde and every other Goliath boy of his generation had played was now occupied by the Tremont Pines Mobile Home Community, the trailers a line of plastic boxes with weeds and gravel and children's riding toys in between.

The complete absence of baseball in Goliath puzzled Clyde. It troubled him. How could such an iconic sport—so *American*—have fallen away? And how had he not known it? What had he been *doing* all these years?

It reaffirmed his belief that this particular sport was exactly what the people needed. Mornings, he backed out of his driveway and into the street, then paused a moment, looking over his house, a square of brick and cement with a few stunted trees and a spot of grass, before shifting into drive and starting down Main Street. If his fingers held some magic-disappearing powers, or if they were attached to a remote-control bulldozer, his own house would have been leveled to make way for the field. He considered this possibility every time he left his driveway.

In his retirement, he had not been content simply to view the square of a lit window from the road. He had finally parked his car and approached the Hardings' front door. Lela appeared exactly as she had on the day of Percy's death, standing in the doorway with a drink in her hand. She invited him in, and the radio was still going in the background, the volume turned low so that he could tell music was playing but couldn't quite grasp the tune, the announcer speaking too softly to be understood. He explained he was coming by to see how she was holding up. "I hate this house," she said. She looked around. "You see those curtains? That's all I've ever changed in more than thirty years. Curtains. This house isn't even *mine*. It's never felt that way." He stayed until late, but she said little else.

After that, he visited her more often than was decent. Sitting in her gleaming, plush living room, he found comfort just to be in the company of this exquisitely sad woman, as beautiful and fine as a piece of china. She spoke of her inability to grasp what had happened. "He wasn't so unhappy, really," she said. "I can't figure out what I was supposed to know about it before he did this. Everyone looks at me. They want me to say what happened. I don't *know* what happened." Her son's family, the little ones and the wife, were nearby, but remained mostly unseen. Ryan, her son, came out only once each evening to say hello, his wife appearing to ask if she might get Clyde a little coffee. Clyde always politely refused. Lela spoke fitfully on the other couch, lifting her glass to her lips, setting it down. More often, she stayed quiet. The seconds ticked by on a massive grandfather clock. Finally one evening she grew tired of his visits.

"Clyde," she said, looking at him almost tenderly, "I don't know why you keep coming here."

The next day he heard talk in the Tuesday Diner that she had packed up and left early that morning for an extended visit to her sister in Iowa. The other lunch-eaters—everyone knew he'd been visiting at the Harding house—watched him, but he was careful not to let his humiliation show as he went to his usual table, opened the menu before him, and began looking it over even though he knew it by heart. His neighbor Rosamond wasn't there, but he was certain she knew what had happened. He remembered how indignant she had been when he mentioned Lela weeks earlier, how she had hurried away. He might have known this would happen.

Later he told Ray, "There's a heart inside me yet."

"There is that," Ray answered. "I've seen the proof."

They were in Ray's trailer, heating soup on the stove in the late afternoon, the sun shining through the window and falling across the table in a wide column of thick light. Clyde was finding it more and more unbearable to be alone inside his own house, especially now that he had begun to imagine it stripped clean to its foundation. It felt as if he were losing something significant, with Lela's leaving, even when he reminded himself he had hardly known her. Clyde did not know how he would fill his evening hours. It seemed impossible to go back to reading newspapers and watching television as before.

He watched Ray stoop to stir the pot on the stove, then reach to find a box of saltines on top of the refrigerator. Since Penny's death, Clyde had kept up a sort of running conversation with his wife about their son, as if she were there observing the boy's growing up with him, his thoughts always a question or an answer to what she would say. It was a continuation of a conversation that had begun before Ray was born, in those old days when Penny and Clyde, upon hearing the news that she was pregnant, first began to imagine themselves parents, a ridiculous and happy adventure that seemed unique to them—they might have been the first parents ever.

Incredibly, Ray had been a low-weight baby when he was born, barely four pounds. There was quite a bit of worry and attention from the doctors the day of Ray's birth and the days afterward, but, looking back, Clyde instead recalled the bird that flew into the room seconds before Ray emerged. It was August, blazing hot, and the windows were open, electric fans going in the hallways. The bird burst through, dusty sunbeams streaming through the window, its wings flapping wildly.

Penny didn't see the bird, but Clyde, who had insisted on being there for the delivery, told her of it later. The bird—brown and small, maybe a sparrow—circled their heads, then fluttered away. At first she did not believe him. That couldn't happen in a hospital, she said. Later she said it was a sign of special blessing, like the dove descending on Christ. Clyde did not want to read that much into it. Actually, he had heard that a bird inside the house—or inside the hospital, in this case—was a sign of *bad* luck, not good. Contemplating luck seemed useless, though; he was happy enough to have the actual baby there, finally. The bird was a wonder, but also seemed a lapse on the part of the hospital, an intruder, and he complained about it once or twice to his neighbors and well-wishers, the guys from the force who came to see the baby and to bring gifts their wives had bought or handmade.

As the boy grew up, Penny understood that her child was blessed. When Ray was twelve, he went out to the woods to play and returned home touched by a supernatural power. Ray told his parents he had become a true follower of Christ, and moreover, that he would be a preacher. "Christ himself has called me," he said, dirty and sweaty from walking among the trees, pale-faced from what he had heard God the Son say. It was a thing Clyde had never come to understand, a purpose he yet questioned, ceaselessly arguing first with Penny in the flesh, then with Penny in memorandum, her voice continuously prompting and questioning him.

Ray read his Bible through that next year, the year Penny fell sick, and he began preaching on doorsteps just after she died. He was thirteen. People said he was gifted by the Spirit, that God had revealed himself to him. Penny said, *Look, Clyde, just* look *at our boy!* It was a special wonder to her, what Ray had become, she and Clyde going over it in the months and years after her death.

The soup bubbled, and Ray filled their bowls. He set them on the table, then seated himself in a rickety old chair, with loose nails in its meeting places. Every piece of furniture in the trailer was a rescue mission from the dump or a castoff from the county schools. He closed his eyes, and Clyde knew him to be praying. He opened them a moment later, dipped his spoon into the soup, and, drawing it to his lips, blew across its surface to cool it.

Clyde held the hot bowl between his cold hands, thinking of

what Penny might think of Ray's long hair, what she might make of Clyde himself, of his visiting Lela so much, during such late hours, how she might interpret the widow's leaving.

He asked, "You ever do any of that praying for me?"

Ray nodded. "That I do," he said. He took a cracker from the plastic sleeve and submerged it halfway in the soup. The soup had a tomato base, with carrots and celery and navy beans, the vegetables grown in a nearby garden, canned and gifted to Ray. The women of Goliath coddled him, a motherless bachelor. The old ladies, though they didn't always approve of his radical ways—it was possible Ray Winston was *too* religious—loved him dearly. The cracker grew soggy, and he lifted it. "Sooner or later, everyone gets prayed for," he said.

He had a look on him, and Clyde expected him to go on, but he instead continued with his meal, and the two were quiet for a while, the pillar of sunlight through the window beginning to weaken.

"You still say God made the world in seven days?"

"That's right. The world and everything in it, and everything beyond." Ray nodded while he talked, as if recalling an incident he had witnessed directly instead of one he had only read about. Even when he quoted scripture, he seemed to do so from a personal space deep inside instead of simply rattling off something he'd memorized. "He spoke it all into being," Ray said.

"Is that so," Clyde said flatly, remembering that last detail from his own time in a too-warm, too-stiff Sunday School room when he was a child, a ritual he had never subjected his own son to, despite Penny's objections. She had taught him, he knew, on her own, when he was not at home, she and Ray in their own private world of stories and games and play. Ray finished his soup and waited for his father to come to his point. But Clyde was stuck on speaking a thing into existence. It was completely unreal to him, ridiculous, but he, desperate as he was, would

have to try it. When he returned home, or maybe in the morning, pulling out into the street in his patrol car, he would pause
there in front of his house and pronounce it. *Dugout,* he would
say. *Pitcher's mound.*

"We tried to shield you from all that," Clyde finally said, as a
means of shifting the focus of the conversation. It was untrue, at
least on Penny's end, but Ray nodded, waiting for something
more. "We tried to keep you out of the church," Clyde said, laying the spoon in his empty bowl and leaning back in his chair to
digest.

When he returned home, he might say *Penny,* but she, he
knew, was utterly gone from those spaces. Maybe *home plate.*
Dugout. Diamond. He might instead drive past the Hardings' house
and, looking up toward the lit windows, speak, *Lela* again and
again, patrolling the empty streets, driving past the dim houses,
closed up and silent against the cold.

"It was six days," Ray said after a long pause. Outside, the sky
had gone to deep orange and gray at the edges, and Clyde felt
suddenly ashamed of the miracles he was contemplating.

"Just to clarify," Ray said. "God made the earth and the universe in six days. On the seventh day, He rested."

Clyde soon had more proof that Goliath needed hope in the form
of nine innings, Rosamond was further convinced the town had
yet to understand the scope of its grief, and Ray was called to still
greater prayer.

Vincent Bailey, who was still trying not to think about the
strange light he'd seen rise from the trees late that Halloween
night and yet thinking about it anyway, remained separate from
the various goings-on at the high school. He avoided looking
into the faces of those around him, barely spoke to his old friends,
friends he'd had since kindergarten. Ever since the ambulance
had arrived, lights but no siren, crunching up the gravel drive in

front of his house the morning he'd found Percy Harding, he'd had trouble connecting the sounds around him with their sources.

So at first Vincent was not even aware of what was happening: a group of half a dozen junior-year girls in black sweaters and thrift-store blue jeans had started writing suicide poems and leaving them, like Baptist tracts, all over the school.

The school nurse found the poems, neatly written with black ink on pink construction paper and cut with the zigzag edge of pinking shears, among the magazines in her waiting room. *Dark passage,* the poems read, *bright night / turn the key, see the light!* They were hidden in library books and stacked beside the coffeemaker in the teachers' lounge. *Soft, sweet going—mark your path! / the edge of knowing—close your eyes!* Students found them folded and slipped through the slots of their lockers. *The last glimpse of life / shines / like the edge of a knife.* Band members even discovered them inside their instrument cases, shaped into funnels and tucked into the horns of the trombones and clarinets.

The principal cracked down on the culprits, who didn't try to hide but sat together in the cafeteria during lunch period, cutting out poems and eating school pizza. *Right to choose life or its opposite,* they preached. When questioned, their representative, a slight girl with frizzy brown hair and pale green eyes, said, "It's all about free speech. We can say what we want." The principal countered: Thou shalt not invade the nurse's office. "And keep out of other kids' lockers," he said. The members of the suicide cult, after some debate, acquiesced, and the poems were simply left out on tables in the library, on the sink in the girls' restroom. The guidance counselor stepped on them when she opened up in the mornings. Some student had slid a few jagged pink rectangles under her door.

One of the girls had an after school job as a fellow checker at the grocery store where Agnes worked. Her name was Bernice. Agnes had seen her only once before outside of the store. It was

at a Friday-night football game, and Agnes had watched her circling the field hanging onto the arm of a tall, pale-featured boy
who kept the hood of his sweatshirt pulled over his head like a
convenience-store robber. She told Agnes, "None of us really
means it. We don't want to *die,* not really. We just want that particular choice to become socially acceptable, you know? I mean,
no one tells a married, adult person not to have a baby. They
don't say you can't *create* life, do they? They shouldn't tell people
not to end their own lives, either. If someone wants to kill himself, I say, let's throw him a party first, wish him bon voyage."

Agnes said, "What a sad party."

The girl shook her bangs out of her eyes. She shrugged.
"People are allowed to be sad," she said.

Talk of the suicide cult was all over town. The mothers at the
drugstore were indignant over these lapses of the school administration. Shouldn't the school board get involved? What about
Pastor Myers? "Now is not a time to worry over the separation
of church and state," one of them contended, and while there was
one mother who grimaced at this, others nodded. "Yes," they
said. "That's right." The Morning Glories at the diner agreed—
taking God out of the schools was part of the reason they were
in this mess. "This mess and many others," one man grumbled.
Clyde drank his coffee and nodded at the cherry pie on the counter. "I'll take a slice of that," he said. His opinion of the suicide
cult was that young people need to express themselves. "We ought,"
he said, "to listen."

At the start, there were six of them. They were good students,
bookish but not especially gifted, all mildly pretty—with large,
round eyes and sweet, pink faces—except for their leader who
had frizzy brown hair, perpetually damp at her temples, and a
pinched-up mouth, sharp nose. The girls hadn't been especially
popular, though their subversion earned the respect of their
peers, and it was not long until suicide cult sympathizers filled

the hallways. Girls began wearing black ribbons pinned to their blouses, and a handful of boys pulled their laces from their shoes and colored them black with Magic Marker. They tied the laces, tourniquet-style, just above their elbows.

Ray Winston incorporated the issue in his sidewalk talks, speaking in front of the post office: "The worst thing that can happen to any of us is that we might lose hope. The loss of hope is the only real tragedy in this world." Charlotte Branch from the drugstore worried about marijuana in the schools. Wally Thumb at the Tuesday Diner was a proponent of an afterschool counseling program and a countywide curfew. "They should be safe at home come ten o'clock," he announced, and no one thought to question him, to ask how this might end talk of suicide.

The teenagers listened to the adults, and had their responses. One teenager, hearing Wally Thumb's comments, told him, "Most of us already have curfews. Our parents give them to us." It was true that few unsupervised young people walked the streets of Goliath past dark. Another refused to remove his shoelace armband for French class as his teacher requested and was sent to the principal's office. He claimed freedom of expression. "You take my armband," he warned the principal, "I'll come in with my *teeth* painted black."

One high school student—not a member of the cult—wrote a letter to the editor for the town newspaper in which she pointed out that the whole idea of suicide, or at least its recent surge in popularity, had come through the action of an adult, not a teenager. "And not just any adult," she wrote, "but a supposedly upstanding citizen, one of our greatest leaders. We all looked up to Mr. Harding and just *look* where it got us." The letter, signed *A Girl in Grade 11,* spurred more talk. The old women who gathered to can pickles and boil blackberry jam in Opal Mercer's kitchen shook their heads. "What has come of this town?" they asked. The Morning Glories were fired up. There wasn't much worse a person could do, they believed, than speak ill of the dead. The mothers of teenagers searched their daughters' desk drawers and closets, looking for rough drafts of the letter or other evidence of guilt. The suicide cult, noting the decisive anti-suicide tone of the letter, was quick to disavow it. *Not us,* a flurry of pink notes read.

Rosamond told Agnes, "They shouldn't have printed it." They were in her kitchen, finishing tea. That was how it worked with Agnes. Rosamond couldn't get her on the phone for more than a week and then suddenly Agnes appeared on her doorstep, ready for tea. Rosamond looked up toward the window above the sink and observed, "I need new curtains in here."

Agnes reasoned that what these girls were trying to do, both the suicide cult and the letter writer, was not truly to make the world safe for suicide, but to make it safe, period.

"*That,*" Rosamond said, rising to rinse her cup in the sink, "is something to wonder about. A safe world." She swished the water around in the cup, looking out through the window over the sink into the backyard of the house behind her—a clothesline, empty this time of year; a swing set, just as empty. "This world is not safe," she said, then, turning to look at Agnes, "but I wonder sometimes if that means it's not good. You know, does it have to be safe to be good?" Rosamond shrugged.

"But you," Agnes said, "you do hate it."

"I don't hate," Rosamond answered her. "I worry, I have my troubles, I am afraid to drive, but I don't *hate.* It's the one thing I don't do." She turned to open the refrigerator. "Are you hungry?"

Agnes didn't answer. She was thinking of the walks she took most afternoons after her shift at the Lucky Grocery. She ambled past houses with brown, wintered lawns and closed-tight windows, blinds drawn, and felt what she'd felt every minute since returning to Goliath: the life of it was draining away, seeping through the asphalt, dimming the sunshine, thinning the grass, the trees, the cold, tight air.

Perhaps it was nothing more than the talk of the suicide cult that had made Agnes imagine small, desperate moments happening inside the houses she passed. Here, in this one, she pictured a woman sliding out a knife from her butcher block on the kitchen counter, then staring at it, the glinting edge hanging over a raw chicken she planned to cut up for dinner. Next street down, in a hunched-over bungalow, an old man emptied an entire bottle of heart medication into his palm and paused, closing his fist and shaking the pills like dice. One truck driver careened through town, came to the underpass and could not help picturing it: his hand jerking the wheel hard right, the crush of steel against cement. A girl in the ninth grade, inside this white clapboard with the rain gutter hanging loose, was studying the fine, nearly translucent skin covering her slender wrist, watching the tendons rise as she turned it this way, then that, blue veins crisscrossing, threading through.

Now Rosamond set her cup in the sink and turned, took a half step toward the kitchen table, then stopped and frowned again at her curtains. They were the avocado green that had been popular twenty years ago, when she'd first hung them. She said, "Those windows need brightening."

"Mom," Agnes asked, "I have to ask you something." She drew in a lungful of air, then asked, "Why is there a brand-new straight razor in your bathroom?"

"What is that. A joke? A riddle?" Rosamond quipped, but Agnes only watched her, waiting. Finally Rosamond shrugged. "I guess I've had that. I forgot all about it." She sighed.

Besides the talk of the suicide cult in town, there was this: Rosamond Rogers had been seen walking alone along the highway, like some kind of vagrant, late Halloween night. She had stumbled along there like a drunk person, like a woman who had no idea who or where she was. That had happened weeks ago; one of the other checkers, who hadn't even realized Rosamond was her mother, had told her. Also, her mother left work some days before lunch. Agnes, walking to the Tuesday Diner in the middle of the morning, had seen her herself: Rosamond coming down Main Street wearing that awful orange coat of hers, her blue scarf tied under her chin. She scuttled along, her eyes turned down, furtive, her brow furrowed—she appeared to be having an argument inside her head. The sight had stopped Agnes; if this woman in the blue scarf hadn't been her mother, she would have thought her crazy.

Had Agnes said anything about her mother's strange behavior, Rosamond might have explained to her about the small bits of information the others had been thrusting upon her; she *was* hiding from them. Just yesterday a man had stopped her to show her a spot of yellow in a gum tree: a goldfinch perched there amid the bare branches. Impossible, he said, but he didn't explain why the sight of this bird in this place at this time was so unlikely. He instead touched the edge of Rosamond's coat sleeve and added that today was the twentieth anniversary of his father's death.

"Maybe," Agnes said, her voice as quiet, as reasonable, as she could make it, "it would be better to hate than to be afraid."

But Rosamond pretended not to hear her. She turned her eyes away, sipped her tea, and considered how outdated and old the curtains were—she really should change them. She could sew new curtains herself. "Lavender," she said. "Or maybe just a soft yellow."

Late that night, after Agnes had left and the sky outside had gone black, her house put her out exactly as it had the night she'd gone to the railroad tracks in the country. The kitchen light flickered, and Rosamond, despite how she'd hidden these last few weeks, simply could not stay inside. She put on the coat

Agnes hated, tied on the blue scarf, and headed through the freezing cold for Dalton's Bar up behind the post office. The sign outside wasn't lit, but the door gave when she pulled on it, and inside, a row of men at the bar turned to see who was coming in. She found a stool, and the man next to her, a truck driver she'd known years ago, turned to playfully cuff her knee.

"Rosamond Rogers," he said. This jolted her; when had she last heard her own name spoken aloud? "I'll be," he said, chuckling. "Rosamond Rogers has returned, better than ever."

Christmastime came, and the people of Goliath were occupied with their preparations. Electric snowflakes were fastened to the streetlights on Main Street, and Charlotte Branch's nephew painted Santa and his eight tiny reindeer on the drugstore's windows. Ladies gathered in one another's basements for wrap parties, and men, young and old, shuffled off to the drugstore to purchase perfume for their wives and their mothers.

Rosamond wrote her Christmas cards, which she always sent out wide, like a flock of homing pigeons, to her family scattered throughout both Carolinas; to local and distant celebrities—even to Dorothy Blair, care of Hollywood Studios; to old classmates; to certain members of the Harding family; and even to Hatley's people in Virginia. She urged each of them, in a postscript, to visit soon. She helped with the company banquet dinner, held in the high school gymnasium, though Ryan sat at a table apart, with his family, and did not make the customary Christmas wishes. He gave out canisters of caramel popcorn in lieu of Christmas bonuses. Agnes helped Mia with her holiday shopping, and Wally Thumb served gingerbread and cocoa at the Tuesday Diner. Multicolored lights were strewn across rain gutters throughout town, and plastic snowmen and Santas were hoisted up on lawns up and down Main Street and the intersecting neighborhood streets. The air stayed cold, and the sky was low and gray.

Celeste Bradshaw—who had finally felt the baby move, a tiny flutter—organized the Christmas pageant, to be held on Christmas Eve. The children practiced on Sunday afternoons while old ladies sat up in the pews, watching. Dale Myers, the new preacher, was often there, and his wife Tonya helped Celeste with the hand-bell choir. In the last week of preparations, Celeste put a cardboard crown on a three-year-old boy who refused to be an angel. She stuck him in the corner of the stage to play a disapproving and fidgety King Herod.

On the evening of the big event, parents and grandparents came to see, and the air smelled of burning furnace oil and oranges from the children's treat bags. Clyde Winston was not the only one to think on how different the sanctuary felt now from the morning of the funeral, and even how different it felt from all the ordinary Sunday mornings since Percy's death. Mornings, the windows were yellow; everything was bright. Now, on Christmas Eve, they were inside the spot of light in darkness rather than the piece of shadow among so much Sunday-morning sunshine. He was, however, the only one to be particularly bothered by the difference—most were happy and peaceful, waiting for the show to begin. Clyde recalled Lela's dramatic departure, and it seemed now, in his replaying, that she had left the church and gone straight out of town, had not even stopped to pack, that she was in Iowa now, wandering around with her nightgown peeping out from her coat. Around him, the people pressed into the crowded pews were dressed up and smiling.

The children, after a few moments' delay, streamed in through the aisles dressed as the Virgin Mary and her betrothed, three Wise Men, sixteen angels, a donkey, a cow, two chickens, four shepherds with their half-dozen sheep, and last, the mischievous King Herod. Celeste crouched at the front to prompt and direct her cast, and Tonya stepped forward when it was time for the bell carols.

Afterward, parents gathered their children in little flocks and guided them to their cars in the parking lots, and the cars rushed out to houses so brightly lit and warm-looking, they shimmered. After the traditions of Christmas Eve—pajamas and cookies for Santa Claus and fierce reminders that Santa could not visit a house where the children were still awake—were dispensed with, the parents and other adults left the children sleeping in their beds. They wrapped themselves in coats and scarves, flasks and tissues tucked into coat pockets, coffee mugs held in gloved hands, and went out, into the hushed night, breathing in the stark cold. They set out for Christmas field.

Each Christmas, near midnight, Ray Winston came out onto the quiet, well-tended sloping lawn behind the elementary school and stood out, searching the sky for the brightest star. He imagined himself one of the shepherds to first receive that historic news, the redemption for all humankind. The others followed.

While the townspeople drew close behind him, Ray once again revisited that first night. The ground was spongy and cold beneath his shoes, the air deep and frozen, brilliant with stars. Ray stood in the darkness apart from the others, and heard the angel's words: *Fear not!* A command more than a comfort, for the shepherds had important work to do—they were the ones to spread the news.

Behind him, arms were raised to the sky, pointing. He did not see them, did not notice their games. They pointed to this star, then that one, arguing over which was the brightest, giggling a little under the influence of the contents of their Christmas flasks, but still keeping some solemnity about them, wanting the ceremony, this searching of the black sky. *It goes on forever,* some said. *There's no end,* they said.

The people—Agnes not, Ray knew, among them—kept watch, and fiercely they longed for something. Ray felt people's search for something more, for hope, as keenly as he felt the Spirit's long-ago whispered calling. He understood why these people gasped at the night sky more passionately than they bothered with the pages of Scripture—it must have been very grand, that first night—a Creator's call of love to the created. God come to earth. *Listen!*

Clyde Winston was not there; neither was Rosamond. They each stayed tucked warm in their houses, a tiny space of lawn between them, and went about their ordinary evening preparations for sleep, the television left on for noise in both houses. Across town, Agnes was up talking to a friend from college on the telephone, her fingers tracing her map of the Eastern world—Bombay here, now Burma, last Tokyo.

Vincent stood out in the dark field near his own house, feeling the same soundless call to a miracle that he had heard several weeks earlier, when he rose to find a fleeting sizzle of lights in the trees, to sounds he couldn't decide whether to place in the real world or only in his thoughts. Tonight, though, it was enough to simply be out in the night, to be near the place of impact. He hoped not in angels or prophetic stars or home runs or far-off places, but in death, that wholly reliable entity, though he didn't name it directly. He took a cigarette from his pocket and smoked it clean to the filter, breathing in the blackness.

Beyond, at Christmas field, the air was so cold, it turned the trees to brittle sticks and stiffened the grass. The stars above were crystal. The onlookers clasped arms and felt their lungs constricting in the frigid air. They swayed and watched the expanse of black sky, the frozen stars. Ray put his bare hands to the sky, praying, and the people fell silent. They dipped their noses into their scarves, seeking warmth. Those first shepherds had been merely bored, fighting sleep before the angels arrived. The people of Goliath likewise did not know what was coming, what if anything they might hope for.

Ray *had* been chosen. The weight of knowing the truth was this: he bore the burden of bringing others to believe.

Rosamond was asleep now, already dreaming. It was the day she first met Hatley Rogers, a salesman, and she dreamed it exactly as it had happened. She was in her parents' house, the same one she was living in now. She could feel the thick gold light of the living room that afternoon, a warm fall day, the curtains drawn. The salesman swept his hat off when she answered the door, bowed, and took her hand, warm and moist from stirring gravy in the kitchen. His eyes were so deeply blue that at first they appeared almost purple. The late afternoon sunshine made his oiled black hair gleam. She was dreaming it out now while the others gathered in the orbit of the sidewalk preacher. They stood out in the dark, scanning the sky for a certain bright star, and Rosamond watched the salesman take her warm hand and, incredibly, pull her toward him and touch his lips to hers. "There," he said. "I've kissed you now. What about that?"

Finally, then, out on the field, as if a reward for their faithful waiting, their months of voiced and unvoiced sorrow, bits of white began to fall on the people's shoulders, on their outstretched hands. Vincent, alone in his own field, felt it too, and Agnes saw the flecks drift down through the glow of a streetlight outside her window. She had finished talking with her friend and her apartment was quiet now. She thought of Ray and wished he was there watching it with her. Rosamond, dreaming still, invited the salesman inside, closing the door behind him.

It landed on the people's coats and in their eyelashes. "Snow," the people at Christmas field called to one another, laughing. Ray heard them, peering up into the sky himself, still searching. "It's snowing," they said, their faces turned upward to meet it.

SIX

It went on through the night, coming down soundless and thick. The people slept, warm beneath their disappearing rooftops. It was still falling in the morning when everyone woke to watch it, tufts of perfect white dropping across the already white lawns, the snow-hidden cars parked in the driveways, the leafless trees, their branches plumped white. Presents were opened, and children bundled up to go outside and play while their parents watched from the windows. The sky was clean blue; no precipitation had been anticipated. Snow this abundant rarely came to Goliath. Across town, men and teenage boys went out with shovels, but the snow was falling too quickly and they could barely get a patch of driveway cleared away before it filled up again. Rosamond went out to walk to Mia's house, and peering upward, saw that the sky itself was beginning to lose its blue, turning white in patches. Thin clouds swirled up from nothing, and then thickened, accumulating, until, past noon, the sun was hidden by all the white. The lawns were dimpled in places where the carousers and the curious ones had traveled through and the falling snow had imperfectly refilled the marks of their boots and the paw prints of animals.

By the late afternoon, the snow lay up to the windows, and the children wearied of wading through it. Rosamond told Agnes, "You certainly got what you wanted."

The Tuesday Diner, which had closed for inclement weather only once before, during the flood of 1939 (and even then had opened briefly for morning coffee and wrapped sandwiches) didn't open the day after Christmas. Wally Thumb, who had trudged through the snow from his home on Griffin Street to the diner because he couldn't stay away, stood out front and gazed transfixed at Goliath completely covered in snow. It did not look like a place he knew. The factory, like most of the other businesses, was closed. The snow went on the next day, and the next.

Harold Clarkson, who at ninety-six was the oldest living citizen of Goliath, claimed he had never seen such weather. It's one for the record books, he told his wife. A fourth grader who had just completed a report on clouds and condensation at school told his parents this was probably the coming of a second ice age. "The Pacific Ocean is refreezing," he explained. The snow continued a third day, on and off; people had become watchful, waiting for it to let up. Celeste Bradshaw watched it through her father's kitchen window while she busied herself at the table, rolling cookie dough. She cut round cookies from an upturned drinking glass, sprinkled them with sugar. The next day the snow had reached more than four feet, and then it stopped falling and did not start up again. Wally Thumb put coffee on and unlocked the door to the café. He sat at the counter and waited, meaning to give free coffee to anyone who hedged a path through.

The roads were impassable and the sky stayed mottled white, with little sunshine. Families began to run low on groceries, and the men tunneled out to the driveway, where their cars wouldn't crank. They waded out to the gas station convenience store up from the high school. There the shelves grew barer as the snow-in persisted, and as these men set out for home with their loaves of Bunny Bread and canned ravioli, everything was white. It all looked the same—the streets, the trees, the houses, the sky. Mostly going out for these base supplies was a drudgery, but for men who had grown up watching movies about superheroes and cow-boys, it was also an adventure, and they allowed themselves to daydream about their own bravery as they went. The snow had blotted out the shape and color of the streets and the trees and the houses. Familiar landmarks—the cactus plants in Mia Robins's side yard, the low brick wall in front of the Harolds' house on Fulton Street, and the concrete rooster figurine on the sidewalk in front of the drugstore—were completely changed. Suddenly it was possible to get lost in Goliath. *Goliath,* whose half-dozen roads and crossways these men had known all their lives.

One man, after drinking a fifth of cheap vodka while sitting in front of his blazing kerosene heater—ice had downed the power lines on his street—went out for a walk, became disoriented by all the snow, and lay down in it to sleep. He was rescued by his neigh-bor who was on a different sort of mission: his wife had become convinced the weather was a sign of the end times and had sent him out to find Pastor Myers. Dale Myers and his wife Tonya, though, were out in it, too; Tonya was from Alabama and had never seen real live snow before. She stopped as they walked to-gether to scoop some of it up in her mittened hands. Drawing her hands to her face, she touched her tongue to the snow she'd gathered.

Most kept inside their houses. They worked crossword puz-zles and watched television. A teenage girl who lived in a trailer with an ailing father and an always gone mother nested in her closet among her clothes and shoes and junk, holding a flashlight to her notebook. She wrote poem after poem. She was a freshman, too young to be in the suicide cult. She wasn't interested, anyway;

she didn't even wear black. This girl mostly wrote free verse, occasionally devising couplets that rhymed *pine* and *sign*; this *pine* was the act of desiring, not a species of tree. She was glad to be in her closet and away from the others during the snow, yet it made her anxious somehow. All this time alone.

Pastor Ray was out with his shovel, laboring to clear driveways for the elderly, stopping in at a few of the houses to have coffee and hot biscuits. People were glad to have him, but he didn't stay long. He had it in his mind to get to Mia Robins's house by the end of the day. Lately Agnes had been focused more and more on those maps of hers, showing him the countries stacked along the west coast of South America, the small spot of Paraguay. She was restless. He feared what Rosamond hoped—Agnes was preparing to fly away. He had told her he liked her here in Goliath, and though she hadn't responded, the idea of her staying in Goliath with him got stuck inside his head. It grew clear to him the other night as he watched the sky, Agnes's snow finally falling. He was beginning to sense what so many around him had long seen plain: he loved that girl something terrible.

Clyde and Rosamond, in their separate houses across one shared lawn thick with snow, had long guessed the strength of his feelings and were waiting the relationship out, each wincing, but for different reasons: Clyde feared his son's getting hurt, and Rosamond feared the opposite, that her daughter might get caught up in it all and return the sidewalk preacher's love.

She wished for something more, that her daughter might really take off, go somewhere distant and exciting, as Agnes had said she would when she was little. Rosamond stewed over it while she was trapped inside the snow. There was nothing but snow at every window. Since her dream about Hatley—which she now had no memory of, neither the dream nor the originating event—she'd given herself over to cleaning out closets, emptying drawers. She felt a need to filter through such things, to pare down her material needs. And it seemed there was something she would find among the debris, some remnant—a letter? a pin? a recipe? It was something she needed.

More and more she found herself doubting her own senses, what Mia had warned her about months earlier when Percy died. *When Percy died.* There was still a part of her that couldn't quite believe those words. She cleaned and sorted and lost track of the hours. It was ten o'clock in the morning, then it was past midnight.

Rosamond was a little hazy—disconnected—when Agnes came to visit her about a week after Christmas. Rosamond answered the door in her bathrobe, a few clumsy bobby pins jabbed into her hair. It still surprised her sometimes. Agnes was *here,* returned to Goliath.

"You made it," she said.

"I did," Agnes said. "I made it."

Agnes began to peel off her wet things and lay them, dripping, on the kitchen chair Rosamond brought her. A bath towel was laid out on the floor to catch the melting snow.

"Lunch?" Rosamond offered. "Tea?"

"Sure. I'll have some tea."

Agnes ventured further inside, past the open cardboard boxes on the floor in the living room, the piles of clothing still on hangers draped across the back of the couch. In the kitchen, an uneven stack of newspapers as high as the table leaned precariously against the wall. Rosamond took the teakettle from the stove and filled it at the sink. Turning, she saw Agnes eyeing the mess. "I'm cleaning out the closets," Rosamond said, shrugging. "Everything goes." She tittered.

"Okay, fine," Agnes said. The house smelled of the old things that had been unearthed from closet shelves and the kitchen drawers, musty and close. She felt the familiar exhaustion of being with her mother, but fighting it, she cleared a stack of magazines from one of the kitchen chairs. There were some things she wanted to say. Seating herself, she began, "Everything's different from when I was growing up."

Her mother, dressed in her bathrobe in the middle of the day, was frowning to herself, leaning against the counter. She seemed at a loss: what to do now that the kettle was on the burner?

"You know nothing of it," Rosamond said at last. She crossed the room, wincing as she took those few steps, as if the walking pained her a little. She sat down across from her daughter, opened a newspaper, and extracted a coupon circular. "You know nothing of what all's changed." She settled her reading glasses on her nose and peered down at the first page of coupons. "Cat food," she said.

"I just mean it *feels* different. To me. I always knew this was a small town. That was never a big surprise or anything. Never a big realization. It's just, I'm seeing now that everything from out there—well, it's all here too. I mean, this town has its trouble. It has heartbreak and all that. Scandal." Agnes fingered the salt-shaker on the table and didn't look at her mother.

"This house is a sty," Rosamond said, licking her finger to turn the page. She laughed. "*Scandal.*"

"Growing up," Agnes continued, tipping the saltshaker to spill a little, a spot of grainy white on the faux-oak table, "I always thought that the town hated us." She sprinkled a bit more salt on the edge of the white circle. "I guess it did."

"Agnes," Rosamond said. She peered over the half-moons of her reading glasses. "What on earth are you talking about?"

"It's okay. They hate us. They hate each other." She began drawing swirls in the salt with her finger.

"That's not what I said. I only said you don't know what all's changed. Yesterday," she said, "I was twenty years old. This happened *yesterday.*" Rosamond turned the page in her circular and

lifted her scissors. She began cutting out a coupon for fabric softener, turning the page around in her hands as she worked.

When the kettle whistled, Rosamond moved to rise, but Agnes gestured for her to stay seated. "I'll do it," she said. She took
the kettle off the heat, quieting it, and reached into the cupboard
for the teapot. "Do you remember the pinball machine at Jimmy's?"
Agnes measured loose tea from a canister into the teapot. She
filled the pot with hot water from the kettle. "I used to play it
every day after school. I had the high score. One of the kids who
worked there, a boy from the kitchen, a dishwasher, I guess, used
to come out and sort of knock on the side of the pinball machine.
Like knocking on a door. He said he did it for good luck."

"You know, Jimmy isn't there anymore," Rosamond said. She
examined Agnes's salt patterns on the table, uncertain where this
little story was taking them. "Alice took over the restaurant. I
don't know what you mean about scandal."

Agnes leaned against the counter while the tea steeped. "Now
they have some sort of crappy video game there. Warships or
something. Tanks. I walk past, and there's usually a boy there
working the controls, real intent on the game. Never notices me.
I can't go inside. I'm in a bubble or something. I don't know why
that is."

"Agnes, for heaven's sake." Rosamond paused. She looked over
Agnes's head, through the window. "I never thought we'd see
snow like this."

Agnes took cups down from the cabinet. She poured the tea
and brought the sugar bowl to the table. Rosamond had to be one
of the last people in the world—or at least in this part of the world—
to make tea from loose tea leaves in an actual teapot. She liked
this about her. Her mother, sitting there clipping coupons amid
the yellowing contents of a solitary house, her life in piles all
around her. Lonely for a husband who'd left her and a man who

had died by his own hand, a man she'd never had in real life. She
had always insisted on the small elegance of this ceremony, the
making of tea.

"I've caught glimpses of him since he left," Agnes said after a
moment. She took a drink of her tea, then set the cup down on
the gritty salt patch she'd made.

Rosamond stared at her daughter. She put her scissors down.

"He was in the hallway when I was still in high school.
Across the walkway from me at McGraw when I walked to class.
Many times. I mean Hatley. That's who I'm talking about." Agnes
paused. The silence that followed his name was enormous. "And
just a few weeks ago, I saw him in the mountains, at a boiled peanut
stand. I was there with Ray," Agnes explained.

"Of course you were." Rosamond closed her eyes.

"Each time I looked closer a second time, and it was never
him. But this last time he was gone before I could make certain.
Before I could look and see if it really was him. Once I thought
I saw him coming across the lawn toward my apartment up at
school. It was right after we'd said our vows, and I thought, for the
tiniest moment, that he had come to meet James."

"James?" Rosamond asked.

Agnes put her hands to her face. Removing them, she said, "It
doesn't make any sense. How could he know?" Then, "Yes, James.
His name was James." She saw Rosamond's eyes flick down at the
spilled salt, then quickly up, away. It was amusing, actually; despite
the burden of what she was revealing, her mother was itching to
wipe up the spilled salt.

Rosamond thought, *James.* That was the husband's name. The
play husband, Agnes had said. They had met in philosophy class.
She had married him in front of a tree. This was all Rosamond
knew about him. She didn't even know what kind of a tree it had
been, or where precisely the so-called "ceremony" had taken place.

"Once," Agnes began, "he said to me, he asked me, did it ever seem silly to me, the way people live? He meant houses and beds and all. Offices and shopping malls. He said, we're animals, after all. Maybe we should be living in trees or something. James was like that. He didn't always have good arguments for what he was talking about, but he really cared. I mean, he really thought about things."

She smiled to herself. "It's the snow," she said, "making me say everything."

Rosamond looked at the coupons she'd cut. "I have too many for salad dressing. And orange juice. I don't even like orange juice."

"The marriage was never real anyway. Me and James. He'd tell you the same if he were standing here. We lived together for a while. That was all."

"That was all?" Rosamond asked. She took her glasses off. "That was *all*?"

"I want to contact him."

"James?"

"Hatley."

Rosamond touched the table delicately, as if she questioned its solidness. She fingered one of the curls in her hair. "He's long gone. You didn't see him," she said. Then, "Are you sure? I don't think you should. No, I don't think this is right at all." But she rose to get her address book from the drawer. She flipped through and then reseated herself at the table, replacing her glasses on her nose. "You did not see your father. You are mistaken." But she tore a corner from the newspaper, straightened her glasses, and lifted her pen.

"It's the best I have." She handed the slip of paper to Agnes.

They were quiet. Agnes folded the paper. "I don't know what I'm doing."

Rosamond looked out the window, across the white. "It's too heavy," she said. "The roof won't hold." Then, "I should have known that's why you came back to Goliath. I should have known.

It's fine. You'll do what, send him a letter? Try to call him? You just can't *go* to him. He's not there." She sighed. "You'll do what you'll do, and then you'll have your peace." She drank her tea. "I don't think it's like this everywhere."

After Agnes left, Rosamond sat knitting in her corner. She looked about her at all her things removed from closets and cabinets, stacked here and there; she was gutting the house, taking everything out, and she didn't exactly know why. Percy, she knitted. *James.* She was nothing special to him, Agnes had said, and Rosamond worried that this was true. *The marriage was never real anyway,* she'd said.

She worried for her daughter in the same way she worried for herself. Maybe it *was* true. Maybe this boy had not loved her and Agnes, in the interest of self-preservation, had left him. Agnes had said she had seen him, and for a fraction of a second Rosamond had thought she meant Percy, somehow miraculously returned. A ghost. Ridiculous, of course. At least now she could see that much. Enough time had passed, and Rosamond mostly believed it: Percy was gone.

Percy, she knitted. *Gone.*

"It's my business," she said aloud to nobody. She was certain Agnes would never find Hatley. It seemed impossible for him to still exist. "I'm sorry," she said, thinking of Percy. "I don't know what she's thinking," she told her dead mother.

It was New Year's Eve. Rosamond didn't realize the date, but around her, in all the other houses, people readied their modest celebrations. They turned their television sets on. They poured liquor into fruit juice and made up appetizers from what they had on hand—crackers, chipped beef, cheddar cheese. The snow had been with them for almost a week and they were tired of it. They settled into their couches and watched rock band performances on outdoor, New York City stages. Across the way, Clyde

Winston's house was quiet and dark, and Rosamond wondered where he was tonight.

She sat alone in the quiet of her house for a time, then rose, laid her knitting in the chair. She went upstairs, put on a dress and a pair of boots and came down to the hall closet. She slid her arms into her coat.

Amid the dim, snow-covered streets, Dalton's was a pocket of light. There were just a few drinkers sitting along the bar and gathered around the tables when Rosamond arrived. Only men tonight, with giant brass belt buckles snug under paunchy bellies straining against the buttons of their cotton shirts. They were mostly middle-aged or older, with thin, graying hair and weathered red cheeks. They turned and nodded at her, then turned back to their beers sweating on the bar in front of them.

Marty Pickard was among them, sitting alone on the far end of the bar, his face down as if to physically shoulder his embarrassment over the morning he'd jumped off his roof, the dejection he felt: his wife was still gone. His left arm was still in a cast, resting in a denim-blue sling. Marty didn't look up. Rosamond had heard that he had tried another way to end his life—driving his car down a steep grade on a far-off county road—but a tree had caught him from crashing into the ravine, and he walked away without a scratch, his car totaled. Now he kept huddled over his beer, looking up from time to time at the television, tuned to a news program with the sound turned off. Someone had started up the ancient jukebox in the corner, and it was playing something scratchy and old.

Little had changed since the days when Rosamond used to slip out of the house after Agnes was in bed, walking the gray streets between her house and the bar, which seemed to be the only place in town where anyone was awake past nine o'clock. The men in those days were, like the men here tonight, rough-talking factory workers and truck drivers, but they were gentler with Rosamond. They called her sweetheart and squeezed her shoulder in greeting. The women, when they came, were usually younger than Rosamond, and they came attached to one of the men or as a duo, two women out together wearing crooked glossy lipstick, drinking with determined abandon.

Rosamond was the only woman who came on her own, who seemed to have a place there. Even after being gone so long, the others regarded her as a regular. Those men had always been friendly with her, joking, flirting, sometimes even starting up a slow song on the jukebox and dancing with her. Other times, like tonight, they hardly noticed her. They looked down at their own rough hands holding beer mugs and grumbled, wanting nothing more than to slump there on their bar stools and grow drunk-heavy and numb. They craved both solitude and companionship, the snow so thick on the streets beyond.

Lance Dalton, pink-cheeked and terribly thin, a wave to his steel-colored hair, tended bar. He wore a clean white undershirt with nothing over it, as he always did, and he looked thinner and older to Rosamond as he nodded in her direction. All the men at the bar appeared sadder and barer to her that night. Maybe it was the weight of the snow that lent gravity to everything. She settled onto an empty stool and accepted the beer he placed before her.

"Thank you, Lance."

"Tucker's here." He turned a toothpick between his teeth. "Didn't know if you'd seen him yet."

This was the doctor from Winnie the town knew about, the man she had had a fling with some years earlier. He was one of the three men in her life who had said he loved her, the first being her father. She had seen him among the drinkers lined up at the bar, but she hadn't recognized him. Jim Tucker, like the others, appeared much older that night than he might have looked if she'd spotted him during the day on the sidewalk in full sunlight or at the Tuesday Diner the week before, when everything was only frigid-cold, snowless.

He was a few spaces down the bar from her, tipping back his drink with a trembling, bony hand, his washed-blue eyes set deeper inside the folds of sagging skin than she remembered, his hair a few degrees whiter. Could it be this was the same man who had lifted her off her bar stool and carried her, laughing, into the street? Tucker had grown old. He had been getting on even when she had known him well, several years ago when Agnes was a young teenager holed up inside her adolescent gloom, and Rosamond had snuck out nights to sit at this very same bar, among mostly the same aging men. *Jim Tucker.* He seemed as much a ghost as Percy, as the invisible Hatley Rogers.

He appeared smaller than Rosamond remembered, him shrunk into his overcoat, his neck as thin and sickly looking as a turtle's. You could add Tucker to her list of failed affairs, more evidence of her tendency to love the ones who would hurt her the most. In the scant, yellow light of the bar, him quietly drinking his whiskey, he appeared harmless. Frail. Tucker so aged, it frightened her. She could blow that man away through the door out into the street.

Then he happened to turn an inch or two, and he spotted her. Eyes vacant at first, then a snap of recognition. There was life there—in that surprise, that shock, in his pale blue eyes, blinking quickly, his mouth working, finally calling out her name.

Rosamond turned, for he had already left his stool and was standing, arms open, behind her. She clasped his hands, the skin paper thin and slippery over the small knots of bone beneath, and wondered if the snow and the late hour and the lack of light inside the bar—maybe also that old raspy music from the jukebox— had fixed her old and pale same as it did the others.

"Tucker," she said, clasping his hands, "Tucker, how *are* you?"

He didn't loosen his grip on her fingers. "Rosamond," he said again. He looked her up and down and shook his head in disbelief. The other drinkers glanced at them—maybe remembering the two of them back when they were together, maybe not—and returned to their conversations. "I thought you were gone forever."

"Oh, you," she laughed. "Foolish man."

"No arguing there." He winked.

He let go of her hands and pulled out the stool beside him for her to sit there. Long ago Tucker had been a physician with a practice a few towns over, driving out to Dalton's for the pleasure of anonymity. To be a stranger in a small town. After his first wife was killed in a car accident some years ago, he gave up his practice and started teaching science at the high school. He dissected frogs with his freshman biology class. "Sometimes," he told Rosamond, "the old surgeon in me wants to try to restart their tiny hearts. To bring them back."

Rosamond nodded to Lance, ordering her second gin and soda. She turned to Tucker. "Still teaching?"

"If you can call it that." He shrugged, absently smoothing down a few strands of gray hair onto his knobby scalp. "More like giving out assignments and waiting to be disappointed."

Rosamond smiled. She thought of Carol, the woman Jim's daughters had married him off to a few years after their mother's passing. Rosamond had never seen her and had met only one of Tucker's daughters, but she flashed to a dough-faced woman sitting inside a living room carpeted in pale beige, looking out at the quiet white street, waiting for her elderly husband—*much* older than she, Rosamond had surmised—to return home.

"These kids," he was saying, "don't have a bit of respect for the scientific method. For inquiry." He shook his head. Then, laying a light hand on her back, he said, "I'm sorry about Percy Harding. I know you two were close."

Sorrow and gratitude enveloped her like a fog. She ducked,

peering into her drink, then looked up, his pale eyes on her. "I know where you are now," he said, turning away, his hand slipping off her back. "I've been there myself."

Just like that, awkwardness fell like a stone between them. Rosamond felt she shouldn't be talking to him at all. She had forgotten for a moment the specific worry that had brought her here. Now it returned to her: Agnes had Hatley's address and she meant to search him out. Dimly and without naming it directly, Rosamond felt a stab of shame; she *had* had her trouble with men. This town hated her, as Agnes had said. This was true.

She lifted her mug, just as she had lifted her beer can in Clyde's house a few months earlier. A different widower—this one remarried—and a different night. She'd been *here* before, though. Years ago, she had spent countless evenings standing here with this man. Rosamond, feeling the snow, the cold, sweating beer, the room overheated with fattish, ruddy-skinned male bodies, thought: *They should write a song about this.*

She made the toast: "To old friends."

Tucker nodded, lifting his mug. The hand holding his glass shook a little; he was *old*, this man who had once spoken of reviving a legion of dead frogs. A man who was grinning at her now with yellowed teeth. Loose skin hung from the bones in his face, and the operation of his eyes moving in their sockets seemed too obvious, too *anatomical*, somehow. But Rosamond was warm from the drinks and from the sight of a familiar kind face. Tucker. They clinked mugs, giddily aware of how foolish they looked.

During the snow, Agnes sat up with Mia. They watched the news broadcasts. Mia, who wrote to third-world orphans whose names and addresses she found in the back of *Christian World* magazine, who knew exactly three words of Russian, leaned forward to blink at the television screen, simultaneously enthralled with and terrified of the snow.

"*Koshmar,*" she said. Nightmare. Mia had missed her weekly salon appointment due to the weather, and her sparse white hair was limp and flyaway. This snow reminded her of all the other snows, and she told Agnes, "When I was a girl, we went years without a single flake. And then this happened, a snow this bad, and everyone was *buried.*" She had sat up straight and turned to Agnes to relay this, and now, she relaxed back into her easy chair. She closed her eyes. "My azaleas love it," she said. "To them, it's nothing but a giant warm blanket." She laughed. "To think, snow is warm to them, the sleeping flowers."

Agnes had not been out to see her mother again since that week after Christmas. It was too much, what they'd let go of, what they'd said, and also this, the burden of Agnes's new knowledge: Hatley's address. She could not settle down to the work of writing the letter, not quite yet—it was enough just to have the means, a place to send it. It was almost *too* much, more than she'd expected.

"We'll never get out from under all this," she told Mia.

"Oh, we'll get out," Mia said. She took everything Agnes said as it came. She touched a bent old finger to her chin; then drawing it away, she shook it at Agnes. "Any other time, we'd *wish* for this kind of quiet."

Rosamond, for her part, could not talk to Agnes either, couldn't pretend they hadn't unearthed Hatley, if nothing more than just by talking about him. In some ways she believed her daughter when she said her marriage had been nothing, and now it was over, and that was that. She heard the edge in Agnes's voice, how she counted her miseries, how she observed the large and small weaknesses, potential failings, all around her. She wondered what kind of revenge Agnes was seeking, returning to Goliath, searching for Hatley. What kind of grace she hoped to gain. How long would it take for her to dust her hands off and walk away?

Rosamond didn't want to piece out how she and Hatley had caused her daughter's trouble with love. There seemed no point in going there, in drawing the possible lines between their mistakes and Agnes's troubles with this boy, this James. She struggled instead to pin down her specific misgivings: did she hope Agnes would find Hatley or that she wouldn't? She worried Agnes had given up her marriage—had it *been* a marriage?—and come home to pursue her father.

Even when the three of them had lived together, she had had a hard time thinking of Hatley as anyone's father. He was so different from her own father, who had been as mild and hardworking as Hatley was impulsive and charming. Her father passed on before Agnes was a year old, and Hatley attended the funeral wearing a pinstriped suit and a firecracker-red tie. After the funeral, at Rosamond's mother's house, he let baby Agnes sit on his lap and play with the handkerchief poking out of his breast pocket. Though he smiled at his daughter, watching her—she stuffed the handkerchief in, patted down the pocket, then, grinning, reached in and pulled it out again, laughing—he didn't seem truly connected to her. He was, at that moment and all the others, more the fun uncle than a *father.*

Now, sitting beneath the silence of the snow, sorting through her things, Rosamond considered: then and now, Agnes needed more than an uncle. Her daughter had always been stubborn and brave. But that courage was paper-thin. It worried Rosamond, what Agnes *hoped* to find versus what she might *actually* find. She had always believed she'd hear from Hatley when he had grown old and weak-hearted, when he was ready to linger over morning coffee and evening drinks without anyone asking too much of him. She thought he would want it to be that way, for them to simply resume married life, but when she pictured them together again, it was in the musty anonymity of the Royal Motel. The dresser drawers were empty there, the bath towels white and flimsy. They lay on the bed, talking. This was before they'd started sleeping together, when he was still trying to keep her pure, *untouched,* and she kept quiet on the issue, though she somewhat resented how committed he was to abstaining. Yet that was the time she wanted to return to. Before they were married, before they'd lived in this house, before they'd had a baby. If they had ever truly loved each other, it had happened there, in the near blackness of that motel room, the vacancy light through the window sliding down Hatley's glass every time he tipped it back to drink.

One of the most hurtful things he had ever done to her and Agnes was to leave, but even worse was the leaving and the coming back, the leaving again. His not returning—when he finally managed to stay gone—was possibly his kindest gift to them.

Thinking through these things made Rosamond lonely in a way she didn't recognize. It came to her as fear, and she was fretful; her house was too quiet and cold. No matter how far up she nudged the thermostat, she couldn't get her hands warm enough to work her knitting needles.

SEVEN

On the nights Tucker wasn't at Dalton's, Rosamond spent time with some of the other men there. These were good men, mostly—rough but good. Friendly. They bought her drinks, told her stories, laughed with her. And now, as the people in town had begun to do before the snow, the men at the bar, those she knew and those whose faces were new to her, began telling her things. Little pieces of their lives, all in a hush, beery and warm and low, beneath the clamor of the bar. Old shames and recurring confusions. Obsessions. Suspicions. They scooted their bar stools close and handed over pieces of their lives to her. She couldn't guess why except that she was—especially during the snow—often the only woman in the room. She guessed there were other women in these men's lives—mothers, wives, sisters—who couldn't be told these stories.

"I keep thinking about this girl I used to know," a worker from the loading bay told her. His cheeks were blistery red, his jaw gray. "I didn't harm her outright, but I didn't do right by her either. I could have done better. I guess that's what I'm saying." One man told how long he'd loved a woman he'd never spoken to. Another had stolen money from his own brother. A trucker she'd known for years squeezed her shoulder and said, "I used to run around on my wife. This was some time ago." He nodded as if he meant to assign her a job or to thank her for a job she'd already completed. He winked, already feeling lighter, having laid his guilt in Rosamond's lap. "I don't know what brought me of a mind to tell you that," he said.

With or without Tucker, Rosamond drank until she was numb enough to walk home without feeling the cold. The truck driver's revelation and the confession of the man from the loading bay— she didn't even know his name—unnerved her, but she tried not to dwell on them. These confessions were weightier than those she'd heard before. She remembered what Agnes had said: it was the snow making people tell too much. Somehow the sheer blankness of it, its abundance—that and all the time they had for drinking—brought to mind old, cumbersome burdens, and these men ached to lay them down.

Tucker, however, made no such confessions. Instead, he spoke of how amazed he was that Rosamond, having quit the bar for a decade, still existed to walk into it. "What happened to you?" he asked.

She didn't mention how, those years ago, Jim's youngest daughter had come to see her at the office. "I think you know my father," she'd said by way of introduction. She was a dark-haired girl with wide, searching eyes. "Daddy wants to get married," she'd said, and Rosamond's heart had quickened at that until she realized, a beat later, that the daughter meant he wanted to marry *someone else*. It hadn't been that long since Hatley had left her, and Penny had just died. She had feigned a cough to beg a moment to compose herself, then, with cold politeness, she dismissed Tucker's daughter. "If there's nothing else," she'd said, and the girl blinked back at her a minute, then finally hitched her purse up on her shoulder and left.

Tucker said nothing more about Percy, but there was an implicit sympathy, a recognition that she'd lost something of significance. He laid his hand on her back and leaned close to speak to her. She asked how Carol was, and he nodded. "Fine," he said. "Brilliant." She didn't ask again.

Instead, Tucker explained the miracle of the human liver. "A sponge," he said, shrugging, amazed at how simultaneously intricate and simple the human body was. When he said, "I'm seventy-three years old, and I'm still up for anything," she laughed. She didn't know if she should try to believe him, his concurrent faith in this world and his impatience with physicalities. He was a doctor who didn't wholly embrace scientific findings, a teacher who had only a shrugging faith in education. "Age is the disease," he said. "*Life* is the cure."

"You are the only woman I know who isn't afraid to go to a bar by yourself," Tucker said another time. A dubious compliment, but Rosamond took it. She kept her eyes on him over the rim of her glass as she drank her soda and gin. She put the glass down and smirked, staged bravado; in reality she was afraid of her own house.

"Intelligence?" Tucker said. It was a desultory remark; he conjured such one-sided arguments from the smoky, beery air. "Who needs it? It's a mist. It doesn't exist." He rubbed his papery, crooked hands together. "*Curiosity.*" He nodded to himself. "Curiosity is the mark of genius."

Rosamond lingered with Tucker at the bar until late, and then left, always by herself, and walked the frozen streets home.

Once inside, she lay in the dark a long while, falling asleep at last only to wake several times during the night, startling up from sleep. She tried to piece out what frightened her and what she could use for comfort. The blank, bare walls of her house seemed to belong to another time; she was somehow dredging them up, like déjà vu. Her hairbrush and the coffee table and the temperature control knob inside the refrigerator were all things she *used* to know. The bathroom faucet, which took so long to turn hot on cold mornings, seemed a part of some other life, a relic of sorts.

At spare moments, the moments she had to let her mind wander, when her television show broke for commercials or while she was washing dishes or making the bed, she resumed searching for the unnamed thing she'd become convinced she needed to find. She stopped where she was, dishes in the sink, and went searching still deeper in her closets, once more through her drawers. She took things out and moved them. She wrapped up in tissue the pearl earrings Hatley had given her and placed them inside the freezer for safekeeping. There was a peacock-green silk scarf stuck somewhere among her drawers that she wanted to give Agnes. She couldn't find it, and she wondered if the scarf she remembered was actually hers or her mother's or was just an artifact from a movie she'd seen. She took a stack of dated magazines from the back of her closet and set them on the coffee table, thinking to reeducate herself on the movie stars and the recipes she had known in years past.

This was *her* version of curiosity: she wanted to know her own life.

Also, during the snow, just days after she gave Hatley's address to Agnes, a piece of mail—*very* good mail—arrived. There came, in the midst of spotty postal delivery during the bad weather, a handwritten note on thick parchment from Dorothy Blair, responding, in a cramped, black scrawl, to Rosamond's Christmas card. Those Christmas cards sent wide and free all these years, and here finally an answer. The actress thanked her for thinking of her and wished her a joyous holiday and a blessed new year. How nice, she wrote, it was to hear from her very own hometown, a place she remembered so warmly. The envelope was mint green, and it had come all the way from California. Rosa-mond touched the envelope, traced the edges of the stamp. *From your friend Dorothy.*

The aging movie star said nothing about Rosamond's post-script, her invitation to revisit Goliath, but Rosamond could not stop thinking of it, could not keep herself from picturing the regal lady walking at her side down Main Street on a day so full of pleas-ing warmth and sunshine, it could only be spring. The day in Ro-samond's imagination, in fact, was so pleasant, the windows in the houses shining bright as heaven and the street so clean, that it could not really be Goliath. Not unless there was a means of stepping back in time, wearing her vintage high heels in the correct season and year and with the correct celebrity, a person who should have been Rosamond's friend—if not Rosamond herself.

There was more: If one Christmas card had met its destina-tion, perhaps they had all found their addressees, and maybe *that* old man—Hatley would be over sixty by now—was thinking of her right this instant. It could be she had given Agnes the correct address, a current one. She still didn't know, hadn't asked: Had Agnes written to him? And if she had, what had she said to him? What had she asked of him? There was at least this: Dorothy Blair had responded. Rosamond slept and planned and knitted and sifted through her things.

She flipped on every light in the house before she left for the bar each night and kept them on after she returned. One night Tucker walked her home. "Carol won't mind," he assured her before she asked. After seeing her to her door, he pecked her cheek and hur-ried on his way, a little old man wobbling across the white. Rosa-mond stepped into her house. The possibility of Hatley's existing in present time had made the Hatley of the past almost hypothetical. *If* a man named Hatley Rogers had lived here, this was how he would have combed his hair. This was the bed he might have slept in, the mirror that might have, years ago, held his image.

Rosamond left the lights burning all night. She imagined her house was a lighthouse shining out to sea, that it would lead some world-weary traveler straight to her door.

Clyde Winston saw that his neighbor's house had become a spectacle of lights, every window glowing in the dark. He knew he ought to go and see Rosamond, to make certain everything was all right, but he didn't. He went out to patrol, to check on the same elderly folks Ray was out shoveling sidewalks for, to make certain everyone had power and heat, to see that no traveler was stranded, no cars crashed into trees. He knew what havoc severe boredom can wreak and kept a lookout for teenagers kicking down road signs and drunks going for backyard target practice in the middle of the night. Mostly, he reasoned, what people needed to keep out of trouble was to feel like they weren't alone. He kept his Buick out on the streets, still icy in most places, to keep the town from feeling too empty.

The suicide poets, who had gone underground since school let out for Christmas break, were once again finding a way to communicate their message. They taped their construction paper poems on the vending machines at the Laundromat on Main Street and inserted them at random in rolled-up newspapers lying in people's driveways. They taped them to the insides of phone booths and pinned them to the community bulletin board at the supermarket. Many of them weren't poems at all, but only slogans. There were the old ones—"The right to choose life or its opposite"— and a few new ones, grown bolder in their bleakness: "My dead self is my best self," and simply, "Good-bye, World."

The girls themselves became more visible, in their own ways. Bernice from the supermarket cut her hair short and broke up with her boyfriend. One got a job busing tables at the Tuesday Diner. Wally Thumb, who believed in keeping young people busy to keep them out of trouble, considered hiring the girl an act of community service. Sarah, the prettiest one, was caught fishtailing on the ice in the factory's parking lot, in a pickup full of boys. When the police brought her home at two in the morning, she smelled of beer and her makeup was badly smudged, blue eyeliner streaked all the way to her ear.

"Crazy," Ray said when Clyde told him about the fishtailing and the beer and the boys. "Foolish," he said, echoing Agnes's word for her ex-husband.

Clyde shrugged. "It's expected. Wild behavior. *Foolishness.*"

Clyde ate his dinners at Ray's trailer. He had, in his blizzard patrols, conjured up a baseball diamond—a bit of land just beyond the cemetery. The land was smooth, snowed over now, but he knew what lay beneath—gravel and weeds, dirt. Cleaning it all up would be a job. But it would work, it would be perfect. He even troubled to sketch out logos for the team shirts: *Mighty Goliath.* White letters on red shirts. *Mighty,* he told Ray. That was the word to remember.

What Clyde found just as worrisome as the drunk fishtailing was the newest mission of the girls' leader, Stephanie: she decided to read every book in the Goliath Public Library. The library was housed in the basement of the municipal building, directly below the police department. She was the younger sister of a famous Goliath High basketball star, now playing—even more famously—at the state university in Chapel Hill, and she had stationed herself in a faded armchair in the library's tiny reading room, a pile of books at her side. She meant to show everyone just how pitiful the town's entire collection of books—a few bookshelves' worth—was. "I'll be done by Easter," she claimed.

"She'll fail," Clyde said.

"She might," Ray said. He had started growing a beard during the snow, and it made him seem taller and bigger and more primitive looking than ever. A giant from a fairy tale. He frowned. "So what if she does?"

"It'll be for the second time, and all these people watching." Clyde shook his head. "No, sir. That girl doesn't need another failure. People do desperate things in the face of failure." They were quiet for a moment; he could say the same thing about Percy Harding. About Rosamond. Clyde had heard she was frequenting Dalton's again. The rumors were spinning about her once again, about her and that old man, the teacher who used to be a doctor. Hell, the entire town: *something* was going to happen. Clyde was certain. The colossal sadness had settled into the ground and the houses; it was as thick as the snow.

"Ray," he said. "I'm not playing around with this baseball idea. This game I'm planning. I'm here to tell you, we need this as surely as we need air to breathe, food to eat."

Clyde dreamed his baseball dreams and thought about the girl in the library and the boy in the country—the one to find the body—and tried to ignore the house next door. All those lights—it seemed like something bigger than what he could help with.

Most nights, after dinner with Ray, he was out there on his porch, standing brave and still as he could against the cold, letting the stark night air numb his cheeks. His eyes watered. Those young people needed to know somebody was watching them. Dogs barked, and there was the distant sound of tires rolling across asphalt, the rise and fall of an ambulance's siren, far enough away to be little more than a murmur. Closer, the quiet felt unbreakable. The silence seemed to fill the sky as wholly and substantially as water filled a bowl. The trouble was, there were places in this town Clyde couldn't see. Places where he would be hard pressed to make a person feel looked after or even seen.

He had asked around about the boy who found Percy Harding right after it happened and had learned something of his family, of his father, gone from farmer to auto mechanic to farmworker/auto mechanic/handyman in recent years. There were three sisters, popular at the high school, and the mother, a quiet, pious thing—a fixture at Sonrise Baptist. Little was known about the boy, Vincent. He was quiet, people said. An average student, no athlete. Before he found Percy Harding's body, there had been little reason to notice him.

Clyde hoped he was enjoying the warmth of his home and family during the snow, but Vincent Bailey could not bear to be in the box of a house where his sisters watched daytime talk shows and bickered, where his mother drifted from room to room, fussing, picking things up and putting them away. His father used the idle time to paint the front hallway, going about it with little talking, dipping his brush in cream-colored paint, putting it on thick and smooth, white onto white. The old wall was yellowed in places from the oil heat, worn dull in other ways. Sometimes his father whistled, but soft, like he didn't know he was doing it. When he did speak to Vincent, it was to remind him of his chores or to tell him not to get used to all this lying around. The weather is bound to turn, he warned him.

"Go find something useful to do," his father said.

Vincent slinked away, out to the old work building, made of soft-rotted wood with gaps that let through the snow. There were useless archaic parts of vehicles long dispensed of, since everything new was kept in the dome-shaped vinyl shed up closer to the house. Vincent went out there to be cold, to smoke, to take a sprig of rough wood and swallow it whole, to catch what insects— a cockroach here and there and plenty of spiders—he could find. He let each climb over his fingers, across the dirt-creases in his hands, over the terrain of his sweater. He thought that for an insect, the cuff of his jacket could be a highway; the ridges in his fingernails were like cracks in the asphalt. An odd impulse came to him, and he considered it for a long time, watching a black ant reconcile the landscape on one of the folds in his blue jeans. Finally, steeling himself, he lifted the ant to his mouth and dropped it, alive, on his tongue. He closed his mouth and put the insect down his throat.

That night Rosamond dreamed something new, not of Hatley or of Percy or even of herself, but of a woman and a man crushed together against a tree, kissing. They grabbed at each other, and she tried not to be there. But she was, and she felt the hot dampness of the night—it was summertime. She couldn't see their faces, but she felt the man's hand from within—through him, she touched the woman's arm, her hair. But she could feel the other side of it, the woman's side, the rough heel of his hand on her abdomen, her shoulders. Rosamond woke up suddenly, in the glare of her lit bedroom, alone. Misplaced. She did not remember what the truck driver at Dalton's had told her about cheating on his wife years ago. There was only her quickened heartbeat and the clock radio on the nightstand: 3:24 in the morning.

While Rosamond settled back into uneasy sleep, Clyde patrolled, looping the same half-dozen streets over and over again. Agnes measured distances across continents with her fingers.

Vincent Bailey slept on the cold space of floor beneath his bed. He brought down a pillow to lay his head on and a blanket for warmth, but he kept one hand flat on the cold wood floor as if to feel a heartbeat, slow and dull and distant, or else a freight train, rumbling close. He nightmared the train, massive and black and pushing forward with such weight, such power, it bore a tunnel into the mud beneath the cornfield, deep beneath all the snow.

The county snowplows came through on the second day of the new year, and it took a few rounds of their passing to uncover splotches of asphalt. People got out for shopping and visiting, the factory reopened on half time, and the roads were further cleared by the heat of the tires. The next few afternoons the sun warmed the air to just above freezing and there came a dimpled look to the white lawns and on the snow-covered porches, sunshine glaring across, pinpricking the snow. By the end of the first full week in January, trickles of melted snow ran through rain gutters, and the streets were bright with runoff. At night the roads refroze and weren't passable again until midmorning the next day. The downtown shops, the public library, and the supermarket returned to their regular schedules. Then two weeks into the year, the schools were up and running again, the grade school children full of snow stories, and even the high school students were happy to be back. They were so *sick,* they said, of their own houses.

The English teacher at the high school, in adherence to the state curriculum and inspired by the recent popularity of death poems among the students, started a poetry unit. She led her students on a labored trudge through the sonnets of Shakespeare, T. S. Eliot's Prufrock—*Dare I eat a peach?*—and for fun, Ogden Nash. The students were encouraged to compose their own verse, though suicide poetry was strictly forbidden.

But poetry's popularity among the high school students had been fleeting; there had not been a new pink construction paper poem since the girls' leader had begun her reading campaign. Besides, after the suicide cult's poems, adult-sanctioned poetry seemed an insult. They refused to warm to T. S. Eliot, and they claimed Shakespeare was completely unreadable. The first Friday of the in-class readings, only one of them—not a known member of or even a sympathizer with the suicide cult—had a poem to share.

A girl native to Goliath yet not well known by her peers rose to read a poem she'd composed about a doorless house. *No way to enter or to leave, the house held itself closed. The demons could not depart, the angels could not enter.* It was the girl with the sick father who had tucked herself into her closet during the snow. Vincent Bailey, who had listened little, spoken little since he found Percy Harding dead in the mud beneath the railroad tracks, heard the poem clear, and he knew right off what sadness the girl was talking about. After school, he did not get on his bus as usual but instead walked behind the school, beyond the factory, to the trailer park where the poem-girl Cassie Stewart lived.

She and Vincent had been in classes together since kindergarten, and all during that time, she had a history of doing strange things, like the time she stole the class hamster in the third grade or when, in the fifth grade, she raised her hand to tell the teacher something in Portuguese. It was a language, she explained, that she'd learned from the back of a cereal box. Since middle school, she had left threatening notes in the desks she occupied throughout the day, warning students not to write on the desks or to work holes into their edges with their pencils. Yet she was a small girl, with a fragile frame, completely unintimidating, and her notes were simply laughed at or ignored.

Despite her oddities, Cassie remained practically invisible among her classmates. At lunch she usually ate with her cousin Mark, who played with soldier figurines between classes, or else with her aunt, her father's sister, who was one of the cafeteria ladies. Cassie wore T-shirts stamped with tobacco company logos and worn-out jeans a few inches too short for her, so her sock-covered ankles always stuck out. On the day Cassie read the poem, Vincent watched her return to her seat and lay her head down on her desk. She didn't lift it up again until the end of class, when she gathered her books and shuffled out the door, her face revealing nothing.

The trailer park consisted of four rows of trailers, six deep. They were set on the far side of the parking lot from the factory and were separated from one another by a few feet of gravel. Vincent, who had never been in the trailer park before, had no plan for how to find the right trailer. He wandered about looking up at the windows, many of which were covered from within with dark sheets or beach towels tacked up over them. Vincent had never been in a place where so many people lived so close together, and he felt like an intruder ambling through, looking up at those covered windows, listening. The trailer park seemed like a combination of an abandoned town and a refugee camp, the voices coming from the trailers abrupt and loud in moments, hushed in between. He came to suspect the people inside the trailers—behind their blinds and beach-towel curtains—were watching him.

He started knocking on doors. Finally, after he had tried a half-dozen or so, a woman wearing a pink terry-cloth robe answered. She gripped a cigarette between her teeth and squinted at him for a minute, suspicious. He explained he needed to find Cassie for a project at school. "English class," he said, and the woman took the cigarette from her mouth and pointed down the row, said she thought there was a girl about his age living there. "A girl and her parents," the woman said, shutting the door.

He tried it—number 8—and while he waited for someone to answer the door, Vincent wondered what he was doing here. He thought of the long walk home he had ahead of him. He looked up at the dingy-clouded sky and felt afraid of the bigness of it. Of everything. It was how he had felt since that Sunday morning when he had found Percy Harding, and even more so since Halloween night, spotting the light in the trees. The world had gained a coldness that had nothing to do with the snow, melting away to slush now.

Cassie appeared. She stood behind the screen door, yellow light coming from an uncurtained window inside the trailer. The air was full of dust motes. Behind Cassie lay a person sleeping under a blanket on the couch. An old television set blared. The floor was a faded linoleum covered partially with shag carpeting, the furniture a sallow tan. Cassie looked the same as at school—skinny, her long brown hair lusterless, her eyes penciled gray. Like the others, Vincent had never paid much attention to her before.

She said nothing, and he felt awkward, her squinting back at him, waiting. Her face was blank, same as after class, and he couldn't tell if she recognized him. He didn't think she was pretty, but he didn't care too much about that, not now. He couldn't say what exactly he wanted from her. It was something that began with the poem, that seemed now to go with the floor, worn so thin the underlying grid of glue showed through in places; with the lumpy figure snoring on the couch. Vincent could see the back of a man's head—Cassie's father, he guessed. There was country poor, Vincent included, and then there was this: bare poor.

"You got a minute?" he asked. She shrugged, didn't step out to meet him, didn't invite him inside. She wouldn't even open the screen door, just stared at him while he talked. "I liked your poem." She looked at him, no expression. Her eyes were as lightless as blank paper. He asked, "Could you maybe write it down for me?"

There were sounds coming from the other trailers; music blaring, people arguing. A car angled around the corner. Canned laughter erupted from Cassie's television set, but otherwise, the trailer seemed completely still, time stopped. Her blankness gave way to a sort of sourness, her pupils constricting into themselves, hardness narrowing down to a pinprick.

"How did you know where I lived?" she asked. He shrugged. She stared back at him a moment, hesitated, then shook her head. "I don't think so," she said, stepping back into the trailer and closing the door.

Leaving, Vincent chose a rock from the patch of gravel beside the trailer and tossed it up at her door, where it clanked loudly but caused no visible damage. He shuffled away, taking the long way from town to his house, the sides of the unmarked county roads muddy with melting snow.

A few days later, though, he thought through the poem, remembered the shag carpet, the scattered gravel between the trailers. He went again straight after school. Cassie, seeing him there on the narrow spot of porch in front of her trailer, nodded, her eyes quicker now, something livened in them, and she turned to get her jacket.

"Let's go," she said, hopping down the trailer steps and heading off, him following behind.

He couldn't figure what had changed her mind, but he followed her to the gas station convenience store across from the railroad tracks. She walked with head bent, hands shoved into her denim jacket, legs so skinny they didn't touch. At the store, he bought two Cokes and a bag of chips, and they went to sit on the curb out front. They were quiet, busy with their operations, opening the chips, taking long swigs of soda. Then Cassie spoke.

"I thought you wouldn't come again," she said. When he shrugged, like maybe he had meant to never come back, she said, "Okay, I'll tell it again." She set her soda down, closed her eyes, and recited the poem from memory in a throatier, more dramatic way than before. "I could tell you liked it in class," she said. They sat for a minute looking away from each other, swallowing their soda, feeling something important and unknowable stretch between them. Across the way, spots of grass showed through the disappearing white, and in the far corner of the parking lot slouched a huge mound of snow that had taken dirt and grease from the asphalt and had been gathered up by the plow, pushed aside. "I could tell you liked it," she said again.

"I'm the one who found the dead man," Vincent said. He nudged a soda-can top with the toe of his sneaker. "I found Percy Harding," he said.

Yes, Cassie knew. *Everyone* knew. Here, the fames and oddities of their class at school, there was a boy whose daddy was in prison, another who swallowed rat poison when he was three, and one who had a great-great-uncle who went down a waterfall in a padded barrel. Another had been to Winston-Salem for cancer treatments. One had won a baby beauty contest. Vincent was not the only one among them to bear first witness to a corpse. Another, a girl, had found an elderly relative in an easy chair, unmoving. Even Cassie Stewart, on the periphery of the group, knew these things.

"It wasn't even bloody," Vincent said. It was the first he had told anyone of what he had seen, other than the bare facts of it to his father on the Sunday morning he'd found the body, him calling him to follow him out there, come see. "His leg and his arm were crushed to nothing, completely flat." He rubbed his thumb across the label on his soda. "At first I didn't even know it was human, what I saw."

Later he took her to the woods and told her to sit, watch. He fingered around in the ice-crusted leaves, the snow soft and wet under the trees. Finally, there, a worm, small enough so he could do it, big enough so it might impress her. It went down. Afterward she recited more poems about the doorless house, the windows shot through from within, the painted walls scratched at, the graffiti etched on the interior, leering green demons and images of fire. She explained to Vincent that she had written the poems during the snowstorm, but that she had felt the suffocation for a long time before. The days of snow only gave her time to learn how to deprive herself of oxygen. Backing up against a tree, she demonstrated: head bowed, she stopped breathing, slumped, then rose a moment later, her face bluish and pale. In the next instant her cheeks bloomed pink again, life coming back.

EIGHT

The snow was washed clean away by a week-long rain, and the sun broke out to dry the streets. The lawns were still muddy when two young men from outside places—strangers—arrived in Goliath. One, a scrubbed-up boy with a smooth face and a tidy haircut, came wearing a dark blue suit. He parked his slate blue station wagon on Main Street and started knocking on doors. When he was first spied through windows and peepholes, people took him for a Mormon missionary. Because he came in the evening, when folks did not like to be taken from the six o'clock news or the dinner table, Rosamond Rogers was the first to answer his knock. She was still in her work dress and panty hose, tired out from the agonizing task of doing so little—Ryan Harding still did not use her much—and she regarded the handsome young man on her doorstep with curiosity and suspicion. His face was so young and fine and earnest, Rosamond instantly longed to touch it. He grinned, clearly relieved to find a door, *any* door, opened to him, and asked in a singsong boom, "What is it *you* wish to know?"

The second boy arrived in worn jeans and a denim jacket too thin for late January, even with all the snow gone. He materialized on Rosamond's doorstep looking as mangy and unkempt as the first boy looked new and clean. His face was marked with sleep lines as if he'd just woken in his car, a faded orange Volkswagen parked not in the street but in Rosamond's driveway, right next to her own dormant Cadillac. Rosamond had been listening to the first boy's sales pitch, about World Knowledge Encyclopedias, him snapping open a dark leather briefcase with brass hinges, handing out pamphlets and sample encyclopedias, the A and the C volumes, and well, he could go get any letter she wanted from his car. He had it all there, whatever she wanted.

"Just name it." He grinned. "Everything you ever thought of, it's here."

The second young man looked past her when she answered the door and glanced at the encyclopedia salesman, a college boy named Trevor. Trevor, who had been sitting on the sofa amid his sales paraphernalia and the ever-teetering piles of Rosamond's old magazines, rose, expectant. Rosamond felt a twinge of the familiar, seeing that sales-hopeful smile.

"Where is she?" the rough boy asked, his movements springy, quick-snapping, as if his bones were held together with rubber bands. The irises of his eyes were nearly as dark as his pupils. Rosamond and Trevor stared at him, uncomprehending. "Agnes," the boy said, closing his eyes and, with visible effort, calming himself, pushing his fingers through his hair, which was how, Rosamond saw, it had come to stand up in peaks jutting out at odd angles all over his head. "Where's Agnes?" he demanded, his voice tilting high and cracking a little as if he might start to cry.

"You're the husband," Rosamond said, realization coming to her. Here, her daughter's *husband*. The skin on the back of her neck prickled with understanding. This was the man—the *boy*—who had broken his heart over Agnes.

"And you," the boy said. His voice was thin and reedy, out of sync with the look of him. "You're the mother," he said.

It was a shock to both of them, Rosamond imagining Agnes speaking to this boy about her, and this boy, imagining Agnes speaking of him to this faded old woman. Creepy to see a complete stranger come to recognize you and think unsaid things about you. He was the cast-off husband, the living proof of Agnes's free-love marriage, failed, spoken of, but never before seen. She was the mother—whatever *that* meant. Rosamond sized him up, saw his dark eyes, the whites threaded with red, gray patches of skin beneath them. Even his hands were rough and red, hard-lived, and yet he still looked so young; there was that crack in his voice, so like a little boy's. She glanced back at Trevor, who seemed a person she had known for some time now, though it had been only about twenty minutes or so since he himself had knocked on her door. He stood with his hands in his pockets, humming a little, this boy too young to know how to fade away in an awkward spot. She realized after a moment that she was waiting, stupidly, for the salesboy to do something, to handle the situation. Trevor stopped humming and coughed into his fist.

"Where is she?" the boy husband demanded. Then, taking a deep breath, speaking softer, imploringly, "Please tell me."

"James," she said.

She and Agnes had not spoken a word about him since the day she had come through the deep snow and they had sat at the table while Rosamond clipped coupons. Yet Rosamond recalled what Agnes had said before, in the days when she'd first come back home and she wouldn't even say his name. *My play husband,* she had said, *a boy I used to know.* They had met in philosophy class. He had waited for her afterward one day, striking up a conversation about the concept of intentionality. Agnes had paused here, explaining the concept to her mother: objects are defined—they exist—only by their representations in the human mind. A cat is not a cat unless it is thought of as a cat. The same goes for tomatoes, a billboard, the moon.

Rosamond only knew this much, plus the other side of it: the end of their relationship, what little Agnes had told her during the snow. This, as far as Rosamond knew, was the boy husband's first attempt to contact Agnes since she'd left him. Rosamond, believing anything to be possible in this instance, half expected her dead mother to come in from the kitchen or Hatley to appear at the front door. Dorothy Blair might walk in from the hallway. Percy Harding could yet appear undamaged, complete.

"Where," James asked, looking squarely at Rosamond, "*is* she?"

She wouldn't say, and instead turned and walked into the kitchen. She dialed Agnes's number and, while waiting for Agnes to answer, looked through the doorway to watch the two boys in the living room. James stood, arms akimbo, his chin jutting out, and Trevor awkwardly touched his sales things, his briefcase, unsure of whether he should pack up and leave or stick around. She didn't know if she ought to be angry or worried for Agnes. Somehow she also found herself a bit in awe of what all her daughter had done out there, apart from her. Agnes had inspired a mighty measure of devotion, this boy worn out from pining for her.

Agnes answered, and Rosamond told her, "Your husband is here."

Agnes was confused at first. "Who, James? You mean James? Tell him to go on back to school. I don't want to see him." Rosamond balked, though it was the response she'd expected. She didn't know what to say to anybody now, looking past James to the young salesman sitting there, with his sturdy tomes, his cheek so soft-looking, she could hardly imagine he was old enough to shave. She remembered Agnes's talk about spotting Hatley at various spots, the bits of Kierkegaard James had memorized, the semester he spent learning the fundamentals of animal husbandry.

Rosamond remembered what Percy had said, about how *they* should be the leavers. In this case, in just this one, at least, it was Agnes. Agnes was the leaver.

"Tell him to go away," Agnes said.

Rosamond wouldn't convey this message. "Tell him yourself," she said, waving James into the kitchen. He came, and she handed him the receiver. Agnes said something and James tried to reply, but she had already hung up on him. He stared at the phone in his hand, then glanced up at Rosamond, as if for help.

"She was stubborn as a child," she explained.

"I love her," he said, still holding the receiver in one hand, absently raking his dirty hair with the other. Rosamond reached to take the phone from him, and he resisted for a second. He seemed startled, as if he had forgotten he was holding it. He released it, and she returned it to its cradle on the wall behind him. He smelled of sweat and stale laundry and something sweet and warm and spoiled. His jacket was worn white at the bend in the collar, and the cuffs were frayed. Rosamond noticed his shoes for the first time: work boots with fluorescent orange laces.

"I do," he said. "I love her."

But she knew she had to make him leave. "Go on," she said, ushering him through the kitchen, the living room, to the front door. She put her hand on his shoulder to guide him, and he did not resist. "There's nothing else I can do," she told him.

"All right," he said, but then he just stood there at the door a moment. He looked behind her, his eyes moving over her gold sofa, her chair by the window. He seemed to have collected himself a little, or was shocked by the sound of Agnes's voice. Whatever she had said had left him bewildered and slow. Stunned. Finally he nodded first at Trevor and then at Rosamond. "I'll come back for her," he said.

He left, stepping slowly, almost daintily across the front yard. Rosamond stood in the door, watching. She had her hands on her hips, like she meant business, and he paused at the edge of the yard, turning to look back at her before hopping over the gushing rain gutter into the street, walking in the direction of town. She closed the door and went to stand by the window, looking out.

"If it's still there at ten o'clock," Rosamond told Trevor, pointing to the orange Volkswagen—presumably the boy husband's car—parked in her driveway, "I'll call the police."

The pair of them stood together at the window, Rosamond close enough to this college boy to smell the starch in his shirt.

"Maybe she should talk to him," Rosamond said. "I don't know. That was my daughter's husband," she said after a moment, thinking she ought to explain. She felt she had a history with the salesboy. It seemed she had known him a long time. "Today is the first time I ever met him," she said.

Trevor shook his head, whistled low. "That's some crazy kind of love," he said.

She locked the front door against the boy husband, said, "All right, now," and Trevor hastily resumed his sales pitch, opening the stiff black volumes to point out full-color photographs of Cézanne paintings and magnified views of carpenter ants. She turned the pages and after a time rose to fix supper. Later she settled at the kitchen table to fill out the order form while he ate the pork chops she'd fried for him. Rosamond learned the boy was from Pennsylvania, that this was his first sales trip. He'd done well in Maryland, decent in Virginia. North Carolina until *now*— he grinned—had been a bear. The boy spoke and chewed at the same time. "These people won't even open the door," he said. Rosamond had an odd, fleeting thought that the boy was her son. She shook the idea away and yet could not help but feel she and Trevor were somehow connected. Maybe he had come here for a reason. Maybe something inside her already recognized him for that. Or it could be, she reasoned, that the boy simply had that kind of personality, was universally familiar looking. Everyone he met felt like they already knew him.

Late that night, after the salesboy had left to lodge at a hotel a few miles down the highway, the Volkswagen was still there in her driveway, its owner nowhere to be seen. Rosamond called Agnes's apartment. A male voice answered, and Rosamond was startled until she realized it was only Ray. "I'm here with her," he said. "I'll see that she's all right." He offered to call and have James's car towed, but she insisted it wasn't necessary. Agnes got on the phone then, said, "Mom. Why don't you get out of there? I mean, you should come over here. Stay with Mia a few nights, maybe."

But Rosamond had work to do, all the piles from the closets, and she'd just cleaned out from under her bed. Agnes told her in a hushed voice, "He'll leave by the morning. He doesn't care about me as much as he thinks he does. Really he doesn't—nobody does. Don't worry."

Rosamond got off before she thought to question the other thing Agnes had said, about nobody caring as much as they thought they did. She meant Ray, Rosamond thought, and James. Hatley. Rosamond turned it over and over in her mind, all the people Agnes might have meant. Rosamond didn't know if Agnes had tried to contact Hatley, but she was certain that even if a letter had been sent, Hatley hadn't received it. It seemed she would somehow divine it; she would just *know* if a connection had been made.

Rosamond sat on the sofa watching her front door, waiting for James to knock on the other side. She didn't dare take off for Dalton's for fear she'd miss James or the salesboy. She'd even turned her lights off so that if a shadow moved across the streetlight outside, she would see it. She listened for the sound of the boy husband's car starting up in her driveway. Probably she should call Clyde, have him look for James. For James's own safety. She could tell Clyde was home—his lights were on. She wondered drowsily if that coffee cup was still sitting, half-full, on the carpet beside his easy chair.

But she didn't get up from the sofa, didn't make any calls. Tonight she was a piece of the dark; anyone coming in would not see her right off. She was still dressed. Her shoes lay on the floor beneath the sofa, her legs curled up beneath her.

It was near midnight when someone finally knocked. Rosamond, who had drifted to sleep there in the living room, jerked awake, sat up. The knock came again, insistent and loud, and she rose, crossed the room, and opened the door before she thought to check, see who it was. She was disoriented, still wanting sleep, and while she remembered there was something she was waiting for—half anticipating, half dreading—for a moment she didn't remember what it was.

"You didn't look to see who it was. You didn't check."

"Oh, Clyde," she said. Then she remembered: the salesboy. The encyclopedias, her dinner with the salesboy, the boy husband—*James*—wild-eyed and pink-cheeked, standing in her door, looking past her, searching.

"I could have been anyone," he said. She hadn't put her porch lights on or flipped on any lights inside the house, and it was so dark, she couldn't see Clyde clearly. But the whites of his eyes shone, and across his cheek lay a rectangle of gauzy light from an unknown source. The air outside was so thin, it whistled faintly, dry and sharp with cold.

He asked, "You're alone?"

Just as James had done earlier that evening, Clyde peered beyond her, into the dark house. He had always been overprotective this way, and while there had been a time she had appreciated it—had even envied Penny for it once upon a time—now she was annoyed. He was wearing a heavy coat but was bareheaded. The chill outside was so deep, it took Rosamond's breath.

She left his question unanswered. Of course Clyde had spoken with Ray, and he knew James had come. Clyde Winston, that good man, come here to make sure she was all right, to protect her from every danger, imagined and real. She wanted to look past him, see if the Volkswagen was still in her driveway, but she didn't want to let Clyde know she was looking. It seemed important not to give him any information he hadn't already gathered from Ray. She crossed her arms and leaned against the doorjamb. Clyde was the third man to knock on her door that night. She remembered the dinner she'd fixed for the salesboy, how good it felt to watch him eat her green beans, her slow-simmered pork chops. There had also been the boy husband, the dirt on his clothes, the grease in his hair. She shivered now in her dress, no coat, her feet bare except for her panty hose.

"Clyde," she finally said, "what is the matter?"

But he seemed to know what she was thinking. "His car's still there," he said, stepping back, pointing at it—the two cars, hers and the boy husband's, two gray shapes in the scant light. "The car's owner is sleeping inside."

The boy husband was camped out in her driveway.

Clyde said, "I'll tell him to move on."

"It's all right, though, isn't it? If he stays? Let's just let him sleep."

"Rosamond." His voice softened. "I have to. He'll freeze out here."

She nodded. It seemed he was waiting for her to invite him in, but the two of them remained quiet for a long moment. She felt both man-rich and alone standing there, all that had happened that evening, the house empty behind her. Despite herself, despite how beautiful and young and broad-shouldered the salesboy had been, she found herself craving Jim Tucker's skinny arms; she wanted to put her cheek against his fragile chest.

Yet, this was Clyde standing in front of her, not Tucker. He was leaning in just so, a look on his face like he was trying to decide something. For a moment it seemed he might lean just a tiny bit closer, draw his face close to hers, and drop a kiss on her lips. Later she'd wonder if she'd imagined it, but at the moment, standing there in the cold, the pearly soft darkness, that slant of light slipping across his cheek and into his hair as he bent his head closer to hers, it seemed possible. It seemed *likely*. Clyde Winston might do as he'd done years earlier, soon after Penny had died, as he'd never done in quite the same way since. He might kiss her, and then what would she do? There would still be a boy sleeping in her driveway, another in a hotel down the highway, and an old man waiting for her in a bar. Another, her Hatley, long gone, and the last, destroyed—*obliterated*—by his own actions.

Finally, though, Clyde only nodded decisively, matter-of-factly, as if these were the olden days, when so much business was conducted with little more than polite gesture and unspoken understanding. *That'll do it,* his nod seemed to say. If he'd had a hat, he would have tipped it, a horse, he would have giddy-upped, away.

Instead he reached out and touched her arm—his gloveless hand to her thin dress sleeve, cold to cold—and reminded her he was right next door if she needed anything.

"You remember that," he said, and left.

Vincent was not about to give his heart over to Cassie. Mostly he was just curious about her. She was an anomaly in Goliath, dark-hearted and strange. She impressed him in small, unromantic ways. Like the way she didn't seem to care about what anyone thought, wearing discount clothes with such confidence, the gutsy notes she left in desks at school. She handled the demons and other hellish creatures in her poems with little drama and no perceptible fear. "It's pure inspiration," she said, shrugging. "I don't know where the words come from."

They met up nearly every day after school and stopped first at the gas station convenience store. They bought Cokes and talked with Fay, the fat, somber-faced woman who worked there, forty-something and four months pregnant. Her first baby, she said. Her name was Fay and she had cloudy gray eyes and a squishy face crusted over with thick makeup, the blue from her eye shadow creasing in a greasy arc over her eye, her candy pink lipstick smudging, shiny at its corners. She moved slowly, in a way that seemed due to general melancholy rather than the malaise of a body drained by the task of growing a baby. "I don't know how this happened," she said, pointing to her belly, and Vincent couldn't help snickering. Of course she knew *how* it had happened. Cassie, ignoring him, gave Fay an empathetic look. "God works in mysterious ways," she said, and Fay sighed, nodding and frowning. "Oh yes, honey. He surely does."

Vincent teased Cassie for the church talk later, asking what all did she know about the mysteries of God? She said, "You don't know everything, Vincent Bailey."

Cassie was like that, talking down to him. She also had a habit of falling silent midsentence, closing her eyes to let in any poem that happened along. She seemed connected to some invisible source, an electric muse that zapped out poems to her. Sometimes she scribbled the words down on a scrap of paper, or more often on her hand. Other times she let the poem come and go, explaining to Vincent that she was only a conduit—the poem was free to float onward wherever it chose to go. She rolled her eyes and took herself too seriously and believed she was prettier than she really was. Vincent could see this in the way she shook her hair out of her eyes. She told him, "I was born in a Denny's bathroom stall," and though he was fairly certain she was lying, it seemed a strange thing to brag about.

Despite all this, she openly admired him, for his finding the dead body and his newly acquired talent for ingesting inedible objects. "You are so weird, Vincent Bailey," she said, grinning. "You are utterly *deranged.*"

Before he stumbled upon Percy Harding's corpse, Vincent had been the most ordinary kid in school. He'd had ordinary friends and drifted in unremarkable ways through the halls, his eyes on the linoleum squares, goggle-eyed with distraction, occasionally still thinking little-boy thoughts about race cars and survival camping. When Cassie Stewart, queen of the out there, called *him* weird, it frightened him a little. He had been thrown out of ordinary and hardly knew how to walk anymore or what to think about.

Cassie, though, quickly grew bored with the cigarettes, the ants, the worms, and spurred him on to more ambitious conquests. "Come on, Vincent. There has got to be something else, something *better.*"

They were in the woods behind the school, the trees bare and reaching all around them. He had already downed a lit cigarette, and they were just ambling through, Vincent tapping a stick against the trunks of the trees they passed. Cassie was walking coatless, her hands thrust into her jeans pockets. She made suggestions: a slug, a thumbtack, a rock, a caterpillar, a razor, a bee.

He stopped to stare at her when she said razor. "It'll rip my throat open," he said, and she shrugged, pushing her sleeve up to show him a place on her arm where she'd scratched her initials— *CTS*—with a safety pin. She'd picked open the scabs again and again to make a scar. "So?" he said, "That's not a razor, doesn't cut deep enough," and she answered, "It's sharp. It *hurts.*"

He agreed to a caterpillar, though, and bent over to search, the late-afternoon sunlight coming down through the tree branches hard orange and cold, the wind shimmying through. He still ate lunch with his old friends, the group of boys he'd known since kindergarten, though he no longer saw them much outside of school. He wondered: did they know he was hanging out with the biggest sad-case girl in their class? They were friendly-ish when they passed him in the hallways, but that was only for politeness. They couldn't *not* nod at him in passing, and they couldn't uninvite him from their lunch table. Yet it was understood: everything had changed.

He had seen a man crushed by a train, and they could never understand what that was like, how he carried around the picture of it in his head. He couldn't shake the sensation that sound had been sucked clean from this world, that when anyone talked to him now, the words were coming from a long way off, even if the person speaking was right there next to him.

His father never said anything about that morning, but he looked at Vincent differently than he used to, only glancing—quick, maybe even a little afraid—when Vincent was turned away. His boy had been the first to see the dead man, and that set a shadow on his shoulders. That kind of knowledge, of *seeing*, was evil, and Vincent had caught the first of it: full-strength death knowledge.

He often thought about the fact that his father had seen the dead body, same as him, and he wished he could ask him to describe it to him, to hear the sight of it put in his father's words. Once Vincent tried to tell him about how the image of that body was burned into the back of his eyelids—the only thing he ever saw when he blinked—and his father interrupted him, saying, "He was dead when we found him. There was nothing we could do." He seemed stuck on that, for even after he turned away and was silent for a few long moments, Vincent heard him say again to himself, "Not a thing we could do."

Everyone was afraid of Vincent, of what he'd seen, and he knew it. It wasn't just his father—everyone stared at him when he was turned away. Everyone except Cassie.

They kept searching, bent over, pushing dead leaves away with their sticks, digging a little here and there in the mud. Cassie was the only one brave enough to hear about it. She *wanted* to hear about it. There was nowhere else for him to be, he realized. This spot, these woods, this was all. He and Cassie would never find a caterpillar, not in these dead woods, but they looked. The air was deep cold, and the scant wind, when it rose, snaked through his jacket collar.

Vincent had teased Cassie for speaking of the mysteries of God, but he was the one who didn't know what to do with the flash of light that had risen from the trees some months earlier. He intuited it to be some manifestation of God, and it scared him. Though the other viewer, Rosamond, who was the opposite of Vincent in every way—female, older, legendary for being completely un-ordinary— was going crazy, seeking out the light, Vincent wanted only to hide from it.

"Once," he said, "when I was a little kid, I saw sheet lightning in my backyard. It lit everything up—every tree—and it scared me. It scared me to death. I saw it through my window." He was lying about when it had happened, but it seemed right too—he *was* a kid. He didn't look at Cassie. She said nothing, and he continued, "I don't know why it scared me. It was the middle of the night." She was still searching the leaves, poking around the base of a tree with a stick. He said, "I should have left Percy Harding where I found him. It didn't do *him* any good. Telling everyone. It didn't do him any good at all."

Cassie stood up, her back still to him. She had found something; when she turned, she was smiling, her hands closed around something. She arched one eyebrow and nodded. "Just the thing," she said, and opened her fingers a tiny bit, letting Vincent see it there, an overgrown insect with monstrous long back legs, and then held it enclosed in her hands.

He was still thinking of the light in the trees, of Percy Harding's body. Still hoping she wouldn't find anything, and here she was, offering it to him.

"It was the worst thing I ever did," he said. "Telling people. I could have left him that way. Just lost, but not dead."

Cassie was not listening. "Open wide," she said, plucking the creature up quick by one of its legs. Her face was flushed from the cold and her breath came out in visible gasps.

"It's a cricket," he said stupidly. "You want me to eat a cricket," he said.

She grinned, brought it closer to his face.

"All right. All *right*."

He closed his fingers over her wrist, and with his other hand grasped one of the cricket's wire-thin appendages between his forefinger and his thumb. He brought the creature before his eyes and studied it. It was a smallish cricket, maybe the size of a quarter, but there was a bit of muscle on its hind legs, and it had a plump little round body. The ants and worms had been small and had not had a single characteristic, save their jerking movements, to distinguish them from a piece of wood or a chunk of dirt. They were just bugs. This cricket, though, had meaty limbs and a heart beating inside its gushy insides same as any animal. Though he hadn't thought such a thing in years, not consciously at least, Vincent caught a glimpse of his mother's shocked face, seeing him. Always, always, there were his father's uncatchable eyes. A look from a cousin who lived in Tennessee, a boy he hardly ever saw. Again, his friends, those he encountered every day, those he sat with in the cafeteria and watched their mouths open and close, talking, laughing with one another. These came in tiny, soundless snatches, and he let them in.

All right, *now*: he dropped the cricket on the back of his tongue and the creature seemed so huge there, he feared he'd choke on it. But his throat closed around it, and it moved down.

Cassie stood back a few paces, clapping. She threw her scrawny arms up above her head, hopping a little, her eyes closed, and Vincent felt it, what he had done, how he had swallowed the live creature, and he thought through the mechanics of the tiny being's death: first the suffocation, the crushing; then the digesting, the breaking it down, his body taking in another entity for nourishment and energy. Vincent would still be dismantling the creature hours later, his body working to digest it, to piece it out in molecular segments to every cell in his body.

"*Wahoo!*" Cassie cried, dancing around a little. Vincent breathed in, let it out slow, fearful he would be sick and yet also feeling steely-strong and powerful for what he had done. He was still *here.*

"Wahoo and mighty," Cassie sang, and Vincent closed his eyes, felt his blood work, pump through, taking in the cricket, absorbing it.

But later, they were taking the long way back to her trailer, shuffling along above the railroad tracks, the factory parking lot, and she said, "Sheet lightning *is* scary. Especially to a little kid." She winked at him, a lame, awkward gesture that he appreciated but could not reciprocate, could not even smile at. He shrugged and looked away.

Clyde did as he said he would: he ran the boy husband away. But in the morning early, there was the sound of tires on Rosamond's driveway. She woke with a single thought: she should have kept them, those boys. She should have found a way to keep them both right here, in her house.

She had slept lightly and rose quickly now, as she had the last time she thought James had returned, when she'd instead found a half-frozen Clyde there on her doorstep. She heard the car door shut. Then, peeking through the living room window, she glimpsed James standing in the driveway, his arms folded, his shoulder hunched up a little against the chilly morning. She couldn't see his face well from this distance and his shoulder and arm were blocked from her view, but she watched the shape and position of his body.

He unfolded his arms and his shoulders loosened, as if he had somehow renounced the cold. He pushed his hand through his hair in a gesture that Rosamond already found familiar. *Dear boy,* she thought. *Dear lost boy.*

She wanted to rush out, offer him breakfast, but he turned just then and began walking down the driveway toward the road with a determined step, as if he knew exactly where he was going. He was off to find Agnes, Rosamond realized. A crazy kind of love, the salesboy had said.

She knew Clyde was probably watching her, or at least watching her driveway. She didn't know what precisely that meant except that if she invited the boy husband inside, he would see. And then what? She didn't know. She couldn't begin to guess what lengths Clyde would go to to protect her from that skinny little boy.

The kitchen was full of sunlight in a way that made it hard to believe how cold it was outside. Every minute she half expected the boy husband to return. Or maybe Agnes would come. But, for what reason? To seek advice? To chide her mother for not running him off immediately? For letting him call her? For staying in her own house? She remembered how Clyde had spoken to her the night before, how he touched her arm, how the darkness and his voice made her more aware of his body, his physical heft. The moment when it seemed he might kiss her. He would always be there on her front porch, touching her elbow, speaking softly to her. Here to rescue her. So long as she kept herself in peril, Clyde would be there.

That evening when Rosamond walked home from work, the Volkswagen was still parked in her driveway, still empty. She looked inside. The floorboards were littered with fast-food bags and empty chips bags, and the backseat—the boy's makeshift bed—was a jumble of clothing, T-shirts and jeans. In the passenger seat was a pile of books, mostly hardbacks, jacketless. Notebooks too, their spiral bindings coming loose from the pages, a couple of empty soda cans. The driver's seat alone was clear.

She stood there for a long moment, not caring who might see her gazing into the boy's windows. The sight of this car sitting next to her own—the Cadillac Hatley had left her—made it look all the more settled, un-moveable. Somehow, though, the two cars' looking this way, so *grounded,* reminded Rosamond that they weren't actually that way at all. She touched the hood of the boy husband's car, then the pale blue of her own. Why, she thought, the exclusive purpose of both of them was to *move.* The shadows, stretched long across the street, were dimming, bruised-blue clouds creeping into the crease of the sky. At that moment standing there, one hand on each car, it seemed to Rosamond that these cars parked here in Goliath—home of the greatest furniture manu-facturer in the world—were the only things around that *could* move.

She pictured Agnes sleeping in Aunt Mia's basement apartment, Ray keeping watch. Maybe her daughter was planning her own escape. It could be she'd already left. But Rosamond believed Agnes needed to let James in. She should talk to him. If they had been married in any sense of the word, she owed him that much—she owed *herself* that much.

Agnes wouldn't answer her phone, though, and the salesboy didn't show. Rosamond had been hoping he would come for din-ner again. Probably, though, he was already gone, standing on some other front porch in some other town, smiling that hopeful smile.

Rosamond, tired of trying Agnes's phone, of watching her own front door, once again turned on every light in her house—it had drawn them once, hadn't it?—and set out for Dalton's much earlier than usual. When she arrived, there were only half a dozen men standing at the bar, none of them known to her. But she put a song on the jukebox and sat there by herself, snapping her fingers a little, swaying a tiny bit, drinking a gin and soda. There was nothing—*nothing*—she decided, but the music.

A few of the men tried to talk to her a little as the place grew crowded, the night outside full dark now, but she kept listening to the music. And though she didn't drop any more coins inside the jukebox, it kept up, and she kept sitting there, drinking and dancing a little on her stool and saying as little as she could get by with to the men there, the men who must have been feeding that jukebox for her. The music kept playing and her drinks kept appearing and Rosamond never opened her purse. She closed her eyes and the words to the songs came to her, and she sang them softly. Someone pulled her to her feet, and she was dancing.

She danced with every man that night, and she could hardly tell one partner from the next, them just handing her off at the end of each song, these men who surrounded her. Oh, was it ever good to be with *men*. They were sturdy and rough-cheeked and just as drunk as she was, though they showed it less. She clasped her hands behind their necks, damp with sweat, and rested her head against the men's chests, her eyes closed tight, and still that music going.

At last she was with Tucker and she knew it: she recognized the smell of his eucalyptus soap and the feel of his whiskery-dry cheek on her forehead. "*Rosamond*," he said, and she held on to that, the sound of her name said that way.

Later he walked her home and they stood kissing on her front porch. She was kissing an old man who was married to a woman she'd never met, a wife she'd only imagined.

"Don't leave," she said, turning to unlock the door. James's car was still there in the driveway, dark and abandoned-looking. Possibly he was inside it, sleeping. Possibly Clyde was waiting for her to return home to run the boy husband off. He most likely knew she'd been gone all night; probably he was watching her this very minute, watching as Rosamond took the old man's hand, that music still playing inside her head. She couldn't make out the words now, just a strumming guitar and the deep and tender sound of a country woman singing her heart out. She'd drunk so much, she could hardly feel the cold. She could hardly tell if her eyes were opened or closed, if she was standing on her own or if Tucker, old, skinny man with an impressively solid arm, was holding her up.

Finally she managed the door and pulled the old man inside. He didn't resist but said, "Honey, are you sure about this?" By way of answer, she began, her eyes still only half open, to lead him through all the lit rooms.

NINE

The roads were dry for more than a week, but the factory stayed on half time. The encyclopedia salesboy, who hadn't left as Rosamond had feared, succeeded in gaining entry into almost every living room in Goliath. The boy was charming; if he could get someone to answer the door, he was golden.

Working people, bone-tired, listened to his pitch. Teenage girls left their bedrooms to peek in on his sales demonstration, and teenage boys lingered over their own reflections in bathroom mirrors. They pictured themselves in blue sports jackets and crisp new haircuts. Trevor had the most success with the retired set. The old ladies fixed him ham sandwiches, and the old men offered him coffee and a seat at their kitchen tables. They were curious about this boy, this seller of information. They quizzed him on bits of trivia and launched into their own memories of recent history. One elderly man who had moved down to Goliath from the mountains some years ago remembered when his childhood home was electrified. "We called it juice," he recalled. "The old people said, they're running the juice out to all of these hills."

By the end of the week, the salesboy had only sold a few sets of encyclopedias, but he'd enjoyed a number of free meals, and as he told Rosamond, "What more could a guy want?" He winked at her, a salesman's wink, and Rosamond recognized him at last. Here she was, frying steak for a young Hatley Rogers. He was younger now, this reincarnation, than she had ever known him— younger and pure-hearted. This boy was clean, earnest, whereas the Hatley she'd known had always been smooth-talking and dark. But there the same wink, the same grin. It gave her enormous satisfaction to set a plate of food before the salesboy and watch him eat it clean. She found herself imagining all the meals she might prepare for him; those dreamed-up dinners stretched out for months. Years ago, when she'd first loved Hatley, she had been young herself. Too young to love him like this, with meat loaf.

But Trevor had to move on at the end of the week. "I've already stayed too long," he said. Rosamond accepted this but made him promise to come back through Goliath the following spring. "I'll buy the next edition," she promised.

The other boy, Agnes's James, was spotted everywhere in Goliath that week. He ambled up and down Main Street, where Rosamond lived, and was seen shuffling along the perimeter of the factory parking lot. There he spent his first few mornings kicking at the loose gravel and—as it appeared from the break-room windows and from across the street at the gas station—talking to himself. He swiveled on his heel, pacing, then shook his head and grinned to himself. When a couple of the men went out to question him, he said he was the lost husband of Agnes Rogers. They asked: did she know he was missing?

Sometimes he drifted up Main Street and through the residential side streets. He often sat on a bench behind the church and watched the river gurgle by. He washed up at in the men's room at the Tuesday Diner and rinsed his T-shirts out at the all-night Laundromat. He always wore his denim jacket and faded blue jeans and sneakers that were so old they appeared to be held together with little more than crusted mud and habit. The habit of holding on.

He took lunch at the Tuesday Diner, claiming a booth in the back to himself, and during that first week stayed hidden behind the menu propped up on the table before him. The Morning Glories, sneaking looks at him on their way to and from the men's room, watched him twist paper napkins in his hands. He studied the faux grain in the Formica-topped table and always ordered the same thing: a grilled cheese and a Coke. Even though they had their own favorite meals, the old men watching him found this suspicious, especially since it was grilled cheese, a sandwich for a child.

He wandered about town again during the afternoon and into the evening hours, and then finally retreated to his little Volkswagen—a two-door Rabbit—always parked in Rosamond Rogers's driveway. Some time during the night, Clyde Winston would knock on his window, and tell him to leave, and he then disappeared down the highway for a few hours or for several hours—once he didn't reappear until halfway into the next day—before he returned and parked his car in exactly the same spot. There he fell back asleep, then woke again and headed back into town.

Though the boy husband's behavior was definitely strange and people talked it over quite a bit, it didn't amount to the kind of upset one might have expected. This was a fourth-generation factory town; Goliath was home to the greatest furniture manufacturer in the South, or that's how most people still saw it. It felt as though controversy and tragedy—despite all they'd seen over the last several months—were things they could either attend to or not. Of course, it was awful what had happened to Percy

Harding, and they were forever grieved by it, but in truth, their lives were still full of the little joys and disappointments they'd always known. The young people were behaving differently— anyone could see that—and among them now was a homeless college boy, clearly more than a little unglued, but he seemed more a symptom of trouble in the outside world, everything that was wrong out *there*. Lasting trouble couldn't come to Goliath. And even though other factories in nearby towns had closed in recent years, and though it had been clear for some time that Harding was not producing as much as it used to, most believed substantial change would never actually reach them.

It wasn't until he'd been in Goliath for a week that the drifter-boy quit ambling around and finally committed himself to pursuing Agnes Rogers, his reported purpose for coming to town. People speculated: had he finally come through a sort of drug haze or was he just waking from a trance of some sort? Or, it could be it took him this long to work up the courage to speak to Agnes. Some thought he'd simply forgotten why he'd come. This was a particular favorite, especially among the Morning Glories. They laughed over it, this hippie-boy who couldn't remember what he was doing in Goliath. The ladies at the drugstore were worried about the town's safety—there's something that's just not *right* about him, they said—but also about the boy himself. "He's a danger," they told one another, "to himself."

Finally, though, on a Sunday afternoon, he picked his gaze up out of the stubby weeds in the ditches along Main Street, shook his stringy hair out of his eyes, and looked toward August Street. No one knew for certain when he had determined where Agnes was actually living. Though it stood to reason he had simply seen Agnes enter or leave the house during his wanderings, a few claimed he just *knew* where she was.

Rosamond had hardly heard from Agnes since James had come looking for her. She was busy enough with her piles of things to look through, her cupboards to tidy up. She had also begun seeing more of Tucker outside of Dalton's, and all the while, she kept going into the office, whether Ryan occupied her or not. Yet, just through quick phone conversations with Agnes, Rosamond understood how firmly resolved her daughter was *not* to speak to him. Agnes had begged her to have his car towed. "Call the police," she'd said. "Throw him off your property." Rosamond had countered, "Tell me again, why is it you want this boy, your *husband,* to leave?" Agnes had nothing to say to that, but she knew two things. One, her mother had never asked a man to leave. Two, her mother would understand her so much better if she had.

James, awake now to his purpose in coming to Goliath in the first place, set one worn-out sneaker in front of the other. He crossed the factory parking lot—empty since it was a Sunday—and headed down Main Street, through downtown, onto the residential section.

The afternoon was amber-colored and brisk, the air gritty with specks of old, dead matter, trees and such, dry dirt. The bitter cold had lifted, though, and for the first time, spring seemed possible, if still a way off. Out front of Mia's house, the daffodils she'd planted in the fall—the very ones she claimed had loved the snow—had pushed the tips of their first leaves through the dirt. The overgrown camellia bushes up closer to the house were budding, tightly curled and drooping from their own heft, and the autumn mums, just below her mailbox, were blooming dusty purple, their second bloom of the year.

James noticed none of this. He strode up Mia's driveway in a military fashion; he didn't march, but kept a neat rhythm, his jaw was clenched tight. Inside, Mia was on the phone. Her neighbor, an old friend, was telling her about some trouble with her plumbing. Agnes was downstairs on her couch, dozing, the television kept on to mark the time.

Ray wasn't there, but she knew exactly where he was: in his

trailer, studying scripture and sipping plain hot water from the lid of an old thermos. He would still be distracted by what he had read when they met later for dinner, still be thinking about the words of the prophet Isaiah or the Sermon on the Mount, all those blessings laid on the poor and unfortunate. The grief-stricken and the humble. They planned to meet up later at her place for dinner. She would prepare a lasagna from a recipe one of her customers had given her.

The knock on the door startled her exactly as a different knock on her mother's door had startled Rosamond several days earlier. Agnes didn't start up quickly to answer as her mother did; she instead thought, It's *him*. She didn't know how she knew it, but she did. James had arrived. She wished Ray was there, and she was glad he wasn't. She knew she would have to talk to James, not because her mother had urged her—Rosamond's motives were all wrong—but because she believed talking to him would free her. After she spoke to him, she could go anywhere. This came to her the instant the moment finally came—she'd been waiting for James to show up as much as she'd been dreading it.

She stood up in a slow, deliberate unfolding, and walked to the door. She was in sweats and hand-knitted slipper socks. Sunlight cracked into the room as she pulled the door open, and, in the very last second, before the door cleared and the person who'd come knocking was revealed, she hoped she was wrong. Maybe it was someone else—what had made her so certain it was James?

But there he was, standing in full, cold daylight. She hadn't even seen him close-up yet. *Him.* Her legs felt jittery and loose, but her vision was clear, unflinching. She felt every ounce *here.*

"Hi." His voice, almost timid, didn't match the demanding thud of his knocking. His hair was wild, his eyes rimmed with pink. He gave her a small, defeated smile—to acknowledge, perhaps, how ridiculous the situation was, what a mess he'd made of everything. He shook his hair out of his eyes and waited for her to say something.

"Hi," she finally answered. The word was not tenuous, as it had been when he spoke it. Instead, in that one word, she heard more certainty than she actually possessed. Agnes stepped back, inviting him in.

Once, when she was a child, a woman snubbed her mother in the grocery store. Agnes was young enough to be interested in the packaging of the products on the shelves—even the frank, single-colored labels on the no-name canned vegetables—and was busy trying to sound out the letters on a box of soup mix when her mother spoke. She said hello, and Agnes looked up to see the person her mother was talking to, a woman in a gray coat and lace-up ankle boots. She was older, her pursed-up lips half buried inside powdered wrinkles. Agnes could see the clear plastic of a folded-up rain bonnet bunching up out of the woman's purse. She waited, but the woman said nothing, just kept pushing her cart down the aisle, maneuvering it between Rosamond's cart and the shelf. It was clear, though, that she had heard Rosamond; Agnes saw her startle at the sound of her name. She watched the woman raise her eyebrows in the way a dog pricks his ears, except instead of stopping to listen, the woman strolled on. Her mother called again, but still, the woman acted as though she hadn't heard a thing. She moved on down the aisle away from them, and Rosamond stood watching her go. She returned quickly to choosing a can of green beans, but Agnes saw that her neck was flushed, her eyes blinking fast, and a thought took root somewhere beneath Agnes's consciousness: there was something wrong with her mother. People simply didn't like her. It didn't occur to her then to wonder whether they had cause not to like her. Agnes was a child. What mattered was: what did their disliking her mother say about her?

It wasn't too many years later that the toy airplane came to town and whisked her across the sky, and she was convinced she would someday leave Goliath.

Now she watched James step into her apartment. He moved in a sort of half-hop that reminded her of a boxer circling up, readying for a match. He looked into the mini-kitchen, touching the refrigerator door handle, the countertop, a banana, a crumpled dish towel drying on the back of a chair.

"Come in," she said again, gesturing to the living area just beyond the kitchenette. James kept on his feet, looking around. He laid a finger on the painted cinder-block wall and paused a moment to examine her down-under map, where the North was at the bottom and the South was at the top and Australia was in the middle of it all instead of tucked into its usual corner.

She found herself suddenly thinking of that woman in the grocery store. It seemed odd that it would come to mind now, with James standing here, taking in her Goliath apartment. Her mother had seemed surprised that day, though Agnes knew Rosamond believed she had long been separate from other women, even before Hatley. Maybe the old woman's open shunning, though, had put it on a different plane. Agnes couldn't remember anything that blatant happening to either of them again. After that, it was only a small coldness, a looking away too quickly, striding swiftly past them on the street, in the aisles of Charlotte Branch's drugstore, at the PTA open house.

James grinned. "Agnes and her maps," he said.

She smiled wanly at this, wincing. How happy he sounded. He had always been that way—alternately happy and desperate. James knew no middle ground.

"Have a seat," she told him, and she did so herself, taking the overstuffed chair. He stood there a moment, just turned from the map on the wall. His eyes were a darker blue than she remembered. So dark, they were almost steel-gray, black. His hair, thick shocks of dingy blond, was longer and wilder than the last time she'd seen him. He looked thinner and tired; the skin on his face seemed to have rumpled slightly, like a worn piece of fabric. Finally he found his place on the sofa, dipping his head a little as he approached it, as if slipping inside a car. He ran his hand through his hair and looked at his shoe, his foot resting on the opposite knee.

She breathed in deep and let it out slowly. "Tell me what you're doing here."

He looked at her quick. Then he grinned, as if they were sharing a joke. "Agnes, I'll tell you. This is a hell of a place to find. Wasn't on any of the maps. Had to stop at every gas station, asking. Finally around Hickory, someone knew where the hell Goliath was." The shoe resting on his knee began to jiggle. "I just set out in this general direction. Just figured I'd run into it sooner or later." He laughed. "Sooner turned into later."

One thing James didn't know was that she had noticed him weeks before he had noticed her. She'd never told him that. On the first day of the philosophy class where they'd met, the professor, an awkwardly self-important man who wore the same leather vest to class every day and called on the same three students again and again, posed the question: Is reality perception? James, who was not fated to be one of those three students, laughed out loud. The professor gave him a stern look, but James leaned forward in his desk, eager to hear more. The laugh had been a child's laugh, not derisive or mocking, as the professor imagined it to be.

James continued. "Been out there for a couple of weeks, driving around." She didn't ask, but he told her. "I quit school." He shrugged. His foot kept jiggling and the movement made his entire body vibrate a little. "They had me too boxed in, you know? I was a caged monkey or something."

She laughed at this, and he looked at her sharply. He uncrossed his legs and put his hands on his knees. "Agnes." His little-boy face—those fierce-quick eyes—went grave. "I found a place for us.

The perfect place. An honest-to-God *farm,* Agnes. Chickens and all."

In class, she'd switched seats to be closer to him. Even then it took him weeks to turn around and notice her; it was Thanksgiving before he asked her out. They went to dinner at a Chinese restaurant near campus, and he'd told her of his year of injuries, when he'd broken six different bones in six different incidents. He claimed he was the least lucky person in the world.

Even then, when they were saying everything about art and living freely and Plato's shadows on the cave wall, she only half believed it all. Everything—the old lady's snub in the grocery store, her father's leaving, her mother's dramatic scarves, her own map habit, every term paper she'd ever written—seemed put on. Fabricated, or at the very least trumped up. Made too much of. She had only been playing at life—not a single thing had ever felt completely *real.* This whole time she was still waiting for it, waiting for real things to begin happening.

Maybe she had begun waiting for those real things that day in the grocery store. Maybe her whole life would be different if her mother hadn't called hello a second time. If she hadn't held herself so tight against the truth.

Agnes didn't have the heart to laugh at James again. She asked, as gently as she could, "When did I ever say I wanted to live on a farm?"

"I didn't think . . . I don't think . . ." Then he shot up. He was on his feet. His hands were in the empty air, palms up, and he said, "Agnes, I don't know." He paced away from her. "I don't know what you want *now,* only what you wanted then, or what you said you wanted." He stopped, faced her. She wanted to touch his cheek, to soften it, somehow. To feel his jaw unclench in her hand. "I'm a stupid bastard, aren't I?" he said.

"No," she said, and rose up a little, preparing to argue, but then stopped. She relaxed again into her chair. Finally she said,

"If you are, we both are." She sighed. "James, do you remember what your friend said at the wedding? Your friend with the beret and the long hair? The one who planned to *bike* to Hawaii? Remember him?"

"Harvey," he said. He shook his bangs out of his eyes. "He was going to ship the bike over once he got to California. He didn't think he could actually *ride* all the way there."

"Fine." She shook her head. "That's fine. That isn't what I'm talking about. What I'm talking about is what he said. Do you remember?"

"I remember a *lot* of things," he said.

She ignored this, continued, "He said, 'Life is art.'" She smiled. "Profound, isn't it?" James said nothing, and Agnes went on. "Well, the thing is, what I've figured out: Life *is* art. It's absolutely true. As dumb as it sounds, as *trite* as it sounds, it's true."

"Wilde," he said, nodding quickly, like this was the important thing to remember: the wise dead man who'd first said such a thing.

"Actually, I thought it came from Harvey himself. That's what I'm trying to *tell* you—"

"*Oscar* Wilde," he said.

"What *I* am trying to say is that it's true for you: Life is art. You have this, this way of going about, of *moving,* of finding things. Finding art."

He considered her words, then laughed. "I'm a fucking stupid bastard," he said.

"*You* are art," she said. "And I'm just me."

He turned away from her. "Shit," he said. He was facing another one of her maps—this one a common world map, every continent in its regular slot. "What *is* this place?" But he turned to her, away from the map; he meant Goliath. For the first time since he'd entered her apartment, he was a person she knew. She was returned for an instant to the girl she was in college—only months earlier, after all—and she understood it once more: she would *have* to leave Goliath. She had loved this man after all. *This* man. And despite everything, despite how stubborn he was, how peevish and small, there was something she still loved about him. A being who couldn't possibly exist here in her hometown. In the town where her mother lived. She had believed that: the simple act of living could be that significant, that ethereal. It could be a thing you performed, a thing you hung on a wall or farmed with: an ideal. Completely abstract, *dreamed*.

James hugged his arms to him and closed his eyes for a long moment. Opening them, he said, "You asked me what I'm doing here. I'll ask you the same thing. What are *you* doing here, Agnes? We never wanted this. We never *wanted* this."

He was right. She had changed the rules, the rules that made them, them. Agnes and James. She had changed from the girl who had stood under a tree on top of a mountain on a windy, pollen-filled spring day and committed herself to this man, to their life. To biking to Hawaii. To farming or painting or panhandling or living off thin air, living off the sweet blue nonsubstance of philosophy. She had been there, had loved it, and had changed—was changing—and didn't know how or why. And there was no telling in this moment where she would end up.

Agnes rose, went to him. She stopped just short of reaching up, just short of walking into his arms. Instead, she touched her fingertips to his elbows and looked into his tired wild eyes. But he pulled away from her, crossed his arms, and stared hard into the empty space just over her shoulder. His face both pink and weathered, unshaven and soft, there at the temples a little blue knot of veins pulsing through. He blinked quickly, his lips twitched. He was going to say something, but then the lines in his face changed and she saw him as clearly as she ever had. James a little boy, his jaw in a tight, unmovable line. Whatever he was going to say, whatever argument he was going to offer, was lost now.

• • •

James left then, shuffling away—being sure, she thought, to saunter out the door and up the steps slowly enough that Agnes could have stopped him if she'd wanted to.

She realized he had thought *this* would be enough. Just showing up. He thought that was all she wanted from him. That all she needed was for him to come looking for her, to pursue her, to want her that badly.

She closed the door and set the ingredients for dinner on the counter. It was almost a surprise to her: how little that was, his showing up. Her thoughts skipped fitfully to her father. *Father* wasn't a word she even thought, not even in that tiny, dark way. She only thought *Hatley.* Even to herself that was all she said. And *James,* gone.

She was thoughtful and slow, peeling the papery skin off the garlic. She tended to the ground beef browning in the pan more closely than she needed to. She wanted to be careful now, in this moment. She wanted to live it true, to act the way she was feeling. She added a pinch of sugar to the sauce. Oregano. Basil. Salt. She was desperately sad but not regretful. Sadder than she'd imagined she would be, seeing him. She didn't feel free at all, as she'd hoped to feel. She didn't feel relieved. Instead she felt burdened— her insides turned to something dense and sour and surprisingly tender—and quiet. She focused on the cooking; the cooking would save her.

Ray arrived when the lasagna was still in the oven. "*You,*" she said, and she saw how he smiled at that, at her teasing him. He had arrived in his green work jacket and faded blue jeans, his eyes tired from all his studying. Here was a man who lived half in a thought world and half in true daylight. In eternity and in the present. Who believed in what he could not see, what he could not even *imagine*, and yet was content, was happy with only this: dinner.

"I was beginning to think you'd never get here," she said.

"I was beginning to think you'd forgotten." When he pointed out he wasn't late, she shrugged. "This is the kind of day that began aeons ago. I think I've been in here boiling lasagna noodles for a century."

She didn't tell him about James; she wanted to keep it to herself for a little while. She wanted to figure out on her own how she felt about things. To miss James or not, to be glad or regretful. She wanted not to think about it for a while. To sit down at the table and enjoy a good meal with an old friend. To save all the thinking out for later.

Also, she worried James wasn't really gone—he'd left too angry to keep away. It seemed impossible that it was really over, the two of them. The story of Agnes and James, experts in what it meant to live as an art form, to be as beautiful as all that.

The next morning, when Agnes called her mother, she learned she was right: James was still there. He'd parked the car in Rosamond's driveway and wandered off into town, the same as he had the week before. Rosamond didn't know exactly where he had gone or how long he'd been in her driveway; he hadn't been there the night before when she went to bed.

"Why are you asking these things?" Rosamond paused. "Something happened. You talked to him." It was what Rosamond had claimed she wanted, but now she pronounced each word as if she wasn't sure she liked the way it tasted. "You talked to him," she said again, this time more of a question.

"I did," Agnes said after a moment's hesitation. She was still feeling unmoored, out of sorts. She had claimed a direction, though, and following it would take her there, all the way to the place where she could be certain, positive she'd gone the right way.

"I talked to him. I told him I had no interest in farming. I reminded him: *Life is art.* And *then* I cooked the most beautiful lasagna you've ever seen."

Rosamond was quiet. Agnes could feel her physically pulling back, away from the phone, as if an invisible line connected them and she'd felt that line tug just a bit.

Finally she sighed. "I don't believe it. Well, no, I *do* believe it. I do. Think, honey: he didn't leave because he didn't care about you. The fact that he *cares* has already been established. He left for some other reason. You remember that," Rosamond said. "He left because of something you said."

"Exactly."

"But he came back. Doesn't that tell you something? Whatever you said, it doesn't *matter*. He came back. He's here; you can still do anything you want. You think about that. You just *think*."

At first, though, James had determined he would leave Goliath—and Agnes—forever. He had driven as far as Greensboro, nearly two hundred miles east, before he stopped at a gas station, punched his fist into the roof of his car, slipped back in, and turned the car away. He was too pissed off to leave and too pissed off to go back. He drove with the windows rolled down because he liked the chill and the sounds of the interstate. The engines, the tires on the pavement, the sounds of motion. He was low on money and he should have gone somewhere else—he should have gone home to his parents' house in Virginia—but he didn't. He just drove on, fingers sore from gripping the steering wheel, eyes raw from lack of sleep.

He parked his car in Rosamond's driveway, walked into town, and went inside the Tuesday Diner for a fried egg sandwich and a cup of coffee. He explained himself to a teenaged girl with frizzy brown hair and a face covered up with freckles.

"I just couldn't leave, you know? Hell. I love her, you know? I just do."

Stephanie Jameson, the former leader of the suicide cult, was in the back booth—she hadn't known James had claimed it as his regular midmorning spot—with her own cup of coffee, doctored with several teaspoons of sugar. On the table before her was a book about herb medicine. It was the first time she'd ever skipped school, and she had chosen the Tuesday Diner because she figured sooner or later someone would make her go back to class and save her from her boring book. She didn't care about the trouble she would get into. Trouble seemed nothing these days, or better than nothing: something to distinguish her from her brother, Dusty Jameson, the basketball star. The news, coming to her through her parents, a foreman at the factory and a full-time mom, was that Dusty was excelling in his studies at the university. He had even begun to talk about majoring in premed. Her parents were completely absorbed with this information, with his phone calls, parent weekends, his term papers, his games, but Stephanie found the scruffy boy in front of her infinitely more interesting. She could tell by looking at him that this boy was an artist. A free spirit, a nonjock.

James apologized for invading her space. "I'm used to sitting at this table." He laughed. "I'm a real creature of habit." He was rough-looking but young-acting, drumming his thumbs on the Formica and humming and ducking his head down to talk, whispering too loudly.

He asked Stephanie about the book she was reading and she shrugged. "Actually," she said, "I'm sitting here, waiting to see if anything can stop that clock." She nodded to it, a plain white-faced wall clock hanging on the opposite wall above the restrooms. "It's been going since I was little."

He turned to look at it, then back at her. She had a short, pointed nose and a long, thin face. Her eyes were the palest water green. He wiped the grease from his sandwich off his lip and took a sip of black coffee. "How old are you?" he asked.

She paused, then said, "Tell me about this girl, the one you love so much."

"She's not just a girl." He set his cup down and leaned forward, his own reckless hair falling into his eyes. "She's my fucking *wife*." And he told her the story of him and Agnes, which began, in his version, when he quoted Kierkegaard to her after class. "I still remember the saying," he said. He grinned, tapping his fingers to the sides of his breakfast plate. "It went: *Be that self which one truly is*." He finished his coffee and pushed his plate back. "It's nice, isn't it?" He laughed. "It's bullshit, too. Utter *bullshit*."

So James stayed, returning to his daily pattern of wandering, lunching, sleeping, driving away, and sleeping again. The weather went gray and drizzly for a few days, and the boy husband, as Rosamond still thought of him, sloshed about, those ancient sneakers of his gone to mush. One afternoon Clyde Winston, who remained wary of the strange young man, walked into Charlotte Branch's drugstore and found one of the PTA mothers helping James select a miniature sewing kit to remedy a tear in his jacket. "You'll need to lick the thread to make it easier to put it through the needle," she explained. Clyde watched James squint down at the package the woman was holding. He nodded.

It depressed Clyde, how the town seemed to tolerate the boy husband. Since James had actually come to Agnes's apartment, he knew his son Ray was keeping an even more faithful vigil. He never left except to go to work, Clyde knew. And though Clyde had finally quit running James out of Rosamond's driveway at night—it didn't seem to do any good—Ray was committed to sleeping on Agnes's couch as long as she'd let him.

It didn't appear she'd be asking him to leave any time soon. She seemed grateful for his protection. Also—and it could just be his imagination, he told himself—but Agnes had begun to regard him differently than she had in the past. She was watching him now, not just glancing his way, not just exchanging those teasing looks they'd always shared. For the first time she seemed to actually *see* him looking back at her. "You again," she said softly, finding him just waking on her couch. She wore a loose terry-cloth robe over her cotton nightgown. Sometimes she hurried from the bathroom to her bedroom in just a towel, her skin pink from the shower. "You need a break from me," she told him when she came out dressed for work. "You'll soon get tired of being around me so much." She went into the kitchen and started up the coffee.

He told his father, "I don't mind doing this. Staying here, looking after her. James is nothing to worry about. I really don't think he is, but I'll stay on. I'll stay right here."

Clyde said nothing, only worried more. James found the frizzy-haired girl again at the library, sitting in her favorite chair, a pile of books on the floor next to her. He learned her name—Stephanie—and what she was planning to do. He was impressed, but she frowned at him. "I've stalled out in the reference section," she sighed. "*The Complete Encyclopedia of Fishing.* That and Plutarch's *Caesar.*"

And though he professed to love Agnes, he didn't approach her again for several days. She explained it to Ray: "He thinks he wants me because he wants *something.* He thinks it's me, but it isn't—I'm just a thing to pursue until he figures out what he really wants." Ray said little, but agreed. Hearts are deceitful, he said, and few people are brave enough to see what they're really looking for.

When enough time had passed since they'd last discussed and disagreed about James, Rosamond asked if Agnes had heard from him. But Agnes wouldn't say. "I don't have anything I want to tell you about that," she said. "New topic, please."

Rosamond considered her daughters intentions. Maybe Agnes was just stubborn or immature in her own right, or maybe she was avoiding James to protect herself. That brand of self-preservation, of guarding your heart, Rosamond knew well, though she didn't recommend it. She had spent the last three nights with Tucker, him walking her home in the blue darkness of late night, the air cold but growing milder. It was mostly foggy now, damp feeling. Rosamond suspected people already knew about her and the married old science teacher from Winnie—there was no hiding anything in Goliath. Still, she wouldn't speak of it outright.

She said, "You don't want to be alone." Agnes couldn't answer that. She didn't know what to say of her own solitude, of the solitude of her mother. Her opinion was that her mother had spent years in a loneliness of her own creation.

She instead spoke of Ray. "He's *here,* Mom. He's here all the time." Rosamond couldn't tell from the tone of her voice what she meant by it, if she wanted Ray gone the way she had James, or if she found his presence a comfort. She sensed it was some sort of a compliment, the pains he took to look after her. "He just stays and stays," she said.

Tucker flashed to mind, and Rosamond felt the prickle of desire startle through her. She hadn't felt that way about him ten years ago, when they first met. Then she had only enjoyed his attention, the reassurance of being wanted. Years and *years* ago, with Hatley, she had felt the same sort of buzzing at his touch, but she braced herself against it. She had been nervous with him. She thought of Clyde too, how he had almost kissed her. She hadn't spoken to him since, but she had noticed he no longer bothered running James off. She was both relieved and vaguely disappointed. James would stay near, but Clyde had taken this step away from her.

She asked Agnes, "But what is Ray doing staying there?"

For years Ray Winston, her best friend's son, had stood out on the sidewalks, proclaiming the Good News, and while she knew he was sincere in what he was saying, it baffled her. Annoyed her too, how anyone can be so certain about that sort of thing. Life and death and sin and heaven's peace. There was a sort of draining weightlessness in the pit of her stomach at the very thought of anyone saving anything. Her next words came out shaky, equal parts earnest and mocking:

"Tell me, Agnes, is Ray only there to save your *soul*?"

Since she had taken up with Tucker, Rosamond walked down the Main Street sidewalk to and from work with disciplined plainness. She felt as if she were hiding everything—no one truly *knew* her—and also as if she couldn't hide a thing: every one of her sins was written out plainly on the sleeves of her coat.

Still, others approached her, told her things. And at least in Rosamond's mind, the confessions grew heavier, even as they began to happen more and more in the daylight, in the town's most innocuous places. Mary Hunt, the librarian, pulled her aside at the magazine rack one afternoon and told her how she used to prick her babies with diaper pins. "I didn't mean to hurt them, but a little stick, a snag maybe, would happen, and then oh, the feeling. The feeling of holding my crying child in my arms. The peace of their finally quieting. Why, I was their *mama*. I fixed it every time." Wally Thumb at the Tuesday Diner confessed, "I used to call my son an idiot." He shrugged. "I used to *mean* it."

The disclosures always came from a person Rosamond knew, at least in passing, and they were stand-alones; once they passed these bits off to Rosamond, they never mentioned them again.

Another, a girl with cotton blond hair whose mother Rosamond knew from Harding, stopped her on the sidewalk and whispered to her all that she and her boyfriend had done together in the vacant lot beyond the cemetery. "I promise to quit," the girl said. She walked with Rosamond past the school, up Main Street. The man who had pointed out the goldfinch in the bare tree months earlier brought three tiny green-speckled eggs out of his pocket. "Blue jays," he explained.

At work she typed memos for Ryan Harding, who continued to fetch his own coffee, to push papers around his desk, to make phone calls. She lunched at her desk, stared out the window at the parking lot, at the sky, marbled with thin, white clouds. At quitting time she walked home, avoiding eye contact with others. She felt all the more fragile—worn down by shame—for their confessions. Every few days she deposited a blanket on the hood of the pretend husband's car, more often a sandwich wrapped in waxed paper. Nearly every black midnight she went to Dalton's. She and Tucker huddled close there, as if leaning into a tiny flame of warmth between them. She worried that Percy's ghost witnessed her betrayal, then felt ashamed for *that,* her simultaneous claim on one woman's living husband and another woman's dead husband.

She woke disoriented, half remembering what the others had told her, her own late nights at Dalton's. The morning's first cup of coffee brought her to the here and now. She looked close but not *too* close in the bathroom mirror. Untangle, smooth, apply face cream. She was growing old too quickly, those reflections in the mirror, the skin puffy beneath her eyes, loose on her neck.

Yet Tucker was truly ancient. He spoke of immortality, of *physical* immortality, the belief that aging, a disease like any other, could be cured. "I eat living food," he told her. She observed: the mornings he woke at her house he consumed a half a grapefruit, no sugar, at her kitchen table. Some nights they dined together, again in her kitchen, him slicing eggplant and spring onions. "Living food," he explained, "living man."

He explained everything to her at the bar. "I nap religiously two hours every day after school. I exercise—with caution. I *pickle.*" He laughed, holding up his sloshing half glass of whiskey. Tucker slept fitfully beside her in bed, mumbling and lurching in his sleep, and was only sound by morning, looking small and baby-like lying on his side, his cheek against the pillow, lips slightly parted. Rosamond loved him then, to see him resting, finally subdued, peaceful for a moment, herself just waking. Carol thought him to be sleeping it off at a friend's house, too exhausted and night-blind to travel the interstate in the dark. Rosamond couldn't let him sleep long; he had to rise early these mornings, drive back to Winnie, to those high school students learning the complex workings of a single living cell.

One night he told her that the principal of his school was suggesting he retire next year. "Retire," Tucker grumbled. "What I am supposed to do? Just quit working? Just *stop*?"

He rarely spoke of Carol, and even more rarely of Francine, his first wife. Once he said, "You know, it's funny. I never felt guilty about remarrying. That seemed, I don't know, necessary. But this, what *we're* doing, I feel guilty. Guilty toward Carol, sure, but really, more guilty toward Francine. It feels like she's the one I'm cheating on here." He smiled sadly to himself and Rosamond felt cut off, removed altogether. Later he said, "I'm glad of this. What's happening between us." And she smiled, nodded, and thought: Here is a man I can never hope to truly know.

Tucker had tricks. He played a game with the other drinkers at the bar. The game began with his casually dumping out a box of matches on the bar, as if he had no idea how many matches happened to be in that box. Rosamond knew he'd already counted them out, that he knew there to be exactly twenty-one matches spilled out. "I never worry," he told the others, drawing three matches from the pile. His hand shook as he plucked them out and dropped them before him. "Anxiety," he said, watching the other player take two or one or sometimes the full number allowed per turn, three matches, and then frown down at them, whatever his choice. The loser was the one to take the last match. "Anxiety is the door to every infirmity." Rosamond saw that Tucker was playing the game wrong. He should act fretful and uncertain—it was a part of the trick. He was supposed to pretend that he had to concentrate hard on every choice. There were seven matches left. He extracted two and announced, "I will live longer than anyone here." His opponent scowled, and in his next turn, Tucker left a single match. The other man, the loser, slumped into his beer, shaking his head.

Later he knocked on the hood of James's car. They had returned home to find the boy husband sleeping inside it. He chuckled. "Old boy." Then, "You can't leave him out here like this."

Rosamond shrugged. "Doesn't feel so cold tonight." She didn't point out what Agnes had said so many times in the past two weeks—no one was keeping him there. He could start up that car and drive away any time he wished. Agnes spoke as if there'd always be a boy sleeping in her mother's driveway, waiting for her, or a man camping out on her couch, protecting her.

Tucker took Rosamond's hand and they walked up the driveway together. "I'm going on a trip to the end of the world," he said. He paused while she unlocked the front door. Entering, he added, "My brother lives in Wisconsin."

Rosamond noticed a fresh scowl on Ryan Harding's childlike face one afternoon when she brought in a letter to one of their distributors he'd drafted and she'd typed. He was to sign the letter, but at the moment he was busy balancing a pencil on the pad of his thumb and talking on the phone. Rather, he was listening, with great attention and apparent annoyance, and then he jerked his hand back, letting go the pencil before catching it, leaning forward to scribble on a notepad. He was consumed for a long moment before his eyes flicked up at Rosamond. She placed the letter on his desk and left him.

She did not feel cowed. Rather, Rosamond was emboldened by Tucker's affection and by a recent good deed: she had finally gone out early one morning, knocked on the sleeping boy's car window, and invited him in to take a shower. She sat in her kitchen and listened to the pipes fill with water, and later she nodded to James when he came down to the kitchen to thank her. "I'm grateful," he said, clean now but still scruffy-looking in his old T-shirt, his hair wet, his face clean but now both rough-looking and fragile, endearingly young. She rose, handed him a wrapped ham sandwich, and said, "You're welcome to the shower. Any time you like."

Later she learned he had gone to Agnes's that same day, waited outside for her until she returned home from work. Agnes broke her ban on talking about James to tell Rosamond, "I wish you hadn't let him in the house. You're encouraging him, and it's not right. It's cruel, actually. Mom, listen, you have to get him out of your driveway."

Rosamond claimed she couldn't turn him away. "It's simply not in my nature," she said.

Agnes would say no more about James, but Rosamond wanted to keep her on the phone a bit longer. She spoke of other things. She wanted to tell her about what the people in town were passing on to her, all their big and small confessions, but she felt duty-bound not to. Instead she told Agnes, "Tucker eats according to the days of the week. One day he'll eat for invigoration. Turnips and onions. On the next for stability. Sweet potatoes. He'll drink buttermilk. And finally, just one day a week, he'll take some protein for strength. Hard-boiled eggs, mostly."

Agnes said, "This man's a *doctor*?"

Some days Ryan Harding dismissed Rosamond at noon. When he did, the afternoon was long. She caught a soap opera she hated but had been watching now and then for many years. The stories were terrible, but the clothes were good. The heiress was on trial for murdering her twin sister, but Rosamond liked the cut of her dress. It was a simple design, in a good, dark fabric. Possibly she could replicate it on her own sewing machine upstairs.

One afternoon she rose, flipped off the television, and stood looking out her front window. She watched James's empty car in

the driveway, a twin to her own heartsick Cadillac. The sun thudded against its windshield as a heartbeat, its rays throbbing.

She found her shoes where she'd left them by the front door
and stepped outside without bothering with a coat. The air was
chilly and the dull-colored grass was sun-dappled. The trees she
passed under had branches so brittle, Rosamond could hardly
imagine life still passed through them, that in less than a month's
time, they would begin to bud, hopeful, with tiny green leaves,
small things. She needed a few essentials from the drugstore,
maybe a magazine. It calmed her to attend to a small, manageable
task. Toothpaste. Aspirin. Just as she had the day Percy died. She
counted it a blessing that she could have a simple need and meet
that need in a crisply efficient manner. She was wearing a nice
pair of navy pumps and had a smart little matching pocketbook
tucked under her arm. Her dress was almost as well constructed
as the murderess's on television. On the sloped lawn of the grade
school, the sprawling branches of the oak tree were lit orange
gold from the sun.

The lawns she passed were empty, and the school, at this late
hour of afternoon, was nearly abandoned, just a few teachers' cars
in the lot. Rosamond was thinking of shampoo while her other
thoughts, the undertows, touched on an odd memory, come from
nowhere. She had been twelve years old when she was baptized.
It happened in the feeble old river behind the church and was
done by Pastor Eugene Grady, almost sprightly in those days, more
than thirty-five years ago. Rosamond remembered how sudden
it felt, the second she was submerged, everything blanked out in
an instant. She gripped the pastor's arm and felt no different coming up except for the goose bumps that rose on the skin of her arms
and a bit bewildered—it had felt so distant, so private inside the
river that split second. Emerging, she was greeted with the shout-
out praises and clapping, the congregation assembled on the banks
of the river, her staunch mama and grinning daddy included. She

had felt embarrassed standing before everyone, her hair dripping, river water clinging to her.

She remembered it now—the chill had returned her to that time. The baptism had been for show, she knew that. To satisfy the expectations of the church. Of the town. There had been no rebirth in that river. Or, if she had come back to life, it had been short-lived. She had died all over again since then, and more than once.

The bell announced her arrival. She nodded to Charlotte Branch, sitting on her stool behind the register and testing her curls with her long fingernails, an open newspaper on the counter before her. There were a few customers inside—a woman at the greeting cards, her back to Rosamond; a man and a woman somewhere unseen, talking. Her hands were cold from the outdoors. If she closed her eyes, she would see the gold outline of the sun-struck tree out front of the grade school.

She would buy a toothbrush for James. He needed so many things. Soap, real soap, with no perfume in it. No moisturizing agents. And Agnes, what of her? What of Dorothy Blair who had written her a note? *She's coming*—her heart thudded. Dorothy Blair *had* to come. The straight razor Agnes had found. An old-fashioned brush and mug she'd picked up at the flea market. She'd been preparing for the boy husband's arrival without even knowing it. She was *supposed* to invite him in. Now Rosamond looked around the aisles of the drugstore, her navy pumps staccato on the linoleum tiles.

Then a voice came up behind her, saying her name. It spoke just as she reached to touch a tube of toothpaste.

She turned, and there he was, looking smaller and older and finer-boned than ever before in his great blue overcoat, his thin gray hair, shiny scalp beneath, the shape of his skull pronounced in the too-bright glow of Charlotte Branch's fluorescent lights.

"Tucker," she said, and he blinked back at her.

He said, "Rosamond, my girl. I thought I'd lost you."

She left her shopping basket on the floor, took Tucker's hand without a word, and led him down the aisle, past Charlotte perched at her register. Charlotte did not even pretend to read her paper, but openly stared at Rosamond and the old man. They escaped through the door, onto the sidewalk. She tried again to speak to him, but he seemed confused, muttering only about how pleased he was to have found her. His cheeks were damp and his mouth twisted strangely, and she put her finger to his lips. *Shh,* she told him. Everything was okay.

She led Tucker, a minute elderly man who watched the sidewalk as they passed over it, silent. Though the lawns were yet empty and though no one stepped out their front doors, the blank window-eyes of the houses took in the sight—Rosamond Rogers pulling along a confused old man, lost inside that gargantuan blue coat, squinting stupidly in full Goliath daylight.

Later, after she got down her whiskey bottle to soften her own prickliness and to ease Tucker's speech, after he told her the administration had spoken, had commanded that Tucker *would* retire in the spring, after he explained how he'd heard the news, called in a substitute, feigning sickness, and had driven straight to Goliath, she went out to the driveway and knocked on the boy husband's car window. She invited him in for dinner. This wasn't until Tucker had talked himself out, had confided a number of misgivings. He had parked his car by Dalton's, then not known what to do when he found it wasn't open. Then Tucker confessed that he loved his wife. "I do, God help me. I love her." He spoke softly. He was drunk and trembling, alternately blinking and opening his eyes as wide as they would go, looking about Rosamond's living room. Trying to focus. Tucker, his wrinkled old cheeks rough with new-grown stubble. A man who loved his wife.

Rosamond cooked for the boy in her driveway after all this, a canned ham and mashed potatoes and green beans flavored with bacon grease, after she and Tucker had gone drunk-dumb, and he had cried and she hadn't, and after she finally called on her neighbor Clyde Winston to drive Tucker home to Winnie. And after she'd remained in Clyde's Buick and watched as Clyde walked with Tucker up to a large brick house and a woman came to the door, looked at Tucker, nodded at Clyde, said something, and took Tucker's arm. This woman was fair-haired and taller than Rosamond had expected, younger-looking too, even from this distance. This woman, *Carol,* reclaimed Jim Tucker, pulling him in by his elbow and closing the door behind them.

It was so late by the time she had returned from taking Tucker home and had heated up the ham that James was already asleep in his backseat nest, and it took her some effort to wake him. But then, finally roused by her knocking, he emerged, rubbing his eyes and asking, "What now? What's wrong?"

Rosamond said, "Come in, eat," and he nodded.

Inside, she served him and they fell into talking. She told him about Dorothy Blair's note, about her old movie career, and James listened. He told her about what had happened the day before, when he'd made a second attempt to talk Agnes into going back with him.

James said, "I love her, you know? I really do. But I'm beginning to think it may be I just love everybody. Maybe not in the way people usually mean it, but it's like, I just wish goodness all around me." He ate a bit of ham, moaning at how good it was, and after swallowing, said, "When I saw that man with her, that fucking—sorry—that *guy,* I just got so angry. I thought I could smash his face in, big as he is." "I don't know, though, I don't know. Maybe I'm not supposed to just love Agnes. Maybe I should be loving everyone." He saw the doubtful look on her face and clarified: "You know, *platonic* love."

He slipped into an old story then, about taking Agnes to see some old-time poet who recited his lines in the buff back when they were still at McGraw together. The auditorium had been packed. He was the kind of poet, James said, that everyone loved. The people's poet. Rosamond felt misplaced, hearing this. She stabbed a green bean with her fork.

The dinner, the talking, happened after Clyde turned from Tucker's house and walked back to the car. Silently they drove home, streetlights sliding past their windows, the smooth hum of asphalt beneath the tires. They arrived, and Clyde said, "I think we should spend some time together, you and me. I think we should talk."

"Talk?" she'd asked. They were still in his car, parked in his driveway, and Clyde had just turned the engine off. He kept his face in profile, and from that vantage point, Rosamond studied his ear. The top, that curl, was grayish, but his lobe was pale pink and fat.

"What will we talk about?"

He shrugged, then turned to her. It felt soft and dark inside the car. "Just things. You and me. We should spend some time together. We're both alone, you know. A little company wouldn't hurt either of us."

But Rosamond shook her head. "Thank you for your help," she said, and she touched his hand, still resting on the steering wheel. He looked down at her hand, lingering, and then up at her face. After a moment he nodded, and she unbuckled her seat belt.

"Agnes never wore the clothes I picked out for her," she told James during their midnight dinner. "And she would never let me comb her hair. When she was little, she ran around here like a jackal, scruffy and wild." James smiled, and she knew what she was doing, feeding him the stories that would keep him here, hoping to win Agnes back. Already she missed Tucker. She missed Clyde too, in a detached way. All the years they'd known each other, the time, so long ago, when they were together. The night not so long ago when he'd almost kissed her. And now what he'd offered her. Company, only that.

"She was always different from these other girls," Rosamond continued, "these girls who just want a boyfriend. That was never Agnes. She never wanted a thing."

TEN

The middle of February arrived, and James stuck around. The weather made its last pre-spring lapse to cold, and grade school children cut paper hearts for Valentine's Day. Rosamond was certain people had seen her leading Tucker down the sidewalk. They likely knew James was now sleeping on her couch, that her own daughter despised her. She took her time dressing for work, careful with her face powder, her lipstick, her shoes.

She was mistaken. They *had* seen her walking a withered old man, bent to peer down at the sidewalk, but they didn't talk about it. This was no flashy affair, no shameful flirtation with the richest and most powerful man in town. Instead, Rosamond was only a middle-aged woman who was growing old too fast. Her style of dress was outmoded and somewhat pitiful in its earnest tidiness, obsessively color-matched. She'd guided her senile old lover up the sidewalk as if he were a nursing-home escapee and she his dutiful accomplice. It was too sad to talk about. They pitied her, and it didn't bear mentioning.

Beyond that, so many had made furtive confessions to Rosamond, they felt their own shame when they were near her. Even those who hadn't said a thing began to avoid her in public. This went beyond the disdain they had always felt for her, the snubbing Agnes had witnessed so many years ago. Now there was something frightening about Rosamond Rogers. Something unnamable and even more unsettling because it was elusive.

The fact that Ray's truck was parked outside Agnes's apartment so many nights did not escape the town's notice. Yet even this failed to stir up much talk. They loved Ray Winston—that odd, harmless man—and couldn't believe he was really having an affair with Rosamond Rogers's daughter. It had been clear since the two were children that Ray was infatuated with Agnes, but the pious preacher would never take part in any truly scandalous behavior. Besides, there were other troubles in Goliath.

The shifts at the factory had never picked up since the snow. It was the longest they'd worked short like this, just half days, and sometimes even half weeks. They watched television, flipped through the A volume in their encyclopedias in spare moments: the aardvark and his curious mating practices, Erik Archarius, a Swedish botanist, and Antarctica, that frigid, sunless continent. There was an edgy quiet to the streets in Goliath, to the houses.

These people could not stay idle forever. Most were third- or fourth-generation Harding workers and did not even consider looking for work elsewhere. Living on less pay was tough going, though. The electric bills were high from the cold spell, and many couldn't pay the full amount. Some started to look for second jobs, putting in applications at the hosiery mill the next county over, at the General Electric plant in Hickory. But most tightened up, held grim—they'd seen hard times before. Harding Furniture had always pulled through in the past.

Yet, there was something different to *these* hard times and the people knew it. They understood they were different from the rest of the world, separate. Some of them had been at Harding for more than forty years. They could not look on a piece of furniture without guessing the grade of wood, the amount and quality of varnish applied, the location of the seams hidden inside upholstered pieces. They saw the world for its people and the pieces of wood surrounding the people, cut, glued, and painted to accommodate them.

Cassie Stewart's mother, who worked in the finishing room, was one of the ones to go looking for a second job. Cassie met up with Vincent after school and told him about it. Her mother was picking up a few shifts at a family restaurant chain down the highway. "She pulls fries from the grease, fixes the drinks," Cassie told Vincent. "She mops the floor at closing." Her father, she said, couldn't work. "He's on disability," she explained.

They were in the old shed behind Vincent's house, him having talked her into riding the bus out there after school, assuring her he'd walk her back to the trailer park later.

"I'd like to meet *your* mother," Cassie said. "Let's go inside to find her."

Vincent shrugged. "She's just my mom."

"That's what everyone thinks about their mother."

Vincent shrugged again. He was beginning to wonder why he'd brought Cassie out here. He'd swallowed a lit cigarette, smoked only about halfway down, but she'd been only mildly interested. Nothing had impressed her since the cricket. He had an idea for a comic book he wanted to tell her about, but he was afraid she wouldn't listen, or worse, that she'd make fun of it. Cassie shook her hair out of her eyes and pulled from her cigarette and Vincent wished she hadn't come. His brain was somehow quieter, though, with Cassie there, prattling on about the odd things that interested her. The girl lied constantly, recounting to Vincent any number of unlikely happenings.

"My mother is a gypsy," she went on. "If she could, she'd take off and never come back. But my father, he's heavy baggage. Do you want to know what happened to him?"

Vincent nodded. He was thinking, though, of his comic book. It was to be about a superhero who didn't fly or spring across skyscrapers, but instead powered through the earth, tunneling through beneath buildings and roads, fissuring the asphalt on highways. His name was Boulder Man, made of rock, he emerged from the dirt to right all kinds of wrongs, with an incredible superpower no other hero possessed: the ability to flash forward, to catch bits of the future. Just tiny bits: a woman's hand fitting a key inside a front door lock, a man gruffly hanging up the phone. As the story unfolded, these disconnected flashes finally came into focus, and the full picture of what was about to happen—murder, world dictatorship, grand larceny—became known. In an instant Boulder Man would spring into action, tunneling through rock and earth.

"His forklift upended," Cassie said, lighting a cigarette. She waited a moment, exhaled, then spoke again. "It pinned him to the ground. Now he has chronic back pain. Every moment that he's awake, he's in pain. So he just doesn't wake up. He takes his pills, he sleeps."

There would be close scrapes, of course. Times when Boulder Man almost didn't get there, when the victim, dangling over a cauldron of molted steel, would slip and the superhero would swoop upward, through the floor tiles. The villain—the evil owner of an international company—had hoped to detain him with embedded explosives, but Boulder Man had evaded the traps and now caught the victim, diving with him back into the ground, tunneling away like an underground missile.

Cassie spoke of the others at school, about their teachers. She hated Ms. Chatley, the biology teacher, an alarmingly pretty redhaired woman rumored to have posed nude for trashy magazines in her younger days. Some students claimed to have actually seen the pictures, proof positive. Now she taught tenth graders the rules of genetics and raised mice in cages in the back of the room.

"She wears a wig," Cassie said. "You can tell." Then she shrugged, her thoughts shifting. "We need something better. Something bigger," she said, and Vincent knew what she meant, that she'd shifted suddenly from her father's ailments to the biology teacher to a more daring, imaginative feat. Something better than a cigarette, more disgusting than a cricket. She looked around her, at the soft wood, the wet dirt.

"Something *dangerous*. Something like a bullet or a wasp. We could find a giant spider, something scary. Vincent, we need to *show* someone. Someone else needs to see exactly what you can do."

Boulder Man, Vincent imagined, found sustenance in red-glowing subterranean insects found so deep beneath the earth they were not yet discovered by those who tread the simple ground above.

"Something more," Cassie said, and her eyes went distant. "Something unbelievable. Something very, *very* bad."

The next day Cassie had it, the ultimate swallowing trick. She wouldn't say what, but she was giddy and dumb-acting, whistling as they hurried out the back doors after school. "It's perfect," she said.

They crossed the gravel lot to the convenience store, and Fay was there, as always, shiny with sweat and melted makeup, whiny-voiced, telling Cassie about what she planned to do with the baby when it came. "There's a lady down the street who will keep him. She'll bring him up here for my breaks." The woman smiled weakly, accepting their dollar bills, leaving their sodas on the counter for them to take. "You two better be getting on," she said, gesturing to the door. "The day's turned out nice."

"Hold on a second," Cassie said, grinning at Vincent. She pulled something from her jacket pocket and cupped her hands around it. She opened her hands. "We have something to show you."

Fay was too surprised to speak, to protest the sudden appearance of a small white mouse, transparent pink in the ears, the toes. Cassie plucked it up by its tail, its tiny point-feet wheeling in the air. The mouse squeaked, scrambling for a solid surface, a means of escape. The pregnant woman opened her mouth, then shut it, no breath escaping her.

Cassie nodded, said, "Go ahead, Vincent."

The mouse repulsed Vincent; he hated that squirming creature, its dot-eyes, its pointed ears. At least it was tiny. The creature was so small, Vincent didn't see it at first for a real mouse, but rather for a toy, a trinket Cassie had found in her cardboard jewelry box, something cheap and old from a fair. But it writhed, its itty feet, its whiskers. Vincent realized where the mouse had come from. It was one of the members of the colony kept in wire cages at the back of the red-haired biology teacher's classroom. Here was a real live creature for Vincent to put down his throat.

Before, that day at school, he had been thinking more about his comic-book hero, and he had even thought of mentioning it to one of his friends, a boy named Thomas, nicknamed Squirrel, who was forever doodling fierce, spiral-eyed house cats. Squirrel got his nickname from the way he talked, high-pitched and quick, chittering away, telling stories of his father, a truck driver, and his older brothers, legendary basketball stars and bear hunters in season. Vincent had happened to sit on Squirrel's end of the lunch group and had caught a glimpse of his drawings. He asked him about them and Squirrel lit into it, telling him of the primal nature of cats, the world's stealthiest predators. "You can't escape it. If a cat wants you, you're toast." He talked on, of wolves, of spiders, of the college basketball tournaments gearing up for March.

For a moment, standing there in front of the quivering fat pregnant woman, Cassie's darting eyes, Vincent thought he wouldn't do it. He wanted to walk out the door, across the parking lot, to the side street where Squirrel lived. Vincent might tell him about Boulder Man. He imagined the two of them bent over Squirrel's desk, and Squirrel listening, excited, wanting to hear more, sketching the muscled, rock-solid figure of Boulder Man, oh man, oh man, adding an alley cat, a rooster.

Cassie was watching, though, and Fay—she was scared and angry both, pale and flushed, sweaty, wide-eyed, speechless. There was something of her look that worked both ways on him: he wanted to run and he wanted to stay, too. He wanted to see just how bad it would be, how *evil,* swallowing the itty bitty rodent, seeing just how scared, how angry Fay might become.

He *was* different. Even his choice of comic-book hero told him that. He had been changed by that morning crossing the railroad tracks, and by every moment since then: the cigarette, the ant, the spider, the cricket, this. He had seen the spirit silvering up out of the trees, but he wouldn't think on it. Wouldn't remember it. *The weather's bound to turn,* his father had said. *Don't get too used to all this lying around.* He hated Fay's simpering look, the disgusting fact of her pregnancy. Cassie was looking at him, her eyes spiraling like one of Squirrel's cartoon cats, and though he hated her as bad as he hated Fay, he at least *knew* her, knew her story of being born in a dirty public stall, her poetry of demons, her caginess. That was the thing that cinched it, right there: he understood Cassie. They were exactly the same.

He took the mouse by its tail, Cassie passing it to him. The rodent arched its back, squirmed, squeaked too softly for Vincent to hear outright; it was more like tension in a taut wire—he felt it. He dropped the creature on the back of his tongue and downed it quick, his eyes tearing, gagging hard but keeping it in, pushing it down. He was weak from it, and he held on to the counter, steadying himself. Fay started to cry. Cassie grinned.

"Why would you show me that?" Fay asked. "I just don't know

why you would show me that!" She put her plump fingers to her face, shook her head. She seemed unable to find sufficient air. "I didn't do anything to you, I didn't," she gasped. "I just don't know why you would show me."

Vincent wanted to walk through the door. He knew he and Cassie would never return to the store. He wanted to leave, but his feet were stuck there, he couldn't move, listening to the low hum of the drink coolers, witnessing Fay's torment, Cassie's clapping. She hopped around in a sort of dance. Vincent felt the sunshine glow, too warm, through the glass front of the store.

Rosamond believed James: he loved Agnes better than anyone else. It had been true of her love for Percy, and of Percy's love for the company. The factory loved Goliath. They had cared for each other, the factory and the town, for more than a century. Ray loved Jesus—he was made for the disciple's life.

At work, Rosamond took her seat behind her typewriter and tried to find something useful to do. She rose for coffee, for paper, to collect the mail. Near midmorning Ryan, with a loosened tie and a wrenched-out look on his boy face, emerged from his office. He walked to her and tapped the corner of her desk. "You got a minute?"

Rosamond rose, surprised, and followed him into Percy's office. Once inside, he stood behind his desk, turned to face Rosamond, and nodded to the door, indicating she was to close it, then sank heavily into his chair. He did not wait for Rosamond to sit, but confessed right off the thing Rosamond knew was coming, but hadn't really expected. No matter what the numbers said, the short days, she had never believed it would really happen.

"We're stopping production the last day in March," he told her. "On the thirty-first, we'll finish."

Her first impulse was to forgive the boy, forgive him everything. Forgive his arrogance, his curtness, forgive him for being from a place as haughty and vaguely northern as Baltimore, forgive him for having a chubby beauty queen for a wife, a wife who was also, like Baltimore, haughty and altogether too northern. It seemed necessary as well to forgive him for having a beautiful, uppity mother, a woman Rosamond's dear Percy had loved. But the clock above his head ticked off a few slow seconds, and Rosamond thought of Jim Tucker, that lost, gorgeous man. She thought of, months before, the night she'd gone out to stand on the railroad tracks, the letter opener cutting deep into the skin on her palms. Rosamond was tired. She had no mercy in her.

"You've ruined the company," she said. It was a lie and she knew it, and though she also knew there was nothing else for him to do, she could not help but think the disaster and the boy sitting before her were related to each other. Percy should have never married that cold woman, should never have had this boy. Ryan said nothing, but she saw him flinch ever so slightly, saw his chin quiver almost imperceptibly. The boy rubbed his hand across his face and shifted his eyes away from Rosamond's. She both hated him and pitied him.

"There were weaknesses," he said.

"You've ruined it," Rosamond said again, sighing, surprised by her own meanness. She felt hatred rise in her, empowering her, and she enjoyed a moment's clearheadedness. What Percy had worked so many years to fight, what he had *died* to avoid, was now actually happening. Rosamond sniffed. "Shall I prepare a memo?" she asked.

She attended to a few details, not including the memo, which Ryan said was unnecessary, and left work early. She did not want to think about the factory. She walked home, noting the sunshine, the blue in the sky. Spring might come to Goliath, even after all that snow.

She found James lying on her couch, watching television. He hardly looked at her when she came in. She went straight to her bedroom closet.

Rosamond threw an armload of clothing on her bed, thinking she would go through it later. Instead she focused on the other items she found, cheap and valuable possessions she'd crowded in there over the years. She didn't know why the carved-wood music box found wrapped in tissue in its own shoebox was important, didn't remember that Percy had given it to her for a birthday gift years earlier, and was surprised by the song it played—"Moon River." The movie she remembered, Audrey Hepburn lounging wistfully on the fire escape, plucking her little guitar. She wrapped the music box back in its tissue, then in a couple of layers of newspaper, and took it to the driveway. She opened the trunk to her Cadillac and carefully tucked it inside. She stood looking at it for a moment, a small bundle of newspaper in a trunk big enough for a corpse. She ought to vacuum every inch of her house, hidden and not. Her fingers itched to scrub the closet's inside walls with Pine-Sol. She imagined a clean new house, all traces of the past, every scent, scrubbed out.

James didn't look up from the television when she passed him on her way back to the bedroom. She changed out of her dress and got down to work, pulling out all the boxes from the top shelf, sorting bits of costume jewelry and hair combs, old greeting cards, notes from Hatley addressed to her with postmarks from all over the country. She pawed through the closet's contents, and then through every inch of her dresser drawers with an almost manic attention, feeling that all of her other attempts, the clumsy heaps of newspapers and kitchen linens stacked in the bathroom, were but prelude to this right and true purge. She threw out old photos and old books, bundled together a number of clothing catalogues. Bit by bit she packed up the trunk and then began to pile boxes into the backseat. She worked in an old pair of cotton trousers and a loose button-down with dried paint on its sleeves, her hair tucked into a bandanna, wisps of it slipping out and sticking to her forehead. She felt magical and dumb, loose and all wound up. She worked through the afternoon and into the evening.

At dusk she brought James the crinoline she had found, kept after some distant, formal event. "My wedding?" she asked, but of course he didn't know. "Should I throw it away?" Again he only shrugged. She decided to do just that, and having disposed of it, slumped into the chair beside the couch. The phone rang again—it had been ringing all afternoon, all evening—but Rosamond and James ignored it. "I'm losing everything," she said, thinking of the factory, of smug Ryan Harding reduced to red-eyed exhaustion, the crinoline, the music box. "Everything," she repeated, and the dear stupid boy laughed.

"Come now," he said. "That can't be."

She remembered a bright happy afternoon from her childhood and described it to James: "Years ago, this town had a wonderful little tradition. A *beautiful* tradition." She smiled at him and he turned his empty, tired eyes to her. "I was seven, eight, nine years old. That part doesn't matter, though. Listen: it was magnificent."

She had not gone up in an airplane as a grade school child, nor had she played baseball or stumbled upon a flattened, bloodless corpse. Instead, young Rosamond had stood on Main Street out front of the drugstore and watched a parade. It was a spring parade, May Day and Easter combined, back when the town bothered with such things. The day started crisp and warmed early. Rosamond was in a blue gingham dress and patent leather shoes to stand on the sidewalk with her father and older brothers and watch the high school marching band, the spangled majorette, the smiling girls with batons. The men from the First Bank of Goliath came through in soapbox cars, beauty queens waved from

floats pulled by tractors, the finely coiffed members of the Ladies
Auxiliary pulled along little red wagons with homemade quilts
and prizewinning quart jars of pickles nestled inside. Then came
the Boy Scouts with their American flags, their salutes, and the
church elders with their tracts, their declaration *He has risen! He's
alive!* They shouted such things, they sang them. The spring children, those with birthdays in March, April, or May, walked together, and the fire truck lumbered through. The librarian dressed
like a Pilgrim, and there was a float from the chamber of com-
merce with an American flag made from tissue-paper carnations,
a painted sign: *Peace Is the American Way.* The factory president and
the mayor came through last, walking in their suits, waving and
calling out hellos, shaking hands, everyone convinced there was
no better time, no better place. Later the children hunted eggs in
the cemetery and everyone gathered at the church for the start
of the revival.

She told James, "It was a *miracle,* that parade." Then, "We should
do it again. Yes, you've convinced me," she said even though James
had said nothing. He hadn't even spoken of Agnes the last couple
of days, and though he brought in several of the books from his
car, he only lay on the couch, watching television and looking
through her old newspapers. He called them a riot, chuckling
at the archaic sales circulars, the price of a pound of butter from
thirty years ago.

But Rosamond was serious now. Ryan Harding had told her of
the end of the factory, what would become, she knew, the end of
Goliath, and she took James's hand, pressed his fingers to hers. He
started; she had his attention. She said, "The parade, we'll do that
for me, for the town, for Dorothy Blair. We can do it. And"—she
leaned close—"the other thing is for you. We will plan a visit.
James, Agnes will come home. You need to talk to her. She's *my*
daughter; I can get her to come."

. . .

Clyde knew that the wandering vagrant Ray was protecting Agnes from was sleeping inside Rosamond's house now, and he didn't like it. He told Ray, "We've got to get that boy out of here."

Rosamond had a history of keeping the sort of secrets that might harm her worse if others knew. Hatley Rogers, at one time, had been one such secret, and Clyde sensed there were more. She was harboring this James, this person Clyde's own son was busy protecting Agnes from, this boy Agnes wanted gone. Clyde was still thinking baseball and planning, having found his spot, dreaming up a Saturday in early May for the game, but he couldn't let go of this worry over Rosamond.

She'd been in his thoughts almost constantly since the day he'd driven the elderly science teacher home for her. He remembered how she'd brushed him off, refused him, and yet he couldn't quit thinking about her. A million times he wanted to cross the lawn, but he remembered her sitting in his car that day and stopped himself. Rosamond had touched his hand in response to his invitation and left. He had watched her go. She went straight from his car to that boy's car, tapped on the window, and invited the boy inside.

Clyde managed this much: spotting her coming home from work one afternoon, he had gone out on his porch and called to her before thinking better of it. "Everything all right? Rosamond?" She had turned, squinting at him in the strong sun, confused and hurried. She answered yes, everything was fine, and turned to unlock the door. "I'm here," he called to her. He stood there in socks, his hands in his pockets. He watched her fumble at the door. She had lived in that house for more than twenty years, and there she was having trouble fitting her key in the door. "Just so you know, I'm here, should you need me." She finally managed to unlock the door, but she turned and looked straight at him. She said, "Thank you." It stopped him, the small exchange across that distance, his front porch to hers. For a moment she kept her eyes on him. "You can call on me, if need be," he said. He was aware he'd already told her that—how many times over the years? It had become their refrain—but he said it once more: "Remember, Rosamond, I'm right next door."

She had slipped into her house then, and Clyde had retreated into his own quiet hole. Tonight he kept the television off and didn't sleep. Instead he brought out old photos and looked through them until he found it: a snapshot of Penny, young and smiling, years before her illness, with Rosamond, also young, also smiling. The shot was from a summer birthday party, Ray's or Agnes's, impossible to tell which one, since both of them had summer birthdays. Neighbors gathered in one backyard or the other, the kids played, the men grilled hamburgers, and the women talked. Clyde was probably behind the camera, the one to frame the two friends in his view, to press the shutter. Hatley must have been around too, somewhere in the background—Rosamond was smiling too freely for it to have been one of his absences.

Now Clyde recognized something he must have always known but never felt, never put in a conscious thought—Rosamond had loved that man, loved him as intensely as Clyde had loved his own Penny, as intensely anyone ever did love another person. And more: she had truly loved Percy Harding. He remembered the night of the visitation, how she'd not attended but come home from some other place in one of those old-fashioned dresses of hers, the whole of her a mess, her eyes empty and crying, her stocking feet stepping up the porch steps real slow. Percy Harding had never done anything to deserve that kind of heartache.

It was a tremendous gift, the devotion Rosamond had given these men, each of them: Hatley, Percy, and the old science teacher. And now this college boy sacked out on her couch. A frightful phenomenon, a woman who could love like that, and not a single one of them had proven himself worthy.

Tonight Clyde looked out from his front porch to Rosamond's darkened house, no longer lit up at every hour—that much had gone back to normal. The boy husband was somewhere inside. If Clyde could have reached across the lawn and pulled Rosamond out through one of the windows and set her somewhere else, somewhere safe and level and warm, he would have. He was not usually given to such ruminations, but with the street dark, the sky hazy with stars, he viewed the landscape before him and re-membered that he was in fact on a planet. A careening body on a path amid other careening bodies on their own paths, far-flung rocks in a sea of endless black space.

But Clyde *was* worthy, he believed, or he could be. Worthy of that woman's fierce love. He was strong enough, steady enough to bear the weight of it, that giant love. To receive it and not turn away, not run away.

Clyde could withstand it. Withstand it and be blessed by it. Blessed enough, strong enough to return that mighty love back to her. He could love her. This was more than simply wanting to or stumbling onto her front porch or rescuing her from a crowded mailroom: he could love her as severely as she loved him—*if* she loved him.

Later, while Clyde Winston slept, while his son Ray bedded down on Agnes's couch, James awoke. He rose from bed—Agnes's childhood poster bed, where Rosamond had put him—and felt the quiet of the house. He looked out the window, viewed the same alien landscape Clyde had, and found his jeans in a pile at the foot of the bed. He dressed, then stepped out of the room, looking around. Each room was still and quiet. It seemed he could even hear Rosamond sleeping in her bedroom above him. James moved down the hallway, through the living room, its large window black but for the small gleam of the streetlight outside, and then stepped into the kitchen. He went to the cabinet beneath the kitchen sink and lifted the key to the Cadillac from its nail.

This town had let him lurk about its streets for a bit. It let him be the drifting stranger, the heartache boy who loved Agnes Rogers and poured his heart out to the girl with the frizzy brown hair who planned to read every book. And with time, Goliath might let him do more: it could let him all the way in. But Agnes never would.

James was twenty years old. Life was rushing on somewhere away from this town, and he had to go with it.

While he collected his jacket and lifted the key to Rosamond's Cadillac from its peg beneath the kitchen sink, Rosamond slept soundly. James stepped outside. Her car was packed up with everything she valued, and she was lying asleep in a bedroom that contained so few possessions, her drawers, her closets emptied. In Agnes's apartment a few streets over, Ray rose and kept watch in Agnes's kitchen, the soft light of the moon spilling through the window.

James knew something of the Cadillac's history, the years it had sat there like a museum piece on Rosamond's driveway. No way would it crank. He slipped inside anyway—cold leather seat, tight, unused steering wheel—and tried the key. The engine turned, the radio coming on, a country station, and he sat for a moment, stunned. He turned the radio down, but not all the way off. The song was one he had never heard before, but Rosamond would have recognized it, an old-time love ballad.

He didn't waste another thought on the miracle of that years-neglected car coming to life. He didn't even remember the mementos and valuables Rosamond had packed into the trunk, didn't even glance in the backseat to see the boxes piled there. Didn't know what he was driving away with. The car coming to life like that was a gift, a sign—his leaving in it was meant to be.

He eased the car out of the driveway, waited until he was a ways down the street to turn the headlights on, and headed toward the highway. Half a mile down the road he parked the car, ran back through the gray, ducking through the streetlights, and returned to Rosamond's driveway, where he started up his own car. Past Lucky Grocery, turn into the highway, park his car in the mattress store lot, which used to be King's Motel—the site of Rosamond and Hatley's courting—and scamper back for the Cadillac a half mile back.

Rosamond lay wrapped up in blissful thoughtlessness. Agnes, a few streets over, smelled something like mint in her sleep. The night grew a degree darker, preparing for dawn. Ray finally left Agnes's apartment, locking it tight behind him with his spare key, and walked home, coming up the hill near the highway and just missing the final reparking, James giving up his two-vehicle scheme at last, abandoning his Volkswagen, spewing off now in the Cadillac. James drove hard toward the black mountains in the west.

ELEVEN

At first no one noticed the missing Cadillac. Clyde kept inside his house in the early morning, reading the paper and drinking coffee in his easy chair, and the others, those who passed the house and the car every day on their way to work or school, felt there was something off, something missing, but not a single one of them put his finger on just what the missing thing was. They shuffled along.

Rosamond rose as usual, went down to the kitchen, called for James, returned upstairs, and dressed for work. She knocked on Agnes's old bedroom door, then searched every room. Even as she searched, she knew he was gone—*really* gone. Yet she opened each door, peered in every empty closet. How had this happened? She had had a *plan,* after all, to bring him and Agnes together, and she'd even told him about it. She rechecked the downstairs shower and the hall closet. She looked on her front porch.

Rosamond dressed, took some coffee, and rushed out for work, thinking she might yet find him. He could appear on the sidewalk, or she would find him sitting in one of the booths of the Tuesday

Diner, slumped over a bowl of oatmeal. Going out onto her front porch, she saw the Volkswagen was gone, saw the driveway was empty, but at first didn't even realize her own Cadillac had vanished. She crossed the lawn, stepped onto the sidewalk, and looked again at the empty driveway. A beat later, she knew what was missing. The Cadillac. And James. James had really left.

The morning was as clean and gold pink as any Goliath morning. A light rain was falling, cool and sweet. Rosamond returned to the house, wrapped her toothbrush in a paper towel, slipped it into her purse, and clattered back out the door and onto the sidewalk. She already knew she couldn't sleep in her house tonight.

The missing car and the rainy weather would later be recalled as foreshadowings of what was to happen. Those given to notions of fate and premonition would think the two occurrences were related to the message Ryan Harding set out to deliver that day. He made no grand lunchtime announcement as Rosamond and others guessed he would, but instead followed the same route every piece of furniture journeyed, from block of wood to finished piece. He went from the rough mill to the cutting room to the gluing room, to the varnishers, the driers, the finishers, and finally the loading dock, clearing his throat, and in a gesture that was uncharacteristically personal, he spoke to each worker individually, using tones as low as the *shuck-shuck* of the machines would allow. He let out the news, gave the end date, and shook the hand of each worker, thanking them for their years or decades of service.

Most of the employees took the news quietly, both shocked and unsurprised. A few uttered words of anger, many cursed, others were simply resigned—it had to be—but none looked Ryan in the eye even when they shook his hand. Each worker immediately thought of Percy Harding. He had known this was coming, of course. The great man had *died* to avoid this task, what his son moved through the factory rooms now to accomplish. They felt

Percy Harding's desperation, his sadness curling around their shoulders, swirling between their feet. Some breathed it in, held it. It was too much for them, first that the factory would, after all these years of speculation, finally close, and second, that a human being had actually stepped onto a railroad track for *this*. The connection made the closing seem both astoundingly huge and triflingly small—tragically insignificant.

Later the machines were stopped for the day, and the sun came out, burning away the last of the clouds. People moved numbly out to the bright sidewalks, to their cars parked in the lot behind the factory. Some stood a moment, looking back at the factory, that rectangle of cinder block and mortar—it had become so familiar to them, they could hardly see it.

They moved on then, but they were reluctant to enter their houses. They lingered on the sidewalks, on their front lawns, talking or just standing around, staring at the rain-wet grass, the asphalt. "I thought I'd hear the trumpet calling," one man said, "when this day came." Others spoke of the inevitability of the news, comparing hunches on how long they'd known this day was coming. "I knew since I started here," one of the loaders said. "I still don't believe it," a woman from the varnishing room said. In her confusion she'd forgotten to change, and she was still wearing her blue work apron, the pockets stuffed with rubber gloves.

Eventually they set out lawn chairs and converged in one another's driveways, on sidewalks and front porches and in the shelter of carports. They drank iced tea and talked about what all they'd seen through the years, what they remembered, where their memories fell short. The weather seesawed, going light, then dark; sunshine, then light, indecisive rain. The people stood out, let the rain spit on their shoulders, dampen their cheeks. Someone took out a guitar, plucked at it a bit; someone else remembered a song from a long time ago; and someone else composed something new, a dirty poem with the best words beeped over by his wife.

There were moments where the sun shone bright enough to thoroughly warm the people, and moments where it beamed too hot. When the children came home from school, cars were lined up in the street to section off a place for them to play soccer, using trash cans for goal posts. Small groups of women came together in kitchens and started cooking. Plates of spaghetti, pork chops, quick apple cake, and instant brownies appeared. The air was chilly when the evening came, and they passed the platters of food around, neighbor to neighbor.

The evening grew dark and now rum was mixed into the iced tea, the poems were rhymed less often, dirty more often. Some started up their praying, their counting of blessings and misfortunes and the ideas of where work might come from now. One woman lamented that she had never purchased a Harding sideboard though she'd always wanted to, and another spoke of a cherrywood dresser Harding had put out decades ago, how she'd finished those dressers, how beautiful they were. This spurred others to thoughts too sentimental to voice, even with the children playing there, even with the rum loosening their tongues. The people drew up into themselves more and more as night came. By full dark, the streets had grown companionably quiet, and then, thinned out, all the people retiring to their own beds inside their own houses.

Rosamond Rogers was among the merrymakers, drinking spiked iced tea and moving through the crowds, and when the others turned in for the night, she walked down Main Street, onto August Street, to Mia's house. She had not told Agnes about the missing Cadillac yet, or about James's leaving. It was still such a surprise to her, a shock; the factory was closing, James was gone.

Mia answered the door in her nightgown, and Rosamond explained she didn't want to sleep in an empty house tonight. Mia nodded. "It's what I hated most, when Lee died. I still haven't gotten used to it, not all the way." The two stayed up for a while, watching television. She said, "I knew this would happen, the factory shutting down, the day I went up in that airplane. Rosamond, do you remember that day? I looked down and saw this town, so small."

Mia rose, crossed the room, a bent old woman in a faded apricot-colored nightgown. She snapped off the television and went to the linen closet to get sheets. "It's comfortable enough," she said, meaning the couch. "You'll sleep well here tonight." She and Rosamond worked together to tuck the sheets into the couch cushions. "Your uncle slept here, after Lucy died. Some of your cousins, when they couldn't bear their own homes." She shook her head. "Everyone in this family has slept on this couch or else downstairs, where Agnes is, at one time or another. I never know who will be next." She said good night and left, but then, pausing in the hallway, she spoke quietly. "It was when I saw that nothing is ever as big as you think it is. Nor as permanent. I saw that on the day we went up in the little airplane." She was quiet for a long moment. "Well," she said, and Rosamond waited for something else, but she slipped away, into the hallway.

In the morning, Rosamond went down to tell Agnes what had happened.

Agnes handed her a cup of coffee. "What do you mean, the car is gone?"

"*Both* cars. Agnes, I thought he loved you," Rosamond said with a degree of reproach, and Agnes sighed. "Maybe he did, Mom. I know *I* did. Is that what you want to hear? That I loved him? Well, I did. But not anymore. That's what you're not getting. What you won't hear me say."

The two set out to walk over to Rosamond's house, and Agnes said, "I think he really did love me, at first. Same way I loved him. But this, him coming here, sleeping in your driveway, that was something different. He was stuck, and now, thanks to your car, he's gotten himself unstuck."

"That doesn't mean he doesn't still love you," Rosamond pointed out. It was still early, their going out across the still-gray sidewalk, a bit of sunlight just opening the sky up. Goliath had returned to its normal morningness, dogs barking from backyards, the houses lit only in pieces, the people inside those houses waking, getting their showers started. "His being stuck, or whatever you want to call it, that's a different issue. His *loving* you is a completely different thing."

They arrived, the two of them standing on the blank spot of driveway, and Rosamond gestured to the house. "Everything inside is gone, too. I've been packing everything up, and I can't tell you why. Don't ask me." Agnes stood looking at the house. "I put the boxes in the trunk," Rosamond explained.

Agnes had to see it. She swept past her mother, into the house, and began looking through the rooms, opening closets and cabinets. She found there was only a single orange coat hanging inside the hall closet. The photographs had been taken off the walls. The furniture and the television set remained.

Rosamond walked past her, into the kitchen.

"It's clean," she said, opening the cupboard, empty. The shelves were wiped down, even the old stains scrubbed off the lining. "Look," she said to Agnes finally coming in behind her. "Look how clean it is."

"It's all gone," Agnes said. She opened drawers, looked through the refrigerator—at least there was that, a butter dish, a bottle of mustard, some milk—went out to the living room, and looked once again in the hall closet. "Everything is gone," she said. They looked in the bedrooms, found little left save a dropped button, a few things hanging in Rosamond's closet. The shelves above were empty. Agnes remembered all the things, precious old things and bits of junk, the detritus of her mother's years of aloneness, of collecting bits of vintage clothing and knickknacks, things Agnes herself had despised—old things, not stylish. But Agnes had

had some attachment to those things as well, the clothing her mother had worn all her growing up, the dishes she'd eaten off of as a child. In her old bedroom, the four-poster bed remained, but every piece of clothing—blue jeans, flannel shirts, sweatshirts, a pair of sneakers she'd drawn on with a Magic Marker—had vanished. Board games she'd shoved back into her closet, a child's jewelry box with plastic baubles and a folded two-dollar bill tucked beneath dime-store bangles, all gone.

"Mom," she said, "he took everything."

"Not everything," Rosamond corrected her. "I gave most of it away. The Salvation Army came and got it, one big mound." She looked around her. They were standing in her bedroom. She put her hand to her face. "Goodness. There was so much stuff."

"My things too." Agnes looked at Rosamond. "I can't believe you've done this."

Rosamond looked at her, quick, as if she were suddenly alarmed at everything that had vanished. Agnes took a seat on the floor beside the dresser. The searching had exhausted her.

After a moment Rosamond took a surviving cardigan in her hands and seated herself on her bed. She fingered a tiny hole in the shoulder, thinking of how she might go about the work of repairing it. She didn't care one toss about the car, and though she already missed all the things she'd packed inside the trunk, she felt light, unencumbered, sitting there inside her house, as hollow as a cave.

"I'm glad it's gone," she said. She sighed, wishing there were knitting needles in her hands. "I should have cleaned this house out long ago."

"All your clothes. Even your *underwear*. Your panty hose has disappeared. Your jewelry." She laughed short, like a hiccup. "I just want to know why. Were you planning on moving? Did you know Harding was closing? Mom, did you plan to give him everything? I wouldn't be surprised. Not a bit. You probably packed everything up and *gave* him the key. You've given everything away. You're too young to go senile like this, to throw out your whole life."

Rosamond dropped the cardigan. She turned to Agnes. "Don't talk to me about throwing my life away, little girl. Just go on, go check groceries in this miserable town. Marry your sidewalk preacher. Or no, just go on doing what you've been doing, which is not deciding. Not deciding about living here, about Ray, about James. You never really decided about him, you just waited for him to go. You wished him away."

"That's right," Agnes said flatly. She rose to her feet and closed the closet door. "I wished him away. It wouldn't hurt you," she went on, "to wish a man away. Your pining after every single one of them doesn't seem to do you any good." She stepped into the hallway, then turned back. "Mom, you cannot leave this life, do you hear me? You can't just get rid of your*self,* do you hear?"

Rosamond didn't answer. Later, when they left, she wiped the dampness from her eyes and concentrated on feeling unafraid. She strained to recapture her boldness. They reached the end of the driveway and went in their separate directions: she up the sidewalk toward Harding, Agnes back to the apartment to get her car so she could go to work.

Agnes felt strange, walking away. She was oddly dry-eyed, disconnected. Her mother had in effect told her to leave Goliath, and she wanted to. It made her dizzy, though, to think of going *anywhere*; even Winnie, the biggest quasi-city within an hour's drive, seemed too much for her. Her maps had told her nothing, only labeled the places of the world, but gave no direction. There were no dotted lines, no pathways.

She stayed numb all morning, tallying groceries, beans, bread, milk. What would her mother do in her bare house? Could she even continue without Harding? After work, she took a supper of canned soup and spent the evening watching television sitcoms, compact installments of play-life, complete with play-laughs. Ray called, but she told him to wait, to come by in the morning. She felt too contemptuous and raw to talk to anyone tonight.

"What a prize," she said to him in the morning when he arrived. They were speaking in hoarse whispers on her aunt's front porch; her mother was inside, sleeping on Mia's couch. She had explained what had happened, how James had taken her mother's car, how she'd confronted her mother's empty house yesterday. Now she was wrapped up in a terry-cloth robe with her hair pulled up in a loose ponytail.

"What a prize he turned out to be," Agnes said. The air was cool and she shivered. She rubbed her eyes and looked at Ray. "I just don't believe he's done this. He took her car, the most valuable thing she owned."

A piece of hair came loose from her ponytail and Ray reached out, almost touched it. He stepped toward her but stopped. The sun had risen just high enough to clear the earth and flood the street with light, as palpable and delicate as mist. Fresh green sap was rising in the trees, and though the lawn was still brownish from the winter cold, it was also damp and softened, warming itself in the sun. Agnes's eyes were sleep-swollen, and her face was pale and bare. She looked out across the street, squinting.

"It's good he's finally gone," Ray said. "We can at least be thankful for that."

"Not coming back," Agnes said, and now she broke down, dropping her face into her hands. Ray touched her arm, and she collapsed into him. "He's never coming back," she said, clinging hard to Ray's shoulders. She pulled back, wiping her eyes with the sleeves of her robe. "I *wanted* him to leave. I don't know what I'm saying."

"Everything will be all right." He drew her back to him. "I promise," he said, fulfilling in that instant another need Agnes had inherited from her mother: a man to promise her something.

He stopped, loosening his hold, and looked down at her. "Agnes," he said, "hear me. *I* won't leave you. If you want me, I'm yours, and I won't leave."

He pulled her close once more, and Agnes closed her eyes, re-thinking his words, testing their effect. She rested for the moment on the strength of those words, and for now it seemed possible—she could stay here with Ray. She could just stay and stay.

Yet, Goliath itself was falling apart. The ditches were weedier than they had been in years past, and the sidewalks were webbed with cracks. The panel of orange and green color blocks on the post office—once so modern-looking—were faded and outdated now. Agnes couldn't stay here with Ray even if she wanted to because the *here* was disappearing. Beneath the homes, foundations had been weakened by insects and moisture, and aboveground the caulking had grown thin, rattling around the windows. Water slipped through worn places in the rain gutters and the overlapping roofing tiles.

People didn't know it full-on, but they sensed Goliath was fading more rapidly now, with the factory's ending. In their gut-level panic, they looked around and tried to see the things that were shining like exploded buildings in their last moments, fading away.

Rosamond was not the only one to lose things. Across town, items were turning up missing in almost every house. At first the objects were insignificant, and those who were missing odds and ends were not completely sure they had not simply misplaced that jar of mismatched buttons. Or the unbroken package of cigarettes they were pretty certain they had picked up at the gas station the night before. Half-eaten loaves of bread disappeared. Tubes of toothpaste. A pair of socks. A handful of change left out on the dresser.

Times were strange during the factory's last days, and most people were either not paying attention or considered the small losses to be of little consequence. They had much larger concerns. To some, a missing book, a lost coffee mug were outward signs of inner confusion. It made sense they would misplace these small things now—they were losing the entire factory. A roll of mints, the tarragon from the spice rack, a travel-size sewing kit. It was unsettling but not tragic. The result of fuzzy-mindedness, but not much of a material loss.

The dispossessions had begun the day the closing of the factory had been announced, that afternoon when the people had met in one another's driveways to eat fried chicken and apple cake, to pick half-remembered songs from the strings of untuned guitars. The thefts quickly escalated, though, to items of greater value. Opal Mercer's gold earrings disappeared from her jewelry case one morning when she was out walking with a neighborhood lady. She reported the loss to Clyde Winston, who advised her to wait a few days, see if they turned up. Possibly she had only misplaced them? But then money went missing from Hank Derrick's pickup. He had parked at the Tuesday Diner, taken down a few bills where he kept his cash tucked into his visor, then returned to find a single twenty-dollar bill was all that was left. Dale Myers, the young pastor at First Baptist, could not locate his brass tie tack. His mother had given it to him when he'd first graduated from the seminary and he'd never preached a sermon without it. It was his wife Tonya who called the police. She and Opal Mercer agreed: something *had* to be done. "It's got to where you don't even feel safe," Tonya said.

There were more losses: Celeste Bradshaw's crystal candlesticks, her father's antique spectacles, china figurines and collectibles from the homes in Mia Robins's neighborhood. Mia herself lost nothing, and her exemption worried her: was it possible Rosamond was the thief? The thefts had been mostly small things, but Mia figured that if it was Rosamond, she wouldn't be stealing for monetary gain. And she couldn't blame Rosamond for resenting the people of Goliath: they had judged her. Shunned her, even. Mia had never understood how people could despise a person who had been through so much. Yes, Rosamond had taken up with the greasy salesman, but then he'd also left her. Her *and* her little girl. Where was people's compassion?

But still she defended Goliath to Rosamond. "The people here are good people, but they have their shortcomings. I'm sorry this town hasn't been better to you and Agnes." She gave a simple, modest smile then, and sniffed a little. Surely, no, Rosamond wouldn't steal a thing; and to prove this to herself, she set her pink trinket box—with her dead husband's gold tooth inside—on her dresser. On the *edge* of her dresser.

"It's a stranger," she opined to her neighbors. "It's someone from the other side of the county, coming in taking our things."

Women gathered at Charlotte Branch's drugstore to tally the missing items, and the Morning Glories held court at the Tuesday Diner. Rumors of Rosamond's house being ransacked by that drifter—the boy they had even begun to *like,* or at least tolerate—were passed around. They worried he was still lurking about, even after Clyde Winston assured everyone James-from-elsewhere was gone. Or what about the other one? The one with all the books? The encyclopedia salesboy. Remember him? It might have been his plan from the start, to steal from them. He could be living in a tree or in a hole in a ground or, defying notice, in somebody's musty old basement. Had anyone actually *seen* either of these boys leave? James's orange Volkswagen was found near the interstate, the keys in the ignition—further proof he hadn't left quite yet. The Morning Glories kept a lookout; the women took out their jewelry drawers and took inventory.

Rosamond did not think about James or the salesboy. She didn't even think about Tucker anymore, and she quit watching

Clyde Winston's windows to see when his lights went out at night. She found with relief that she missed almost none of the possessions she'd lost. She still heard her daughter's voice telling her, *You can't get rid of yourself,* but only in the quietest moments. She tried to stay busy instead.

On the day she had packed all her things away, a new thought, pristine and certain, had come to her. It had grown muddled in the days since, with the end of the factory being announced and all the talk in town about the thefts. But now the thought returned to her. It warmed her. An enterprise of sorts. A *mission.*

There would be a parade: a spring day, as bright and smooth as an Easter egg, the frothy floats, smart American flags whipping in the breeze, the notion that Goliath could yet be what it had once been—if only for one afternoon.

"Imagine it, Mia," she said. "Just *imagine.*"

Mia, who recalled the parades nearly as completely as she remembered flying day, who was happy to have her sister's wayward child safe in her house, the wayward child's child safe in the basement, who after these years of widowhood was simply happy to have another warm body parked beside her on the couch in the evenings, didn't question Rosamond. The thought that Rosamond had been the thief seemed downright silly to her now: of *course* it wasn't Rosamond. Her faith once again restored, she clicked about gathering supplies—paper, pens, phone book—and the two of them got to work.

It was like the old days, Rosamond poring over the lists of names and numbers, further dividing the citizens of Goliath into sublists: prioritized, starred, and question-marked. She had done much the same work with Percy's old client lists, the main furniture stores from here to Portland, the hotel chains, even a few individual buyers—all the places they'd sold to. The letters of gratitude thanking them for their business. And others, the invitations to Goliath, to the High Point furniture show. Occasionally there had also been the letters of apology. Of correction. The explanations of delays. Percy had dictated them all, standing, leaning against his desk, his tie loosened, shirtsleeves rolled up, brow wrinkled. And then it had been up to Rosamond to tidy those letters, to fix the wording just a tiny bit—not so much that he'd notice, but just sort of simplify his sentences a bit. Pare them down just the *smallest* bit. She typed them up, he signed, she addressed and stamped, and out they went. Remembering it now, she could see the old dark-wood stain of her desktop. She could feel the thin office carpet beneath her shoes as she slid into her spot behind the typewriter, lifting her fingers, setting them on the keys. There, from the hallway, came the smell of the ammonia floor cleaner the janitor used on the linoleum.

Mia had been wrong when she had said nothing was as big as you thought it was. Some things were so big, you could walk right into them with room to spare. Agnes had been wrong too: it was possible to get rid of yourself by doing so, by walking into big sadness or hope or, oftener, both.

So while the people of Goliath catalogued their losses, Mia and Rosamond began their telephone campaign. They worked together from the lists Rosamond had made, taking turns on the kitchen extension. Rosamond dressed in her work clothes and sat at the table as if it were her office desk, legs crossed, spine straight, speaking with a pleasant, professional-secretary lilt. It felt so much like the old days, she had to stop herself from announcing that she was calling from the office of Percy Harding.

Yet unlike the old days when everything had been so busy, when the people she called—the suppliers and the customers and the board members—had had a professional interest in what she was calling to tell them, the townspeople they called from Mia's kitchen telephone were not receptive to Rosamond's vision. The high school band leader politely declined to participate, saying they had the state competition to prepare for. He had been a friend of Mia's oldest son Donald growing up and seemed embarrassed to have to tell her no. "I'm really sorry," he said. Charlie Brinks, from the Jaycees, would inquire about procuring a horse and wagon for the high school homecoming queen, even though it had been many months since her coronation. Also, horses trained for parade walking were hard to come by. "Mia," he said, "this whole thing don't look too promising. A parade? *Now?*" John Truman, the mayor, told Rosamond there were permits she'd have to procure. Mavis Sloan, representative of the Baptist ladies, said they would consider putting up a float, but she wasn't promising anything. She brought the matter up at their next meeting, in the church's fellowship hall, and the ladies discussed it. A parade, they murmured to one another. A *parade.*

Rosamond kept making her calls. Maybe it would be the world's smallest parade. Maybe it would fail completely. Maybe she would never know a single moment of peace, and maybe Dorothy Blair had not actually written the note—Rosamond imagined the aging movie star had a personal assistant.

The very idea of a parade was so absurd, it was laughable, but it was also unthinkably tragic—the greatest insult to the dying town. For years, the town had hated Rosamond Rogers for her scandalous behavior, but since they had witnessed her leading a confused old drunk man—her *lover*—down Main Street, she was plainly ruined. Now they pitied her, which was in some circles another form of hate. The woman excited all the wrong feelings of guilt and dismay.

Rosamond wrote invitations to television news anchors, to the county commissioners. She made a trip to the drugstore to tell Charlotte Branch to spread the word: Dorothy Blair would be the honored guest at the parade. Charlotte pursed her lips. "Will do," she said, but she was as doubtful as anyone else. She watched Rosamond click out the door, and she predicted: this will be the loneliest parade ever.

Toasters disappeared. Family Bibles. Rhinestone brooches. The pink trinket box with the dead man's tooth inside remained untouched, but Mia discovered one morning that an antique bisque doll, the size of her thumb, had vanished. She had bought it for a nickel when she was a child—maybe sixty-five years ago. It wasn't especially valuable, and she'd kept it in the drawer in the kitchen where she stowed rubber bands, ink pens, and her spare sunglasses. She asked Rosamond, "How did they know to look there? Rosamond, who is *doing* this?" She looked around her. "Where else have they been, in this house? Have they been *everywhere*?"

James was not spotted through the first week of March, though people kept a lookout for him as they made their way up the sidewalk to the factory, as they stopped by the Tuesday Diner, as they picked up groceries at the supermarket, them casting questioning looks at that Rogers girl, bad enough she was Rosamond's daughter, and worse—she was the one to bring the boy trouble to Goliath in the first place. It could be she was harboring that boy, the one she'd supposedly sent away.

Clyde Winston kept up with the town's thefts—he kept them scribbled down in a pocket notebook he'd bought the week after he retired. As he went around town recording the losses, he approached the people of Goliath at the post office and the diner with sign-up sheets for the baseball game. "As likely to fail as that parade," Charlotte Branch muttered to herself, though she posted the sign-up sheet. She mentioned the parade to every customer.

May third, Clyde told everyone. It was the same date Rosamond and Mia were repeating into the telephone, the date of the parade. Rosamond and Clyde agreed that the parade would take place in the morning, the baseball game in the afternoon. May third, May third. People were told the date again and again. Many lost the A volume of the encyclopedias the salesboy had left them. Other books. A couple of tarnished old forks from silverware drawers. Clyde kept patrol—how could he *not* find the thief? He was always looking. His baseball campaign had more traction than Mia and Rosamond's parade campaign, but still, enthusiasm was slow to lift off. Everyone locked their doors during the day. At night they woke at the smallest sounds.

Some prepared to leave Goliath. A sprinkling of For Sale signs popped up on front yards, and a few put in their applications at the Broyhill plants in Lenoir, the Corning plant in Hickory. Items continued to go missing during the day, and they began to disappear in the evening hours as well. One man sat watching television in his living room and came into the kitchen for a snack to find that the cookie jar—with the cash hidden inside—had vanished. It made no sense. Rosamond told Mia, "People need this," she said. But she meant the parade, not Clyde's baseball. "People need to celebrate, to *march*."

Ray Winston appeared on doorsteps in the evenings, inviting each household not to the parade or the townwide baseball game, but instead to the Goliath First Baptist Church revival, to be held the first week in April. He had made a promise to Agnes and his face fairly glowed with his newfound purpose. Yes, he would stay with Agnes. The knowledge of this commitment increased his fervor; he was a man of God. Ray was to be the speaker this year, as he was almost every year—a man like Ray Winston was born to preach at times such as these.

"Be quenched for an eternity," he said to the people, and he had made such petitions before. Now it seemed his zeal was even grander, more impassioned, than in the past. "Come, taste eternal life!" His eyes were as steady and calm as ever, but his huge hands shook a little as he held them out, palms up. "Come down to the church," he said. "Come, *believe*."

. . .

The people of Goliath were mistaken about when the thefts had begun. The first had not happened on the day of the street mourning party, but rather a week earlier, when Vincent swallowed the white mouse. Afterward, he and Cassie left Fay there crying, and stepping out onto the asphalt, Cassie said, "I have something for you."

Vincent later concluded it was a show of good faith on Cassie's part, her leading him down the street, then around to the back of a little gray house on Mimosa Avenue. She was showing him she would match him crime for crime. There was a neglected, shaggy lawn out behind the house, a lawn chair with its nylon loops worn loose and droopy on the back porch. She gestured to Vincent to stay quiet, then turned the knob of the back door—it was unlocked. They slipped inside the quiet, darkened house, Vincent following Cassie, who moved quickly over a stretch of faded linoleum in the kitchen, crossed the narrow hallway, and entered a bedroom whose bed was neatly made—a navy spread smoothed up over the pillows.

Vincent was still feeling too numb from the mouse-swallowing, from watching the fat pregnant lady cry, to feel afraid, and Cassie was quick-moving, silent. She plucked a pearl earring from a bowl of jewelry on the dresser, pressed it into his palm, and, pulling him to her, kissed him hard. Vincent barely had time to react when Cassie jerked back, turned, and led him through the back door across the lawn, just beginning to lose its winter pale. The day, as Fay had pointed out, was a day borrowed from the approaching spring, light and warmish.

In the street, Cassie burst out laughing as she bounded ahead. "I told you I would do it, Vincent Bailey," she sang back to him, though she had not said anything like that before. The most surprising part of all of it was the kiss. He still held the earring in his hand, its post jabbing into his palm, and watched her skipping out

front of him, her brown hair whipped out behind her, her entire
figure bouncing up and down, a quick-swaying girl, all skinny
elbows and worn-white jeans. She insisted, "I *told* you."

From there the thieving and the kissing kept up, growing more
intense with each theft, and when Cassie skipped away each time,
Vincent felt a degree colder to Goliath, to the people they were
taking from, and came a bit closer to this strange girl, this skinny
trailer poet with safety-pin scratches on her arms. Once, in one
of the houses, her kissing him quick and fierce as she did each
time, each time a bit longer, when she pulled away, Vincent held
her arm. She stopped and watched him trace the letters carved
into her arm. It seemed he could feel the quiver the same way
she did, that shivery feel of half-numb, half-livened skin.

Vincent had stopped swallowing cigarettes and crickets. He
and Cassie were only stealing now. For all the complaints that
rose up in town, they found easy entrance into the houses. Even
as the thefts grew in frequency and consequence—they grew bolder
each time—people left their back doors unlocked. There were
half-opened garage doors. Open windows whose storm screens
popped out with little more than a tap, front door keys easily discovered in flowerpots and ledges above doors, beneath the paws
of front-porch ceramic cats. But Cassie and Vincent mostly used
those open back doors, and if they happened upon a house whose
back door was locked tight, they simply moved on to the next.

Cassie took it in her mind to steal only valuables. "No more
matchbooks," she said. She lifted bits of jewelry and crystal pretties and, as often as they could find it beneath mattresses or left
carelessly out on dressers, thick wads of cash. "The purest profit,"
she said.

In the beginning, their spoils, except that first earring which
Vincent kept in his dresser drawer and put in his pocket every
morning, a sort of good-luck charm, were abandoned in the woods

or in trash cans out front of the gas station. Then when they began lifting items of greater worth, Cassie kept them stored beneath her bed. She was dreaming of motorcycles. "Harley-Davidson," she said, then "No, a Black Widow." A few raindrops from pearl-pink sunset clouds were tapping against her window. "We'll take off on a souped-up chopper," she said.

Vincent agreed, though he couldn't really imagine leaving, couldn't really see himself on a Harley-Davidson. For him, the thieving was about each lift, each kiss, each giddy moment of escape, spilling out into the street, watching Cassie skip ahead, her sometimes enjoining him to skip too, grabbing his hand, insisting, "Come *on,* Vincent." He allowed himself to be dragged away down the road into the graveled lot by the trailer park. She led him into her trailer if her mother wasn't home, the two of them tiptoeing past her sleeping daddy on the sofa, back to her room to pull the stolen items from the waist of Cassie's jeans or from her pockets, and to touch each thing, tally up their earnings, inventory their goods.

"You'll be a road captain," Cassie dreamed, and Vincent nodded, half listening to her. At home his father, who hadn't had much work in months, had started going out to the field of junk every afternoon, looking around. Vincent watched from his window. He picked up the various pieces of metal, parts Vincent didn't even know the names for, but he tried out words for them anyway, remembering *U-joint* and *oil cylinder* from the time he was a little boy and his father was a busy man bent over the hood of a car or hammering at a sheet of metal, the whir of the electric sander. Long ago. His father picked through the junk, gathering a pile. Vincent slipped out to the junk field after him, looking through the grease-covered pieces his father had salvaged, holding them in his hands, feeling their heft, pondering their past lives inside various automobiles. He wondered at their worth.

Cassie said, "Since we were in kindergarten, I thought there was something different about you. You never liked kickball. You never played unless you had to."

Later he'd asked his father what he was doing with those pieces. His father snorted, shaking his head, and Vincent thought that was all. They were just finished up with dinner, the two of them the only ones remaining at the table, and Vincent was reminded of the day he'd found Percy Harding. He remembered the supper his mother had served him that afternoon, the quiet at the table. He thought it would be that way again, his father not speaking except to say how hard it was to forget a sight like that, and he went into his own thoughts, of stealing, of kissing Cassie, the improbable motorcycle she was dreaming of.

His father finally spoke, confessing he was building a car. He said, "Now don't that beat all," and his words were soft, unconvinced. "I'm building a car from nothing."

"You, on your bike, your chopper," Cassie murmured. She'd returned the loot to its hiding place and was now lying on the floor and squinting up at the ceiling. "Driving into the blue."

His father had continued, "I plan to build it from nothing but junk." He spoke quietly, thoughtfully, fiddling with his fork. "I aim to use only what's out there."

He left the table then, and Vincent was left with quiet until his mother returned, smiling at him, asking if he'd like some popcorn to take into the living room. He could watch some television; she'd tell his sisters to let him choose the program. She collected the dishes and took them to the sink, turning on the tap, bubbles rising. She sighed, looking back at Vincent. "What do you think?" she'd asked, and to Vincent, it was sadder than any deflated parade, his mother at the kitchen sink, hoping he'd want some popcorn. She was trying to love him back to a different time, when comfort and peace came as easy as that, but he knew it wouldn't work. He could not be returned to the safety of being a child, not after seeing Percy Harding razed to the mud, not after swallowing that mouse, not after seeing the fear and anger on the pregnant lady's face. It was more than that. Being around Cassie, just knowing her, had delivered Vincent to a different way of existing, and there was no going back.

TWELVE

Rosamond Rogers was everywhere. She made phone calls, went to the Tuesday Diner early for coffee so she could flirt with the Morning Glories, talked with Charlotte Branch at the drugstore. Her continual presence put people in mind of the day several weeks earlier when she had walked an old man down the sidewalk in the late afternoon, all the houses watching, while the grade school cheerleaders practiced their jumps on the school lawn.

Something about revisiting that sight—Rosamond walking ahead, holding the bent old man's hand, his face turned down to the sidewalk—spoke to the people. They found their thoughts returning again and again to the incident, and even those who hadn't seen it began to remember it as if they had. They couldn't stop themselves from re-imagining it, and in their restructuring, they searched out an inkling of perception: there was something different about Rosamond Rogers, something besides her hair, which had in just the past few weeks gone gray well beyond her temples. She seemed to grow older daily, her brown eyes gone soft, the wrinkles around her eyes and her mouth spreading, deepening. This belief was unexplainable and almost fearsome in its intensity. They reperceived her kindness to the old man and keenly felt her humiliation. They still pitied her in a way that bordered on hate. And yet, that pity had softened a tiny bit. Or, rather, its direction—its aim—had shifted. Now, it almost seemed this woman had, through her actions—that long walk— carried the humiliation of the entire town.

They continued to outwardly mock her idea of a parade, though, all the more for her insistence that Dorothy Blair, a movie star, ancient now and hidden for decades, would reappear. Secretly, though, many mused in their own minds about the strange woman's power to make things happen. In the past she had earned Percy Harding's respect and even his affection. Maybe she really could conjure up the only person from Goliath to achieve a scrap of fame. She clearly had enormous faith in her own vision. The people began to think about what else she might be able to do.

But Rosamond was growing tired, these weeks of pleading for help, for participation in the parade. Her knees bothered her, walking from work to the Tuesday Diner, where she had a glass of sweet tea and watched through the window as people passed by. She had found lately that her heart beat too fast for small efforts, and now, walking home, she had to stop to catch her breath. She worried, in an idle, useless way, that she had belatedly acquired Tucker's old age, or maybe some of Mia's weaknesses. As if the cell-level decay of old age spread like a fever.

"You need sleep," Agnes told her. "You're exhausted." She believed her mother should give up the parade: "Does this really seem like a good idea to you?" Rosamond shook her head, dismissing her daughter's worries, certain she couldn't possibly understand why such a celebration was necessary—*vital*, she said. But then, Agnes was young.

"We have to have the parade." She used the voice that Agnes

hated—the same voice Rosamond had been using for years, the one that chided and scolded and was certain of its superiority, or at least the superiority of the words it said. Usually Agnes turned away at that voice or even left. But now her own apartment was just a set of stairs away, so Agnes touched her mother's shoulder. They were sitting in Mia's kitchen, all the lists and sign-up sheets and the proper forms in various states of completion spread out before them.

"All right," she said. "That's great, Mom."

Cassie spoke of her motorcycle dream every afternoon, but for Vincent, the stealing was only about the thrill. He couldn't care less about the motorcycle she was talking about, and he knew he'd never leave Goliath with her. He only wanted to take things, and he still had the impulse to ingest bugs and paper clips and to dig out the little rough pieces of car parts fallen away, into the debris of metal and foam and rubber out there in the junk field. He didn't want to leave Goliath with Cassie, to spend the rest of his life thieving with her—he only wanted to kiss her. He craved the quick-hot feel of the kiss, and it wasn't just her tongue or her mouth or even her body there so close to him. It was the danger of it, and the action. At his own house, it seemed all of them, even his fluttering sisters, lived underwater, everything distorted, distant, and unreal. He agreed with everything Cassie said about their leaving Goliath, traveling west, just to get to the stealing and those kisses.

Cassie was ever hopeful, and she'd quit cutting her arm. She said, "Vincent Bailey, we won't be living here forever. Remember I said this. Remember it when we're someplace else." They were lying on the floor in her room, their arms entwined. Her eyes were closed. "I can almost believe we're already gone."

A few weeks into their spree, though, they were discovered. It happened in an ordinary boxy brick house. There had been no back door—the basement door behind the house and down the steps was locked—and they had used an unlocked side door that opened into the laundry room. They moved into the living room, where everything—the sofa, the throw pillows, the curtains—was cream- or beige-colored and trimmed with lace. A tiny old woman was dozing on an easy chair, her thin, veiny hands clasped together in her lap. Vincent turned back, gesturing to Cassie that she follow.

They retreated to the laundry room, fearing the old woman would wake, but a person was there, a woman coming in through the very door they were aiming for. She was old, though not as ancient as the lady snoozing in the living room, her hair brown and gray, not white, and curled to her shoulders. This woman was done up in a blue dress; Vincent even noticed, in a flash of looking her over, realizing they were caught, that she wore matching high-heeled shoes. She stood in the closet-sized room facing the thieves and set her purse down on the washing machine. She then attended to her white gloves, pulling them off finger by finger. It didn't seem she had even seen them. Vincent wondered for a moment if the woman was blind.

He turned, meaning to find another way of leaving, but she stopped him. "Hold on there, you. You just keep where you are a minute." They stood then, Cassie in the doorway behind him, her head already cocked, ready to spar, but Vincent couldn't think clearly. The scene was coming from a long way off, the picture before him something he believed and couldn't believe at the same time. The woman was looking at Cassie, who was puffed up, her hand on her hip, as if she meant to take exception to this woman, as if they had any good reason to be standing here in a strange house, as if the woman were the intruder and the house rightly belonged to Cassie and Vincent. Her eyes shifted to Vincent, his joints twitching with the confusing flux of impulses streaming through him. Run, his mind was calling, *run*—but his muscles kept still. He didn't even blink.

"Ma'am?" he finally tried, and the woman stared back at him. She was looking at him as if she was trying to figure him out. She shook her head and stared hard again, her arms crossed, brow furrowed. "Ma'am," he said, "we were just leaving."

"You're not leaving," the woman said. "You're not going any-where."

"You can't keep us here," Cassie put in, "you have to let us go."

"Go?" the woman asked. She was squinting now, as if she were looking into a great light, trying to focus on a thing that couldn't be seen with naked eyes. "Where would you go?" Then, "Have you got it? Whatever it was you came to get? Whatever it is you're stealing from my aunt? Yes, I've heard of you. The thieves. Everyone is looking for you." She took a step toward them, and Vincent, in the corner of his eye, saw Cassie reset herself. She put her other hand on her hip, holding her ground. He heard her draw in a breath, about to speak, but the woman spoke first.

"Why," she said, "you're just kids. You're *children*."

"You better not tell nobody," Cassie said. She moved forward and Vincent shot a hand out, touched her shoulder. She shook it off, her eyes narrowing on the woman. "You better just let us go."

"What is it?" the woman asked. "What is it you need?" Cassie said nothing, and the woman looked at Vincent. The afternoon was bare and bright and growing too warm in that small room, crowded with washer, dryer, detergents, laundry baskets filled with crumpled clothes at their feet, towels stacked up neatly on the dryer. The smell of fabric softener filled the room. Vincent thought of his mother, who seemed to spend half her life at the washing machine, sorting, filling, shaking, folding. The woman followed Vincent's gaze toward Cassie, then turned her eyes back to him.

"What do you need? You might get more, you know, asking rather than taking. You might be surprised, what people will give you."

"We don't need anything from you," Cassie said. "You better

just let us go. I mean it, lady. We don't need *anything* from you."

Vincent grabbed at her hand. She yanked it free, though, and he whispered, "Let's go." But Cassie came closer to the woman, and Vincent saw for the first time just how tall she was, taller than him, taller than the woman they were trying to steal from. It was as if she'd grown a foot standing there, staring each other down. She brought her face close to the woman's face. Vincent, still half thinking about his mother, about Cassie's kiss, which he was missing, and his father's field of junk, somewhere out in the free world, finally recognized her: it was the sidewalk lady. Here they were standing in the house of the sidewalk lady, whose real name Vincent couldn't remember; he knew only that she was the one who dressed in those outdated dresses, in high heels and white gloves, and was always walking up or down Main Street. Cassie was holding the woman's eyes, her hatred so thick, Vincent was now afraid of them both—weird lady, weird girl.

"There's nothing you people have for us," Cassie said.

The woman paused, looking at them. "Then you'd better just go," she said, though she kept blocking their way to the door leading outside. Her hands were on her hips and her eyes had narrowed to slits. "You can go out the front. You can just walk out the front door. Go on, free. I won't tell, but you'd better quit your stealing. That's all I'm asking, that you stop. And I'm asking it for your own sakes."

Vincent steered Cassie by the shoulders. She was stuck for a moment, unyielding, and Vincent had to push her so hard, she nearly lost her balance, steadying herself against the dryer.

"Let's go," he whispered, "Cassie, *come on.*"

Finally she budged and they tromped back through the living room, where the dusty old woman was no longer sleeping but blinking to attention, looking them over, and out the front door, bright sky opening up above them. They stood for a moment there, full in the glare of Goliath, and walked down the road, past the bank, the diner, the drugstore, back up toward Cassie's trailer.

"No bike, Vincent, no way," Cassie said, her entire face clamped solid as stone, her eyes pinpoint hard and shining. "We're buying you a yacht, an airplane. A *jet*. Forget the chopper. You and me are going to *fly*."

But Vincent wouldn't hear her. He dropped her at her trailer and left with a mumbled good-bye. He shuffled away, dropping into the woods behind the quiet high school—it was nearly five o'clock—and walked home, his head bent, watching his shoes, the grass, dead leaves, still with the sidewalk lady's face in mind.

After Vincent left, Cassie went into her bedroom, slid open her closet door, clicked on her hidden flashlight, and sat down among clutter on the floor beneath her clothes. She rose up on her knees to squeeze her hand into her pocket, and extracting the peachy pale trinket box she'd stolen from Mia Robins's dresser, settled back and opened it. She didn't know exactly what she was expecting—a coin, an earring, a thumbtack, she didn't know—but what rolled into the palm of her hand made her stop. She stared at it, at first unable to even see what it was—a ball of foil, a rock, *something*—and then finally: it was a tooth. And from there, her actions got stranger, harder for her to explain even to herself. Once she saw it was a tooth, a human tooth extracted from some unknown person's head, she put the thing in her mouth. She rolled it across her tongue, felt for its grooves and dents, tasted its met-alness, its oldness. And finally she swallowed it. It wasn't alive, as Vincent's latest conquests had been—it was even better: it was *human*.

There had never been anybody for Rosamond until Hatley arrived at her parents' front door and offered her sewing bobbins, notions, and thread. He set out his wares on her mother's piano bench. She reached out and touched these beautiful, useful things. He married her, but even then she suspected him a ghost. They were *all* ghosts. Thin as vapor, nothing solid about a one of them.

Then she'd had Percy and Hatley both, and Percy more and more—distracted, but also an enjoining spirit, one that sought her, that told her his secret thoughts about birds and furniture work, one who went to her for the comfort of easy conversation, the comfort of someone sitting still and *listening*. Rosamond believed she had loved Percy in a quiet, pure way. She had simply paid attention. But this comfort had not in the end been enough. Nothing had. And then there was Tucker, whom she had abandoned to another woman twice now. She had not been to Dalton's since she returned Tucker to his wife, and she'd heard nothing from him. She thought of him, his fights against retirement, against death itself, his odd diets, his practiced shrugging off of worry. *Worry*. It was Rosamond's oldest friend.

The two young men, one to show her volumes on every subject in life, the other to claim to love her daughter, the both of them needing looking after. And now came this boy here today who meant not to give her anything, not sewing pretties, or to seek soul-comfort, but to steal from her. He did not steal as James had done, only taking the car when love had failed him, but came with full intent to take what he wanted, just as he and that girl had taken from everyone else in town. Finally, Rosamond saw her deficit plainly: she had nothing for him to take. Everything, every *thing*, was gone. There was comfort, knowing this—all she had was herself. All she had was the moment in front of her now, and her parade-planning, the future.

These were the details she remembered: Hatley, sewing notions; Percy, cardinal; James, car; teenage boy, wild-eyed girl. Hatley's eyes, the parade. A tiny glimpse—there Agnes as a baby. She had been skinny, forever whimpering, and slow to latch on for nursing, but tough. Agnes had been tough from the very beginning.

Rosamond rose from her chair leaving Mia tucked soundly

into her easy chair, dozing in the glow of the television set, and
stepped outside, turning to walk across town to her old house.
She made her way slowly, and once there, she did not go inside,
but stood on the sidewalk out front, looking up at it. Her house
had gone dead, lightless, and she peered deep into its dark, empty
windows. There was something left inside it, she thought. Something important, a thing she'd forgotten. But she could not think
of just what it was.

She continued on to Clyde's house, knocked. He answered the
door in stocking feet, exactly as he had those months ago when
she came by just days after Percy's death. Behind her, the sky had
dimmed but not gone dark yet. Another sign spring was coming.

"Rosamond," he said. He seemed happy enough to see her.
Again, just as she had last time, she suspected he had somehow
known she'd be here, had been waiting for her. And if he noticed
how she'd changed, he didn't show it. He stepped back, inviting
her in.

She had been in this exact spot before—here, in Penny's living
room, everything in shades of tan and navy—and yet she'd never
been *here* before: in this moment. She'd never entered this house
with nothing but her tiredness. She felt blank, standing there.

Without a word, Clyde stepped into the kitchen, and when he
returned, she'd already slipped her shoes off and was sitting on the
couch. She had come to tell him about the teenagers who were
robbing the town, to offer a description, but such a thing seemed
impossible now that she was here. She'd get to it, she would. But
first she would drink a beer, talk with Clyde, this person who had
known her so long. She felt such relief, sitting here. There was
nothing for her to explain, no accounts to give. Nothing clever to
say, and no strain to make him feel—to wholly experience—the
attention she planned to give him.

She took the beer and shifted over a few inches, making room.
Clyde hesitated, glancing first at the recliner, where he had planned

to sit, and then at the spot Rosamond had made for him. He chose the couch.

She said, "I know who the thieves are."

Finally now he seemed surprised. "Who?"

She shook her head. "In a minute. Later. First, I want to ask you something."

"What's that?"

"Did you mean it? About you and me spending some time together? Do you remember what you said the night—"

He nodded. "I meant it," he said. "I mean it."

Rosamond nodded back at him, and they were quiet a moment, each contemplating the deal they were negotiating. Spend some time together, he had said. Talk. She couldn't predict what all that might mean, their agreement now to *talk,* and she was fairly certain he knew no more than she. Such an arrangement had felt like too little before, but now it seemed so full, the small abundance of only that, spending time together.

She said, "They're children. The robbers. A boy and a girl."

"A boy and a girl," Clyde repeated. "Their ages?"

"Teenagers."

"Wait, now. How do you know?" He turned to face her. "You saw them?"

Rosamond paused. "Oh, let's wait," she said. "I'll tell you later. You know what we need? We need wine. I'll get some. In a minute. Everything, in just a little while." She closed her eyes a long moment. The day she stood in the driveway, one hand on her car, the other on James's. She had imagined herself leaving, actually leaving Goliath. She smiled to herself; Clyde couldn't know what she was thinking. And yet she smiled for that moment when she'd thought about driving away—she could have gone to South Carolina, her mother had people there—just knowing she could, and now, for this moment. Here, Clyde so close to her. He'd stood on her porch at midnight not so many weeks ago and almost kissed her. Now she thought she knew why he hadn't.

"For the moment," she went on, looking at him, "let's just talk. It's what you promised me."

He hadn't kissed her then because of everything standing between them. Because it was too cold, too late, and everything was off: she was waiting for James and thinking of Tucker, still lost in Percy. There was a boy sleeping in her driveway and Clyde was coming to save her.

She said, "Tell me anything. Whatever you know. Tell me about baseball."

Clyde took a long drink of beer, then set it down on the coffee table. He sat close to her on the sofa and put his hand on her back and began to move it up and down her spine, exactly as he had done as a comfort to Lela Harding back on the first Sunday of October, when the air was mild but growing cold. Rosamond leaned into him, as Lela had done, but she leaned in closer, listening.

"No one knows when baseball began, it must have been a very long time ago," he said. "But the first World Series was in 1903. That much we know."

Vincent expected the phone to ring the night the sidewalk lady found him, or for the police to show up. His mother was busy tending to dinner and housework, no idea her son was about to be arrested. His sisters carried on with their phone talking, television watching, bedroom door closing. He hadn't thought much about them since he was little and they were all-knowing. Now Vincent began to wonder about the secret lives of the females he lived with. The oldest was enrolled in community college, working toward a nursing degree; the middle one was almost finished with high school, keeping a steady boyfriend this year; and the youngest was coming to small fame these days as some sort of genius in her science classes, especially biology. She had turned quiet and brainy, reserved and sometimes grumpy, watching television and chewing on a candy bar.

His mother, moving about the house with a laundry basket on her hip, looked on these things—the odd hours, the boyfriend, the candy bars—with a raised eyebrow, concerned. She asked Vincent, "Are you coming along okay in school?"

He shrugged. "Sure, fine."

She nodded though she looked uncertain, and later, coming down the stairs to fix himself a snack, he found her standing at the washing machine behind the kitchen, checking his jeans pockets. At the same moment that she pulled something out— something small enough that she had to extract it carefully—he remembered that he'd forgotten the stolen earring there. She examined it in her cupped palm, not seeing she was being watched, pressing a finger to it, squinting, and finally set it on the shelf above the washer. Vincent came around the corner then, stomping through the kitchen, but she said nothing of her discovery. That night at dinner, his father sat at the head of the table, presiding over green beans and pork chops, and Vincent's sisters, sulking and chattering at turns. His mother's eyes slid to Vincent, and she gave him a little smile.

The phone kept quiet past dinner and no knock came at the door. His father sat in his chair in the living room, watching television, and Vincent could barely stand for him to just sit there. He wanted to lift him up from his chair and bring his fist against his father's tight jaw. He pictured himself calling the police and making his confession. His father kept on watching television, and everything stayed absurdly quiet. Later, after everyone had gone to bed, Vincent rose and looked out over the parts yard, odd pieces shining in the small light of the moon, their sizes and shapes warped by the mix of shadow and light. He hoped for a sudden, torrential rain to rust it all away.

In the morning, his sisters moved about in their blur of hair spray, shoes, and book bags, preparing for departure. His mother, downstairs in the kitchen, opened and closed cabinets, cooking breakfast none of the girls would have time to eat. His father was somewhere downstairs or else out drinking coffee, Vincent imagined, making a measured start to the day, looking over the junkheaps.

When the upstairs hallway was at last empty, Vincent slipped into his parents' bedroom. He went to the dresser and took his father's pocketknife from a pile of change beside a wallet and a half-eaten roll of antacids, the contents of his father's pockets. Vincent wrapped his fingers around the smooth, heavy pocketknife, hiding it in his fist, then came down the stairs, taking off for the bus stop. He slipped away to the woods before the first bell and played with making swipes at the ends of his fingers. The cuts bled like mad, dripping unto the exposed roots of trees. The blood fallen to the dirt was dark brown, quickly gone, camouflaged in the earth; on the sidewalk, it was true red, bright in the glare of the sun.

Celeste Bradshaw, who was five months pregnant now and gaining more weight than her doctor thought wise, woke one morning struck with indecision. She had difficulty choosing which maternity blouse to put on, and she didn't know if she should drink tea or coffee with her toast. Should she *have* toast? When she did her grocery shopping, she walked up and down the produce aisle and couldn't choose among the apples.

The spring rains stirred up mud in the ancient river running behind the church and deposited puddles in the gutters and soggy places in the newly green yards across town. Tadpoles swam in the puddles and children sloshed through the water-soaked lawns. The river rose in its banks but did not flood. It was the red-brown color of Carolina clay. Many evenings when the children were sent out to play, faint splotches of rainbow appeared in the skies just as the sun was setting.

Celeste made her confession to Rosamond: when she was a child, she had led a grown man her daddy knew into her backyard and taken off all her clothes. "I just stripped down to nothing." He hadn't told her to, and before he could even react, she'd already run, screaming, back to the house. "I can't imagine what he must have thought of me," she said, "of what I did." She told her all this out front of the post office late in the day, just before it closed, everyone headed home from work. She tugged gently on the cuff of Rosamond's sweater as she talked, as if she were her daughter, and when she was finished, she did an odd thing: she hugged Rosamond. "Thank you," she whispered, and hurried on.

This was the last confession Rosamond was to hear. She didn't know it then and felt little different, walking to Mia's house. There were new things blooming in her yard. Mia stood in her housedress and a pair of sandals and pointed out each one. "The periwinkle, the irises, the very last crocus." It would be months before Rosamond would realize what had ended that afternoon, with the bit Celeste told her about taking her clothes off for that man. And then she wouldn't question why the random disclosures had ended; she would instead wonder why they had begun. Beyond that, she would want to know if any of it had really helped the townspeople. And always, always, why her?

The last beam of sunlight fell gold and heavy on the streets and the rooftops and the windshields of people's cars. Rosamond had given a thorough description of the young robbers to Clyde but had also assured him that they wouldn't do it again. Clyde asked her how she knew. "I just know," she said. "Or at least I know about the boy." Still, he would look for them. She didn't know if he planned to tell the police.

Now she told Mia, "Let's put the irises in the parade. We'll let the spring birthday girls carry them." They still discussed this, the parade that nobody else yet wanted, and they still acted as though it would happen, no matter what the rest were saying, no matter how few people had agreed to run a float or collect a marching band. Agnes had told her to get some sleep, but Mia had prescribed fresh air. Fresh air *helps* you sleep, she had explained.

Mia shook her head. "By then we'll have daisies. We should use the daisies, especially if the girls are young. Irises are for the old ones. For the old ladies like us."

Around town, James's name was spoken less often. The townspeople had gone a day, then two days without anyone losing anything. The girl at the library was still reading the fishing encyclopedia and nursing the tiny crush she'd had on Agnes's husband—he really *could* be hiding out somewhere, couldn't he? Marty Pickard's broken arm, now healed, was regaining its strength. Since Janice left, his elderly mother had been going to the market for him, but now, Agnes noticed, he was having a go at it himself. One evening he asked three ladies at the Lucky Grocery how to poach an egg before he found one who was willing to give instructions.

"Put some vinegar in the water," she said. "That's the secret."

"My wife used to do fix poached eggs," he explained.

Celeste Bradshaw took her time selecting her shoes in the morning. She lingered over her morning television news shows and took a nap before leaving for the day. She picked up the phone, dialed a friend's number, changed her mind, and set the phone down again. She wandered into the Tuesday Diner and took a survey—what should she call the baby? Her husband Ronald was certain it was to be a boy, but Celeste knew better. She told Agnes, "It's a girl. No question." She had caught up with Agnes at the post office. In all her baby distractions, Celeste Bradshaw checked her mail constantly. She could not keep herself at home. Agnes was picking through the sales circulars, about to leave. "Ruth," she said when Celeste asked for her vote. So few in town knew it: Agnes had been a student of foreign languages. "It means friend," she explained.

Then it was the end of March and, with it, the end of the factory.

Old-timers, referring to the legends of the start of Harding Furniture more than a hundred years earlier, were shocked to learn that the children didn't know the most important year in Goliath history: 1890. In that year, the thirty or so laborers employed by the Harding Furniture Company moved from their shed in the woods to join fifty new-hires in a massive, just-built brick building in town. The factory was huge and shining new in those days, the glory of Furniture South, and the pieces first crafted there were the finest in the Carolinas, commissioned by special order and shipped by train to a new hotel resort in Asheville. The workers were the most skillful furniture-crafters in the nation, led by Grady and Samuel Harding, brothers, and then, later by Samuel's son Leland, the husband of famed evangelist Martha Harding and father to Percy Harding. In the beginning, the workers arrived in boater hats and dungarees at six every morning and worked sawing, shaping, hammering, gluing, and varnishing logs of hardwood cut from the nearby Carolina forest until noon, when they gathered at the loading bay to chew on cold biscuits and stare down the twin lines of railroad track trailing off into the trees.

No one from that original team, of course, was there to see the last piece of furniture shipped away. No one even spoke as though it was the last. The final item was a set of cherrywood head- and footboards, lightly varnished, still smelling of wood, with the pattern of an oak tree, its branches stretching out to form the dome of the headboard; the footboard was made of oak leaves touching. The workers left at the completion of each step: first, the rough mill workers, having fed the last of the heavy logs through the saws, swept the floor, unplugged the machines, and clocked out. Next the cutters, who tooled the wood and carved the intricate tree pattern; then the gluers, who pieced the two halves of the headboard together. The varnishers wiped the varnish on, then set the pieces between the drying fans. Throwing away their gloves and their cloths and gathering their coffee mugs and personal radios, they left.

The finishers took the pieces from the fans, checked that the varnish had sealed smoothly, and then wrapped up the pieces and settled them into their box. Once it was finished, loaded onto the last truck, the loaders waved to one another and pretended it was the close of any other workday, going out into the nearly empty parking lot, driving away.

It was eerie rather than sad for the workers, setting out. These people with loose, unsettled plans for their futures, those who had jobs lined up and those who didn't, returned to their homes and parked their cars in their driveways. They sat there for a moment before stepping out. The factory closing was like the sun burning out; despite the warnings, the announcement, no one had believed it would actually happen.

Celeste began at the Tuesday Diner telling others she'd finally chosen a name. "Ruth," she said. They would call her Ruthie, which seemed somehow less primitive, more hopeful. "Ruthie," she told her neighbors and the Morning Glories. She burst into her father's sterile workroom.

"We'll name her Ruthie," she said.

"All right," he answered. "That's fine," and he nodded, returning to the dead man—a retired telephone pole climber—on the table before him.

THIRTEEN

Harding's closing day was a Wednesday, the first night of the revival. Rosamond waited for Agnes to come home and walk with her up to the church. Mia wasn't going with them. She claimed she experienced her own revival every morning, sitting at her kitchen table to read from the books of Daniel and Romans. She said she already knew how the Rapture was going to happen. She told Rosamond, "He'll come through that door." She meant Jesus, returning to call the believers to the heavens. "We'll go up in the clouds." Mia nodded to herself, then settled in her chair to watch a game show on television. When Agnes arrived, she repeated the information about Jesus's coming, and added, "I hope you'll be here when He comes."

Rosamond found her pocketbook, and the two, mother and daughter, set off. The rain had stopped, the sun had shone hot all day, almost as warm as summer, and the puddles, drying, were losing their tadpoles. Inside the church, people drifted into the pews, pausing to chat in the aisles before they took their seats. The heating system was slow to catch up with the changing of seasons, and it pumped too much warm air into the sanctuary. People began to fan themselves with bulletins left in the pews from Sunday. Rosamond and Agnes sat near the back.

At precisely seven o'clock, Ray Winston came through the back doors and started up the center aisle, walking with the same lope and slouch he always did. He was Ray, and he wasn't Ray, dressed as he was now in dark slacks and a pressed white shirt, buttoned tight at the cuff, no tie. He called out a hymn number and a shaky a cappella rendition of "Standing on the Promises" trickled through while Ray took a seat in the front pew, head bowed. He prayed through the hymn. A few old congregants— those who had heard and believed the story of the bird flying into the hospital room—sang out strong. Odd, Agnes had never seen Ray preach before. She'd never come to the revival before and had hardly even chanced upon his sidewalk lectures. When she had, she'd only caught pieces of them, never heard a full message. Beside her, Rosamond, still seated, rooted about in her pocketbook for a tissue, then snapped it shut. She exhaled deeply, lifted her chin, and set her jaw in a tight line. She was always very solemn in church, no singing.

The song over, people slipped their hymnals away and seated themselves. The sanctuary fell quiet, and Ray began. "There once was a city called Jericho."

Ray did not preach as a typical Baptist pastor preached. He stood in front of the pulpit rather than behind it, his huge hands open at his sides. He faced them, slumping a little, and he spoke so quietly, the people gathered in the pews had to lean forward and keep very still to hear him. The lights hanging from chains above them illuminated everything in splotches of yellow, and the stained glass windows shone their brightest at this hour, the sun low in the sky, shining directly into them.

"It was a great walled city. Militarily impenetrable." He looked over those assembled before him; the church was nearly half full.

A fair number for a revival, though he knew their numbers would thin as the week wore on. He shrugged, hooking his thumbs in the belt loops of his slacks. He was freshly shaven, Agnes noticed, and his hair was still wet from his shower, combed back and tucked behind his ears.

"Joshua," he said, "was new at the job."

James, Agnes knew, was gone, despite all the rumors about his sticking around and stealing things. She hadn't known it at first, though, had not been able to quite believe that he had left. James, who had claimed to love her so intensely. Gone with her mother's ancient Cadillac, itself a monument to the most crippling approximation of love.

Beside her, Rosamond shifted. The grim straight line of her jaw relaxed a tiny bit; she had heard the story of Joshua and Jericho before. She couldn't place exactly where she'd heard it—it must have been in church some years earlier. Her parents had taken her as a child. It could be she had simply absorbed the story at some point, like so many other legends, so much history.

Rosamond's mind drifted to other things. Clyde wasn't here—he attended church even more seldom than she did, even with his own son preaching—but she already knew she'd walk there, to Clyde's house, afterward. She'd been up there most nights since she'd gone to tell him about the thieves. She cooked dinner and he told her about baseball and Venus flytraps—they were vanishing, he'd read, from the wetlands of South Carolina where they'd once flourished. Such comfort, she thought, in so little. Words she only half listened to.

At this moment she could have been there with Clyde, or she could have been with Mia, making their parade plans. But Agnes had asked her to come here, to sit in the too-warm sanctuary and watch the stained glass windows glow absurdly orange.

Ray was nowhere close to the part Rosamond remembered, when the walls crumbled to dust and the Israelites took the city.

He retrieved a well-thumbed Bible from the front pew and turned its pages until he found the passage he needed: "When Joshua was near the town of Jericho, he looked up and saw a man standing in front of him with a sword in hand. Joshua went up to him and demanded, 'Are you friend or foe?' " Now Ray shrugged again, looking up at them. "A fair question, wouldn't you say?"

In truth—a truth Agnes hated to admit—she had been hurt by James's leaving. Worse than the fact that he had stolen from her mother; he had *left*. Ridiculous that she should feel this way, after begging him to go. She had grown used to it, though, the idea that he truly loved her. While he had been there in Goliath, wandering about, pursuing her in his half-assed way, there had been proof: love existed. *Love,* Agnes thought now. She had called it *love?*

Ray was a slow preacher. He was only in the first verse of his message, still contemplating everything simple and profound about the question, friend or foe. "Will you kill me or will you help me?" Ray asked. His next words were spoken so casually, it could have been he was speaking only to himself. He said, "He can only help. It's his good nature *to* help. It's our nature to resist that help."

Love—now, *this* day—had a thickness to it, Agnes decided. A viscosity, a fullness. This discovery had something to do with James's leaving and her mother's house coming undone, vanishing, and now Ray's preaching with agonizing slowness. Her mother was a statue beside her, cold as marble. Love was *thick*. It was quiet and so slow, you never saw it coming. A person can be startled or charmed or hurt into *thinking* she was in love, but that wasn't the same.

Agnes believed: one could not live unless one intended to. That was what she had loved about James, what she loved about Ray, watching him now. Any kind of living besides *intentional* living was merely a series of chemical reactions, electronic impulses. Brain waves. Heartbeats. The mechanics of living, but not the truth of it.

"The stranger had an odd response." Ray gave his listeners a half smile, amused. "This stranger Joshua met at the gate to Jericho, the very entrance to the promised land. He answered that he was neither friend nor enemy. In fact"—he took a step toward them, ducking his head a little as if to enter through an invisible doorway that wasn't quite tall enough—"he claimed to be the captain of the host of God."

The room relaxed a little, Ray coming to his point. People resumed fanning themselves. Somebody coughed.

But Agnes was still. She watched Ray shake his head at the unlikelihood, the impossibility, of such a thing—the captain of the host of God, neither friend nor foe, standing before Joshua. Here was Ray, preaching, delivering what glimpses of truth he'd been convinced of. Convinced of in soul knowledge, heart knowledge, head knowledge. All three, he'd once explained to her. He'd also told her that worship could not be called worship unless it was done in spirit and in truth. He said nothing's true—not accurate like a fact, but *true,* like something you'd stake your life on—without its being soul true.

Tonight Rosamond would go sit on Clyde Winston's couch and drink the wine she'd left in his pantry. She might cook a little dinner, or maybe he already had. It could be he was heating up two frozen Salisbury steaks in the oven this very minute, anticipating her coming. She rarely thought about Tucker anymore, and little about Hatley. And though the loss of Percy still gripped her—an ever-present undercurrent to her thoughts—the pain no longer choked out all her breath. This was Rosamond calmly in her church pew, relaxing into herself. She had come tonight for this, to let go of those old sharp pieces.

"The captain of the Lord's host." Ray laid his Bible on the pew and stepped closer. He passed the first few sparsely inhabited pews and stopped. He whispered, "I believe this is the Christ speaking here." He leveled his eyes on the people. "Christ speaking here, before Bethlehem. Before the angels and the shepherds and the inn that had no room for him. Him coming to Joshua, saying, 'Take off your sandals, for you are standing on holy ground.'" He was only whispering, and yet, because they kept still as stones, the people heard him.

"'Take off your sandals,'" he said again, louder but still nothing more than his regular speaking voice, "'for the place where you are standing is holy ground.'" He bent down; everyone watched. He was undoing the laces in his shoes. His work boots. Agnes recognized them.

"Come," he said, rising up, holding the back of a pew for balance as he pulled them off, "*believe*." He leaned over again to slip off his socks, then stood before them, barefooted.

Outside the streets were quiet. The sun had sunk into the crease of the sky, though its reflection off the earth's atmosphere lingered; it looked like melted butter smeared across the bottom of the sky. Clyde was sitting on his porch step, watching the sun set and thinking of Rosamond and the Goliath thieves. He expected they were out there yet, not yet done with their crimes. He kept a protective eye on the houses lined up on Main Street, but he didn't venture out to patrol. He too was coming to terms with a sort of peace this evening. His dead wife speaking through whatever it was—consciousness, physical space, what have you— that separated them, saying, have *this*. Take it, she said, this happiness, this rest.

And now, while Agnes rejected the idea that a person could or should fall in love, beside her, her mother Rosamond was accepting that very thing, the falling. Allowing herself to slip into easeful love finally now, after all her years of straining so hard to reach it. No, Agnes believed, love was not so easy, not a thing to tumble into. It required standing, alert, taking that step—not *falling.* Love was a decision, it was action. Rosamond worked it all out in the physical realms of comfort: yes, go to Clyde, put the pan on the stove, cut up the potatoes, heat the oil. Agnes told herself to stand here watching Ray. She couldn't look away.

"*We,*" Ray said, "are standing on holy ground." He raised his hands so everyone could see what he meant—this church, this street, this town. "Believe it," he said. "This place is sacred. It's *blessed.*"

Ray never made altar calls. He instead invited others to prayer, lowering himself now to his knees. "Let's talk to him, Christ. Here he is, standing before us, not our friend, not our enemy, but our God. We are standing at the gates of Jericho and he is about to tell us what we need to hear: how we can claim our city. Our promised land." Now Ray returned to his natural repose, that shrugging humility.

"But today, before our marching orders are issued, before he tells us how we are to reclaim our city, we're called to kneel here on *this* holy ground and to pray."

The people closed their eyes. They remembered the red brown water of the river and the baby frogs in the street and the look of the closed-up factory, the one they'd left that very day. A few streets away, above the post office, the light in the basement of the municipal building—the library—was burning late so that the girl, the former head of the suicide poets, could read. She had reportedly completed one hundred books now, and had been given her own key to the library so she could read there in her library chair at all hours.

On the other end of Main Street, Mia Robins caught her breath. Her trinket box, the one that held her late husband's gold tooth, was gone. In her yard, the daylilies bloomed on even as the sun dissolved away. The thieves—the *real* thieves—had taken it.

Agnes, inside the sanctuary, kept her eyes open. She didn't

bow her head. She watched Ray and remembered that she had come to Goliath for a reason. She saw Ray's lips move in a silent prayer, and she understood: whatever it was she had come for, the start of it was happening now.

Rosamond, who had stepped forward, had come to kneel, to—as Ray implored them all—*believe,* had her own eyes closed. She didn't see the dark figure just stepping inside the church, standing in the back. She was half praying, making her requests, half remembering, thinking of the crackle of light she'd seen rise from the trees that country-black Halloween night. She had never told anyone what she'd seen. And while there were a dozen plausible reasons—heat lightning, transformers sparking, planes flying, asteroids falling—she believed it had been Percy Harding. *And* God. It was all the good things coming to her, igniting there on the dark horizon. In a way it was Clyde too. Every good thing. It was this moment, every head bowed. They were coming to faith, coming to believe in the parade. She believed that they believed, and the power of that belief kept her eyes closed, caused her to let loose of her physical bearings. She was there again standing on that railroad, the spot where Percy had died, receiving this, the *colossal sadness,* and the other side of it the hope, the promise. A parade. She believed.

Love itself, Agnes understood, was not desperate, but the belief in it—the *hope* for it—could be.

The man in the back of the church, a stranger, had gray in his beard but not in his hair, which was sleek black. He wore a wrinkled plaid jacket and his shoes, well worn, were bogged with red clay, the mud of the river. He made no movement to take a seat or proceed another step into the church.

A few turned back to look at him, but said nothing, and he in turn looked out over the pews from behind, the people's shoulders bunched together, their heads bowed. Some of them knelt facing the pews. A few had moved to the aisle as Rosamond had done and were huddled there, their faces in their hands. Others sat staring straight ahead at the stained glass windows behind the altar, or they fiddled with their belongings, their pocketknives and purses.

The man did not move his eyes away when Agnes turned and saw him. It had been more than ten years since he'd left, but she recognized her father at once. Utterly changed, gone old, and yet it was him. Black hair, houndstooth sports jacket. Hatley Rogers was his own legend, even after all this time. She glanced back at Ray, standing now, looking at the stranger and then at her. He was no phantom; Ray saw him as clearly as she did.

Rosamond, who had risen, returned to her pew, noticed her daughter was upset but misjudged the reason, reached over and took her trembling hand. She saw everything in its simplest light this evening. And it *was* simple, all of it. She couldn't tell what was starting up between her and Clyde. She only knew that it was good and she could accept it plainly. She could accept the comfort of his couch, of his hand on her back.

And she had comfort left to give, to take her daughter's hand now, to close it inside her own, to still it.

At the close of the service, the people rose from their places, wiping the dampness from their eyes, and shook one another's hands. They gathered their families and their belongings and stepped out into the freshly dark night. Agnes looked, but Hatley had already redisappeared.

Rosamond murmured, in a voice so quiet Agnes couldn't tell for sure she was even talking to her, "A lovely service." Agnes said nothing, and Rosamond squinted at her. They stepped across the parking lot. "Did you enjoy it?"

"That's a strange word," Agnes said. "It was a good message, but I'm not sure I *enjoyed* it. I don't think that's the point of it."

Rosamond sighed at her daughter's exactitude. "Never mind,"

she said. She meant: there are many ways to think of the word *lovely,* so many ways to see it.

It was odd to say, but Rosamond's not seeing Hatley annoyed Agnes. And she was relieved too that her mother had not seen him. Relieved and annoyed and worried and happy. He had come back to them. All this time had passed and now here he was, or there he had been, standing in the back of the church.

They walked on past the elementary school under whose oak tree Agnes, ages ago, used to eat her lunch. They passed the coin laundry and the houses, all the houses Agnes had known her whole growing up. They seemed unchanging, but they had changed. Porches had been painted, roofs had gone to disrepair. One of the houses had a coffee-can wind chime hanging from its eaves. Agnes tried to remember: had it always been there?

In that moment, walking beside her mother and yet so very far away from her, Agnes wished she could wipe it all away with the sleeve of her sweater. The houses, the television-lit windows, the school and its oak tree—all gone. Her father had returned, and yet he hadn't. She could try loving Ray, and she couldn't.

Mia was likely at the house, doing some odd household task. Once Agnes had come home to find her aunt polishing her chopping block with linseed oil. Completely necessary, she had answered when Agnes asked what she was doing. It was in those moments Agnes was reminded that her aunt Mia and her mother were related. Undeniable. They shared a gene for championing useless tasks, a familial characteristic Agnes had missed out on.

Hatley, she thought. Nothing more than a trick, she imagined. An illusion. Although. He *could* appear, any second. Every tree was suspect, every shadow.

Now she said with a sudden energy, "No. I didn't particularly enjoy the service, but I can tell you did. I'm glad you have that, Mother. I'm glad you have the capacity for faith."

Rosamond did not know what to say to that. She couldn't tell if Agnes was making fun of her or if she meant what she said. Rosamond had never thought of herself as a person who had a capacity for faith. She had not regularly attended church since Agnes was a child.

Finally, though, she said, "Maybe I do."

Agnes turned off toward Mia's house, at the corner of August Street, and Rosamond continued on to Clyde's house, still puzzling over what Agnes had said. Agnes, who knew her better than anyone else, and yet also not at all.

She found Clyde on the front porch steps. "I've been waiting for you," he said, and scooted over, making room. He said, "The boy went on too long, didn't he?" It took her a minute to connect to what he was saying—he meant Ray.

She shook her head. "Just long enough," she said.

Later they went in together and she stepped out of her shoes and then slipped into the bathroom to take off her panty hose. Her calves were sore from all the standing and walking she'd done; it felt good to be bare-legged and free under her dress.

She put a frozen chicken pot pie in the oven, turned the timer on, and returning to Clyde in the living room, she picked up his hand and led him to the bedroom. She was tired, she said. "Exhausted," she explained. "Just exhausted." The room was tiny, the bed neatly made, and on the wall there hung a painting of a tree with an owl in it; by the window was a framed cross-stitching of the Lord's Prayer. They lay together on the bed, she in her dress with no panty hose or shoes and he in his dark slacks and thin undershirt and socks. They were side by side, only their hands touching. She remembered when Penny had made the cross-stitching on the wall. So intricate, the different colors of thread—it had taken her an entire winter. Ray and Agnes had been little then, preschoolers, and Rosamond had been thin and fidgety and forgetful.

She had still been driving the Cadillac in those days, she remembered, and was still wearing the scarves Hatley had bought her back in their motel days.

They lay quietly for a while, and then Clyde said, "Rosamond, I don't know what we're doing here."

Rosamond answered, "We're just waiting to see what happens next." The light was getting too sparce to see the cross-stitch, to make out the owl in the tree, but she could see Clyde's face, his cheeks scratchy with stubble, his nose and chin pale and a little lumpy, like biscuit dough. When he turned to look at her, his eyes were dark but shiny. She could see them yet, in this light.

"That's all," she said. She let loose of his hand and slid her hand up his arm, drawing closer. "Just resting here together."

The sky was full purple when Ray arrived at Mia Robins's basement door. He looked down at her, clearly tired out from the sermon—it had emptied him—and yet she couldn't believe how solid he was, how *here*.

"Hello, you," she said.

He paused. Something in her tone caught his attention. "Hi," he said.

She took his arm and led him back out the door, across the small concrete slab of porch and onto the back lawn. "We need a blanket," she said, and left him for a minute, going inside to fetch one.

"All right." Ray was easy. He'd take a blanket on the ground or not. He'd sit with her at the table or leave her alone, if she'd rather. He would be here or not be here—whatever she wanted.

She returned with a sleeping bag one of Mia's sons had owned and unzipped it. He helped her spread it on the cool grass.

They lay there next to each other, holding hands. The sleeping bag wasn't long enough for Ray; his feet were on the grass. They looked upward, watching the sky deepen, the stars appear. The first few came so slowly, Agnes had half believed they'd never come, but then the rest emerged too fast to catch them all. She was thinking of her father, expecting him to show up at any moment. She felt safe there with Ray, and she settled into the quiet, wondering.

Cassie Stewart was alone in her room. She had gone to the revival and had seen Rosamond Rogers and the others kneel in the aisle and in the pews. She had heard the sidewalk preacher carry on about Jericho, the stranger who was the Christ, and the holy ground. Her father was asleep now on the sofa, and her mother was filling drinks at the fast-food restaurant down the highway.

It had been a week since she and Vincent had been caught by the woman in the blue high heels, and Cassie had grown bored waiting for their crimes to go public—no one, it seemed, knew anything. She hadn't heard from Vincent since he dropped her off that day, had barely had a chance to speak to him at school. He had turned cool toward her, and she was tired of writing poems. She lay on her bed and played a game with the half-empty bottle of her father's pain pills she'd taken from the bathroom. She lined the pills up on her bedspread. They were tiny and white and completely round—she marveled at their uniformity, at their miniatureness, like a dollhouse tea service. She checked the digital clock on her nightstand. Every time the number five or zero appeared without her mother's coming home, her father's rousing himself from the sofa, or the phone's ringing—Vincent's call—she took a pill. She washed each down with a sip of ginger ale.

Vincent was in his father's garage. His fingers were wrapped up in gauze, applied by his mother who had found him when she arrived home in the early afternoon, his fingers delicately slashed and bloodied. She, crying, had wrapped his cuts too tightly and his fingertips tingled at the first. They were numb now. He was watching his father solder together scraps of metal to patch up the side door of the Buick he was resurrecting, the torch a soaring blue flame he maneuvered, its light reflected in his safety goggles. He planned to take an engine from a smashed-up Chevrolet. He would use the exhaust pipes off an old Fiat, would custom-order the windshield to fit the frame of the Buick.

Agnes, lying on the blanket with Ray outside her apartment, miles away from the Bailey house, said, "I'm not sure what all you were talking about in the church." The trees beyond them rustled in the night breeze. "I understand it," she said, "but I don't believe it." They lay holding hands, and Ray rubbed his thumb across the first knuckle of her index finger. She pulled his hand to her mouth and, opening his fingers, kissed his palm. "I only want to. I only *want* to believe."

"No one believes on his own," Ray told her. "True belief is the work of the Spirit. One only has to allow it, to open up to it."

Vincent's father removed his safety goggles and whistled. He had turned the side of the car smooth with his flame; it looked as if it all belonged together. He said, "You're a damn fool to cut yourself like that. Your mother is wrenched apart over you."

"Someday all of these houses will be empty," Agnes whispered to Ray. "Someday soon everyone will be gone." She thought she saw Hatley then, picking his way through the far trees, but as quick as she looked straight on, he was gone. She moved closer to Ray and gripped his hand tighter. "I *want* to believe."

"The wanting comes first," Ray told her. "That's the first part of it."

"Damn fool," Vincent's father said. His face still held the marks from the goggles. He was sitting on an overturned bucket. Weary, he let his head drop back against the wall. The Buick sat hollow in front of them. "We'll have to wait until your fingers heal to start the painting," he said. "If you keep yourself whole, you can help with the painting." Since the day Vincent found Percy Harding's body, his father hadn't looked at him. Now he did look, but quick, closing his eyes and rubbing at his eyelids with his thumbs. "Damn fool," he said again, softly.

"The wanting, the thinking it out, finding out you need to believe, it's always the first step to anything. That's where everyone starts. You're starting just fine," Ray said.

Vincent nodded. "All right," he said. He was imagining holding the blue flame to the palm of his hand, to his cut-up fingers: pain that bad, he thought, wouldn't even feel like pain. It would be something else, something *beyond* pain. He still carried with him a superstition of thick blue skies and the flight of birds. Since that morning, he didn't trust a thing until he saw it move in some way. He looked for breezes to move tree limbs, for light to flicker in the windows of still houses.

"I can do it," he told his father.

Cassie lay in her bedroom watching the clock, keeping up her game, the window long black, until weightlessness came to her limbs and everything felt disconnected. Then she slept.

Revival was on for five days, and Ray preached on the fall of Jericho every night. He spent the second night speaking more on the stranger's imperative to Joshua to remove his sandals and connected it to the story of Moses and the burning bush. He spoke on the preeminence of *I Am,* the forever God. He worked his way to the part where the Lord ordered Joshua to lead the people in a nightly march around the city, and finally, the last day: the sounding of the trumpet, the people's shouts, and the crashing of the wall. He invited them to imagine the rubble, the dust in the air. He enjoined them to recall—Jericho had been militarily *impenetrable.* "Believe me when I say," Ray told the people, "God is all-powerful."

Before what had become of Cassie Stewart was known, Stephanie Jameson, the girl in the library, had sensed something was wrong. That night, after everyone had left the revival and settled into their houses, after Rosamond had taken the chicken pot pie from the oven, had her dinner, served Clyde, and later returned to fall asleep on Clyde Winston's bed, after Pastor Ray and Agnes lay on the sleeping bag, talking and waiting, Stephanie the library girl remained in her library dungeon. She had finished the encyclopedia of fishing—a book she'd admit she hadn't read word for word, but she had at least looked at every single page—and risen to stretch. She rolled her head on her shoulders to work out the kinks, rubbed her eyes, and then felt it, something *strange*.

For a time, since she met the drifty-boy—*sexy stranger*, she'd called him in her diary—her reading campaign had been a sham. She hadn't really read those hundred books. For a time she kept the library as a hideout, a place to go and remember her encounter with the drifter-boy, to rework the comment she'd made to him again and again until it sounded first existential and brilliant, and then plainly idiotic, and then once more utterly inspired. So *deep*—she wasn't sure herself what she had meant. She'd realized this was what she had wanted the whole time. Writing all those poems, the whole bit about having the right to choose life or its opposite, all that time what she'd wanted was something to think about and the space and quiet to do just that—to think. Then, after the thinking, she actually settled into reading. The night of the revival, while Ray was preaching about holy ground and walls collapsing, she picked up Plutarch. She couldn't *believe* the Goliath library had the book, no matter how crappy and hard to read the translation was.

What she actually heard was nothing: a fleeting and random cessation of activity, all the small noises of ordinary life pausing, a flicker of silence. Chiefly it was the dehumidifier behind the librarian's desk gurgling to a stop, but Stephanie, struggling through the first agonizing pages of the misfires of Caesar's youth, did not recognize it. She hadn't heard the constant rumble of the dehumidifier before, and now she only heard its absence. She heard quiet, a quiet that went on and on, the streets emptied, the night birds stilled, the summer insects not started yet.

Even after word of yet another grave event—a girl in the trailer park found dead—found its way to the Tuesday Diner and the post office, to the high school, Pastor Ray preached on Jericho. His message felt that important; nothing could stop it. On the third night, he reminded his listeners of the Lord's directions. The people should *march* around Goliath every day for a week. "On the final day, the day of completion, they would circle the city seven times, then give a shout," he told them. Cassie Stewart's tragic death was in the newspaper, and people talked it over on their telephones. It was different from the death of Percy Harding; this time the sadness was greater than the shock, and people attended to it in quieter ways. They tried to recall the girl: so few had known her. On Friday, the last night of the revival, Ray Winston stood before the gathered people and said, "Only now can anything we say or do be true. Do we believe? Is God all-powerful even now? All-knowing? All-*loving*?"

Stephanie, who left the library near midnight still feeling ill at ease, learned of Cassie's death from one of the original six suicide poets the next morning at school. Sarah, the pretty one, stopped her in the hallway before the first bell. She explained what had happened, the overdose. She was crying, and her voice was hoarse. "Someone actually did it," she told Stephanie.

Stephanie didn't cry at first; she slumped against the row of lockers. She said, "This is *so* sad," but her words sounded too thin even in her own ears. "I can't believe this," she said, and Sarah nodded.

It was another nothing thing to say, but it was how most of the other young people, learning the news, felt. Over the next few days, they told each other it was her right, her *choice*, echoing Stephanie's own words from months earlier, but they couldn't even convince themselves. None of them was bold enough to say the other thing, the later mottoes about one's dead self being one's best self. Alone, they simply whispered Cassie's name.

Pastor Ray continued preaching about Jericho on the streets even after the revival. He couldn't stop. He had left his other question—whether or not people could still trust in an all-powerful God now—unanswered, and instead focused on the thing he meant for them to do. He stood in front of the church and told those passing by, "He told the people to circle the city seven times." He said it standing outside Lucky Grocery, sitting at the counter at the diner. He continued, "Today I'm only asking you to do it once. A parade." He kept his usual unassuming air, preaching as if it didn't matter too much to *him* if they listened, which had the desired effect of putting the imperative on his audience. It was their job to listen, to do: "There *will* be a parade in Goliath." He folded his arms, said, "The question is, are you with us? Will you be among the ones to recapture our own town?"

Finally it made sense to the people. A parade. It really could happen. There might be this much left to Goliath: a parade, a baseball game. The death of the girl in the trailer park saddened them, but maybe there was more to the world than sadness. This universe, if not Goliath, was big enough for both hope and sorrow to exist simultaneously.

Mia spurred them on with her phone calls, "I just really want this to happen," she said. "Oh, I fear for Rosamond if it doesn't," she intoned darkly. Often there was a pause on the other end of the line, but it didn't seem right for anyone but her closest friends to inquire. Even then she didn't bring up the missing trinket box with the gold tooth inside, or her suspicions, but only said, "She has her heart set on this, you know."

People knew. And if they'd ever felt pity for Rosamond, they felt it now. She had grayed and wrinkled practically overnight, and they'd noticed a slowness about her—gone was her perky *snip-snip* down the Main Street sidewalk. Now she walked with care; she spoke with care. They'd even seen her kneel with care in the center aisle of the church during the revival. "She's sorry," they told one another, though no one could put into words exactly what crime she had committed.

They found sign-up sheets for Rosamond's parade and Clyde's baseball game at the diner and the drugstore. Wives signed their husbands up, and children found the news when they returned home from school: they were leaving Goliath, moving elsewhere, but first they would play baseball and they would dress up as a caterpillar or in their Scouts uniform. They would carry a flag or a baton or a bag of candy, and they would march in a parade. Throughout town, the sad news came through the ordinary gossip channels, but the other news, the idea that there were things yet to be done in Goliath, last moments, came through their telephone lines, from the sidewalk preacher.

Clyde Winston and Marty Pickard, whose wife had finally called after nearly five months' silence, met during this time to clear the lot behind the cemetery for the baseball game. The rocks gave easily in the mud, and Marty, working the far end of the lot, pitched them into the ditch beside the field. She was coming back for a visit. "Don't think too much of it, Marty," she'd said. "I don't know anything for sure," she said. Near noon, Harold Clarkson arrived to help clear away the bits of gravel from the field. Working together, the three men bent over rakes they'd each brought from their own garages. Harold, ninety-six years old, rested often, and Marty favored the arm he'd broken months before, but Clyde kept at it for hours, working hard, talking little.

"The thing about it," Clyde said, "is that baseball always was. There's not a moment in time when it began. It probably started with a boy and a stick tossing a ball in the air, seeing if he could hit it. That's all. Just a boy and a stick." The three men watched the trees bob in the whispery breeze, and they felt the sun, warm on the backs of their necks.

The young people were anxious about their current situation; they were all sad in the way of Stephanie Jameson, and there was nothing for them to do about it. Together, they faced a confusing loss—the loss of a person they'd never cared much about, a person they'd paid hardly any attention to. That strange trailer park girl who read her poem just that once, who hung out with Vincent Bailey, himself a normal kid turned scary odd, a kid they didn't know what to do with, whether to let him go off-the-edge-weird or try to pull him back. They had mostly in the past ignored Cassie Stewart, but now they couldn't think of anything else but her. It was a frightening phenomenon, peering into their closet-door mirrors and realizing that here was a person who could in a matter of minutes down the pills, press the blade, drive into an overpass.

Ms. Chatley, the sexy biology teacher with cages of mice in the back of her room, turned her classes into mourning sessions, claiming these children—they heard that word *children*—needed an opportunity to express their grief. Most of the students rebuffed her efforts, but instead carried their sadness with them, hearing in the slam of lockers, in their friends' voices, in the scuffling sounds of shoes on linoleum tile, a confusing strain of hope. A parade? A baseball game? It was disorienting, almost frightening, that hope.

Vincent Bailey, who was not in Ms. Chatley's section of freshman physical science and who had not attended the revival, was called into the principal's office a few days after word of Cassie's death had circulated through the school. The principal peered at him over the smudged lenses of his bifocals. "You've lost a good friend," he observed, then waited for a response.

Vincent nodded, suffered a few moments' wordless inspection, and was finally dismissed. He shuffled back into the 8:05 scramble, everyone rushing to homeroom. He stood by his locker, watching all the other students pass. It seemed to him, in that moment, looking out on the others, that the mouse he'd swallowed months earlier for Cassie had not yet died but was still alive inside him, trying to find traction on the slippery walls of his stomach, attempting escape. Odd to think of the mouse, and then when he did, it seemed almost natural for his thoughts to shift to Boulder Man. Vincent imagined the superhero, his chiseled rock muscles and molten metal eyes, his iron fist thrust forward, surging through the ground, the linoleum tiles of the hallway buckling and rippling from below. He saw Boulder Man emerging from the earth, clods of dirt falling from his hair, and he also saw his father standing by the junk pile, the same as the day he'd spied him looking about. This time, though, in Vincent's mind, his father raised his hands and the junk parts floated up to meet in mid-air. His father orchestrated the entire engine-construction in the air by beckoning the parts with his fingers, waving them together, watching their connections like a magic show. While he imagined this, the tiny white mouse inside him scratched and gnawed, desperate to find a way out.

Stephanie, the former leader of the suicide cult, worried she would stumble upon a construction paper poem. A forgotten one, fallen through the slats in the lockers, swept up and redeposited on the floor of the cafeteria or in the girls' restroom, or simply a snatch of pink tucked into the checkout envelope in the back of a library book. She was always searching as she shuffled through the hallways, and the students around her, who were very sad but still felt guilty at the shallowness of their grief—it was impossible, it seemed, to be sad enough—walked about without looking at one another. Their eyes flitted away, and they bumped their elbows into doorjambs and locker knobs as they drifted.

And Vincent, standing in the hallway, waiting for the day to end, hated every single one of them. All of the numb, black-sweatered, skittery others passing by him. He spent the day sinking away from them, and when it was time to go home, he started out by foot.

FOURTEEN

The next week the people of Goliath busied themselves planning a parade, a baseball game, and a funeral. The employees of Goliath Bank and Trust met in the board room to drink coffee and plan their float. One of the tellers proposed they go patriotic, and the branch manager, who liked the idea, wondered aloud: Stars and stripes? An eagle? A second teller volunteered expertise with tissue-paper carnations, and at last a flower mosaic was sketched out on the back of an outdated memo.

Hatley Rogers had stayed in Goliath after the revival. He rented a one-bedroom trailer and wandered about as a lost man, standing outside the downtown shops. He peered into the windows. Whether he was studying his own reflection in the glass or the people inside was impossible to tell. He walked down the residential streets, on the sidewalks, and ventured down to the old river behind the church, inching so close to the edge his shoes were muddied. He ate at the Tuesday Diner. The waitress who took his order—ham on wheat, no mayo—lifted her eyebrows in question at Wally Thumb, who only shrugged back. He didn't know the man. The stranger took his meals alone.

He had aged as badly as Rosamond had, though it was likely his decline had not come as quickly. The dazzling blue-purple eyes that had won him entrance into so many living rooms during his years as a door-to-door salesman had faded to watery gray. He walked a bit crookedly. His hands trembled. People were reminded of the last great Goliath-wanderer, the drifter boy, who had been as young as this man was old, and they worried—though the thefts had stopped, the thieves had not yet been caught. This stranger walked with a limp, though, and rested often in his wanderings, and there was comfort in this: How much harm could an old man do?

Agnes alone recognized him. Since the night of the revival, she had spotted him throughout town and followed several yards behind him, along the streets, beyond the river, behind the factory where the trailer park met the woods. She ducked behind trees and kept her distance, wanting only to watch the man who had been her father. She was not ready to speak to him, and he likewise didn't approach her. It tortured her a little, though, how aimlessly he seemed to wander: Why *had* he come back?

Rosamond, occupied with the parade campaign, with sitting out on the front porch with Clyde Winston most evenings, watching the street before them disappear into darkness, remained ignorant of Hatley's reappearance for a full two weeks. Besides everything else, there was this fresh tragedy, this Cassie Stewart, to grieve. Rosamond recognized the girl from the papers: one of the thieves. She had spoken with that girl, she had *caught* her. She could have saved her.

Vincent—tortured in an entirely different way by Cassie's death—walked home from school each day. He went slowly and refused the offers of half a dozen drivers who stopped and asked if he wanted a lift home. Each time the driver pressed, asking again, before finally shrugging and taking off, watching Vincent in the rearview mirror until he disappeared. One concerned motorist even went home and called the police, asking that they go out there and pick him up. Vincent walked in the weeds and yanked at the tallest stalks as he went. The wounds on his fingertips were scabbed over, healing but still sensitive, stinging with the weeds.

People in town deliberated over which position they would play at Clyde Winston's baseball game. All the old men wanted outfield, while the young men and many of the women put in their requests to play first base. The principal at the high school put an asterisk next to his own name and wrote *pitcher*. Members of the volunteer fire department met at the station and planned to deck their truck with streamers and to invite children to ride onboard for the parade. They would have a spaghetti dinner fundraiser after the parade and game were over. Pastor Myers and his wife set out to visit the Stewarts at the trailer park and gently inquire if they needed any assistance with the arrangements. The funeral was planned for Friday.

Charlotte Branch made a basket of candy and Tylenol for the Stewart family and asked one of her afternoon girls to drive it over. The afternoon girl, a junior at the high school, spied Vincent walking through the weeds on the side of the road and, as so many others did, offered him a ride. He looked straight at her before shaking his head, and the girl was discomfited. She called her friends that night: Vincent Bailey had a murderous look about him. The stare he fixed on her was so frightening, she couldn't forget it. She had trouble sleeping, and she couldn't stop talking about it. She conjured up a complicated theory about how Vincent had killed Cassie Stewart and then made it look like suicide, and though her friends were tempted to believe, they didn't. "She was his only friend," they countered, to which the girl replied, "Maybe Vincent Bailey doesn't *want* any friends."

Vincent, upon arriving home from each afternoon's long walk, stood looking at the car his father was building. He had been putting it together, not in the air, but on his worktable, with his own hands. The outside was completed, and already the motor was in place. His father had even pulled the brake lines through and positioned the tires. Vincent pulled back the old sheet that covered the car. He put his hands on the hood and waited until he could convince himself it was warm, the engine trying to cool after a long ride. He lifted the hood and bent over, touching the pieces inside. Afterward, he lay down on the grass, outside of the garage, and pictured airplanes falling down on him. He was waiting for his own suicide to happen, but he couldn't coax it along. Vincent stared into the sky and hoped for someone to come, to start up that handmade car and drive it right over his chest, concentrating on the fantasy until he heard his ribs crack under the crush of black rubber.

Yet everything Vincent saw—sky, cloud, tree branches shifting in the wind—beat with import, with an insistence that the world on some level—be it only the molecular level, the level of chemistry or physics—make sense. He couldn't sink quite low enough to dissolve it all away.

New For Sale signs had popped up in all the front yards, and by the end of the week few Goliath houses weren't on the market. Charlotte Branch, alone in her store, sighed to herself. Those houses would never sell. Her store stayed quiet all morning, and she was reminded of the autumn afternoon months earlier when a breathless, stiff-acting Rosamond Rogers had swept into her store and purchased a letter opener with a cardinal carved into its handle. Instead of sitting at her counter and reading a magazine, Charlotte stood by the window and looked out at Main Street. The parade sign-up sheets were full, and Charlotte was glad. Let Rosamond Rogers have her day. Let her have the retired police chief; everyone could see that happening. Let her bury that cursed letter opener and get on with it already.

Every young person in Goliath besides Vincent Bailey had plans to attend the funeral, but Cassie's parents at the last minute canceled the service. They were leaving Goliath, taking Cassie's ashes with them up to Virginia, where Cassie's mother's sister lived. A short obituary in the newspaper gave little information save Cassie's dates of birth and death, but the science teacher, in her efforts to help the student body grieve its loss, announced a last-minute memorial service to be held after school on Friday in the library. Few planned to attend.

The rumor Charlotte Branch's afternoon girl began about Vincent's having killed Cassie had leaked out all over the school by then. A former friend of Vincent's was gathering his books at his locker when one of his classmates told him. He closed his locker, shaking his head, and told the small group gathering around him, "No way. Vincent wouldn't do that." Other students countered, pointing out Vincent's strange behavior since he found the corpse of Percy Harding, and one even said, "He planned to kill her from the start. That was the whole reason he started hanging out with her." This girl applied loose psychology: "He saw a dead body and then wanted to make one himself. He wanted to kill somebody."

This had begun a division among the students. A girl named Holly Bligh, who lived out even deeper in the country than the Bailey family, told her friends at lunch, "The truth is, we *all* should have been Cassie Stewart's friends. The reason she died isn't because Vincent Bailey was her friend and somehow talked her into taking those pills. No. The reason she died was because we *weren't* her friends. It's all on us." She shoved her trash into her lunch bag and strode out. The cafeteria fell quiet, and the students finished their lunches in silence.

The girl's lunchroom pronouncement was followed by a short speech by one of Vincent's old friends one morning in home-room. Squirrel Jones said, "Vincent Bailey is a friend of mine. He didn't kill nobody." Stephanie Jameson, still rattled by the moment in the library when the world fell quiet, shifted in her seat, listening. Later, the student body president ended the morn-ing announcements he voiced over the PA with "Godspeed. Be kind to each other."

The students banded together and began to speak up on the Vincent/Cassie issue less and less in Ms. Chatley's class. One student even told her, "This is about us, Ms. Chatley. No of-fense, and we know you mean to do a good thing here, but this is about *us*."

Stephanie began to think she might say something. Make some sort of pronouncement, officially withdraw her old pro-suicide platform. It had sort of gathered up inside her—the urge to say something—while she listened to Squirrel Jones and the little girl from the country and even this student, the boy who opposed the biology teacher's attempts at forging a grief circle. But it was so little, what she could say, and in homeroom class, she looked around and saw that no one was listening to her anyway. She was no longer the leader of anything.

By the end of the week, most of the students had fallen into the Vincent camp, and when Ms. Chatley announced the after-school memorial service, no one had to say they weren't going. They never said anything at all, even the former leader of the sui-cide cult, who continued to observe how little noticed she had become among the students. It was right back to the days before any of this—before the first poem, before the clock and the diner and the hours she'd spent reading in the library.

The walkout at the last bell, the students filing into the woods and surrounding Vincent Bailey—everyone knew he skipped his afternoon classes to smoke there—was completely unplanned.

The afternoon was warm, and the sky full of high white clouds. He had put out his cigarette and was now trying to doze against the trunk of a tree. The sun burned through his closed eyelids, though, even in the shade of the trees.

When the stream of students arrived, surrounding him, Vincent stood up, observing each face. His fellow classmates, maybe twenty or thirty of them, stood among the trees. Some had backpacks dangling from their shoulders, some stood squinting at him, curious, and others folded their arms and simply waited, somehow confident Vincent Bailey, who had held his peace for so long, would speak now. He said nothing for a long moment, looking from face to face, to the branches overhead, squinting into the bright sun a quarter of the way down the sky.

Finally he spoke: "I have one of her poems."

Stephanie watched him from among the others. He closed his eyes and began to recite the one about the doorless house from memory: *No way to enter or to leave, the house held itself closed. The demons could not depart, the angels could not enter.*

He finished the poem and left, simply walked through them, and the others went out to the buses, which had waited for them, or began walking home. As they went, though, they rehearsed Cassie Stewart's words silently inside their heads.

An auction was held the following week at the factory. There had been announcements in all the newspapers, and traffic from outside Goliath clogged its streets. Walt Roberts, who had been just a few weeks earlier the lead machinist, sat on a stool in the warehouse and called out bids on electric fans, half a dozen hand trucks, and a number of rusted heat lamps. Rosamond Rogers, sitting at a table that was itself scheduled for auction, kept a record of what was sold and to whom, and one of the girls from accounting accepted the checks and wrote the receipts. Anthony Harding, Percy's older brother, the one who, months earlier, had called the workers together to relay Percy's death, returned to town for the sale. He stood in the back with his arms crossed, saying little. In the afternoon, he walked through the empty rooms and touched the walls, as if to check how secure they were, and then he left, slipping out before the auction was finished.

Marty Pickard was one of the loaders called on to strap office chairs into the beds of bidders' pickup trucks. He set the mammoth microwave oven from the break room inside one bidder's trunk and helped load the soda machine into a moving van. His wife Janice, who had arrived for her visit a few days earlier, rose from her lawn chair on the front porch when his truck pulled in the gravel drive. He swung out, and she took the steps down to the walkway. "Babe," he said, laying his hands on her shoulders. By that word, *babe,* he meant to convey the disconnection he felt, the surreal quality of a day in which the factory was broken into pieces and auctioned away. She nodded. "I know," she said.

Office supplies, the coffeemaker, the worktables, the unused desk blotters, all was auctioned off, carried away, and then the great cinder-block building was as empty as a cathedral. Rosamond left carrying a cardboard box filled with the little nothings she'd found in her desk drawers—pens and such—and started up Main Street.

She intended to go see Ryan Harding once more, to have her say, to explain what needed explaining, forgiving, and to do what she could to give Percy's ghost rest. She felt a sort of presence—or rather the *chance* of a presence—similar to the inkling, the hope she'd held those first days after Percy died. The feeling someone had just left her or would be joining her soon. Walking up Main Street toward the Harding house, there might be clues in the newly budded trees, the damp grass. Small confirmations, encouragements. *Yes,* go on. The early evening breeze was supple and green-smelling.

It was dusk when she arrived at the Hardings', and though

the house was mostly dark, Rosamond was fairly certain Ryan
was somewhere inside. His sweet-faced wife and children had
left town weeks earlier—returned, Rosamond assumed, to
Baltimore—and though there was little, if anything left to do, it
seemed he just wouldn't leave on the night of the auction. Rosamond herself had already been officially released from her secre-
tarial duties by the powers that be, the conglomerate that had
purchased the factory and the Harding Furniture name, and so
now *she* was free to go. Funny that this had only occurred to her
at the end as she took the steps to the door. She peered into the
vine-and-leaf patterned stained glass windows flanking the massive front door, though it was impossible to see anything inside,
dark as it was, ornate as the stained glass was, and finally pressed
the bell.

In an instant, she realized she *could* go. Away from Goliath.
There were no longer any official duties keeping her, and this
recollection brought on a sudden inward spasm of fear. If nothing
held her to Goliath, could it be nothing held her at all? And yet,
she kept standing there. There, at the entrance to the Harding
home, all that heft and polish she'd always felt approaching the
house, or walking inside it, or simply passing by. She remembered
the night so many months ago when she'd crossed the lawn to beg
a tea bag from Clyde, how unmoored she'd felt.

Another reason Ryan wouldn't leave, or at least not so quickly:
he had something of Percy in him. Didn't he? She checked her
shoes, exactly as she had done that other long ago night when
she had stood in this same place. Again, she wore pretty shoes,
but not the same red pumps she'd worn before. These were simple
beige, but with an elegant bronze buckle. This time she had no
coat to adjust, so she straightened her blouse, her skirt. He *had* to
have something of Percy in him. This was a thing to cling to, a
reason to stand here, to press the bell once more, to wait.

Finally there came noise, a shuffling from within the house. He appeared, and this time he didn't look too young to manage a company. His hair was just as blond and his eyes as blue as ever, but he was squinting hard at her and holding that squint a beat longer than was comfortable. He was unshaven and wore a baggy gray jogging suit. It took a moment for Rosamond to place it: he was wearing his father's clothes.

"Rosamond," he said at last, and stumbled awkwardly for a moment before inviting her in. She sensed she wasn't altogether welcome, but she thanked him and followed him inside, feeling strangely dignified in how unwelcome she was. She had not approached the Harding house since the afternoon of the viewing and had not stepped inside it for quite some time, years. Seeing it now, she was taken aback—the place was wide-open and dark, nearly empty. Gone were the massive pieces of furniture and the clusters of crystal and bronze knickknacks, the antique sewing boxes and the bud vases, the paintings on the walls. Instead, there in the sitting room—the very room where Martha Harding used to hold her prayer sessions—was a recliner, an aluminum TV tray at its side, and a desk lamp perched precariously on the windowsill behind the chair. The foyer, where they stood, was empty, and Rosamond could feel the grit of dirt and dust beneath her shoes. Everything was scantly lit, and the house smelled of dust and coffee and souring milk.

"I pared it down pretty good in here when Cathy and the kids moved back to Baltimore," he explained. "The movers took it all away." He folded his arms. "I'm in the study, packing." He paused. "It's good you came by." He unfolded his arms and laced his fingers, stretching his arms out. He'd gone from squinting too coldly to smiling too warmly. "It's fitting, you know? You being here? I'm going through his desk."

His desk. Of course he had had a desk at home, probably used the same kind of pens—with an extra-fine blue tip—here that he used at the office. He probably drank coffee at this desk, paid bills

there. Made calls. She had never before pictured it, though—
Percy's *second* desk—so she expected it to look exactly like his
office desk, sleek, with deep drawers and metal drawer handles
in the utilitarian style of those days when Percy first took over.

But the room he led her to was as full—*plentiful* was the word
that came to Rosamond—as the rest of the house was sparse.
Here, in Percy's study, the walls were lined with mahogany bookshelves, and the bookshelves were crammed with leather-bound
books and knickknacks, framed pictures of Ryan as a child,
Ryan's children, a few clocks set in crystal—gifts, Rosamond
supposed—and a miniature marble bust of an unidentified man
of historical import. The desk itself was massive, made of dark,
polished wood, and its surface was mostly clear, holding just a
telephone and a cup of pens and pencils. Rosamond also noticed
a half-empty plastic bottle of some kind of cheap liquor; she
couldn't make out the label. Behind the desk, a window looking
out over the side yard trees let in the pink orange light of the
setting sun.

"I wanted to pack up his desk myself," Ryan said, shrugging.
When she'd last seen him, she'd accused him of bringing down
the company. Of *ruining* it. Now here this boy, slightly drunk,
standing in Percy's study, unable to pull a single book from its
shelf. He shrugged again and touched the back of Percy's chair.
This boy who could not bring himself to sit in his dead father's
chair.

"Do you know," Rosamond asked, "what your father did the
day you were born? He went to work." She smiled. "Maybe that
seems awful to you. It did to me. At first it did. I remember wondering about what he was *doing* there, in the office, when his
brand-new baby boy and his wife were at the hospital." She shook
her head. She was standing, leaning against the back of a chair
facing Percy's desk. "You have to understand something about
your father. He loved the furniture business. He *loved* it. He once

said to me, 'Rosamond, do you know what we are doing? We are making *furniture*. People buy these chairs and sideboards and tables and headboards, and then they bring them into their *homes*.'

"It was noble to him. Going into the office on the day his son was born. And the other days he went, all the days of your growing up. It was *noble;* he wanted to pass it on to you. His favorite thing in this world—his *only* thing in this world—and he wanted to give it to you."

Here Ryan smirked. "I guess he did just that. He gave it to me."

She hesitated. "He didn't mean to do this to you. He didn't." Then, quieter, "I was very fond of your father."

He stared at her. "You loved him."

We should be the leavers, Percy had told her once, many years ago. *You and I.* The *leavers.* He was speaking philosophically, perhaps hypothetically, but not practically. He didn't mean they should actually leave, together or alone; instead, he meant they should be *capable* of leaving. He was speaking of what ought to be possible, and that was all.

After a long moment she spoke: "Yes."

What she wanted to do then was to turn and hurry back down the bare hallway and out the front door, down the steps, away. Exactly as she had run away the day of the viewing. She wanted to clatter down that rambling driveway as clumsily as she pleased, to release herself to barefoot wandering across the sidewalks.

Instead she asked Ryan, "Where are the boxes?"

He brought them out and a pile of newspapers, and together they began taking the books off the shelves, solid old tomes Percy had likely never opened. They wrapped up dusty picture frames, opened the desk drawers, sorted things. What remained unsaid was a fact too obvious to bear stating: Ryan had not, as Rosamond once said, ruined the company. They worked long and spoke little and made small discoveries along the way: a wooden ink blotter from who knew how long ago, rubber bands gone brittle, a mess of paper clips, the suspect bottle of Scotch, and a stack of gift chocolate, still wrapped.

Rosamond thought of asking how Ryan's wife was, his children. She might also ask about Lela; she'd heard she was opening a plant nursery, of all things, in Idaho, where she'd been living with her sister for so many months now. One of the neighborhood ladies had connections to the Harding cousins in Raleigh, and the news, what little the Hardings knew of Percy's widow's current situation, had found its way to Goliath through these connections. It was also known that she had just moved out of her sister's house and taken her own apartment. She wasn't coming back. Also, she was growing her hair long, as it had been when she'd first moved to Goliath more than thirty years ago. "It suits her," Mia had said, though of course she hadn't actually seen this new Lela Harding with her own eyes. "She'll be all right," she predicted. "She was never meant for Goliath." Mia had a way of talking, no matter her limited knowledge of a topic, that made Rosamond lean toward believing her. "She'll be just fine," she said.

So while Rosamond was curious about Lela, and she wanted to mention her in a generous light, to show she bore her no ill will—she had, in the space of the last several months, given up a good portion of her disdain for the woman—she did not want to break the easeful quiet between her and Ryan. How companionable it was now, all the sifting and the sorting and the packing.

They spoke instead only of the material things directly in front of them, this thimble—a thimble in his desk drawer?—this sports magazine, this half-gone roll of antacids. They chronicled every little thing, simply speaking the names out loud—eraser nub, receipt, box of pencils. Rosamond thought they might find important papers, like insurance policies or bank statements, but they found only incidentals—thank-you cards and newspaper clippings—and she didn't ask. Likely, she reasoned, everything important was in a box at the bank. She was glad of this: it was so much better to find the crumbling rubber bands, the half-eaten roll of Rolaids. They kept on, working together in a way they hadn't in all the months she'd been Ryan's secretary. She relished the rhythm of it. She had spent many long hours working with Percy in much the same way, in a small room not unlike this one, the two of them bent over papers on a desk, talking, sorting. After an hour or so, she opened the chocolates, and soon after that she drank some of the boy's terrible gin.

As she was leaving, she thought it again: *You didn't ruin anything.* They paused together there a moment at the door, and he folded his arms, said, "I'm glad you came." She nodded. She kissed his cheek, then patted it. He grimaced a little; it was a reminder he was a baby yet. So *young.* She was still a little unsteady from the gin and she worried he'd insist on walking her home, but he said only, "Careful, now," and let her go, standing in the doorway, still in those baggy old running clothes, growing smaller, standing there, as she descended back to the street.

The people still living in Goliath were idle inside their homes. They were holding on for three things to happen: Rosamond's parade, Clyde's baseball game, and the unlikely sale of their homes. The houses were priced so low that the Morning Glories at the Tuesday Diner, who were among the few resolved to stay put, joked that the Jaycees could buy up all of Main Street and the following October stage not just a haunted house as they had during Halloweens past, but an entire haunted village.

In the evenings after supper, families and couples and old friends trooped down the sidewalk to the lot Clyde had snagged for a field. They were a motley arrangement of old men dressed in wide-collared golf shirts and ladies in culottes, fathers in khaki shorts, exposing the palest, hairiest legs, and middle-aged women—the mothers of Goliath—in pastel jogging suits. The teenagers wore jeans and rock T-shirts, and the little girls had uncombed hair that streamed wild behind them when they ran. The lucky children, those whose mothers weren't looking, had shed their shoes and darted barefoot across the grass and dirt, weaving through the adults tentatively flexing their hands inside their baseball gloves.

There were two teams. Clyde had appointed Harold Clarkson and Marty Pickard, who had helped him clear the field, the coaches. They set about training. Marty directed his team to break up into pairs to practice throwing and catching; most were clumsy at it, scrambling off to retrieve lost balls, a few even putting their hands over their faces to protect against their partner's erratic lobs. He bobbed among them, punching one fist into the open mitt of the other hand, issuing encouragement. *Good throw. Good catch. Good hustle. Good eye. Good, good, good.* Harold, who had recruited his sixty-eight-year-old son to assist him, had his team sit in the grass and hear a short lecture on the rules and ethics of the game. He explained the philosophy of baseball: *We want everyone to make it home, you hear?* Afterward, he lined his players up and, one by one, his son Grant instructed them on how to hold a bat, how to choke up, how to swing. They did all this without anyone actually pitching the ball. Harold explained: *A man must learn to crawl before he can walk.*

It was hard to tell if Clyde Winston, who stood apart and squinted out at the players, aged nine to ninety-six, was pleased. When Ray came, though, Clyde nodded at the commotion: baseball bats swinging at the air, potbellied men chasing down balls, growing so winded they couldn't speak, old ladies running to base.

He said, "They'll remember this."

Later, during a scrimmage, a fly ball was hit by a retired bank teller, and everyone on field and in the dugout watched the ball soar in a perfect high, short arc, dropping soundly just shy of first base. No one had tried to catch it, and there was a moment's uncertainty before Harold's first baseman, a high school senior, scrambled after it.

Agnes had not used the address her mother had given her. In the end she'd been unable to. Afraid. She had sent no letter, and yet here Hatley was in Goliath. He'd come unbidden. It was as if merely *thinking* of writing him had summoned him.

He ate at the Tuesday Diner, he went down to the river behind the church, and—Agnes finally discovered—he slept in a single-bedroom trailer at the far edge of the same trailer park where Cassie Stewart had died. She was still following him, and the irony of her being the pursuer when it had not been so long ago that she had been the pursued was not lost on her. She told Ray, "I guess I'm getting my due." Hatley had been coming near her, she realized, for years. She was certain: this was the man who appeared across from her apartment at McGraw, the man she had spotted at the boiled peanut stop on the way to the mountains. He had finally come this close. What was stopping him from closing those last few inches?

Agnes told Ray, "He's changed his mind about seeing me." They were sitting at her kitchen table among long-cold dinner dishes, watching the windows go black.

She fidgeted while Ray thought the situation over. "It's why I came back, you know," Agnes said. "To Goliath. Out of all the places in the world, this was the place he might show up." She had told no one except Ray about Hatley's return; her mother, she knew, was sitting upstairs with her aunt Mia, playing cards. Soon she'd leave to spend the rest of the evening at Clyde's house. A good thing, Agnes had decided. She had said as much to Ray, and though he had agreed with her, he didn't seem entirely convinced. It was probably just a surprise to him, what was so clearly happen-

ing now between Rosamond and Clyde. To her, it was a relief—
and a miracle. Since James had come to Goliath and since he'd
left, she'd believed more strongly than ever before that people
should just *love* if they can, when they can. *Who* they can. Because
yes—why not?—it *was* a miracle. Love itself, miraculous.

But all of this was too sentimental to say out loud. Easier to
ponder this father thing, this stranger, to piece out just what he
might be doing here. To worry over the practicalities of why he
had come—why *now?*—and not think too much about the connection between Hatley and who he could or couldn't love.

"He's afraid," she said at last. Ray nodded. He didn't question
her, didn't doubt that the stranger truly was Hatley Rogers suddenly returned to Goliath. She said, "Fear. He doesn't have the
right to *fear* anything."

Finally, though, a few weeks after the revival, the man himself,
looking not so much afraid as displaced—perhaps *chronically*
displaced—and not at all like the half menace/half hero Agnes
had concocted in the space of ten years and a lot of imagining
and fearing, appeared in her checkout line at the supermarket.

"You," she said. An incidental thought came to her: she was
taller than her mother. Several inches taller, in fact. Hatley, now
before her, counting change in the palm of his hand, was hardly
as tall as James. She had always thought that when she saw him
again, at the very least he'd be *tall*.

"It's you," she said again.

The man floundered. He looked up at her. He was jowly, and
there were gray pillows beneath his pale eyes. His blue black hair
shone under the fluorescent lights and the skin across his forehead and above his gray-streaked beard was ruddy on the surface
but betrayed an ashen look beneath.

"Agnes," he said. He blinked at her. "I'd like a word," he said
too forcefully, and he rocked on his heels, his hands gone to his

trouser pockets. She said nothing, and he hesitated, pulling at his beard. He retreated a little: "I was just getting some groceries."

He held his hands, palms up, over his selections: canned ham, canned milk, canned green beans—food to survive nuclear winter. He shrugged. Did it mean: *Can you blame me? Look how defenseless I am, purchasing such things.* You can't fault a man who buys something as banal, as indestructible, as canned milk.

"A word?" he asked again, more earnestly this time. He had put his hands on the counter and leaned across it, toward her. "Please."

Fifteen years. The man—her father—looked like an item of clothing that had been washed too many times. His seams were puckered, his ends frayed, wrinkled to hell. The horrible black dye in his hair was so bad, so obviously an addition to his natural state, she half expected it to come sweating down into his ears.

"Wait for my break," she told him. "Ten minutes."

He nodded and said, "Of course," though there was some question in his voice, as if he wasn't entirely certain he'd make it. He handed her a twenty-dollar bill to pay, then, collecting the change she dropped into his palm, shuffled off to the front of the store. There he stood idly jiggling the coins in his pocket and shuffling his feet to some song he was singing beneath his breath. He examined the bulletin board full of notices for lost puppies and grass-cutting services and ignored the shoppers who straggled through the automatic door, pulling shopping carts free from their tangled line.

She remembered him mostly for his absences. For his leave-takings, those mornings of near-silent coffee and sausage gravy, then Rosamond sitting on the sofa in her bathrobe after he'd left, peering relentlessly out the window as if to summon his return. Once, when Agnes was five, he surprised them both by showing up on Agnes's actual birthday: August fifteenth. He brought a can of apple juice and a pocketful of peppermints. Agnes sat at the kitchen table with her knees tucked to her chest, her father surrendering the mints like a handful of dice onto the table. For a moment, all three of them stared at the red-and-white candies, their clear cellophane wrappers catching the overhead light. She looked up at Rosamond, who had not yet combed her hair that day, a Sunday. Her face was bare. Agnes could tell she wanted to dash off to the bathroom to groom herself, to at least pull a comb through her hair. She was suspended, though, in a cartoonish smile. Finally she said, "Agnes! Thank your father for the candy."

She rang up the next three customers, handed the register key to the other checkout girl, and waved to her manager—she was taking her break—then moved to approach Hatley.

"Ready?"

He turned from the bulletin board full of community notices, his eyebrows shooting up, his plastic shopping bags dangling from his fingers. "Yes, yes. Should we . . ." he looked around, but Agnes jerked her head in the direction of the back of the store.

"Break room," she said. She led him through a set of double doors into the stockroom, stacks of breakfast cereal, laundry detergent, and potato chips forming the nearest wall of products, with towers of boxed instant potatoes and heaps of giant bags of dog food behind. In front was the break area, with a coffeemaker set on a chest of drawers and a table and chairs. They settled into a pair of orange plastic chairs beside an urn of old coffee. Agnes waited for the man to speak. He drummed the table with his fingers and nodded to the coffee. "May I?"

This was not the man Agnes remembered. *This* man was tentatively polite, jumping up to slouch out of his jacket, folding it carefully over the back of his chair. He got busy fixing his coffee, fussing with the packet of cream and the stirrer, taking a careful, hesitant sip from the Styrofoam cup before frowning, then recovering, nodding. "Well," he said, as if sipping that awful coffee settled things. As if to say, well, isn't this pleasant? And aren't we happy to have a moment to chat? It was delusional to Agnes, the way he drank that coffee, the way he held the carafe up invitingly in her direction, offering. "Suit yourself," he said when she refused.

As a teenager, she had walked the sidewalk paths, passing the fire department and the school, this house and another, and wonder: What did Hatley Rogers think the first time he stood in the very spot she was standing in, seeing what she was seeing? Before she was born, he had lived here. He had stopped traveling for the space of several months and just lived here. In Goliath. Agnes had carried this secret hope: she was repeating her father's thoughts. She thought she might have the mind of her missing father, that every thought that had come to him would, in a swirl of spent energy, drifting about for years in the air, heavy with factory exhaust, visit her as well.

She swallowed, pressing her eyes closed, and Hatley took another sip of his coffee. "Piss poor," he said. He took another sip, to confirm, and shuddered. "The worst."

The *worst*. If she had been her mother, she would hop right up and fix him a new pot. Would probably also pull a tin of shortbread cookies from some previously unseen caddy or secret cabinet, and she would produce a crystal sugar bowl. A porcelain creamer of milk.

Instead, she watched him drink the coffee and waited for him to explain himself. He sipped and frowned a bit more, looked around himself, and finally, again pulling on his beard, asked, "You surprised to see me?" And then the stupid old man winked.

She didn't smile. This was mostly because she couldn't do that to his wink, couldn't direct a smile or a grimace or a scowl at it. In fact she could not make her face do anything. She suddenly thought that her break was only ten minutes long, and she also thought, *Fuck it*. Just fuck it all. Her mother, it turned out, was unbelievably stupid. Pathetically stupid. How had she done this? How had she let this man into their lives? It seemed that way—that Hatley had been let into their lives long ago, in the flesh, and ever since in memorandum—even though Agnes of course at the same time understood that her physical existence was a result of *his* existence. She wouldn't *be* if it hadn't been for him. And this angered her more than anything else.

But after a long silent moment in the massive gray concrete-floored room, she ventured: "Why have you come here? I mean, to Goliath? Why now?"

He grasped both arms of his chair and pushed back, but stopped himself from standing. "Agnes," he began.

It was the first time his tone of voice had dipped into a regis-ter she recognized. Now she remembered what it was like to be a ten-year-old girl coming home from school to find her father suddenly there, sitting in the easy chair as if it were the place he kept every afternoon of her life. One afternoon such a visit hap-pened and she had recklessly launched into a discussion of the Revolutionary War. She was in the fifth grade, and it was the most substantial thing she could think to tell him about. She told him: *General Cornwallis, Bunker Hill.* Her father had used the same flat voice he used now, as if the mention of long-dead English generals unnerved him. But young Agnes had continued with the history lesson. Even when he tried to speak, she persisted. She was out of control, wheeling along, spinning from Revolu-tionary War generals to amphibians to the inane television reruns she watched after school. "Agnes," he'd said then and now, and the word was a measure of patience he'd rather not dispense.

"Agnes," he said again. "I have always loved you and your mother."

She stared at him. This could not be true, but something lifted inside her, some stub of hope, a habit of longing.

"I always did," he said resolutely. "I do even now," he admitted, and the quaver of a bumbling old man returned to his voice. He looked down gravely for a moment, as if in prayer, then rose suddenly and turned to the cupboard. He opened a cabinet, pushing around half-eaten bags of jelly beans and potato chips. Chipped coffee cups. A canister of safety pins. "I'll make us some real coffee," he said. He pulled out a box of crackers, shook it to show it was empty, and pitched it into the enormous trash can behind her chair. He found the canister of Folgers and, peeling back the lid, sniffed at it, frowning, then shrugged. "This'll have to do," he said. He poured the old coffee, gritty with spare grounds, into the sink, and rinsed the carafe. The items in his hand clinked unsteadily as he worked.

"We had a baby." He looked at her. "You." He poured clean water into the machine, flipped it on, and returned to his chair. "I always wondered how things went on with you two after I left. I used to drive past schools and think, *She'd be old enough for high school now.* I'd calculate it. I'd say, well, she's graduated now. I'd say, now she's in college. I'd hope you were in college. Knew you were smart enough. I remembered how you used to tuck yourself under the kitchen table with a pillow to read your books. Some days I come up on a table, maybe in a restaurant or when I'm in somebody's house, and I'll kind of look, like maybe I was expecting you to be there, hunkered down like you used to do." He frowned. "I had a hard time keeping you in the right age in my mind. I'd be picturing you at about ten or so, or thirteen. Then I'd stop to add up the years and, why, you'd be nineteen or twenty."

She said nothing and kept her eyes hard, though a version of what he was saying was true on her end, as well: she had never thought he would age so thoroughly. She had imagined being summoned to his funeral—someone from the hospital or house where he died would somehow know to call her. She and Rosamond would attend. She imagined them arriving at an isolated church out in a field of dust, a two-lane highway snaking on past it. They would arrive and find the person in the casket was exactly the same man who had left them, her dark-haired, smooth-cheeked daddy in a casket.

He pressed his fingers against his closed eyelids, and when he opened them again, looking at her, they were reddish in the whites, pink at the edges. "The day I left, I didn't know I was leaving." he said. "I finished my business in Georgia, I sat in my car. It was a terrific old Cadillac, white with gray leather interior, every inch of chrome slicked up and singing. I thought, I can't be a man in this car and drive back to Goliath. I always felt strange in my own skin here. Caught. Your mother's Goliath, this town, is like a pit of gravity. Where good men come to drown."

He paused, looking at his hands, and cleared his throat. "Come again?" he asked, but Agnes shook her head. She hadn't said anything.

"I met a girl in Kentucky. Same deal. Small town, factory. Toaster ovens, though, not furniture." Hatley shrugged. "She had a daddy who disapproved. Same as your mother. Whole damn town was against me. Same as Goliath. Same thing, through and through."

He broke away then, staring past Agnes, into some invisible thought. Her break was past over but she remained at the table, listening. The coffee gurgled and popped through the filter.

"I don't know," he said. "Small-town girls. My business is small towns, though. You know that. Small towns and suburbs. It has always been that way."

He shrugged, the matter of Kentucky settled. "A few weeks ago, I come across this bit in the paper: *Harding Furniture Closing.* I couldn't believe it." He hesitated; his story had run out. He had nothing left to explain. "I wanted to see her. Your mother. You. I couldn't believe it, that the factory was gone."

"I've seen you," Agnes said. "You've been here. And you were at McGraw."

He looked at her, then away. "All of this happened a long time ago," he said. The coffee was ready, and he rose to pour it into two Styrofoam cups. Silently Agnes took hers and set it before her. He resettled himself carefully in his plastic chair.

"Fifteen years," she said, prompting him. "This happened fifteen years ago."

"No, it happened *before* then. That's what I'm trying to tell you. The baby came, you were born." He glanced up at her and then away. "She loved you like she's never loved anything in her life. At first we were in it together. I did the changing, the feeding as much as she did. We bathed you together at the kitchen sink. I was almost scared to touch you at first, you were so little. We got along fine, though, the three of us, holed up in that house together the way we did." He laughed. "I didn't know it would change. But, before long, I had to go back out on the sales calls, and when I came back, it was a done deal. You and her together. You were apart from me. When you cried, you only wanted her. And she, she couldn't stop thinking of you for a second. We'd be together on the couch, talking, and she'd hear you crying, a whimper so small *I* couldn't hear it. From then on, I felt like I was stepping into something. It was something I didn't have a part of." He sat blinking a moment, then took a sip from his cup. "Still, I stayed a long time after that. A damn long time."

"You're blaming me." Her voice was small. He left because she was born, but that couldn't be—when he left, she had been thirteen years old.

"No." He shook his head. "I'm not blaming anyone. I'm the one who did it."

Agnes let her coffee cool in front of her while Hatley drank his. She wished she had a means to record the words so she could reconsider them later, parse them out, but she didn't think they would sound any better later. He pressed his fingers to his eye-lids again, blinked up at the fluorescent lights in the cinder-block rafters.

"Did you do it again?"

He set his cup down. "What's that?"

She pressed her lips together, looked away. Then, her eyes were back on him, quick. "Do you have any other children?"

"Why, no." He seemed surprised by the question. He opened his mouth, about to say something further, then stopped. He shook his head. "No," he said again, quietly. Then, after a moment, he said, "Her family took everything I owned. I mean Colleen's family. They needed this and that. They took it all bit by bit. Bled me dry." He paused. "You're all right, now, aren't you? You turned out just fine."

"I don't know why you think you can ask me that."

Hatley considered. "Doesn't seem a horrible question."

"You don't know what all's changed," she said, echoing what her mother had said months earlier, in the snow. "You can't know a life you just return to, the one you didn't live. You can only know your actual life, the one you're inside of."

Now he nodded. "Yes."

"Have you spoken to her?" Agnes asked.

He sniffed, rearranging himself on the plastic chair. "I have not," he said. "Not yet," he added.

"Then don't." Her cup of coffee sat untouched between them, and the stacks of boxes behind held the large room quiet. She rose and pushed her chair back under the table, then stood be-hind it. "She's been through enough." Her mother *could* love Clyde, could love him and be happy. "It would kill my mother, seeing you. You hear me? It would *kill* her."

"See here?" Hatley said. He rose from his chair and slipped his hand into his pocket. He brought something out and held it up for her to see. It was an ordinary teaspoon, but Agnes recognized it as being one from her mother's kitchen. She'd had that same silverware for years; Agnes saw the scalloped design on the handle, how the spoon was pointed a tiny bit at the tip. It was even worn the same dull gray as her mother's silverware, as if the spoons in Rosamond's kitchen drawer had aged in exactly the same way as this one, the piece of silver in her father's pocket.

"You see what I've held on to?" Hatley asked. "You see what I've kept?"

FIFTEEN

It was during the days, when, unknown to her, her estranged husband had returned, after she'd seen the tide shift among the townspeople, their coming to believe in her parade, after she began sleeping in Clyde Winston's bed, when she was overseeing the final preparations for the parade, it was during these days that Rosamond sat down at Aunt Mia's kitchen table and began to read from the Bible. She started with Genesis: "In the beginning God created the heavens and the earth."

The Spirit of God hovered over the deep, dark waters and the formless earth. After light was spoken into existence, after there was day and night, the first day, there was the second day in the history of the universe, and on this day, God created the sky. It was later, though, after he grew nut trees and vegetable-bearing plants from the dirt, that he filled the sky: first with a greater and lesser light to separate day and darkness; next with the endless stars; and lastly with birds to soar across the blue, to rest in the trees, to call out to each other in the first golden light of the day.

Rosamond went out to the factory's parking lot mornings and

oversaw the putting together of a dozen floats laid out in flatbeds, raised with painted plywood and sanded two-by-fours, draped over with glittering cloth, stapled, glued, and nailed into place. The floats took on the images of wedding cakes and zoo animals, American flags and tic-tac-toe boards. The people hummed, working; they were makeshift carpenters and fashion designers and patriots and candy slingers.

She mingled among them, talking construction and debating the soundness of the different structures. She went up at noon for lunch at the Tuesday Diner with Clyde. He looked good in full daylight—*real*—and she admired him over the rim of his coffee cup. He talked baseball, she talked parade. The weather was breezy and dry, and Rosamond hoped the rain, if it came, would hurry on and be off and vanished before May third. The sky was cloudless.

On the sixth day of the beginning of everything, once there were light and fish and birds, God created the animals to roam over the surface of the earth. Then came the moment. God said, "Let us make man in our image." He fingered a creature out of dirt and breathed life into it. Rosamond considered all of the beginnings. She thought about the floats in the parking lot, and her daughter living in the basement apartment below her and Aunt Mia. She thought of Clyde, that new relationship that was in many ways a very old one, and of the girl who had swallowed the pills and died, that ending. When Rosamond thought about Cassie, her hands went to her chest. She should have protected that girl as fiercely as she protected her own daughter; she should have taken in that sad thief.

But Rosamond wavered. Who's to say what any one of us should do? More than anything, she and Clyde Winston were simply great friends. It was the first time she had ever truly been friends with a man, though there had been a glimmer of it with Tucker. In the evenings, she walked next door to his house, while everything around her was drowning in deep purple and there were spots of streetlights on the sidewalks. She felt better these days, more rested, abler. Stronger.

Hatley Rogers was walking through the same blue-darkness, following several yards behind. Rosamond did not see him. When Agnes had begged him not to bother her, he hadn't agreed, but now, faced with this opportunity—Rosamond was close enough that he could simply call to her, make her turn around and *see* him—he hesitated. His daughter, a grown woman now, a supermarket checkout girl with more than half of a college education, had begged him. He watched Rosamond, a dark form moving ahead of him through the deepening of that precise moment, day turning into night. He had shown Agnes the relic he carried in his pocket: the spoon. Years ago, his last morning in Rosamond's kitchen—even now he claimed he hadn't known it was to be his last morning—he stirred his coffee, put the spoon on the table, and drank. Then, before leaving, he tucked the spoon inside his jacket pocket. He had asked Agnes in the stockroom if Rosamond had ever noticed the missing spoon. Agnes answered that she hadn't, then told him, "It will be too much for her to know you kept this. You can't tell her. You can't see her. She's fine. She's *happy*. Leave her alone. You have to."

Hatley had come, in part, to test it, to see if Goliath could yet drown a man, now that its factory was gone. He had thought— what? What had he thought? That the factory's closing had somehow freed the town? He could see now, walking through, standing in the back of church as he had done a few weeks ago, the Harding auction, the river, which seemed to him to have grown noticeably wider, slower in the past fifteen years, that Goliath was *better* equipped these days to pull a man under, not worse. The factory, he saw now, was the only thing that had made life in Goliath possible. Never mind how small that life had been.

But here she was, *happy*. Since he'd been here, living in his single-bedroom trailer, cooking his canned-food meals on a dime store frying pan, he'd seen it for himself: his own house, the one he and Rosamond used to live in together, had gone dark. He'd observed everything, he'd seen it. Rosamond was living with the man next door. Clyde Winston. Hatley remembered him, but now it seemed an impossibility: Percy Harding gone, Agnes grown up, and another, Clyde Winston, that old sop—his own wife somehow gone—loving the woman *he'd* married, the woman he'd bought that now-empty house for.

Rosamond, walking, her lost husband several feet behind her, realized: we can't tell the difference between the sad thieves and the ordinary ones, those who plainly want to take versus those with honest need. There are, she thought, more sad thieves than mean-hearted ones, more who steal out of their own desperate heart-poverty than out of simple greed. She walked on, considering this, and the color slipped out of the sky, hushed to dark but for the pale moon and the streetlights.

When Hatley was a child, he had believed he'd grow up to be a good man. He and his family had lived in a weathered old clapboard house at the edge of a beach town in Virginia. His mother was a sometime teacher, taking what summer school jobs and tutoring positions she could find but refusing to take on full-time employment. She wanted to be home with her only child. Hatley's father was himself a traveling salesman, often gone. He worked for land speculators and real estate higher-ups, selling tracts of land, mostly the marshy plains of the inlands. Hatley believed he would be good because his mother told him he would, the two of them shelling peas on the porch. Or else they played checkers on the kitchen table long Saturday afternoons, just the two of them in the quiet house. But as a teenager he became a lifeguard on the weekends and found he was popular with the vacationing girls and their mothers. These bathing-suit-wearing, floppy-hatted, red-lipsticked women eventually stole him away from his own mother and the plans she'd laid out for him: college, marriage, everything necessary for an upright Christian life. A *good* life. One entirely different from his father's.

Even back then, though, when he was stealing away with the mothers on the beach, he believed he'd someday return to goodness. Or maybe some high-minded calling. Even as he eventually left his mother alone in that old clapboard house, he believed it. It was this impulse—to be *good*—that had attracted him to Rosamond in the first place. Returning to Goliath now was a surrender to this calling to be a good man. This calling, this pit of gravity, this drowning in a small town—it was all a way of coming clean.

And so, in the name of being virtuous and clean and noble, he dismissed Agnes's pleas, and now, in the soft blackness of a warm spring evening, he called out to Rosamond.

She didn't hear him at first. Hatley had to clear his throat and call again; even then it took a moment for her to step out of her thoughts, to turn and look, see who was calling her name.

He wasn't more than ten feet behind her, not far at all, but it was too dark to see him clearly. His voice, though, damnably familiar, struck her vertebrae, made her shiver. She felt it, the knowledge of who that voice belonged to zinging up her spine, into her neck, spreading out across her shoulders. Her *elbows* twitched. He stepped forward into the glow of the streetlight, and at last she saw him.

It would have been easier to believe it was Percy. In fact her first impression in the rush of thoughts that crushed around her was that it *was* Percy. Her mind scrambled to revise her memory: it was Hatley who had died, Percy who had left. *That* was why Percy's returning was now possible. He hadn't died; Hatley had. The man before her had a thick gray beard—it couldn't be Hatley.

His first words to her, after he spoke her name, were feeble ones. He stood blinking there in the streetlight, his hands thrust deep in his pockets, and said, "I should have called."

"Oh," she said. Every politeness returned to her. Knee-jerk politeness. She would later wonder at that, but now, before she even thought it out—this was *Hatley* standing here—she forgave him his temerity, his hideously bad timing. "Oh, no, that wasn't necessary. Not necessary at all. You did just fine, coming here. You did just fine."

Rosamond believed in a world of order. There was a balance to things, a sort of equilibrium of good and bad that brought on moments like these. The thing that was *supposed* to happen had come about. Her husband left, her daughter left, and now each was coming back to her, one by one.

And yet he didn't even look like himself, especially not there in the odd angle of light, the shadows deep in his cushiony, non-Hatley-like face. He *looked* like a specter standing there. Like a creature not of this physical world.

But he seemed relieved by her words. His eyes relaxed; they knew each other. Finally it *felt* true: this was Hatley, this, Rosamond.

"Hatley," she said. Her hand went to her mouth.

"Yes," he stepped forward, just out of the glare of the streetlight. "It's me."

They were each quiet for a long moment; neither could think, what to say? Finally he asked, "Would you like some dinner, Rosamond?" He stepped closer, close enough to touch her, and put his hand out to cup her elbow, ready to guide her away. She wanted to brush his beard away, all the way off his face so she could see his chin, his cheeks. He must have been planning this, this return, this sidewalk encounter. His eyebrows were raised as if he'd posed a question, but Rosamond felt how certain he was in his hand on her arm. Here he was, claiming her—*reclaiming* her.

What she could do now was refuse to go. "I'm sorry. I have

plans." She didn't pull her arm away, though, and his expression was slow to change—still bright-open, expectant—as if there were something there in the just-blackened night, in the air, that blocked the way, made it difficult for her words to reach him. Invisible particles in the damp, warm air: the grit of friction.

Or perhaps there was a deficit inside him: old-man slowness. Maybe it was just Rosamond's voice in his ear—where *had* he been all this time? In her confusion, she couldn't remember for an instant where he was from. His origins, where his people came from.

Hatley nodded, though, and released her elbow. He was roused to quick action, searching his trousers pockets, coming out with a slip of paper and a pen. He bent over, put the paper to his knee, then, searching for light, hobbled a few feet back, toward the circle of yellow streetlight. Finally he scribbled something down.

He stood upright and walked toward her, his hand stretched out, offering the paper. She took it.

"Tomorrow," he said. "Come in the morning, about nine. We'll have breakfast." He paused, half turned to leave her, "My address." She was still holding the paper in her hands, though she hadn't looked at it yet. "You'll come?" he asked.

She would. Yes, she nodded.

"All right then. All right, Rosamond. I will see you in the morning." He started up the street toward the school. "Come hungry!" he called back to her. He laughed a little and turned to go. This time it stuck—his going—and since he was headed in the same direction she needed to go, toward the south end of Main Street, she lingered there on the sidewalk, still holding the piece of paper in her hand, still not looking at it.

When she finally did look, hours later, she found it was a receipt to a restaurant in Libby, Alabama, a place called Hooper's. He'd paid for one meal, one drink, four dollars and change. Hatley's looping scrawl was on the other side. He wrote with a black pen, fine-tipped, smeared just a tiny bit, but still legible. Hatley had troubled to write out the full name of the trailer park where he was staying—Tremont Pines—though it was the only one in Goliath, the one where Cassie Stewart had died so recently. Unthinkable, going there.

Rosamond was at Clyde's house, had sneaked into the bathroom to take the note out of her pocket. She read it there, leaning against Clyde's clean sink, possibly the most immaculate sink in town. The bathroom was the one room he cleaned with conviction, with scrub brushes and Comet and ammonia on the tile. Another offering from Penny, something she had instilled in him. How *necessary* a clean bathroom was. Rosamond breathed in all that chemical cleanness and looked over the slip of paper again and again. It was as if she might divine everything from the flourish of the script, the extra curl at the top of the two. As if she could see her future in the way he placed the two humps on the *n,* the first generous, almost pudgy, and the second collapsing back into the first. Probably Clyde had always cleaned this bathroom, ever since Penny died, and probably he had started cleaning it a teeny bit more lately, since Rosamond had been coming around. For dinner, they'd had soup from a can and grilled cheese sandwiches.

He was there now, in the other room, watching the late news, waiting for her. And Hatley, in trailer number twelve, a few streets away.

It had been only a few days ago that she'd gone up the hill to the Harding house and granted what pardon she could to Percy's son. The night of the auction, when she'd reminded herself: she could go. There was still that option, that of her simply flying away. Just like Hatley, the younger version, or James, the boy who had broken his heart over her daughter. Percy. Out the bathroom window, down the street, away. Away and *alone.*

In the beginning, God made the heavens and the earth. He put everything in order, the plants and the animals and the rivers and the mountains, and finally the people. Every created thing had its place.

Some years later, there arrived in Goliath, North Carolina, a baby who grew into a girl who was pretty enough and smart enough and pleasant enough, but still lacking in some crucial way. This lack did not have a name or a known origin. It could be she had said the wrong thing, had answered the teacher's question wrong, or that she had given the wrong look to another little girl or boy, or perhaps that she had kept her gaze on one of the other children a beat too long. Or maybe it was only this: the others sensed how much she longed to be a part of them, and it was this longing—the intensity of it—that proved how very separate she was.

And one day, when that girl had grown into a young woman, a man came to see her. It happened when the girl had grown so thin that her bones were as light and inconsequential as those of birds. The man opened his sales case before her. Inside, there were only sewing notions, thread and needles and thimbles, but to the girl, who felt extraordinarily, achingly light in her thinness, her hollow bones, the different colors of thread wrapped up on their little wooden spools lined up together and looked like a single extravagant thing, a tapestry. This was plenty in the girl's eyes. This was everything.

No one was going to stop the teenagers from burning everything down to scorched grass. They themselves didn't know they were planning such an ending. They only knew this: they were willing to search things out. To begin with, this meant following Vincent Bailey home from school one afternoon.

A group had gathered in the woods behind the high school half a dozen times since the walkout the afternoon of Cassie

Stewart's memorial service. Vincent shared what he remembered of Cassie's poetry, but beyond that, he had little to say. They came anyway, just to sit around in the woods and feel apart from the rest of the world. They knew they were all leaving Goliath. By next fall, they would be elsewhere, scattered among other teenagers at other high schools, living among people who had never known Cassie Stewart or Vincent Bailey or Percy Harding. They felt a need to acknowledge all they'd seen, some crowning event. A marking of *their* time. The parade and the baseball game had been dreamed up by the adults, but the teenagers wanted something of their own. They wanted all this without knowing they wanted it—they only knew that they couldn't go back to life as they had known it, nor could they simply wait around for the day they would all leave Goliath.

They felt a compulsion to express something but couldn't collect the thing they wanted to say from all the scraps of hurts and desires inside them. So they went to the woods after school. They watched Vincent smoke. They tried to pay homage to Cassie Stewart, but their stories were meager, and they were clumsy in telling them.

On the first day, there had been more than thirty, but their numbers dwindled, and by the day of the memorial service, they were down to ten. Vincent announced he was walking home. "Anyone want to come with me?"

He walked on without looking behind him, though he heard them shuffle about, hefting backpacks and coming up behind him, talking to one another and laughing, revived by this small call for action—they were finally *doing* something. Vincent led them on the weedy trail beside the county road that Goliath's Main Street faded into outside of town. They formed a scraggly line behind him. Squirrel Jones fell in place two steps behind Vincent, calling to him, "Vincent, what's the plan? Where are we going?"

"My house," Vincent answered.

They continued, and in time, those behind him quieted a bit. They trudged on, half because they truly believed Vincent Bailey had something for them, some righteous call to action, half because they had nothing else to do.

Despite his outward confidence, Vincent didn't actually have a plan settled in his mind. Though he had no idea just what they would do once they arrived, he felt *something* would happen. The times called for it, and Vincent felt anxious and hopeful and angry all at once. His pulse quickened. He and his father had already painted the hood of the car they were building, and he had promised Vincent they could begin work on the driver's side this evening. Vincent had an idea that some of the others would stick around for that, though this seemed shameful thinking—there was a greater call leading through the weedy path beside the county road. The sky was the mild blue of spring, and Vincent caught a glimpse of déjà vu. His body sparked panic and mission and loss.

They arrived, and Vincent led them to the old shed where he'd first begun the art of swallowing living and nonliving things. It was too small for everyone to fit inside, so Vincent stood in the doorway and the others crowded around outside. He lifted his hands, about to speak, and they were all watching him, waiting. Vincent looked into their eager, attentive faces. It seemed impossible to imagine that these were the people he'd been so afraid of just a few weeks earlier, the ones he had hated for that same reason—he hated them because he couldn't stand to be afraid. Afraid of what they were thinking, of what they imagined about him, afraid of what they possessed that he didn't. He'd had entirely too much fear, and now all of that seemed to rupture into something altogether different, a sort of boldness, a new, clear thinking. The washed-out blue from the sky seemed to settle across the others' features, and Vincent believed that what was happening now was also happening in the future, and in the future's future—every action going out in waves, cresting for miles.

He pulled a box of matches from his pocket and shook one out, then stared at it. It was the wrong thing. He'd thought he would light the cigarette, smoke it down slowly with them watching, and then swallow it. It was something he'd imagined since the old days when he showed Cassie the trick. He had pictured these people watching. But he stared now at the match in his hand and it wasn't enough.

Everyone was silent. He had to *do* something.

It came to him, what he should do, what those waves going out into the future seemed to demand, but for an instant he didn't want to. He flashed to his father—they were supposed to paint the car tonight. *Their* car, what they'd put together. If he did what he was about to do, everything would be changed between them. They would go back to the days when his father hung back, silent and afraid of who Vincent had become, of what they both had seen.

There was the match. Vincent looked into the eyes that were watching him; a few nodded back at him. He again imagined those waves rolling out into the future, and it seemed impossible for him not to do what he was staring at, not to complete the deed he was contemplating. This action seemed more important than anything, and it seemed that the plan that was rising up behind it was meant for the others to watch unfold. He had forgotten about Cassie in that moment, and yet all of this was about her, and more: that wave he was imagining seemed to have come before any of them. Something else had started it, and now it was simply carrying them along.

Here Vincent, the boy who had found the dead body beside the tracks, the boy who had carried the news into his own house first, then listened and watched as the news moved out, into town, struck the match. He dropped it and neatly stepped over the tiny bloom of fire.

He joined the others, Squirrel at his side, whispering, "Oh

man, oh man." The group watched the wall of the shed catch with their arms crossed and their eyes alive, jaws set. *Yes.* The fire leaped up the side and one finger of flame stretched around the corner. Another reached all the way to the top, the flat stretch of two-by-fours put together for a roof. There was a joy in their solemnity, purpose in their destruction. The fire crackled and gnawed, and the teenagers watched in awe; it was as if they had invented fire, as if it had never been witnessed before. The orange flames were as gentle as they were vicious, rising up as if to caress the old pile of wood, to cushion it when, after a long time burning, it crumbled apart and fell in a whoosh of flame hot enough to burn the cheeks of those watching.

They stepped back, and Vincent went to uncoil his father's garden hose. He dowsed the earth around the fire, and then drew nearer it with ever-tightening circles. The others threw dirt on the last of it and stomped out the last smoldering embers. In the space of thirty minutes, the shed was burned down to ashes, and the junk parts inside had been charred to black.

Breakfast turned out to be silver-dollar pancakes, orange juice mixed from concentrate, and coffee. Rosamond asked, "When did you learn how to do this?" She surprised herself; she was teasing him.

"This? Pancakes?"

He was standing over an electric griddle with a plastic spatula in his hand. He had insisted Rosamond sit at the tiny two-chair table a few steps away. The counter was a mess of dribbled batter, eggshells, and a torn, half-spilled bag of flour. The night before, he had been salesman Hatley, smooth. Smiling. *Certain.* But this morning, here, was a Hatley she'd seen only glimpses of before. Here a Hatley intent on his task, worrying the edges of the pancakes with his spatula, blinking down at them. There were four silver-dollar-sized pancakes cooking now on the griddle, and a plate of them, covered in foil, on the counter. He had a dishrag tucked into his belt for an apron. He grinned, self-assured but not obnoxiously so. It was the grin he'd given her years ago when she'd betrayed her friend's comments: *you take my Clyde and your Hatley and put them together and you get the perfect husband.* A grin he used to give little Agnes, a baby on his lap pulling the handkerchief from his suit pocket and tucking it in again. The kind of game only a baby could play and not grow tired of, and Hatley had let her, had watched her little face, had given her this smile, a smile he now cast down on the mini-pancakes.

"I'm a one-trick pony," he said. He shrugged. "Pancakes only."

She had had a difficult time imagining the place where Hatley was staying. In the years he'd been gone, she'd only been able to picture him in the room they'd stayed in years ago at the Royal Motel, a gritty, musty dwelling with yellowing walls and a wobbly old dresser. The room where they'd lain next to each other in the dark, hands touching. That odd courtship of theirs. The stories he'd told her. Tall tales. Fat women and skinny men, skinnier dogs. What all he'd seen on the road and what all he'd lived before her. Babies left in washtubs on the front porch, women barely dressed. Old ladies who chattered away, telling him what color the neighbors had painted their bathrooms—even the *ceilings*—the old men telling him their favorite tales, war stories, car stories, hospital stories. Each house on every street in every town had these old stories. And she had turned her face to see his in silhouette. The flash of headlights from the parking lot, the highway beyond.

The trailer was of course larger than the motel room had been, but it felt very small. She felt crowded inside, as if she needed to hunch down to keep from touching the ceiling with the top of her head. The walls were wood-paneled and dark, and the floor was carpeted mossy green. His current automobile, a midnight blue Lincoln rather than a Cadillac, was parked out front.

"That'll do it," Hatley said at last. He turned off the griddle and brought the pancakes over. Two plates, silverware, and a too-large plastic jug of syrup were already on the table. They used cloth napkins. Hatley remarked, "They came with the place." He meant the napkins; he was spreading one across his knee. "Everything you see here." The furniture: a drab, sturdy loveseat, a painted rocking chair, a coffee table. He smiled at her. He had kept up the black in his hair, but not the pomade. It was still thick, but lackluster. The beard still threw her a little—he'd always been clean-shaven, soft-cheeked, when she'd known him before—but it was also the most natural thing about him, gray and very thick. He had always had a strong chin, a solid jaw, fleshier these days—*hairier*—but still there, still strong.

She hadn't seen the dead girl's trailer when she'd walked up. Of course she hadn't known exactly which one it was, didn't know the number on it or anything like that. But still, she had half expected it to be marked somehow. At least darker or emptier-looking than the rest. But they'd all pretty much looked the same on the outside, plastic-sided and narrow, gravel in between. Hatley's had been the smallest, on the edge of the first row.

"After you." He offered Rosamond the plate of pancakes.

But she only looked at them. She seemed caught somehow, snagged in the moment, trying to choose among the tiny pancakes. She said, "What I'm trying to do, sitting here, sitting here and watching you *cook,* for heaven's sake, you're *cooking.*" She stopped, closed her eyes a minute. She shook her head as if to dislodge that particular image: Hatley at the stove. "What I'm trying to do is to imagine what you might tell me. What you might possibly have to say to me."

Once the words were out, she couldn't believe she'd said them. That she'd broken through this little clear shell they'd made for themselves, the pretense of a normal breakfast. Old friends.

He set the plate of pancakes down and was quiet a moment.

She pulled her napkin off her lap and laid it on the table beside her still-empty plate. It occurred to her: it was possible she had dreamed the whole thing up. That the before—the house and marriage and baby, Agnes, the child—had never happened. That they were merely old friends, that was all. She had misinterpreted his intent, those years ago.

Finally, though, he said, "I have always loved you and Agnes."

"Agnes," she said. "She wrote to you, and you came." She had been thinking this through all morning. Of *course*. He had come because Agnes asked him to.

"You came for Agnes," she said.

"No. No, ma'am." There a bit of country coming out of him, that *ma'am*. It meant his patience was tried, his way of talking to housewives who didn't want to believe his sales claims, those who doubted him and the integrity of his product. She flashed to his mother, a stout woman with a stripe of steel in her black hair, sourness on her face. Rosamond had met her only once. They'd made the trip up to Virginia after they'd married, and from the second she met her, Rosamond suspected Hatley had already hurt her. By leaving her, he'd done that. His mother, Barbara, looked disapprovingly on her new daughter-in-law's white gloves, her red high-heeled shoes.

Now Hatley turned from his empty plate to Rosamond. He said, "I never got a letter. Or anything else from Agnes. I never did."

She nodded. "All right," she said. She was ashamed to admit it, but she was glad. She was glad he had come because he wanted to see her and not because Agnes had begged him to. And then, realizing where the tiny rush of relief had come from, she felt sick there in the tiny trailer, the too-thick orange juice growing warm in its plastic cup.

"Why?" she asked. "Why did you come?"

"Hell, Rosamond, what do you think? Why do *you* think I came?"

She blinked. "Hatley, I'm no fool."

"Rosamond, I—"

"I'm *no fool*. You tell me where you've been, who you've been with. You have to *tell* me."

He shook his head. "That's not what you really want to know." She stared at him. Who was this person? "What you really want to know," he continued, "is why I left."

"I *know* why you left."

He raised his eyebrows at this.

"You left," she said, "because you quit loving me. And Agnes. You just *quit*."

"No, that's not right." The lines around his eyes were so deep, they looked as if someone had etched them into his skin with some care. They were sort of perfect in that way, in their precise-ness. "That's not right," he said again. "What happened was I came home one day, and you were cut off from me. You and Ag-nes. You two were like this *unit*. Just you two. When she cried, she cried for you. And you, you couldn't see anything, not any-thing but her." He shook his head. "This *town*, God help me, this *town*. I had to see it," he said. Hatley put his hands up in a gesture of mock surrender. "I had to see this town, see Goliath, without its factory. Without"—he pinned his eyes to hers, kept them—"without *him*. Without *Mr.* Harding."

She shook her head—no. Not Percy. He couldn't *speak* of Percy. Not now.

"I need you to tell me," she said. "I need you to tell me why you came back. *That's* what I need to know."

"And I'm saying I already have. I've already told you." He brought his hands together, one hand kneading the knuckles of the other. Finally, quietly, "I kept a spoon."

Rosamond didn't know what he meant. She leaned into the table, closer to him, as if it were only a problem of physical distance, what she wasn't getting from him.

"A spoon?" she repeated.

He lifted his hands from the sides of his empty plate and dropped his face into them. For a second she thought he might be crying. Crying for her. Crying because of what he'd done, how he'd left her, how long he'd been gone. Crying because of what he was saying now. About Agnes. *Their child.* About Percy.

But when he looked up, blinking quickly, his face was hard again, all tied up, and he said, "I kept a spoon from your kitchen. All these years." It was too late, she'd already begun to cry with him. "I always carry it with me in my pocket." He paused for a moment, and she thought he might lean back in his chair and pull the spoon—*ta da!*—out of his pocket, but he didn't. He just kept sitting there, blinking in a rapid, furious way, his lips working, trying to find a word, a sentence, a story to explain all this. Even his anger didn't have the power she needed it to have, though. Him sitting there, speechless.

At last he said, "What you really want to know is why I left. Where I've been. What you really want is an apology. And I know I should. And I am . . . I am *sorry.*" He curled his hands into fists, one on either side of his plate, his knuckles gone white. "I *am.*"

"All right." She leaned back in her chair. This was all she was going to get from him. "You're sorry."

"I hate this town," he said. He plucked a pancake from the pile with his fingers and dropped it onto his plate. Then he dropped one onto hers. "I've always hated it."

"Okay." She nodded, stupidly. She was crying now unchecked. "*Okay.*"

She was trembling hard, the napkin a damp ball in her hands, her head throbbing. She felt the blood pulsing through her skull so strongly she could almost feel her whole self moving with it. Here, this man, her *husband,* in this tiny trailer with his miniature pancakes, here he was: he had survived. He had come through all these years unscathed.

They were quiet for a long moment. Finally he said, "You always made me want to be a good man, Rosamond. You always did. And now I'm back, I'm back now because I am a good man. Now I *am*. I am a good man."

But Rosamond had her eyes pressed closed. She was reeling away backward, all the way back to the day when she, age twenty-three, still dressed in her office dress, pearls, and shoes, opened the front door of her parents' tidy little brick house. There before her stood a beautiful stranger.

"You look good, by the way," he said after a moment. He dropped another pancake onto his plate, picked up the bottle of syrup. "I meant to tell you, how good you look." He wiped a smudge of spilled syrup off the table with his thumb and licked it off. He smiled. "Lovely as ever," he said.

Agnes had not known how to protect her mother from Hatley. She couldn't even tell if he was still in town; she had been afraid to look.

It was planting season in Mia's yard and she stayed there between her shifts at the supermarket, her hands in the dirt. She and Mia worked side by side with hoes, turning dried chicken manure into the soil where Mia wanted her marigold bed. Agnes knelt and pulled out rotted, half-moldy leaves from beneath the boxwood bushes by the house while Mia watched her. Working in the yard brought out what roughness Mia had in her; she spit into the grass clippings, she swore. Finally she handed Agnes a rake. "Try that," she said. But Agnes wouldn't; she preferred to work with her bare hands, to pull it out bit by bit with her own fingernails. Mia began the planting; Agnes kept working the soil.

Hatley had told Rosamond the same thing he had told Agnes: he loved them, he always had. Rosamond, coming up on Mia's house from Hatley's trailer, found Agnes working in the yard. She was bent over, still digging the weeds and rotted vegetation from under the overgrown bushes. She'd worked nearly the whole way down, from the north side of the house almost to the front door, when her mother came and squatted down beside her. The day was dizzy with sunlight, the sky blue and enormous.

Rosamond would tell her. Or she wouldn't. It was simply such a relief to be here among the soggy green, the heady beams of sunshine. She was wearing good shoes and a nice skirt, but she went ahead and knelt down. She took her pretty shoes off. She would worry about such things later. Right now, she thought: *just let me breathe.*

Agnes, for her part, would *never* tell. She hadn't even told Ray. She wouldn't. She'd had enough telling and thinking and trying; it was time to *do* something. She dug at Mia's weeds until they reached the door, past noon. Then she and Rosamond lay on Mia's driveway. They just picked up, went over there, lay down, and talked about sleeping.

"I could sleep for the rest of the day," Rosamond murmured. Clyde was waiting for her back at his house, and she knew it. Soon she would stand up, go to him. She needed this space, though. This sunshine, this daughter lying down beside her. This unbearably hard driveway. The sky above her, a thing she couldn't see the end of.

"I could sleep here for always," Agnes said.

Mia appeared with a pair of iced teas. She handed one to each of the girls, and announced, "Well, Rosamond. You've been cleared. I've looked through all your things. No trinket box, no gold tooth. You didn't take them." She settled herself down next to them. "I'll bet," she said, "you didn't even know you were under suspicion."

. . .

One week before May third, Parade Day, Vincent Bailey and his gang of mourners of Cassie Stewart gathered around a town map to plan. Stephanie Jameson was not among them; she'd had enough fire and death and suicide. She wasn't reading in her library chair, either, or hanging out at the diner, hoping the drifter would show, the one who so loved a girl named Agnes. She was at home instead, watching television and trying to be normal.

This same day—the same day the teenagers started planning—Ray Winston hit the sidewalks preaching.

He was greeted at every house with the miniature sad smiles people were wearing these days, and they listened to him preach from the Beatitudes leaning against their doors, looking out past Ray, into the street. They tilted their heads, arms crossed, willingly nostalgic. "I hear you," the listeners said, and "Thank you for that," when he was finished. A few were converted, and a few refreshed their worn-out commitments to Christ, but for the most part, these sorts of decisions had already been made. The believers would keep on believing, and those who wouldn't believe were in their own ways committed to their unbelief.

In more than one house there were packing boxes stacked in the doorway, ready to depart. "After the game," one man told Ray, "we're taking off. Don't know exactly where we'll go," he said, "but we're taking off." Others planned to stay and drive up to the General Electric plant in Catawba County to work, and a few were set on staying put. "This is America," they insisted. "Something else will come in, some other business to take hold of Goliath. We won't be sitting here long." One of the stayers invited Ray inside to see his pantry stocked with canned goods, his freezer with cellophane-wrapped packages of ground meat. He led Ray to the bathroom whose cabinet was stacked with toothpaste and toilet paper. He said, "I can survive here for months." He touched the stack of toothpaste boxes, neatly lined up.

Celeste Bradshaw said, "Ray, we're moving." She invited him in, same as the immutable stayer, but she wanted to show him the house's empty spaces instead of its plenty. "This was to be the baby's room," she said. It was not a room so much as a space inside a room, a small, boxy enclave set out by the living room whose windows overlooked her neighbor's hydrangeas. It was an unusual feature for a Goliath home, and Ray imagined the room had been providential. Ray Winston, who had long ago heard the call to a spiritual life from the woods, from his mother's deathbed, told Celeste, "It's as if it was always meant for a baby." And, perhaps it was only a man like Pastor Ray who could see the beauty in a bit of providence going to waste. "God planned it," he said, mostly to himself, "even knowing you wouldn't need it. It's a function of his generosity. An unnecessary provision."

Celeste said, "It's still good, you know? That we had this space for the baby, even if we're moving away now." She paused here, then lay her hand on Ray's arm, whispered, "We're moving to a town called Lewiston, Pastor Ray. Lewiston, *Maine*." She spoke conspiratorially, as if their moving all the way up to Maine was some sort of a scandal. It was an old habit of hers, giving information as gossip. "Ronald's cousin found work for him up that way." She shrugged. She regretted the time when she had hated Rosamond Rogers. She felt both sad and relieved by the passing of Goliath. "We'd never leave this town if we didn't have to."

Ray felt there was something to be said for the small peace of at least having something valuable to grieve. The loss of Goliath, the tentative joy and nervous pleasure of something else to move toward. Ray covered her hand with his own hand for a moment, laying on a blessing, then left.

. . .

Celeste Bradshaw could have been, in an entirely different time, one of the women to find the empty tomb on Easter morning. She might have been the one to question the angel, mistaking him for a gardener, begging him to show her the Christ. She had that same telling impulse, the tendency not to believe what she had seen with her own eyes until she told of it again and again.

Ray was more of a listener than a teller, yet he had spent these years both listening and speaking: knocking on doors, spreading the good news. God had created the lack in him from the beginning just so He could fill it. He had made a man who didn't want to speak, only so that, when that man obeyed, and when he made a life of speaking, he would come to love it, to adore the same task he simultaneously struggled against.

He had noticed how quiet Agnes had been lately, how much time she'd spent away from him, hiding in her ancient aunt's garden, and he had misjudged the reason. There she was, out there pulling weeds and dead plants—this was Mia Robins's garden; there was no end to the vegetable debris in that plot of ground—every second she wasn't working. He had seen the man who *might* be Hatley Rogers, returned after so many years, in the back of the church on the first night of Revival, and then it had been all Agnes could speak of for a week, and then nothing. *Nothing.* It felt to Ray now, walking through the town, preaching through the last days before the parade, that he had gained the town but lost Agnes. He was certain *something* had happened. She had met the man or she hadn't. He had turned out to be the real-life Hatley or he hadn't. Maybe he'd already left. Whatever the case, Ray believed something had convinced Agnes to hide from him. He feared, now more than ever, that she was preparing to leave.

He believed every word he preached; he couldn't say a word he didn't believe. A word he wouldn't stake his own life on. They were meant to circle around Goliath, exactly as the Israelites had circled Jericho, and claim it. *Reclaim it, and then move on.*

That was Goliath's calling, the town's instructions. But now Ray, having informed the town, would be set free. *Released.*

He laid on blessing after blessing. The streetlights winked on, and Ray hurried.

The plan came to him: he would tell her, *Let's go somewhere else.* She would likely think he meant to drive up the mountains and eat boiled peanuts from one of the roadside stands, though there weren't so many, now with the weather growing warmer. She might think he meant running off to Denny's by the interstate for coffee or to a movie or simply out for a long walk. They had not made plans for their own escape from Goliath; his job at the county was still good, at least at the moment, and she could probably go on working at the supermarket for a time. It seemed somehow that they were bound to stay together—their talk on her lawn the night of the revival had cemented something between them. Agnes had nearly said as much, before her great weed-pulling quiet had begun. Now, walking toward Mia Robins's house, toward Agnes's tiny basement room, Ray was struck with the staggering possibilities in this great, lost world. He imagined how he would say it, how he would reveal what he intended for him and Agnes. *I know the plans I have for you, plans to prosper you and not harm you.* The scripture was as near to him as his own thoughts. *Plans to give you a hope and a future.*

But he wouldn't quote to her. He would have his own words. He would say, *What I mean is for you to get out a map.* He had been steadfast, staying in Goliath to preach until the end, and now that he had been faithful with the small things, he glimpsed God opening his hands, revealing the entire planet. Ray could preach anywhere. *I want you to choose a spot,* he would tell Agnes, *any spot, and we'll go there. Just pick. You just tell me where, and I will take you there.*

SIXTEEN

They knew the town well enough to map it out for themselves. Goliath started at the railroad tracks running through the west end, the factory sitting there empty. The railroad was intersected by the highway, called Main Street within the town limits. This was the town's chief artery, other roads branching out from it. At the east end, on the hill, was the Harding house; Lucky Grocery up the highway beyond. Across, the cemetery with the ball field behind. Vincent explained: they would start just this side of the downtown shops, at the houses next to the church and the school. They would work their way east, toward the ball field. This would happen after the parade, during the baseball game, so that no one would stop them.

"No one will even be around," Vincent promised. Since the shed fire a few days earlier, the group had further diminished to eight.

"No one will get hurt?" one of them asked.

"No one will get hurt," Vincent reassured them.

He was calm and self-assured, hunkered down in the woods,

the notebook paper map on his lap. His father had said nothing about the burned-down shed, though his mother had spent half the night on the phone with her sisters, worrying over what to do with him. It was eerie, the quiet his father kept, and everyone in the house felt it. It was a grace, though, this ending for Goliath. Vincent and his followers intuited the town's rightful end. It was pure poetry, and fitting, to burn the town away to nothing. Cassie herself would want it this way. She had wanted it—a fire to consume all the buildings. Vincent felt peaceful and disconnected, planning it, letting go. He had lost his father that Sunday morning, the two of them standing out in the field while the coroner made his notes. His father had looked from the sky to the dead body to Vincent, and everything had changed. Nothing, Vincent knew, could ever be unchanged.

"No one has to worry," he told the others after a long pause, studying the ballpoint roads and the two-dimensional box houses. "We are doing the right thing here, the *only* thing." The others nodded and set their eyes hard. They had their own disappointments. The darkness had settled into the trees around them and the sky was blushing gray pink beyond. Vincent had seen the spirit glittering in the trees beyond the junk pile just that one time, the same night Rosamond saw it while standing on the tracks, half wishing her life away. He had not seen it since, but this night, walking home after dismissing the others, he sensed it just beyond the periphery of his vision—the crack of light, as from the sky opening. Then it was gone, and Vincent pretended not to have seen it at all, not even that first time.

She had not returned to Clyde that day. She had planned to, but the day got away from her in the impossible yet inevitable way of such days. Like the day Percy died. Or when Penny was finally, undeniably sick. Bed-weak and yellow-skinned, faint. Or like the day years ago when Hatley had first left her.

Her thoughts were infused with a sort of numb dread, and she lingered in Aunt Mia's front yard, in her driveway, and later in her kitchen until nightfall.

She slept on Mia's couch that night, as she had before the re-vival, before Clyde. *Clyde*, she thought. She worried: What did he think of her staying gone the whole day? The whole night? She lay on the sensible, sturdy-hard couch in Mia's living room, willing sleep, and kept recalling the day's pulsing blue sunlight. The startling somber endlessness of the sky above the driveway where she'd lain silent beside her daughter, the heady reality of empty air, of breathing it in.

She did little more than endure the next day, still adrift in the Hatley-ness of the previous day, the cloying smallness of his trailer. The parade preparations were in their final stages: the last coats of paint and sprigs of artificial greenery and discussions about the lineup and traffic closings and go-carts and tissue paper. There was frenzied activity in the Harding parking lot, and yet Rosamond remained virtually untouched by any of it. *Untouch-able*, unreachable, until at last, late in the night of the day after she had had breakfast with Hatley, she returned to Clyde.

She let herself in and found him in the living room, still awake though it was already past midnight. The television screen cast a bluish light over his face. He didn't turn to look at her when she stepped into the room, or even when she spoke his name gen-tly. Years later, she would look back on this moment, her stand-ing in the dark, waiting for him to acknowledge her, and realize something in that—his *not* turning to her—made him more himself, more starkly *Clyde,* than ever before. In this moment, seeing his a capacity for stubbornness, for *in*flexibility, a life with him seemed utterly possible. She hadn't even realized how *un*real such a life had seemed before.

"You're here," he said at last. "Well." He spoke coldly, evenly, as if he meant to be ironic, mock surprised, but he couldn't quite pull it off. Instead, his words were utterly flat, and Rosamond stopped, her purse still under her arm. She didn't sit. She opened her mouth to speak, but he gave her a stern look—sterner than she'd ever seen him give before. Even angrier than when Penny had died, though he had been mostly lost in those days. Bewildered. He laughed a short bark of a laugh and Rosamond wondered if he'd been drinking. If he had been, he wasn't anymore. He was just sitting there, slumped down in his easy chair, his eyes on the screen.

He said, "Dumbest movie I ever saw," and Rosamond stepped forward, clicked off the television. Clyde was in the dark now, though she could still see his face faintly in whatever light there was.

"But then you'd probably like it." His voice softened a little with that small joke. He sighed. "It starts with a plane-crash love scene, if that tells you anything."

She smiled in the dark, still wary of how Clyde was acting. "Hate to think where it ends," she said.

He laughed dimly and scraped his hand over his face. In that gesture, Rosamond tried to read him, to decipher what he knew, what he was thinking, and came up with nothing. Nothing she could know for sure, what he would say now, what he could tell just by being in the same room with her, by her staying away, by her coming, finally, now.

He held his hand over his chin and said, "Penny knew before I did." He looked her way but not at her. Instead he looked past her, through the window, into the street, as if there was something to see out there. "She teased me about it. Said she could see it from the beginning. My liking you. She laughed, said I had puppy-dog eyes for you, and you didn't even know I existed." He looked up at her in the scant dark, his hand still on his chin, resting there. "Those were her words. She said, *Clyde, that girl don't even know you exist.*"

"Clyde, I . . ."

She took a step closer, but he held up his hand. "Let me say my piece."

She nodded. "All right."

He sat up in his chair and leaned his elbows on his knees. He was quiet for a long moment, and then, nodding shortly to himself, he began.

"He's back. He's *been* back. I knew you'd see him, that he'd come after you, or you, you'd see him and be after him. I knew it. The first I saw of him downtown I thought, oh hell. The bastard. But I think it's good. You seeing him. I expect you need to see him. What do you think? Do you think it's good?" She couldn't speak, and he shrugged. "Hell," he said, and laughed shortly. "In any case, he's here. I know where he's been staying, and I know you've been there."

He said these words, gave his report, and wouldn't look at her. What she wanted to do was turn a light on, sit down, lean toward him, *touch* him. The backs of her knees ached from standing, and her arms were tired, too, just from holding still. Later she would think she hadn't breathed at all. That's how she would remember that moment, his pronouncing with such certainty—almost *arrogance,* Rosamond thought—what he believed was happening.

Finally he looked straight at her, and she shifted, half stumbled from the suddenness of it, the weight of him looking at her there in the near dark. "What you need to hear from me now is this: I've waited. I waited past Percy. Past *Dr.* Tucker. Past your grief. And now it's time. You make it clear to me what you want. What you're willing to take from me. You know it now," he said. "You *know* that I exist."

Clyde existed. *Yes.* What he couldn't understand, though, was to what degree she saw it now, his unmovable, unquestionable existence. She closed her eyes; again she stumbled a tiny bit, grasped the arm of the couch, finally lowered herself to sit there. The exhaustion she felt was so profound, she couldn't speak. She just sat on Clyde's couch, him a few feet away in his easy chair, and waited. Her eyes were closed. Her tiredness was nearly tangible, a pocket for her to slip into. Sweet oblivion beyond. But she would not give in to it quite yet. She sat there with her eyes closed and waited. Waited and waited for him to come, to sit beside her. She would not waver in either direction, would not sleep, would not stand up to leave, until he came.

And finally he did. He came to her. He sat next to her and she turned to him, lay her head on his shoulder, and touched his face.

She said, "I've made my choice. That's why I'm here."

He kissed her hand. "No more waiting," he said.

"No more waiting," she promised.

The next day was May second, the eve of Parade Day. Baseball Day. Burn-the-town-down day. A ruffle of clouds floated far away, above the mountains, and the *Goliath Star* and the Channel 12 newscasters out of Charlotte predicted more of the same for the morrow. Rosamond was, for the most part, reasonably calm; everything was ready. The only wrinkle—a significant one in Rosamond's view—was that she still had not heard from Dorothy Blair. Of course, it had been a long shot from the beginning, from the day she'd written to her a few months earlier. Beyond unlikely. But she had hoped.

"It's not tomorrow yet," Clyde said. He insisted Dorothy Blair still might come. "Stranger things have happened," he said.

Agnes spent the day boxing up her things and thinking of her mother. She planned how to tell her: she loved Ray. This had finally come to her, whole cloth, the day her father made coffee in the Lucky Grocery break room. When Hatley had explained to her the forces that pulled him away from Goliath—and now the forces that had drawn him back. She recognized her confusion, her years of hoping. He'd never pursued her before. He hadn't been the stranger she'd spotted across the way at McGraw or the man in the checked jacket at the boiled peanut stand in the mountains. She had been waiting so long for Hatley, but the man she truly wanted—needed—was the one to come to her a few nights ago, breathless with promise. *Anywhere you want to go,* Ray had told her. *We'll go there.*

But Clyde, in that dark hour in his living room, hearing all that Rosamond was promising him, had given a specific location. They would go live in a town called Roxie, near the coast. Pecan orchards, he'd told her. A *wedding,* he'd predicted. The beach less than an hour away.

But today Agnes was packing up her clothes, her secondhand toaster, her maps. Ray was making prayer calls on Mia's street, among the old ladies. Mia herself was trying to piece together the mystery of the disappearing trinket box. She looked through her dresser, searched among her unmentionables in the bottom drawer. Perhaps she had put it away and then forgotten. Perhaps no one had stolen it after all. Perhaps it never had *been* at all. She was an old woman, certain in her wisdom, her years, but lost in the day-to-day chores, unable to remember what she'd done just yesterday, let alone several weeks ago.

Stephanie Jameson was trying to reconnect with old, pre-suicide-cult friends in the cafeteria at school. Before the suicide cult made her semifamous at the school, she'd been friends with the academically minded, with members of the marching band. They allowed her to sit with them for lunch, but she sensed it would be awhile before she felt reconnected to them. Which made the whole thing practically useless: her family was moving the following week. So were half her old friends. By the summer, they'd likely all be gone.

Vincent Bailey and his followers were everywhere after school that Friday afternoon. They found cans of lighter fluid in their parents' basements; they bought matches and lighters at the gas station and Lucky Grocery. They got candy and soda too, just for fun, and slipped into Dalton's to use his cigarette vending machine. Stephanie was home doing her math homework, squirming in the pointlessness of it, but persisting nonetheless. She had heard the others, the Cassie mourners, were planning to disrupt the next day's events, but she worked to shrug it off. She didn't care, she decided. At this moment all she wanted was normal, even if that normal included math.

The other people in Goliath ate their dinners, watched their television shows, took their evening showers. Many of them went to bed early, while others stayed up to watch the late shows. A few did as Rosamond Rogers had done so many years ago after flying day: they rose in the middle of the night and scrubbed out their refrigerator shelves. They finished up leftovers, tossed out old newspapers.

The smallest of Goliath's children rose early the next morning, the morning of the parade. They slipped out of their beds and padded about their night-still houses, feeling the importance of the day. They fingered their parade costumes hung at the ready on closet doorknobs. Those who had been issued whistles—the junior baton twirlers—found them and touched them to their lips, pantomiming a great blow inside the gray-wrapped silences of their hushed houses. There were the first morning sounds of birds in the dark trees outside their windows, and sometimes a car sloped down the street, headlights flashing across their front lawns.

Their parents were nearly as excitable, having both dreaded and hoped for this day for some time, but when they arose, they moved more slowly than their children. They stood quietly inside their kitchens, listening to the coffee perk, looking out over their driveways to see if the paper had come. Many had already packed up their things and sent them off, or had them ready for the moving trucks in the hallways or stacked against the walls, and they felt bare and strange and anxious, waiting for the parade day to turn light. It was like the early morning of a long car trip. It seemed that by evening, the hills and mountains around them would be replaced by an altogether different topography. They might change states, cross international borders. When the coffee had finished brewing, they leaned against their kitchen counters and sipped, their children, holding their costumes in front of their pajamas, spinning out across the linoleum floors.

Rosamond woke near dawn, instantly recalling what day it was. She experienced a moment of stark vision, peering through the wall across the street into and through a series of houses, viewing images of fellow townspeople's bedrooms and kitchens, drapes and carpets and pillows, and the townspeople themselves, this family, this person, this child. All of it flashed through like clicks on a slide show, tunneling outward, all the way to Vincent Bailey in the country.

She watched the boy startle from sleep. He woke rubbing at his nose with the heel of his hand the way small children do. He had seen a young child, his hair still wet from his bath, combed straight, standing out in a field of grass, sunshine pulsing down around him in bubbles, bursting open on the boy's shoulders, on the points of the blades of grass. The boy was dressed in a short-sleeve plaid shirt and dark blue jeans and he looked around uncertainly. Blackbirds lifted from the telephone pole beyond the house, and there came the low, distant whistle of a yet-to-appear train.

Vincent shifted, pulling himself out of sleep, and Rosamond blinked her way back to her own reality. Clyde was waking up beside her. She told him, "Dorothy Blair is not coming."

Clyde had come to something like belief in the months since he'd shared a bowl of soup with Ray that night last fall. It had come to him—not really belief, but rather the belief that belief was possible—as he worked to bring baseball back to Goliath.

Discovering the field, recruiting Harold and Marty to help him clear it, and then watching the restorative act of work and the hope that comes with work, watching some small piece of matter changing under the influence of a man's own two hands, all of this had given him cause to believe in believing

His face was swollen and pink from sleep, his eyes only half open. He took a hand to rub the sleep out. He looped his arm around her waist and whispered into the fabric of her nightgown, "Dorothy Blair doesn't matter." Despite what she'd done a few days earlier, going to Hatley, being with him, or maybe *because* of it, Clyde was convinced: Rosamond was as faithful as any person he'd ever known. "This parade, this day is about you, and it's about Goliath. It's about going on with things."

He told her more about the town of Roxie, four hours' drive from Goliath. "Four hours, that's all. We'll get up one morning next week, get in the car, and we'll be there by noon. We'll have lunch in Roxie." He described the town to her. A narrow, tree-lined street ran through the town, little white houses on either side. Painted metal mailboxes at the end of every driveway. Clyde had been there once before. Years ago he and Penny had stumbled through on their way to the beach. "We stopped there for lunch and to gas up, and Penny found an old woman selling carnations out front of the restaurant." Another, a long-haired man down the way, sold watercolors out of the bed of his truck. The ground was sandy there, Clyde said, even on the highway. It was close enough to the beach to smell the ocean. Seabirds flew overhead and displaced sand crabs crawled through the mud.

"We always planned to go back there," Clyde said. Rosamond understood—was grateful, in a way—that Penny would always be with them. After all, she had loved her too. It was no disloyal act, Clyde's bringing Rosamond to the town he and Penny had found together, had dreamed of returning to. Rosamond knew that part of Clyde's happily ever after was to live in the town he and his late wife had once shared. He *needed* Roxie. After all, Clyde had his own heart-secrets, his own past. They would go to Roxie, North Carolina, and settle among the pecan trees, the sandy highways.

Vincent rose from bed and left the house without saying a word to anyone. His sisters were still sleeping, and his mother was in the kitchen, beating eggs in a glass bowl. He stood in the doorway and watched her for a moment, stepping out through the back door, screen door clanging shut behind him, just as she looked up. "Vincent?" he heard her calling, but he was already out the door. The sky was clear and light outside, a little damp in the earliness of the day, the sun glowing fiercely orange at the edge of the sky. His father, dressed in his stiff work clothes, his sweat-worn baseball cap, was in the yard, bent over the car he built. He worked to refit something in the engine it looked like, likely just tinkering. Just admiring his own handiwork, making tiny adjustments. He stood to watch Vincent go by. Neither spoke. John Bailey's eyes slid over his son, held his gaze a second; then he returned his attention to the inside of that car.

Vincent kept on over the hard-packed dirt with his backpack thrown over one shoulder. He walked under the breezy blue sky the length of the old county road. The morning grew warmer as he went and the sunshine was nearly palpable, as if it was no longer coming from the sky but rather from the air itself. The light had no distinct source. He crossed weedy ditches, muddy spots. Before he even came to the railroad tracks, before the gas station, he heard the commotion coming from the factory parking lot, the meeting place for the floats: marching band instruments piping up, the squeals of young children who had been awake for hours now and were starting to go giddy tired, the laughs and calls and admonitions of their parents. It was just past eight o'clock; the parade would begin in less than two hours.

Vincent stepped over the curb, meaning to amble though the gathering crowd, to observe. The parking lot was a spectacle of little girls dressed as butterflies, old ladies in straw hats brandishing too-bright gardening tools. Show tools, Vincent thought. Boy Scouts straightened their neckerchiefs and elbowed one another. One called out to another: no way he could lasso a bag of potato chips with his retractable key chain. The other called back, *Watch me*. The junior baton twirlers were waiting with painted-on stage faces, throwing up their batons and watching helplessly— again and again, the batons, blinking silver in the air, came down in the wrong places. Vincent drifted through, looking from this specimen to another, guessing the old men's commentaries by their expressions and not wanting to, predicting which butterfly would be the first to break down in tears. They were already growing shabby, their felt wings sagging, the glitter falling off as they chased one another through the maze of waiting floats. He viewed the First Bank of Goliath's huge American flag made from carnation blooms, the Jaycee-sponsored barn-replica float complete with a cardboard cow and a real-life chicken. There was even a Harding float, made and decorated by who knew who, with a huge papier-mâché rocking chair and old photos blown up to poster size from the factory's dedication seventy years earlier. A gaggle of very young children hopped around eating popcorn, their animal costumes half on, masks held on with elastic strings. This one had the orange and brown spotted legs of a giraffe. This one had only the yarn-mane of a lion.

Vincent looked on and felt that he was drawn back from every-thing, all of it small and distant. Even the faces of other high school students, the marching band and those on the Future Farmers of

America float, were both familiar and unknown, same as the face of the lost little boy he'd dreamed of that morning. The sounds were strained too, as they had been the morning he'd found Percy Harding. The calm and solemn voices of the authorities were so small, Vincent was unsure of where they were coming from. No one spoke to him, and only a few glanced his way. It could be that he was walking through an event that had already happened, that these players woke every morning to reconstruct the happenings, the parade preparations. It seemed everyone around him knew what was going to happen, but they carried on, pretending.

Vincent shuffled through, emerging on the other side of the parking lot. He came up behind the high school, setting out for the houses. Vincent walked quickly and slowly in fits, falling in and out of thought. He tried to see everything around him, the grass, the bits of trash in the gutters, the houses as a stranger would. See them and just think *green*. Or *old*. Or *pile of rocks there. Weeds.*

He arrived at the convenience store where he used to go with Cassie and stopped. He couldn't keep himself from remembering, and a moment later, he was walking inside. But the pregnant lady wasn't there. Vincent asked, and the girl behind the counter, a punk girl with razor-cut black hair whom he recognized from school but whose name he didn't know, shook her head. "She had her baby," was all she could tell him. She stared at him. "Vincent Bailey." He nodded. Since Percy Harding had died, since Cassie, he'd been famous. She sneered harder. "She's not here," she said again, waiting for Vincent to go.

He stood a moment longer though, unwilling to leave whole and unhurt like this. He wanted to apologize, but he also wanted to give the quivering pregnant lady a chance to seek her revenge. She might materialize. She might come out and punch him. It seemed possible, this strange gold-lit morning, the floats lined up in the factory lot, for the pregnant lady—Fay, he remembered—to

suddenly appear, or for the girl behind the counter to turn com-
bative. Just because he was standing there. Because he was looking
at her without talking. Because she *knew*. She could step around
the counter and jab her knuckle in his eye. She was a girl, and
small but tough-looking. Her dark hair was cut short enough in
front to bristle. She could knock him down, kick the life out of
him. If the wounded pregnant lady didn't appear, someone else
would knock him down. The punk girl kept on staring at him
over the counter.

Vincent didn't, however, see the other girl who was standing
several feet behind him, by the drink cooler. The girl with the
frizzy brown hair, sour-faced and wide-eyed and shaky nervous.
Obscenely freckled, Vincent might have thought if he had glanced
her way, the mood he was in. The mean ways he'd come to voice
his thoughts. Of course he would have recognized her, would
have known it was Stephanie Jameson, the former—now recanted—
leader of the suicide cult. He might have noticed too the way she
was watching him, the look on her face, both shocked and com-
prehending, and then determined. Stephanie seemed to know that
there was something going on. Something about Vincent's voice
had proven it to her. The way he narrowed his eyes at the girl
behind the counter, kept on standing there, the fact that he was
even here in town on a Saturday morning. A repellent, desperate
energy was emanating from him—his brown-eyed, sweat-streaked
face, an almost imperceptible tremor in his legs, his hands, his half-
cocked smile, quick-blinking eyes, staring and staring at this girl
across the register. They—Vincent Bailey and the rest—*were* planning something. Something terrible and unthinkable and irrevers-
ible. Something *huge*.

Clyde insisted again: "Dorothy Blair will come." Rosamond
shook it off; she had other things to worry about. She gulped her
coffee down, rose to stretch, to have the smallest moment of

quiet, of sheer happiness at the arrival of parade day. A *miracle.*
She said, "The butterflies don't know where to stand."

She dressed and hurried down to the factory lot where the
commotion was already in play, the high school band lining up,
those terrible, thick-plumed hats askew, kazoo blowers and their
mothers milling around, unsure where to stand, uniformed policemen passing out their candy too early. Rosamond began to
help with the order, shepherding children and adults, costumed
and uncostumed, here and here, in line, a well-thumbed lineup
page on a clipboard gripped to her chest. She imagined she knew
things about the parade participants: she could see the places they
were going. What all was in store for them, beyond this day, after
the parade, the baseball game. This woman, squat, with broad
shoulders and a round, flushed face, a gluer from the factory
whom Rosamond had known since grade school, would be living in a town whose water tower, lime green, rose like a stilled
hot-air balloon over the top of the post office. Another woman,
a young long-haired and tall woman Rosamond didn't know by
name, would work in a supermarket bakery. Rosamond flashed
to the woman's hands icing a great white sheet cake, carving
smooth white over the spongy yellow. This man, a member of
the Morning Glories, would live in a house with pale pink curtains
on his bedroom windows. He would peer out onto a backyard
he didn't know. This family, the butterfly child and her parents,
would get in a car and drive a long way, the little girl staring out
the window at the changing landscape, everything going flat, then
cement and steel, then loping and grassy. Some of the flashes
were nothing more than a glimpse of a house or a square of carpet
or a clothesline. Sometimes a parked car, a patch of asphalt, a strand
of pearls coiled on top of a dresser.

She caught sight of Agnes walking through the crowd with a
cumbersome tray of paper cups, coffee for the parade workers from
a booth Wally Thumb had set up in one corner of the lot. She

too imagined she could see what would become of Agnes: Agnes bundled in a thick coat walking a broken and muddy cement walkway between squat, featureless buildings. There were children out there, in Agnes's future, and a far-off place. Far, *far* away, just as Rosamond had always imagined. She stopped her the next time she passed close, asked, "Where are you going?" Agnes only nodded to the other corner of the parking lot and lifted the cardboard tray of coffees she was to deliver. Rosamond's mind was slow and gummed up this morning. "No," she said, "I mean, where are you and Ray going?" Agnes shrugged, and Rosamond saw anew how pretty her daughter's long dark hair was, how clean and simple and beautiful her face was. Agnes couldn't answer, and Rosamond finally admitted, "Agnes, he loves you."

She looked back at her mother among all the happy, half-frantic townspeople. There passed between them a flicker of understanding. Later they would have to talk about Hatley. About what had happened, about what *would* happen, whether either planned to see him again. But for now they only exchanged a brief and unfamiliar satisfying look. A *recognition*. Agnes nodded.

"But I don't know where we'll go," she told Rosamond. "We haven't got everything figured out."

Rosamond was called away by one of the mothers from the drugstore who had volunteered today to help coordinate the parade. She wanted to know if Rosamond would give the all-clear signal that it was time for procession to start. The woman raised her eyebrows. She tapped on her watch. "You see?" she asked. "It's ten o'clock exactly."

Rosamond squinted at the factory lot. Somehow the jumble of costumes and people and instruments and vehicles and cardboard barns and carnation flags had arranged themselves in a crumpled line, with a cherry-red convertible nosing into Main Street. The convertible held a lumpy balding man dressed in a gray suit, the mayor of Goliath, and his similarly dowdy wife, nodding and smiling at something he had said. The line of floats crossed the lot and curled back into the street behind, every one of them at the ready. Rosamond, looking down Main Street, saw that both sides of the street were thick with people on blankets and lawn chairs, every citizen of Goliath waiting for her go-ahead.

She fleetingly thought of Dorothy Blair; a part of her half believed the parade would be a complete miracle, that the ancient movie star could still appear. Just like in a movie, at the final scene, everything perfect. But she wasn't here and it was time. It was fine. Everything, she saw, was perfect enough, and Rosamond gave a nod to the convertible driver. Let the parade begin.

As the cherry-red convertible eased out and began its slow creep down Main Street, the mayor and his wife lifting their arms to wave, as the spectators began cheering from their lawn chairs, waving little American flags the First Bank of Goliath had passed around, Rosamond stopped: she had forgotten something.

She hurried down the Main Street sidewalk, picking her way around the people in lawn chairs and those sitting on the curb, all the way down to her own house, which she'd shared with Hatley, with Agnes, where she had finally lived by herself for the years it took the boy husband to come and drive it all away. She came up the porch steps and threw open the door. Stepping inside, her eyes adjusted to the dark of the house, and she saw she was not alone.

There in the middle of her living room stood the thief, the boy named Vincent. His hands were at his sides, and it was impossible to tell if he'd done anything before she arrived. He appeared a bit older than when Rosamond had last seen him just a few weeks earlier, his hair a little longer maybe, and impossible as it was, Rosamond was struck by how tall the boy was. He had just come to her shoulder the day he tried to rob Mia's house and now seemed much taller than she was. He stood blinking in the sudden gush of light Rosamond had let in.

"I've forgotten something," she told him. Then it occurred to her to explain, "There's nothing left in here." Vincent said nothing, watching her. His face was set hard and distrustful, and Rosamond saw that it was his expression that made him seem older. He wasn't really so tall.

"This is all that's left," she continued and opened the closet door. Her coat was hanging there. A sadness that rigid—what she saw in the boy—was dangerous. "All that's left is a coat in this closet. That's all I have here. But then," she went on, "you're not here to steal from me. I can tell you're not." She paused. She touched the coat, slid the shoulders out from the hanger and folded it over her arm. "I don't know why you're here." Vincent said nothing. "Did you just need a place to rest?"

She felt inside the coat pocket and pulled out what was there: the letter opener she had thought to give the Harding family months ago, when Percy had first died. "Whatever it is you're planning," she said, clenching the smooth blade in her palm, touching the tip of the carved cardinal's beak with her finger, "whatever it is you aim to do here today, whether it be during my parade or Mr. Winston's ball game, I'm going to ask you to reconsider." She held the letter opener out to him, opening her fingers so he could see. "Isn't it pretty?" she asked.

"Lady," Vincent said. Rosamond saw now he had something in his hand, a notebook with a pen tucked into the spiral. His hair was greasy and he looked as scruffy as the boy husband had when he'd arrived on her doorstep months ago, looking for Agnes. "You don't even know me."

Looking down at the tiny carved bird in her hand, she said, "I know who you are. You saw him. You saw Mr. Harding and it's hurt you, looking at death like that. Looking at that *kind* of death."

He was quiet a moment. They could hear the sounds of the parade happening outside the door, folks on lawn chairs cheering up the street. The sunshine flowing through the open door was as soft as cream, like warm milk spilling all over Rosamond's back and across her shoulders.

"I shouldn't have told anyone," he said at last. It was the same thing he'd confessed to Cassie back in the fall. "I just shouldn't have."

She frowned at him, still holding out the letter opener until she looked down and saw it. She closed her hand around and slipped it back into her pocket.

"You couldn't have changed anything," she said. "Vincent," she said, remembering the name that Mia had given her months ago—the boy who found Percy's body was named Vincent. "You did the right thing."

"I took a different way coming home. That's how come I found him. I shouldn't have." He looked at her. "I should *not* have come back that way."

"You did just fine," she said. "You did just fine. What else was there for you to do?" And he grimaced at that—at how far off she was from understanding his true thoughts, his real fears. A person can be illogical and grieved, too. A person can think ridiculous things and then those ridiculous things could be more harmful, more *real* than anything that actually happened, than anything a person could prove was true. He should not have found the body—this was the only thing he knew in this moment or in any moment since it had happened. He should not have come that way at all.

She said, "No one knows another's heartache. No one knows, truly knows, another person's troubles."

He was quiet a moment, and Rosamond thought, *there.* She thought she had him, that she had done it: that she had *saved* him. This boy, this sad thief. She thought he could see the truth in her words, in how much she understood him, how achingly and honestly she lived her own losses, how she carried them with her in her coat pocket.

"Listen," she said after a moment, "I have to get back to the parade. You should come with me. You can sit with me. I'm right next door"—she gestured in the direction of Clyde's house—"watching."

He wouldn't go, though. Instead, he turned instantly back to stone, back to a boy with a frozen look, a boy who could not be reached—who didn't *want* to be reached. She sighed. "There's nothing in here that you can't have." She looked around, the rooms empty but for furniture. "You can *have* this house."

She left then, hurrying out to the parade, and Vincent sat in a square of light coming around the thick gold curtains in the living room. He listened to the parade, the whistling of the junior baton girls, the calls and clapping of the townspeople lined up in the streets. The others—the band of Cassie Stewart mourners—gathered unseen in the other long-empty or just vacated houses and prepared with their matches, their cans of lighting fluid, ready for the end of the parade, signaled by the high school marching band's final row of drums disappearing up the far end of Main Street.

Up on the other end of the street, lingering up near the starting line, the factory lot, Stephanie Jameson stumbled stupidly, aimlessly about. Some odd-crazy thought, or a protective instinct: *something* was coming. She worried it was the factory itself, something there. Then she was certain it was the high school. She was tormented by what she knew and what she didn't know. A creepy steely edge to Vincent Bailey's voice. A rumor, what his crowd was up to today, what they had planned, some kind of trouble. But Stephanie didn't know. She didn't know what might happen or who it might happen to. She couldn't even say: was there truly any danger? Any danger in any of this?

Rosamond went next door to watch the parade from Clyde's porch steps, and she was alive and happy and scared for the boy thief's sake and not even caring at last that Dorothy Blair hadn't come. She didn't tell Clyde about the boy, but she looked around, hoping to see him out here, in the open. The giant American flag passed and she said, "Look, the flowers haven't wilted." Here came the monstrous plywood rocker, wagons of the the Ladies Auxiliary, the spring birthdays, from March through June. Tiny pink-cheeked girls carrying heavy-headed daisies.

Vincent Bailey sat alone in Rosamond's old house. He listened to the parade-noises through the shut front door and took stock of his equipment: a matchbook courtesy of his old man's dresser top, a can of lighter fluid he'd purchased at the Lucky Grocery the week before.

The high school was closed up tight, of course, the double doors around back locked with a chain. Still, Stephanie walked around the building, peeking into the windows, all empty, but still, what? What was it? *Something* was going to happen. She felt it now same as she'd felt it the night of the revival, the moment everything was so very still and quiet. The night Cassie Stewart, a girl she'd barely known, had swallowed those pills, one right after another.

Finally she determined to tell someone. She came around the hill behind the high school, around the patch of woods, through the factory parking lot, the first floats returning, everyone clamoring, excited and exhausted at the same time. People were shaking off their costumes, their headgear and animal paws, their glitter and wigs and smeared makeup and cowboy hats. Everywhere there were girls in jeans with lipsticked ragdoll cheeks. The policemen in their uniforms, still carrying their baskets of candy, threw the last of them out among the retired parade walkers. Stephanie stopped in front of one of the policemen, but he didn't even see her; he was squinting in the midday light, looking for someone among the crowd. She put her hand out to catch one of the mothers' arms, but the woman turned, told her the parade was almost over. "You need to sit down a minute, take a breath," the woman told her, then was pulled away by one of her children.

Stephanie went on then, past the parade people, crossed the street between floats. The pizza restaurant was closed tight, but the door to the Tuesday Diner gave when she pulled on it. Inside, there were two customers: a pale-featured woman eating a sundae and a black-haired man with a newspaper, sitting in the very back, in the boy drifter's old seat. Wally Thumb was freshening the man's coffee, and he looked up at her. "Something is happening," she told them. "Something *awful* is happening."

The marching band—the grand finale—stumbled past, their movements shaky but earnest, their steps mismatched but faithful, committed to the task, the orange plumes from their helmets wafting in the breezy blue spring air. Rosamond spoke now, told Clyde, "They're to be together." She sighed a little, both wistful and excited and still a tiny bit incredulous at the turn of events. "Ray and Agnes," she said. "They're to be together.

"They're to be *happy*," Rosamond insisted, and the girl Stephanie Jameson searched the faces before her: the wan sundae eater, the gray-bearded, black-haired man, Wally Thumb himself, pausing there with the coffee carafe in his hand, his mouth opening to speak.

Vincent dropped the match in Rosamond's house, long emptied. The flame sprang out bright orange blue, and Vincent, having locked all the doors, checked to see all the windows were shut tight, whispered the months-old poem: *No way to enter or to leave, the house held itself closed. The demons could not depart, the angels could not enter.*

SEVENTEEN

The parade, later recalled with the generous glow of things long past, was extraordinary: the sparkling butterfly girls, the serious-faced Boy Scouts with their American flags, their salutes, the church elders with their tracts, their declaration *He has risen!* The high school band marched almost in sync, and the cardboard cow looked as real as any cardboard cow had ever looked.

Afterward, nearly every citizen turned out to play in Clyde Winston's baseball game. They were clumsy at it, but no one cared. They let old ladies walk the bases and permitted children limitless swings and pitches that were so slow, the ball seemed to hang suspended over the plate. Both teams swelled fifty or sixty strong. Crowds stood out in left field and punched their fists into their gloves, hunched over, watchful. The line of players waiting for a turn at bat started behind home plate, circled around, and continued past third base. Observers sat in lawn chairs all along the sides and in the grassy space beyond. Others picnicked in the cemetery or tailgated in a patch of gravel below the field.

Teenagers fell into the woods and children played everywhere, swirling through the spectators' blankets and lawn chairs and through the maze of grave markers in the cemetery just beyond the playing field.

This time the ball was barely nudged by the bat and the batter seized her chance while the other team scrambled after the ball. Next came a lumbering teenager who loosened up with a few practice swings before hunkering down over the plate, squinting. The bat made contact with the ball in a soul-satisfying pop and no one caught the fly. The bases emptied. From among the spectators, cheers and impromptu baseball songs gave way to chanting and stomping. Clyde stood on the sideline between third and home with his hands in his pockets. He told Rosamond: "It's good. Everything I'm seeing, it's *good*."

Harold Clarkson, in a stiff blue baseball cap that looked awkward and new and altogether too big on his old gray head, paced out front of the makeshift dugout, calling out to his team the sort of directions and encouragement Little League coaches offered their players: *Keep your eye on the ball* and *Catch that ball* and *Attaboy, attagirl*. They ignored strike-outs and kept swinging until a good twenty players had had a turn. Marty Pickard stood near third and nodded encouragingly at any player who looked his way. Ronald Bradshaw covered second base while his wife Celeste sat watching the game with her hands resting on her pregnant belly, a fertility goddess in a lawn chair.

The people were so caught up in their game that the first hint of smoke to waft up to them went undetected. It grew stronger, and the high school principal, who was pitching for Marty Pickard's team, paused, baseball in hand, arm cocked back and ready to throw. He looked toward the street below them, hidden under the belly of the hill they were standing on, and a few of the other players turned to see where his gaze was searching. Before the smell was full enough to pronounce the word *fire,* their eyes began to sting from it and Mia Robins, squatting over home plate preparing to swing, called out, "Smoke." She let her bat drop. The young girls behind her, waiting for their own turns at bat, giggled, believing *smoke* to be a weak old-lady cussword. But then one of the Morning Glories in the outfield pointed out a whorl of gray rising like a tuft of pulled cotton through the blue sky and pronounced it: "Fire." It was calm, how he said it, and that was what the people would remember most clearly, the unearthly peace that first enveloped the news. For a long moment, the citizens of Goliath were perfectly quiet, soul-still, and the fear did not touch them.

They looked on, watching the smoke rise up through that gold-dust air, and a moment later, the fire was high enough to catch glimpses of, the orange-yellow flames shimmering up at the crease of grass-hill and asphalt-street. There was the sound of it, a low-buzzing crackle so soft at first it seemed to be coming from the people's own thoughts, from their imaginations, but then growing more intense when their attention was turned to it, and a few whispered, "I hear it." The smell turned from just faint smoke to things burning, the familiar scent of wood going to ash and smoke, the heat-fueled process of separating the natural, which burned easily, and the unnatural, the synthetics, the polyesters and nylons, splitting to soft plastic and fumes.

The people left bats and drink coolers lying on the ground. Others went with their baseball gloves still on their hands, not thinking to take them off, and the picnickers mindlessly rolled closed the tops of their potato chips bags and propped them against the grave markers, as if they meant to return to them soon. Clyde Winston turned to take Rosamond's hand, and the two went with the others.

The field emptied, Clyde and Rosamond moving down the hill with the others, still mostly quiet though others were calling to one another, training their eyes on the stretch of road below them, down from the cemetery, until they finally saw it: a smear of orange far down, beyond the untouched houses, the saved ones on the left side of the street, and then, nearing, an identical orange smear, a *breathing* entity, reaching up on the other side. Twin fires: the one on the church side of the street was further along; the flames surged above the trees. Inside these houses, the houses of ordinary people, of bankers and factory workers and teachers, the synthetic carpet fibers smoldered and melted and moved, almost invisible, igniting the seats of sofas and surrounding the legs of kitchen tables, the linoleum curling and turning hot synthetic yellow beneath.

There was fire beyond Main Street; above, on August Street, where the old, well-pensioned people lived, their gardens scorched from the radiant heat alone, a stack of newspapers burning on one back porch—the back porch of the only August Street house to catch fire. This house—two down from Mia's house—burned in the middle of a street of unharmed white and gray houses. The kitchen was engulfed, fire pouring through the cupboards, jars of homegrown green beans and strawberry jam exploding one by one on the basement shelves. Below August Street, on the tiny unnamed graveled path that led up to Dalton's bar, where the few houses were little more than cinder-block boxes, the air was thick and sooty, embers flying recklessly, finally catching on a tree whose limb, engulfed in flames, crashed onto the roof of a toolshed. In a loosely joined neighborhood of old pines and sturdy brick carports on the other side of the cinder-block shacks, the flames of one house—that of the owner of the pizza restaurant—ignited the roof of another. The upholstered dining room chairs burst into flame and snagged the gauzy dining room curtains, which were gone in a second, the windows briefly flashing orange as if quick-lit from inside. Bed linens caught, rugs caught, bookshelves collapsed. Flames reached up the interior walls and curled the edges of framed photographs of the restaurant owner's children until the wall itself, entirely consumed, crumbled apart. Finally the roof gave way, sending a whoosh of sparks into the street.

These fires in process were farther up from Rosamond Rogers's house, which had been lit before the others and was burned down to smoldering now. Rosamond and Clyde stopped there. The house was old-time stucco, and the roof had held, but Rosamond could see the insides were hollowed out, the giant living room window cracked and gone, everything blackened inside. She stood amazed at how completely the things inside her house had burned; even at this distance, she could see the gold couch in the living room was gone, burned away, and though the walls still stood, everything on the walls had been consumed or else turned to ash. Her beautiful fleur-de-lis wallpaper, which she had hung herself right after she and Hatley were married, scorched now beyond recognition. She thought of her kitchen: had the refrigerator survived? And the upstairs: was there a scrap of furniture, of carpet, of curtain left anywhere? The smoke was still thick: it was impossible to see anything or to register the loss of anything for certain.

Rosamond stood several yards away in the street, her hands folded in front of her face, and Clyde drew close. He reached out, touching her arm, and she leaned into him.

"The boy," she whispered. "Where's the boy?"

Farther up, where the houses kept burning on either side of the street, and above, on the side streets, the fires roared loudly, steadily, and the people had to yell to make themselves heard. They stood back in the street, but even there, their faces burned. On one side of Main Street, the low square windows had turned black and now cracked apart, falling in chunks into the scorched boxwood bushes below. The owners of the houses, a few young families on one side, older, working folks on the other, could only stand in the street, watching. None of it was real to them in that moment. No one yet began to think, *who?* The sight before them was enough. Most of the children were stunned to stillness, terrified, but a reckless few hopped anxiously about, and the grown-ups had to grip their shoulders to keep them from going too close. The watchers looked hard into the stretching blazes those first moments before the fire trucks arrived. They stood with the shoulders of their children gripped tight in their hands; above, on August Street, Mia held tight to her sobbing neighbor's hand. And even as they stood silent, chilled with fear, with unbelief, they marveled at the fantastic display of destruction, those leaping hot flames, at how *alive,* how sweeping and magnificent the great red fires were, how beautiful extinction could be.

Wally Thumb's first impulse, after three or four seconds of speechless surprise at seeing Stephanie Jameson burst hollering into his diner, was to protect the girl. His second thought was: of all mornings, this was happening *today*? He hadn't even planned on opening this morning, the morning of the parade, but had changed his mind at the last minute, figuring there would be at least one hungry customer to come in, one person who wasn't so committed to the parade that he couldn't tear himself away for a cup of coffee. Later, when all the pieces came together, when in the week or so Goliath had left, the series of events, the damages tallied, and the details of Vincent Bailey's miraculous escape from the fire became known, Wally would realize he had been placed on this earth for a purpose. That he had opened up that morning for a *reason*. He had had a part, however small, in saving a young person's life.

What he did in the moment, though, was to quiet the girl down. It seemed the most responsible thing to do, especially when he pressed her, asked her what exactly was happening, and she answered that she didn't know. "All right," he said, "You sit down here." He then brought the girl a Coke and went to try to locate her parents.

The man in the drifter boy's corner, however, took the frantic girl at her word. Hatley, who had been watching the fair-haired woman eat her sundae while he sipped his coffee and looked disinterestedly over the newspaper, rose from his table, left a couple of dollars to cover his bill, and nodded good-bye to the sundae eater. This much the three remaining in the diner could attest to. What happened next, or rather why what happened next happened—how Hatley came to be the one to save Vincent Bailey from the fire—was never entirely pieced together, though there were some clues.

Hatley left the diner, hurried the up Main Street, past the elementary school and the post office, past the enormous white Baptist church, a number of other houses, and then to Rosamond Rogers's house. No one was certain what had delayed him—nearly an hour must have elapsed between his hearing Stephanie's pronouncement in the diner and Hatley's dragging Vincent, already unconscious, from the burning house. Some speculated he had first hurried to check on his own possessions inside his trailer before going to Rosamond's house, but others pointed out: Hatley had no reason to suspect fire. Stephanie Jameson herself didn't know at the time about the fire. All she knew and said was that something was happening. Just *something,* which of course could have turned out to have been nothing at all.

In any case, what must have happened was this: Hatley had broken Rosamond's picture living room window—with a stick? a rock? his own *fist?*—crawled inside, and lifted the boy out of the center of the house. How he found the boy was not known; the firefighters suspected the walls were already burning at the time—the place was filled with smoke. It could not have been easy for the man to find the boy, and the boy, out cold, would not have been able to call for help.

The most sentimental among the people of Goliath believed he was something like an angel: God-touched, *special.* Others believed he was simply foolish, diving into a burning house like that. And still others suggested he had his own death wish. What better way to go out than as a hero?

It was only by chance that Hatley's identity was uncovered. Stephanie Jameson spotted him among the other onlookers, recognized him from the diner—the man who had hurried away—and upon questioning him, realized he had pulled Vincent Bailey from the fire. Later, he admitted his name and his business in Goliath: he was the long-lost husband of Rosamond Rogers, father to Agnes. Yet he would never speak of the incident other than to admit that he had simply been at the right place at the right time. It was all he said in the days right after the fire, and then a few weeks later, when a news crew from Charlotte came to interview him about his act of heroism and the call he'd made to emergency services from the neighbor's—a retired police chief's, in fact—telephone.

"Right time, right place," Hatley said, and shook his head. He gave the reporter, a pretty, brown-haired woman in a mannish blunt-shaped pantsuit, a modest grin that was broadcast that evening on a number of affiliated news channels' programs across the country.

Vincent himself didn't know what had happened. He knew only that he had stayed inside the house as the fire built, surrounding him, and then suddenly he was on a patch of cool grass several houses down, waking from something that wasn't sleep but a blink-quick loss of consciousness. He alone saw the stranger, whom he later identified as Hatley, move away through the crowds. Around him, people were milling, watching, stricken, and no one even saw Vincent. At first no one understood what this boy had survived.

Once he dropped the lit match inside his own assigned house, Vincent didn't know if the others had followed suit. He felt instantly and completely alone inside the house that used to belong, he had heard, to a traveling salesman, and now belonged to and had been abandoned by that salesman's ex-wife. Vincent had recognized her also as the same woman who had caught him and Cassie stealing. He had risen at Rosamond's leaving, still shaken by the surprise of seeing her—it seemed she *knew* what he was going to do. She had left him there, and Vincent, rising up, checked, made sure that the doors were locked, the dead bolt on the front door thrown, before he sat and speaking Cassie's old poem—a poem she had written before any of this—he struck the match against the paper.

The fire was a small thing at first, a burst of flame at his feet, but it grew quickly, thriving on the carpet, the sofa, and the curtains and leaping across the walls. Vincent knew at once what a coward he was, for he felt the heat from the fire and shrank away from it. He curled up and ducked his head to his knees, his eyes squeezed shut, humming to himself to block out his fears. Years ago, he had been given a pocket-size blue leather Bible by one of the elders of his mother's church. His mother had put him to bed reading from that little Bible. She read everything, but lingered over the Psalms and the Book of John, which she re-named the Book of Hope. Just a few weeks ago, he had stood up in the woods and recited Cassie's poems to the others gathered there, and before that, he had looted his way through almost every home in Goliath. He had *kissed* Cassie Stewart. And, before that, months and months ago, he had come in from lighting a campfire near the creek behind his house and found a dead body. Even now, crouched down in Rosamond Rogers's house, it was the stillness of that body that terrified him.

The fire was reaching up the walls now, and only the ceiling above him and a few pieces of furniture nearby were intact. The smoke hurt his lungs. And then Vincent lost consciousness.

Finally, a woman watching the fire noticed Vincent sitting on the grass, covered in soot. His T-shirt had burned through in great, black-rimmed holes. She made him stand and called others to examine him. Where had he been? What had he seen? His jeans were scorched and the rubber in the soles of his shoes had softened in the fire. They made gray smudges on the sidewalk. Though his hair smelled of smoke and the creases of his hands and face were black with soot, his skin, his eyes, his mouth were not burned. He was trembling, and the woman instructed him to shake out his limbs. Was he hurt? What had happened to him? The boy couldn't speak. The people, gathering around, looked him over, called to the firefighters and other emergency workers to come see. Rosamond and Clyde, hearing of the discovery, came near, and Rosamond touched his arm, looked close in his eyes. Pastor Ray was ushered close, and he pronounced it: not an inch of Vincent Bailey had been harmed in that fire.

That Goliath should end in devastation and miracle was not too great a surprise to Agnes. She had returned to Goliath because she needed a place away from her boy husband. After that, it seemed she couldn't leave her mother. These things were only on the surface, though. Beneath, Goliath seemed to have a greater gravitational mass than any other place on earth. It was as if a giant magnet was buried there, just below the dirt. Agnes, sensitive to the call of geographical locales large and small, believed that the town, needing witness to its end, had called her to it, kept her there.

This day she had her mother's ancient black camera and she filled the film first with images of the parade—the homecoming queen, the butterfly girls, the old men in uniform, so many Goliath townspeople marching; then scenes from the baseball game, the bat swingers, the base runners, those who stood in the outfield with vacant looks on their faces; and finally the fire, shots of those disheveled and sweaty from the baseball game pressed together, looking on with every different expression of grief, confusion, and wonder. One woman, watching her own house burn, sat down in the street and held her child, exhausted by the day's events, in her lap. Another, a man, stood back with his hands open at his sides, his arms flexed and his face expectant as if he were looking for his chance to step forward, to quell the fire. The fire trucks arrived and an old woman, her thin white hair loose down her back, stood back looking on, her eyes calm and knowing. She seemed completely unattached to the spectacle before her. Weeks later, sifting through the just-developed pictures, Agnes commented to Ray that it looked as if that old woman might simply step into the woods or onto the county road and disappear. "It seems like she will step off the edge of town," Agnes said. "She will step off the edge and just vanish."

There was, in the weeks' long exodus to follow, a quality of the leaving that felt like a magic trick, or as if the magnet Agnes imagined to be just beneath the dirt switched its polarity and now repelled the people, scattering them. After the fire was put out, it was quickly determined that not a single person had been hurt. Those who had lost their houses—in all, the Cassie mourners had managed to burn seven houses and a small portion of the Baptist church to the ground—were the first ones to load up and leave Goliath, though most of them stayed nearby, in the chain hotel down the highway or with friends and family, until the insurance papers could be filed, every loss catalogued. The pizza restaurant owner, Alice Woodall, stayed with her son, Jimmy, and Mia's neighbor, a widow, made good use of the couch Rosamond had recently vacated.

Nearly everyone else had already decided, at the factory's closing, to leave Goliath, but the fire inspired them to make their exits more quickly. Many were already loading boxes into the beds of pickup trucks and vans the very next morning. Others lingered for lunch at the Tuesday Diner, and some stayed for several days, only to stand in front of the bursts of ruins—blackened bits of wood and brick—amid the rows of normal, untouched houses. They picked up empty candy wrappers and bits of tissue paper off the streets, scraps from the Harding Furniture float and the butterfly girls, foam cups from Wally's Saturday-morning coffee service, broken bits of china and ashy clothing and soggy books from the sites of the fires.

Even those who had not planned to leave began to talk about leaving. It seemed impossible to stay, to live among the gutted houses, to lunch at an almost-empty Tuesday Diner. They closed their post office boxes and stopped their newspaper subscriptions. The end of May brought on a new, less hopeful outcrop of For Sale signs.

The signs were the saddest things to Rosamond. She walked through town at dusk the week after the fire and looked into the blank window eyes of the empty houses. She sat on Clyde's porch beside her own blackened square of burnt grass and debris and told him, "These houses will never sell." Clyde was in his lawn chair, Rosamond on the first step below him. He reached down and put his hand on her shoulder. "Let's go on, then," he said. "Yes," she said, and he lifted his hand. She felt light there, with his touch gone.

After a moment, she said, "I love you, Clyde."

He nodded. "I love you too."

Hatley Rogers remained a wandering stranger for some months after the fire. He stayed on, living in the one-bedroom trailer, after Goliath was all but deserted. It seemed, for a time, that he had to stay. That he *couldn't* leave.

What had happened the day of the parade was that he smelled smoke when he first stepped out of the diner. He reasoned in that moment that it was nothing. A campfire. Kids playing. Then there at the top of Main Street, against the grainy bare-treed mountains—spring had not yet reached the top—a smudge of orange. At that, that *tiny* bit of fire up the street, he stood, frozen: he was not this person. This person who would change things, save things. This person who would try.

But, then he began the walk anyway. The walk down Main Street toward the fire. Later he realized that the smart thing to do would have been to return to the diner, call for help. He couldn't say why he hadn't called or in any other way summoned help, or walked faster or ran: it was simply what happened. It felt that way, like a thing that was happening—that had in a way *already* happened—and he was just living it out. Living out the already decided.

It took a long time for him to reach the house. Once there, he again acted without thinking. He first tried to break the window with a rock, and then found a potted plant on the porch, and this time, it worked. The window exploded and the heat, the smoke rushed out at his face. He stood blinking a long moment, his eyes burning, and then he shrugged his jacket off and, wrapping it around his fist, beat out the remaining pieces of glass. He made a hole big enough for himself, now operating under a misguided, panicked single thought: *they* were inside. In his confusion, his fear, he had for a small moment lost his bearings time-wise, *decade*-wise. For the space of that instant—laying his jacket down on the edge of the window, hitching up his leg, and finally hoisting himself inside the house, his throat immediately raw, his lungs burning with the smoke, his arms, his legs, his face, his hands throbbing with heat—in that fleeting moment, he believed they were exactly as he had left them. Agnes, still a girl, not even quite a teenager, and Rosamond, young, her hair still dark and thick. The girl was doing her homework, his wife was washing dishes at the sink. He crawled through that window to save his family, the one he had just abandoned, and instead—after a time of looking—found this boy on the living room floor, his knees drawn to his chest, his arms clutched tight around his head.

In that rescue, Goliath had finally done for Hatley Rogers what he needed it to do: in that moment, rescuing that boy, a *stranger*, he had become a good man. He stayed behind for that reason alone. He couldn't leave the town. Not now, so soon after he had reconciled himself to it.

He knew he would not be allowed to stay there, that somehow, even completely vacant, the town would only abide his presence for so long. He walked the neighborhood streets, visiting and revisiting the burned, abandoned houses, the school his daughter had attended. He stood before the lawn with the enormous oak tree shading it, watched the tree shadows on the grass shift in the breeze. He could have been that girl's father and her mother's husband; at one time he could have chosen that. He could have persisted, he could have survived Goliath. He could have, but he hadn't stayed long enough, and now it was too late.

He walked time and again to the river behind the church, which he had begun to think of as *his* river. He loved the sound of it, the unbroken steadiness of the water moving: an unhesitating, constant force.

He finally decided it was time to leave, though, when late the following autumn, there was a cold, soaking rain that turned much of Goliath to mud and flooded his beloved river. Both Agnes and Rosamond were gone by then. Rosamond had left in Clyde Winston's Buick in the dark early of a morning late in May. He had not spoken to her again since the morning he'd made those miniature pancakes, the morning he'd implored her to stay with him. He didn't have the heart to. He stood on the sidewalk several houses down and listened that morning to the sounds of their final partings, the car doors opening and closing, the clomp of the trunk closing. His view of the car in the driveway, loaded up, Clyde and Rosamond piling in, leaving, was obscured by the enormous holly tree in Rosamond's neighbor's yard—the one on the other side from Clyde. He watched the car slide out the driveway onto the street, then forward, gone. It happened so quickly.

Hatley needed a life of rest now, old rascal that he was. So he set out across the street, across Rosamond's driveway, on past the rubble of her house, the sooty remains. It was early, not quite seven o'clock yet. Then, using the spoon itself to dig, he buried it, his only Goliath souvenir, in the soft red brown earth of Rosamond's backyard.

Later he drove all night, back to the motel in Florida where he'd lived before he'd seen the news item, Harding's closing. There he subsisted on vending machine foodstuffs and coffee from the motel office. A few weeks after he'd returned, he bought a can of shaving cream. In the motel's dark-tinged mirror, he shaved his beard off slowly, systematically, stopping to clean the razor, to observe his progress. When he was finished, he wiped the scraps of shaving cream from his face and stood looking into the mirror. He touched his newly smooth, pinked-up face.

Vincent Bailey spent the rest of the spring and much of the summer lying around, watching daytime game shows and thinking of the number seven. He had never imagined they would be so successful. They'd planned to burn it all down—they'd mapped out every house on a two-mile radius out of Main Street—but still, *seven*. It seemed a big enough number now that it was all done, now that those homes had *actually burned*—gone from normal and good and untouched to ash and crumbled glass and fallen roofs. *He* had done this. Percy Harding, the aged, saintly man, had killed himself—and tormented the young person to find him in the process—but he, Vincent Bailey, with the help of those *he* had persuaded to join him, had burned down seven homes *and* part of a church.

Of course he had failed on the other part of his plan, the part both Mr. Harding and Cassie Stewart had accomplished. He didn't know how to feel about this. It was easier to think *seven* and to guess the price of laundry detergent, to name three of the original signers of the Declaration of Independence. To sleep. It had been determined, through a conference among Vincent's parents and a social worker and then later approved by the authorities, that Vincent would attend the alternative high school in the fall. He accepted this with no argument, retiring to his couch, watching hour after hour of junk TV.

Years later, it would astound him to recall those weeks of television-watching and sleep: his thoughts, during that time, were entirely confined to concrete entities. He could only picture the tangible entities right in front of him. He did not imagine or reason or argue or even remotely philosophize. For weeks, it was as though that part of his brain was simply switched off, and he could respond only to the images on the screen, the voices in the house. What he was eating. The pillow beneath his head.

All this mental vapidity was made easier by the actions of his mother, who herself seemed to have taken a vacation from meaningful thought. She was all action, protecting and coddling her son as she'd never had the courage or perhaps the strength to do before. She would not allow his father or his sisters to enter the living room where Vincent lay convalescing on the couch. That alone was very hard for her—there had been a terse but surprisingly short argument with Vincent's father and a round of *not fair*s from his sisters—but once it was accomplished, this rule established, her way was cleared. She could dote on him as much as she pleased. She brought him his meals on a tray and spoiled him with candy bars and comic books. It was as though he was five years old, not fifteen, and she was nursing him back from strep throat and not from an organized, wide-reaching, and altogether too successful arson scheme. Never mind the suicide attempt. She suggested he get out his colored pencils and work on his comic book drawings. She could pop him some popcorn if he liked. He should invite a friend over to keep him company. What about the Jones boy? What about his cousin David? Should she call him?

She touched her son's forehead and smiled down at him. "I am so, so sorry," she said, and now understanding flickered faintly somewhere beneath his self-loathing, his nonthinking self: what had happened to him—as far back as seeing Percy dead in the mud—had in a sense happened to her as well. This woman, his mother, *loved* him.

Years later, after Vincent had served his time at the delinquent school and settled into a job at the hospital as an orderly—a job, it turned out, that suited him, his being near people all day, helping them, smiling at them, a job that required patience and gentleness and a special attention to others' dignity, and yet also allowed him a tidy reserve of emotional space—his father, an old man now, said to him, "Everything turned out all right for you, didn't it? You turned out just fine." Vincent said nothing; he had begun to see a weakness in his father, a slowness to his speech and his movements and also a worry in his eyes that he now realized had been there all along. His father insisted, "Everything turned out just fine," and looked away, not believing in his own words. Vincent understood at last: it was his father who had been afraid.

Also that summer, while he lay on the couch and drifted mindlessly through daytime non-soap-opera programming, a girl from school visited. She came almost every week, and he came to anticipate, however dimly, her visits.

"Stephanie," he said when she arrived in the doorway. He moved over to give her room to sit on the sofa.

She accepted and asked him how he was. "How's your throat?"

This was the tacit understanding between them: they could discuss his still-sore throat, the dreariness of this particular summer, the specific punishments, both parental and of the Goliath Police Department, of the other arsonists. All this was fine so long as they didn't speak aloud the actual *cause* of any of it. She could ask about his throat, still raw from the smoke, but not about the man who had saved him. It was fine for Stephanie to recount how she had hurried to summon help on the day of the parade so long as she didn't get into why help was needed. They could laugh about how his mother hovered, snacks at the ready, but Stephanie dared not wonder aloud why she was being so nice. She was sure that her own mother, in the same situation, would *not* be bringing her treats and offering such gentle, affectionate care. Her own mother would likely keep her locked up in her bedroom—no phone, no TV—for months. Years.

They had their reasons for avoiding such subjects. Vincent was doing his best not to think at all, and any of these topics would have required just that. But also, Stephanie only wanted to be *near* a person who had lived through the things Vincent had lived through; she didn't necessarily want to know everything. It was the same reason she'd read all those books, why she'd so many months earlier written about the worse thing she could imagine doing—killing herself. She wanted full, outright, out loud *life,* but she wanted it secondhand, weakened just a tiny bit. She did not want to actually *confront* anything.

Still, she managed to say one thing that may have seemed significant, weighty, perhaps, to Vincent if he'd had ears to hear her that summer. It was hot both outside—throbbing blue, sunstoked heat—and inside, the television's volume turned low, the whir, in the hallway, of a fan. Mrs. Bailey was in the kitchen, cooking something brown-smelling and sizzling for dinner—a dinner Stephanie would most likely be invited to join the family in eating, as her own parents were up at Chapel Hill, getting her brother settled into his summer, athletes-only dorm room. Vincent's sisters were upstairs in their bedrooms or else gone, out of the house—they had jobs, boyfriends, church activities—and Mr. Bailey, who never said much anyway, was outside working in his garage. Stephanie, sitting next to this quiet boy in the middle of all this heat and stillness and unseen cooking, felt removed, like a character in a book. Not quite real. It was as if, in this moment, the entire house was only a backdrop to some stage in her mind. Anything she expressed now would be erased, *gone,* the second she spoke it.

"I think you needed to do what you did. I really do," she began, looking into the television screen and not into the human face beside her. "Cassie Stewart was dead, and us kids, we needed to *do* something about it. Maybe it's wrong to say, but I think they kind of deserved it. I mean, the adults, the people in charge of everything. They should have kept all of this from happening to us." She glanced at him, shrugged. "Maybe I'm wrong." Then, returning to look into the television and remembering what the drifter boy in the diner had once told her, she added, "*Be that self which one truly is.*" She laughed. "It's kind of bullshit, isn't it? And it's also kind of exactly right too. Don't you think?"

A few weeks after the fire, Agnes and Ray threw a quick, happy wedding in the Baptist church. Only a small annex, a storage facility had been damaged by the fire, and even that needed little more than a fresh coat of paint. The parts they needed—the sanctuary and the fellowship hall—were sound as ever.

The day was green and pink and blue, full of springtime, the breeze light and warm. Mia wore a lavender dress—mulberry, she called it—and cried more than Rosamond did. Clyde kept taking pictures—he insisted on getting everything: Ray standing awkwardly at the front of the church in a stiff-looking moss-green suit, Agnes walking down the aisle on the arm of her mother. She cradled a gigantic bouquet of Easter lilies from Mia's garden in her arms. The cake-eating, the toast-making, the dashing through the shower of rice, the driving away in Ray's pickup, all were captured with Clyde's little point-and-shoot. Agnes wore a pale blue dress that wasn't a wedding dress but was still, everyone agreed, lovely. Just *beautiful*, Rosamond said. She left her hair down but let Mia pin a few tiny daisies—for good luck, she said—behind her ear.

There were no bridesmaids or flower girls, no groomsmen. Pastor Dale Myers married them; his wife Tonya played the organ. The church was quiet, so few people inside, the carpet so thick. Mostly family and a few old friends of Mia's and Clyde's attended, plus one or two of the other cashiers from the Lucky Grocery and Agnes's taciturn but nonetheless loyal, good-hearted manager. The day's biggest surprise was the arrival of Charlotte Branch from the drugstore. She brought a date, a plumber from the other side of the county. When she and her fellow went through the receiving line, she grasped Agnes's hand tightly and smiled more kindly than anyone had ever seen Charlotte Branch smile at anyone. "God bless you," she said, and the plumber, a narrow-faced, grinning man, nodded.

After the wedding, Ray and Agnes moved into Ray's trailer. Mia was packing to move in with her son Donald in a town thirty miles east of Goliath. Her mother and Clyde had already left Goliath, just a few days after the wedding. "Come visit," her mother had said, and Clyde, in a fatherly way that befitted both roles—he was her father-in-law *and* her quasi-stepfather—squeezed her shoulder. He winked at her and repeated the offer. "We'd love to have you anytime," he said.

She and Ray were unsure of what to do, where to go—whether to leave at all—after Rosamond and Clyde drove out together to the coast. Ray had promised her they could go anywhere she wanted, just get out a map and point, but Agnes had not known where to point. She couldn't know, she told him: it wasn't *time* to know. Ray accepted this, and the two kept working, Ray with the county groundskeeping, Agnes with the Lucky Grocery. At the moment their jobs were still there, even with all the vacant houses all around them, all the people moving out. Ray took down Agnes's maps and studied them for himself, along with his Bible, in the evenings. He prayed over them, trying to piece out just where God meant for him to go. He felt it worse than Agnes did now: they must go *somewhere*.

A week later, Agnes dropped an open magazine onto the kitchen table where Ray was studying scripture. "There," she said. She'd found it: an article about a missionary training school in Pasadena, California. "It's not Africa, but it *is* the first step."

He read the information aloud to her. "'Before leaving for the mission field, come to us, allow us to train you and to enable you to better meet your calling . . .'" He put the magazine down. "I thought my whole *life* was the mission field."

Yet they agreed: it looked good. They would go. The courses wouldn't start until August, but they decided to take off as soon as possible, reasoning they could find jobs in California for the summer. They would leave all this—the sidewalks Agnes had walked, the doorsteps Ray had preached from, the roads and buildings and houses and smells and sights Ray had known, prayed over; what Agnes had loved, then hated, then loved again.

In any case she was ready now. More reluctant—*sad*—to leave Goliath than she had ever imagined she would be, but ready all the same.

"California," Agnes said. She stood over him where he sat at the kitchen table and fingered the curls caught inside his shirt collar.

"The *world*," answered Ray, turning to look at her, reaching up to catch her fingers there at the back of his neck.

Rosamond and Clyde's quick departure had been at Rosamond's insistence, and Clyde was agreeable, as anxious to leave as she was. Agnes, after eighteen years of growing up there and ten months of living as an adult in Mia's basement, three weeks in Ray's trailer, had been ready to leave; Rosamond, after more than half a century, was *beyond* ready.

"Why should I want to stay? Even for a few more days?" she'd said to Clyde. "Especially now, when there's nothing left?"

And yet she found the actual leaving, the packing up and going, enormously difficult. *Heartbreaking,* she told Clyde. Heartbreaking *and* wonderful, she said, and he nodded. Of course he understood. In many ways Clyde had loved Goliath—and loved *in* Goliath—more than she had. Still, Rosamond showed it more: she sniffled, she walked the Main Street sidewalk once more alone; he read the paper, patrolled the streets.

What amazed her was how little there was—as far as actual preparations—to the leaving. She packed her clothing and what few keepsakes had escaped both the house purging she'd done months earlier and the fire: the cardinal letter opener she'd never managed to give away; a necklace Tucker had given her; her teapot, fire-blackened across the back but still in one piece; the Easter lily from Agnes's wedding she had pressed inside the biggest book Clyde owned, a dictionary he'd had on his shelf for decades. She packed all these things as briskly as she could and looked out, glimpsed the ashy ruins of her house next door. A light rain was falling, graying the sky, darkening the trees, the street.

The morning of their departure, she filled a thermos with coffee and double-checked her purse for the essentials: wallet, lipstick, sunglasses, white gloves, which she still took with her, even after all these years. They were long out of fashion, she knew. But Rosamond was Rosamond: she wore a blue shirtwaist dress and matching pumps, and kept her gloves tucked into her purse, in case she felt like putting them on. Or maybe she would do this: she would roll the window down and let her bare hand out to feel the air rushing through her fingers.

She shored herself up in her seat, her dress laid straight and nice across her knees—she *was* excited, excited to be traveling, if nothing else—and took the road map Clyde handed her. She would direct, though it was wonderfully easy: point the car east and just *go*. One could drive across the state and on into the Atlantic Ocean on that same highway.

Clyde finally opened the driver's side door, got himself settled behind the wheel, his own For Sale sign in his yard, the house locked up tight. They planned to return for the furniture and the appliances, his vacuum cleaner. His easy chair.

She wouldn't give him everything—she shouldn't, she believed. There were things a person should keep, thoughts one should just hold on to. No matter how much, how fiercely, a person loved, there were yet pieces to hold back. To keep.

They hadn't discussed it, but Rosamond knew before they started the path Clyde would take: he would go the back way, looping through the town, out behind the factory to the county roads and then beyond to the highway.

Now they started out, driving past the Lucky Grocery, the waterbed store where King's Motel used to stand, away from the high school, the factory, the Harding place. Beyond her own house, the drugstore, Dalton's Bar, the cemetery, the Baptist church. Past the downtown shops, the Tuesday Diner, the municipal building with its thousand-book library tucked into its basement. Rosamond held her purse in her lap. Clyde, beside her, was quiet. In a moment, she knew it would begin, the traveling talk, talk of gas mileage and tire-wear—Clyde would be that sort of traveler, she knew. And she would be the one to tell old stories, remembrances, to wonder aloud about the houses they passed, the people in their yards and on their porches.

But for now, leaving, they were quiet. Past the pizza place, the drugstore. Rosamond pressed her lips together and touched her gloves inside her purse. Clyde reached over, laid his hand on hers, closed it around her fingers. Past the grade school lawn where Rosamond's daughter, her Agnes, had once sat on its green lawn in the shade of a wide-branched, thick-leaved oak tree, eating her lunch. Past the factory, its parking lot. The post office up the way. Clyde slowed the car to creep over the railroad tracks.

EPILOGUE

Some years later, in the spring, a shining black Mercedes coasted into town. It rumbled slowly, leisurely, across Main Street, and a tiny elderly woman in the backseat looked through the window, over the cemetery, now in remarkable disrepair—weed-filled and overgrown. A few thin white clouds floated above the markers.

The car rode on, past Rosamond Rogers's house, a blackened skeleton of a structure. Next came Clyde Winston's house, and then the house where a row of coffee-can wind chimes still hung on the eaves, though the house itself had long been vacant. Down the way, there were the pair of burned homes standing opposite each other, and the other homes, some standing firm, virtually untouched; others were damaged by the passage of time and the weather. Here a tall gum tree, uprooted by a storm a few years earlier, had fallen onto the roof of a two-storied clapboard. The tree had smashed right through one of the dormer windows and the house was left open, its upper room exposed to the sunshine. Everywhere, the lawns were overgrown, shingles had fallen off rooftops. In the trailer park, many of the trailers had lost their plastic skirting and most of the windows had cracked apart and fallen out of their frames.

The old woman and her driver passed the elementary school, the post office, the great white Baptist church on the corner. At the factory, the parking lot's asphalt was broken and weedy; kudzu was growing up the sides of the loading bay. The great brick building still stood, sturdy as ever, but a number of its high, square windows had been blown in by the same massive storm—with hurricane-force winds—that had felled the gum tree on Main Street. The downtown shops were all closed up, though the old woman could see inside the Tuesday Diner. The tables still stood in tidy rows, and the old blue Pepsi fountain was still there, in tact, behind the counter.

It was a breezy blue-skied day. The stand of dogwoods across the street from the factory lot were in full white bloom, the oak tree in the elementary school yard had just begun to leaf. The earth was damp and warm; the telephone wires were dotted with speckled-throated brown birds. Robins and sparrows, finches.

The Mercedes turned up August Street and rolled past another fire-gutted house, then pulled into the drive at number 195, Mia Robins's house. This was the address Rosamond Rogers had written across the bottom of the letter she sent to Dorothy Blair some ten years earlier. Now finally, bent and old with a wrinkled face chalky with powder, the aged movie star had arrived. She wore a fur-lined driving jacket and authentic kid gloves, though it was warm outside in the blue-bubbled spring sunshine. The man driving the car was young and smartly dressed, an attendant hired by her children to assist her.

She sat for a few moments in the parked car. Simply looking over the fallen pieces of her hometown—*a little place called Goliath,* she had described it in a magazine interview more than a half century ago—had wearied her. Her eyelids, thin as tissue paper and blue-veined, fluttered as if they meant to open but couldn't. Not quite yet. The attendant, a boy named Christopher, opened the door for her, but she shook her head so he would wait, let her catch her breath. She wore silk stockings and patent-leather black-and-white spectator shoes. Her dress was simple combed cotton, but the color was such a brilliant shade of indigo, it gleamed even in the shadows of the inside of the car.

Beyond the open door, past the young, able-bodied attendant, Mia Robins's garden was a thick knot of vegetation, of thorny vines and drooping, enormous flowers, smooshed purply black blooms and wasted roses, crumbling into dust. Bright yellow crocuses nosed through the heap, and there were outbreaks of wild pink azalea bushes, unchecked shoots of burgundy and orange straw flowers and tangled periwinkles, their blossoms smaller and darker and *ferocious* in some way—tiny and determined, of deeper color than any the old lady had ever seen. Dorothy Blair could see much of it from the backseat, and then better, more pristinely, more *materially* once she gestured for the young man and he took her thick-knuckled old hand, her thin, trembling elbow, once she was helped to standing. There, she was so close, and there were masses of them—butterflies, large-winged and blue and orange and yellow, living their simple butterfly lives, their flitting from one bloom to the next, their lift, the quick flights, their lighting on the thinnest petal, opening and closing their wings. That opening and closing caught Dorothy's attention; it seemed an absentminded gesture, a tic of a sort, a careless, graceful movement.

"They're alive," she said, only a scrap of what she meant to say, so slow, these days, were the connections, brain to mouth. These were the only words she could offer, and the young man smiled.

"Yes," he said, "they're *everywhere*."

Clearly the house was abandoned, the woman who had written the letter, had invited Dorothy, the Rosamond Rogers of exuberant good wishes, of praise and hope—Goliath, the letter had claimed, was *so* proud of its most famous past resident—was no longer here. She had left; everyone, it seemed, had left.

And so the two began walking together toward the high school, she limping along, creaky jointed and unsteady, he upright and robust, practically twitching with warm-blooded young health. She was well into her nineties now, a grave old woman trying to return to an old place, a place that existed mostly now in her mind, in dim, muted-colored memories. She kept her eyes down on her feet, muttering to herself a little. The young man knew from experience it wasn't necessary to try to decipher her words, to respond. He continued wordlessly, matching her creeping pace. Any onlooker who had also witnessed another mismatched couple more than ten years earlier making its way up the other side, up Main Street, might have noticed the similarities: it was just like the day Rosamond guided Jim Tucker up this way, except now, on August Avenue, the man was the young one and the woman was old. It was she who was now lost in time and space, she whose steps were so uncertain.

The butterflies, the street, the trees, the weedy lawns, the fallen tree limbs, the crumbled houses—all were clearer to her now as she walked past them, stopping every so often to peer into sun-lit places and into the shadows beneath the trees. Clearer now were the ashen splinters of the fallen houses, the grass growing in patches through the rotted floors, the For Sale signs, now fallen over in the grass or else nearly covered with high-reaching weeds, their lettering faded. Also, the church, across the way, was more damaged in person than could be easily seen from the road. On the northern side, the side nearest the railroad tracks, across the field from the river, a portion of the roof had caved in, the doors on that section gone, so that its pews were open to the sunshine. The old woman stopped and looked inside where weedy wildflowers and grass grew right through the weathered carpet, reaching above the pews in some places.

Next she and Christopher made their slow journey across the street, making such agonized progress he longed to simply pick the old woman up, cradle her, carry her across the asphalt. Finally, haltingly, they came to the patch of woods behind the old high school. She motioned to the young man: they would stop here. Stop here before these woods, which hadn't been woods at all, year and years ago, when she'd lived here. During that time, there had been a small clearing. Nearly everything else—the row of houses on Main Street, the high school, the grade school, the Tuesday Diner, the drugstore—had been nothing but trees and birds. In those days, there were only a few storefronts, a scattering of houses, the old factory motel. The river behind the church—a tenth of the size it was now.

In that clearing in the woods had stood a house made of blue-painted clapboard and hand-poured cinder block. There, before the trees had reclaimed it, grown back, before the high school was built adjacent to it, when the train bustling through was the very heartbeat of the town, when Harding Furniture had not yet reached its full glory, there, years ago, had stood the house where Dorothy Blair had grown up. There, where Vincent Bailey had smoked his cigarettes, where he had swallowed the cricket, where he had recited Cassie Stewart's poems. Where he had led a band of young arsonists. Where Ray Winston, at an even earlier time, had spent his time in the wilderness, where he had met his God just before he lost his mother, *there* was the house where Dorothy Blair had lived.

She stood looking into those woods a long time, shivering a little with an old woman's chill. She could *see* it, the place where the house used to be, there, her old bedroom, the kitchen, gas stove, table. A fireplace in the front room. A rickety, rough-lumber front porch. The trees were just coming to green now, and the sun came dappled through, lighting up last year's fallen leaves.